KUNTANA

Kuntana

A novel about power,
love and betrayal.

DASH STARKEY

www.dashstarkey.com

ISBN:
Paperback
978-0-6487919-2-8
Digital Media
978-0-6487919-3-5

Cover: Michelle J Photography

First Printing, 2021

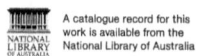

A catalogue record for this
work is available from the
NATIONAL
LIBRARY
OF AUSTRALIA   National Library of Australia

All of my books are dedicated to
Love and Life
... I hope you find yours.

Elle, my love and my life.

My baby girl **Emily**, the light of my life.

Cliff and Heather Starkey, for their amazing love and encouragement. I couldn't have done it without you.
Michelle J Photography for her amazing cover photo.

THANKS

Geoffrey Brook Starkey

A man who has inspired many characters, wore many hats and has many stories to tell.

Colin Starkey

A brother who has his own unique adventures and is always looking for the next challenge.

Darren Starkey

Definitely the daredevil of the family, who's only mellowed slightly with time.

Michelle J Photography

A husband and wife team that lives life through the lens. Amazing photographers who take the most incredible photos of the Snowy Mountain brumbies, dingoes and other very Australian wildlife.

Emma Heather, Jessica Murree & Alivia Murree

Three girls who have grown into amazing women. Keep following your dreams. We are so proud of you.

Emily Mullins

You have grown into an incredible woman, always dreaming big. You make me so proud.

30 YEARS IN THE MAKING

The idea of Kuntana was born several years before my beautiful daughter Emily was. It was the early 90's, and I finally committed to something that I had dreamt of, since childhood. The thought of writing a full novel was, to say the least, overwhelming. Possibly made worse by the fact I started writing it by hand. A year later, I moved to an electric typewriter. Things moved a little quicker. As time went by, as sections were added and removed, and as I improved, the story was transposed onto an early IBM Thinkpad, bought second hand at a government auction.

This novel was written in a time I sought control in my own life. It reflects the strong personalities who I came in contact with in my daily life. Those who could achieve, via legal means or otherwise, ultimate power. Power is an intriguing thing, often fleeting at times, so I decided to explore what such power costs. Kuntana holds the culmination of my research.

The story grew. For me inspiration arrived in everyday moments. Firing a 357 handgun that had enough kick to knock the arse end off a mule. Being handcuffed by a county sheriff friend, whose day job was to round up cattle rustlers. Racing on foot across the city with a briefcase jammed with cash. Life offered the opportunities, my writer's eye saw more.

Entwined in the story is the Australian outback: something I adore. A land of harshness, hidden by its beauty. Something also reflected by the characters. Fluttering between Brisbane, Stanthorpe and the property Kuntana, this story of strength and struggle, is entwined with love and devotion. Set mainly in Australia, the story also carries the reader to far away places such as Japan, the Amazon and the United States of America.

I hope you enjoy the story and find some of the turns as surprising as I did.

PART ONE

Pain of Life

~ 1 ~

THE TRUTH HURTS

Brisbane River, Queensland, Australia.

'Are you sure?'

'Yes, one of our contacts stonewalled his enquiries. Got friendly with him. Likes to brag too, especially when he's drunk.'

'What do we know?'

'Vanished for many years, apparently went to South America. The Colombian boys had a bit of trouble with him, he vanished and suddenly appeared in our neck of the woods.'

It was quite blissful to glide across the water, the bow first slicing then distorting the city lights reflected on the fragmented moonlit surface of the Brisbane River. The lights and sounds of the city had been quite spectacular from river level, giving Amelia a new appreciation for it all. The bustle faded as they travelled further upstream. Now the sounds of the bush were disturbed only by the rhythmic plunk of the small engine. An occasional light from a house could be seen set back from the river. Most around this area built away from the river's edge in fear of another 'flood of 74.'

Amelia should have felt cold with the wet winter breeze coming in off the river. Instead, she felt unusually warm and had to open her jacket to cool off. Their pace quickened with the encouragement of the tide. Amelia's pulse also quickened as the reality of a face to face meet approached. The night was cool and overcast but it did not dampen their desire to complete this task.

'Not far now.'

Spoke Rosario. A malt factory, silhouetted by the moon, passing on the left their only indicator of location. Looming around the bend lay the Moggill Ferry, the Stradbroke Star, now motionless, resting from its day's work. Their small craft pulled alongside one of the large cable wheels. Amelia carefully manoeuvred on the slim cable edge, using the wheel for balance. Rosario, by her side had already tied the craft, cleared the side in a swift leap and turned to see who could view them. All that could be seen was the old man seated against a far wall, slumped on the ferry's controls, mumbling incoherently to himself and an empty scotch bottle, spittle dribbling from his mouth and running down his unshaven chin. Ignoring the drunk Rosario nodded his intention to proceed.

As they walked along the outline of a stairwell a few metres ahead to the right was visible. The turret it was attached to was large, sombre and forbidding. Its high metal walls were dotted with small, barred windows from which escape was clearly impossible. Amelia looked at it and felt sick at heart. Using Rosario's hand for balance she descended into the blackness, her heels clicking on the crude checker plate metal. Rosario followed close behind, eyes checking and rechecking for any movement. A sequenced tap on the iron door was responded to by the opening and closing of a peephole.

Scraping metal soon followed as the door creaked into life. Stale air from the bowels of the ferry rushed to greet the new visitors. Inside the pungent odour was worse. Poorly lit, the room was rank with the smell of humanity and suffering and untold horrors, yet hauntingly silent, as if empty of inhabitants. There was an incandescent light dangling on a wire from the metal ceiling. It cast a pool of white over the centre of the room, leaving the walls in deep shadow.

Within the shadows stood the two boys who had brought Sal here. One, a scruffy fellow with a loose hanging ponytail and fluff for a moustache. The other had strong Italian features draped in dark hair slicked at the sides. Both carried the over confidence of youth.

Seated beneath the light was an unkempt man, slumped in a chair. Eyeing the newcomers, squinting against the blurring effects of alcohol. Attempting to raise a hand to shield the light, he remembered they were secured to the chair arms. In his day, rope would have secured him but the youth of today preferred these new plastic zip tie things. His legs too were secured and painfully at that. The square edge of plastic sharp against his flesh.

'Hey buddy, answer the lady when she speaks to you.'

Rosario and the two boys moved further into the

darkened shadows, the red glint of a cigarette the only evidence of their whereabouts. Placing a chair next to his, Amelia spoke calmly to the man, making conversation as if she were meeting him under different circumstances.

'Salut, Sal. Parli inglese?'

Up close the man looked like a frightened rabbit, obviously knowledgeable of such a situation, but more used to creating one. His rugged square jaw concealed by his tanned, withered skin drooped in surprise. A slight nod answered the question. His white thatched head swayed with the rocking motion of the ferry, but he understood.

'Do you know who I am?'

Hurriedly shaking his head side to side, Sal's eyes darted about the room, refusing to look into the deep dark pools of mystery set in such a beautiful woman's face.

'Surely you jest me, Sal.'

Speaking softly, as if to an elderly relation, Amelia held her voice firm but tender, full of understanding.

'This picture may help.'

If Sal looked scared before, it was nothing compared to the new terror that flowed through his veins.

'Don Ricoldi's son. Nicosia?'

'Yes Sal, and there's me beside him. A lot younger though, I don't think I've aged much, do you?'

Desiring to flee but unable to, Sal's eyes intensified, the white trying to smother the pupils' small specs. His Adam's apple bobbed, recognising the seriousness of this interview.

Still speaking quietly as if sharing a private joke, Amelia leant to Sal's ear.

'I know you shot him.'

'No. No, it was not me. You are mistaken.'

'I never make a mistake Sal.'

'No. You are wrong. It was not me.'

Resting her arm along his, Amelia patted the back of Sal's hairy hand with her fingers slightly. In any other circumstance, Sal would have smiled and maybe laughed.

'You shot him in cold blood. In front of me. Women shouldn't see those things, Sal.'

'No. It was someone else.'

Resting the heel of her palm just behind his knucklebones, Amelia clawed his fingers with hers and started to raise them slowly.

'I do not blame you, Sal. We all have a job to do. To earn money for our families. So, if you tell me who ordered the hit, we may be able to work out a deal. This type of business disgusts me so.'

'I know nothing.'

The declaration was emphasised by a painful cry.

'Aaagh!'

With each word his fingers were bent up and back further and further until an audible crack was heard.

'I know you did it, so who ordered the hit.'

Amelia's voice was calm and friendly.

'No.'

A second crack.

'They'll kill me.'

'I can protect you.'

Refusing to acknowledge Amelia, Sal's eyes searched the darkness for respite.

'Obviously, my words aren't strong enough. Rosario!' She rasped.

Rosario's intimidating figure stepped from the darkness. To Sal it was the grim reaper himself.

'Giorno del giudizio.'

Judgement day. Murmured Rosario as he approached the pair.

'Rosario, our friend Sal is not being too co-operative. In his best interest, maybe you could have a word with him.'

Rising, pacing to the rim of light, Amelia waited, facing the darkness. This was the part of business Amelia detested the most, yet in abhorrent acts was where a powerful reputation was earned. She wished to run and scream but knew she had to hold steadfast. Sal's whimpering reached her ears. She knew Rosario's fisted hand would strike any moment, with each blow she involuntarily closed her eyes, hoping, preying she could be back at Kuntana. A drizzle echoed off the walls as the man's bowels betrayed him. A small laugh rose from the far shadows.

Counting to ten, bracing herself, Amelia spun and approached Sal again. Strategically placing her hands on his, her wild eyes penetrated his cringing exterior.

'Why make this hard for yourself, Sal? Tell me who ordered the hit, and we can work things out between us.'

'No. I do not know.'

'Non mi sento a vena!' *I am not in the mood!* 'Give me a name.'

'I don't know his name. A man in Palermo hired me.'

'A name.'

'I know not.'

'Rosario!'

Rosario's large form emerging from the darkness made Sal physically recede in the chair.

'No. I know not.'

Blood trickled from his mouth after the next barrage of fists.

Standing unseen was Roberto and his companion, both young and eager to be involved in such an environment. Roberto's chest swelled, he had managed to work himself and his best friend into the best crew. Foot soldiers, for the second in charge of the Ricoldi family, Rosario.

'Not bad hey?'

Grinned Roberto as the centre room action disrupted the response.

'Again who?'

'A man. No name.'

'Te ne pentirai.' *You'll be sorry.* 'Roberto! The vice.'

A simple request striking fear, for imagination was Sal's greatest enemy. Imagination was seducing him in the horror that may come. A vice? What for? Curling his fingers under in anticipation, a streak of pain fought against him.

'Don't worry Sal, this won't hurt your fingers. No. I'd be more worried about your manhood if I were you.'

'Si, si, it is coming back to me.'

The boy was kneeling between his legs, the fist of before was holding his head back to restrict the view. The grinding zip made him react in a way like fingernails drawn down a chalkboard.

'A name Sal.'

'A man, stocky, short.'

'A name, otherwise, I can't stop him.'

His manhood receded from the cold touch. How could they? In all his years he hadn't stooped this low. This woman with the wild eyes, no emotion, how could she stand by and watch this?

'Si. Yes, it is coming back. Name starts with...V. Yes. Vinny, no. V. V. Vance, no. Vito! Yes, Vito was his name. He had a cigar. Foreign. Stank lots.'

'Are you sure?'

'Si. Si. Vito.'

'Stato un pazzo afarlo.' *You were crazy to do it.* 'Don Ricoldi's son.'

With a wave of the hand, Amelia's assistants once again vanished to the darkness. Perspiration ran down the man's forehead. His eyes quivered in indecision. Tongue chalky and dry, his voice tremoring as he spoke.

'You were the hit, not Nicosia.'

'Sorry?'

'You were the hit.'

Years of mental anguish and doubt bloomed to the realisation of what she dreaded all along. Nicosia died because of her. She should be dead now not him. Running in an endless replay, Nicosia's death swirled vividly before Amelia's eyes.

As it had done a thousand times before, the memory played again.

****

'Where is he Rosario? He should be here by now.'

'Don't worry Signorina Amelia. He will come. Look, there he is.'

Nicco waved from across the busy intersection, a bouquet in his free hand. Amelia had been waiting for him for over an hour. Final preparations for his surprise birthday party had taken her most of the day. His impression was that they were going to the movies and a quiet dinner. But her news was too important.

Outside the cinema it was busy, people scattered about, waiting for friends, lovers, and husbands. Amelia hoped to tell him the news later, yet she could barely conceal it any longer. Running to the curb, Nicco darted amongst the Fiats, Opels and assorted European cars. A pure Italian male in full flight, gesturing and abusing, making himself seen and heard. It was true what they said about the Italians, thought Amelia. Hot headed, obsessed with women and her favourite, great lovers. Dark hair slicked in the day's fashion, his best suit pressed just for her.

Rocking her arms in a cradle fashion, Nicco stopped still, shook his head, and looked again. Smiling, Amelia nodded, rocking her arms once more. A Cheshire cat grin filled Nicco's well-cut face, eyes illuminated with excitement, his movement became inspired.

'Can it be?'

'Yes Nicco, my love. Our first-born is due in seven months.'

Mounting the curb, arms spread wide, Amelia anticipated them wrapping her in the warmth they promised. His kisses would drown her, sending both into a frenzy.

Whap! Whap! Something whistled passed Amelia's ear.

Rosario yelled something about the ground, but Amelia's eyes were transfixed on her husband. A large wet crimson patch seeping across his chest. '*Nicco!*' Flowers lay scattered on the pavement, Nicco on his knees amongst them, head bowed as if in prayer.

****

The memory lingered but the present circumstances drew her back quickly.

'You fucking bastard!'

Amelia's temper could be restrained no more. With a mighty blow of her heeled foot, she planted a kick in the centre of Sal's chest. The force so strong, it literally knocked him backwards onto the floor.

'You missed?' Incredibility. 'You missed the target? How dare you call yourself a hit man? You should have killed me, not him, you incompetent bastard.'

Kicking with unabated fierceness, it took both Rosario and Roberto to remove her from the bloody mess on the floor. Roberto's companion, Christopher, looked dumbfounded. Firstly, at the mess on the floor, then to its creator. A greenish tinge flushed his face, before he threw himself to a dormant engine, emptying the contents of his stomach. If nothing else, he had a newfound respect for Mrs Ricoldi.

'Amelia?'

'It is okay Rosario, I am fine. Just a little emotional for a second, that's all.'

Straightening her clothes, showing no expression at all, Amelia indicated for Roberto to approach.

'Roberto, are you sure your friend is all right?'

'Yeah sure. It's his first confrontation, that's all. Once he dumps it, he'll be fine.'

'That's not what I meant.'

'Oh.'

Momentarily pausing to absorb the impact of Amelia's statement, Roberto looked to his best friend. If Christopher decided against all this and leaked any information to the police or anyone, they'd both be dead. This business was tough, but he trusted Chris with his life.

'Yeah, he's okay'.

'I sure would miss you.'

The statement hit him like a slap. Out of character, Amelia had the desire to soften the moment.

'Considering I've known you since you were a snotty nosed little hoodlum.'

There was always a warm spot in Amelia's heart for Roberto. He showed great promise. Normally she wouldn't encourage this lifestyle, but it's what he always wanted, since he was small, and strangely it suited him. As it had suited his father. He was well versed in extortion, terrorising high school students while still in primary school. It all came naturally to him. She would hate to order the hit on her godson.

'Okay sparrow.'

A name she affectionately called him, out of reach from his contemporaries. 'Clean up quickly. Thanks.'

A smile of understanding passed between them. With a

nod to the lifeless soul on the floor, both Amelia and Rosario exited quickly, breathing deeply as each escaped the suffocation of the room. Wiping her hands clean, Amelia automatically reached for Rosario's, cleaning them as if he were a small child.

Rosario knew such things pained her, but it was the law of the jungle. To win, you had to be the strongest, the most powerful and, unfortunately, the most hideously feared creature alive. Amelia had played this role well over the years, but the pain of it was taking its toll. Tonight, was the first time her emotions had taken control.

'Rosario. We have a problem.'

~ 2 ~

FRIENDS

Issaquah, Washington, U.S.A.

'Freak! Don't touch me!'

I still can't believe those words escaped from my mouth. Through the rumour mill at high school, it was discovered my friend Jesse, was, dare I say it, a lesbian. A word forced from my lips. I for one didn't know this. For over sixteen years, nearly all my life, she had been a part of my world as a best friend should. To outsiders it must have been obvious. Spending all her free time in the local garage pumping gas, repairing lawn mowers, tinkering with cars and motorbikes. Continuously wearing her dungarees and steel capped work boots.

Admittedly she doesn't really look that way. Long and seductive hair layered shaggily around her face, giving a warm and friendly appearance. Always smiling and laughing. Take the prom for example. She wore the most exquisite dress you ever did see. Long, slinky and silver, accentuating her natural shapeliness. Even I, who normally looks proportioned correctly, appeared frumpy compared to Jesse. An endless quantity of guys clamoured to be next to her or be seen dancing with her. Many girls passed an admiring look too. You couldn't help it, she looked good. Stunning.

Tell me she was going to become a model or was dying of cancer, and I would have accepted it. Tell me she was that way, and I would have said 'no way!' And I did the first time I heard it. You mean to tell me I've been hanging out all these years with one of them?

Jesse and I hung out all the time. We even wrote children's books together for the church. The church! Imagine that. Many of her stories were so sweet they'd run from your mouth like honey. Being the visual artist, as we called it, my job was to design the accompanying pictures. It sure was fun. My biggest artistic task was to paint Jesse's old Indian motorbike, black with yellow flames and things. That darn bike. Found in some backwoods somewhere and it took her a year to rebuild. All I ever heard about was that bike. The carburettor needed this, the fuel tank was full of sludge, it needed a special fuel cap, the cylinders were worn and the conrods were bent. Yaddah, yaddah, yaddah. That stupid bike didn't even run.

Well anyway, I'm straying. Halfway through the big paint job was when I discovered the secret. Placing the information at the back of my mind, I didn't even think about it till we were working on that darn bike. Jesse lent over my shoulder, hand on my neck and thumb behind, as she had done many a time before. Her breath, paused to praise, cupped my ear and I freaked. Thus, my earlier statement.

Curious about what caused this psychotic reaction, she grabbed my arm. Freaking even more I let her know I was up on 'her little plan.' She, looking bewildered, listened to my scathing enlightenment. 'Her lesbo fantasy!' Dumbfounded, as I continued, she only interjected a single syllable word. 'What?' Proceeding like the proverbial bull in a china shop I hit harder.

'Are you or are you not in love with me?'

A stranger's silence followed.

'Yes.'

Eyes pleading to explain penetrated my impulsive reactions, yet I bolted for my life. What a way to start my final summer vacation. By mid-summer we still hadn't spoken or caught up. Confused parents questioned but no answers were forthcoming.

Danny Lorenzo changed all that. Danny was the dream date, every mother's dream. An extremely good-looking young man, eighteen years old, dark black wavy hair, sparkling black deep-set eyes, a complexion of a bronzed god, and very gainfully employed in his father's meat works business. An executive at that. I must admit, the late model Porsche increased his appeal as did perfect manners, which were never lacking, or at least not in public. Never without a beautiful date, I was ecstatic when he asked me, (me!), to go on a drive to the point. Considering how I like astronomy and everything he explained, it would be the best vantage point, uninterrupted views, and all.

Trapped in a car with Danny was like being on the bottom of the ocean, caught in a fishing net, with an octopus.

'You're lovely, just lovely.'

He was fast. Caught by surprise he had my arms pressed tightly to him, his mouth hot on mine, then, incredibly, it was sliding quickly down my throat to my breasts. Sure, some girls did that thing on the first date, not me. Beating my fists on his face achieved nothing, his desire increased with each blow. Initially, I was paralysed with fear, recalling my mother's words.

'Oh honey, how exciting. This is the type of boy every girl dreams of marrying. Born with manners, looks and money. His parents are such good churchgoers. Supporting the community wherever they can. I'm so excited for you.'

Face buried in my bosom, all I could feel was his repulsive tongue on my skin. Arching my back in reflex, trying to dislodge him, his hands holding my buttocks, squeezing, forcing me against him.

Mother also believed in love and respect, and this wasn't either. Thankfully, the fear passed, replaced quickly with despair and finally disgust. Fighting off a man who felt he had a divine right to any female was difficult, but my survival instincts kicked in. Actually, I kneed him in the groin while searching for the door handle, and within a split second I was tumbling to the ground. Scrambling to my hands and feet, I jumped up screaming. I found myself left in a cloud of swirling dust, as he slammed the door behind me and drove off. His horrid laugh echoed in the distance.

Hell. (Forgive me Father) From this point it took me forty minutes to find a phone, and an hour to decide who to call. Ma and Pa had gone away for the weekend, allowing me to stay home by myself for the first time. Trusting me in the hands of such a respectable young lad. Jesse said it was no problem to pick me up.

A nearby log, crumbling from life's beatings and white from the sun's torment offered the only respite. My eyes, a dyke ready to burst. Small droplets building to a crescendo of emotion. Look I used that word. Having never really thought about it, there are many duality meanings to words. Twenty minutes it took me to settle down, dry the eyes and stop my chest heaving under the sadness, then I heard the rumble. The Indian. Gee Izzy, how could I treat a friend that way, my best friend? Tears sprang to my eyes the moment I saw her. Poor Jesse, she assumed I was crying over Danny.

Wrapping me in her leather jacket, I was bundled onto the half painted Indian. Cool air brushed away my tears, as Jesse took the ancient motorbike gently down the sloping curves. Holding her waist tightly, my head gently resting on her shoulder, I had no mind for any dual meanings. I was so happy to have my best friend back.

Coming to a halt in the quiet suburban street I called home, we dismounted. Never had the cream stucco house, green shutters at each darkened window, in a mixed-up Mediterranean style, look so ominous and unwelcoming.

'Izzy. Would it help if we talked about it?'

'What?'

'Danny. What he did... or tried to do.'

Shaking my head, sprinkling tears to the ground, Jesse's hand reached out for my cheek. The heat burned my chilled skin as her thumb wiped away the last remnants of saltiness. Standing, staring at each other, a lifetime of words and no voice for them.

Piercing pale blue eyes searching my face, responding to my actions. Stepping forward, her heat still seeping through my now blushing cheek. She wrapped me in her arms, a feather soft kiss landed on my forehead. With my eyes closed I could sense her love for me. From that point in time, I am sure I loved her. More than I ever expected.

Secure in the domain of my room, Jesse hesitantly assisted me under the cover of my bed. Carefully she tucked the sides tightly making me secure and warm. Slowly brushing her locks away from her face, we came eye to eye.

'I'm sorry.' Was all I could mutter.

A weak smile filled her face. I shivered once again. Like the friend of the past Jesse lay beside me. My body secure under the blankets, her lying loosely above. Her presence offered a peace I had not felt since childhood. I drifted off into a deep sleep.

Sunlight burst through the window, celebrating the birth of a new day. The veil of darkness and all its evils removed. Rubbing sleep from my eyes I remember seeing Jesse's dressed body and arm merging to form a protective arch over my still wrapped form. Smiling, my hand searched out hers, as if to say, 'I've missed you.'

Studying my concerned face, her eyes drifted to the familiar family photo on my side table. Pa in his freshly pressed black clerical robes smiled out to us. Ma in her favourite pink skirt and jacket set, white blouse rustling in the autumn breeze. And me, Izzy, a ten-year-old smiling with metal braces gleaming in the receding sunlight, embraced by my proud parents as Jesse and I hold up the trophy we won at the science fair. Side by side, our proudest moment ever, together. Eyes returning to my face, their fire extinguished, Jesse whispers four little words that shattered my peaceful existence.

'Don't ever forget me.'

With those words hanging in the air, Jesse rose and left my room, and my life forever. No words could describe the pain I felt. All the hazy fancies of childhood were long forgotten, lost in the limbo of someone else's life. Adult ideals had intervened, and there was no turning back. Gratitude surfaced in the sea of sorrow. Gratitude for teaching me that love is limitless, no boundaries able to capture it. Amazing how life's lessons hit you in the face with the power of a sledgehammer. I think I would have preferred the sledgehammer.

Without knowing it, Jesse taught me how to be non-discriminatory, something I already thought I was. Ignorance must have held me in this belief, that or the lack of action made me feel secure in the thought that I didn't discriminate. To do nothing is as bad as discriminating against someone for any reason: race, creed, colour or sexual preference. For the good and the bad of it all, I am eternally grateful to Jesse.

Surely, she would not have chosen such a persecuted lifestyle, in such an already difficult world, unless it came from deep within. That is what I hope, for my Christian upbringing could not bear to face any other reasoning.

Rest assured I am not that way, having since had an intimate interlude with a person of the opposite sex. Enjoying it thoroughly. My time with Jesse will never be forgotten, but in gloomy times like now, the joyful thought of her brings happiness to me. The thought of my one true friend. Jesse is just one memory I dredge up when life is suffocating.

My other most memorable moment is time spent with Uncle Timba. Funny really, his name, considering how tall and straight he was, like a tallow wood. When I was little and wouldn't eat, Uncle Timba had a special way of preparing toast. He cut thick slices of bread and with a long fork, held them over the open fire. Then he placed the slices between his giant palms, patting down each side to remove any cinders. I ate so many slices that, to this day, I love the smell of burnt bread.

San Francisco, California, U.S.A.

Well anyway, that male, previously stated as satisfying my sexual preference, was just caught in a rather risqué position with a One L, a first-year law student. What a creep, saying it was an accident. Sure, he just tripped over and landed on her. Be real. So here I am, sitting alone, waiting. Such a dank, musky bar, at least it suits my mood better than those trendy café bars. My mind still not understanding why I'm waiting alone for my horrid ex, Jerome, to appear.

All of society's misfits appear to be in the bar tonight. Businessmen, amidst midlife crisis, are trying to seduce girls young enough to be their daughters. Perpetual drunks stand to one side plunging the last of their money into the blinking gaming machines. The barman, in standard pretend listening mode, is polishing glasses with a towel slung over one shoulder.

Three freshmen are leaning on the alcohol polished bar, jesting and joking. Bet they've left their girls at the dorm so they can play up or something. Look at the way they stand, trying to look irresistible. One looks a little wimpy, while the other, with broad shoulders, stands with his back to me. The third is particularly cute, for a white guy. His manner is slightly different, confident, bordering on an air of superiority, yet still enticing and svelte in movement. Oh, they're looking this way. At me? If only I could hear what they were saying. Surely it would be good for a laugh.

****

'Okay boys. The bets on the table. Whoever doesn't get laid tonight loses.'

Moving closer to his companions, using individual eye contact to heighten the effect.

'And you all know what that means?!'

Rubbing his hands, licking his lips in excitement, Carl eyes his competition. Girls throw themselves at him in no uncertain terms. With reason too, Carl was what many would call a jock. God blessed, a handsome figure of a man. He keeps himself in fairly good athletic trim, even taking into account all the alcoholic bouts his young body has suffered thus far, inches taller than his companions, hair rich and full. Having a father with plenty of money also helped. This brilliant idea was therefore conceived in his own conceited mind.

'Got your eye on anyone yet, Mike?'

Patrick realised it came down to he and Mike, as it always did. It wasn't that either was painful to look at, next to Carl though, they looked less exciting. Hidden behind the façade of being gentlemanly, the truth was neither desired to have numerous random sexual partners, espe cially not to win a bet. They weren't prudes but their conscience sometimes took control.

Mike took in Patrick's expression, reading his face as if it were a favourite story. He remembered when he first stepped into the dorm, there was Patrick, auburn hair neatly combed, carefully trimmed, and set in place, his hairline already receding at eighteen. Unpacking his clothes in a pedantic manner, his body's pale complexion reminding Mike of uncooked dough, that, or a nightclub pallor. He was physically on the verge of going fat, but not quite yet. Hands carefully manicured, his fingers strong and clean yet his face always cheerful, encasing a welcoming smile.

Mike considered Patrick his base in the confusing world of university, the knowledge this one man had made up for any shortcomings in the beauty side, even though

Patrick was not always willing to see it that way. The two had been inseparable since the start of the university year. Sharing notes on their courses, eating, and hanging out, and basically having a great time.

'She's quite a good looker, over there. The second table on the left. Looks as if she's waiting for someone.'

Mike tilted his head in the direction of the woman he saw.

'No deal Mikey boy. She's coloured.'

Responded Carl harshly.

Frowning in incomprehension. 'So?'

'Everyone knows they're easy.'

Jested Patrick.

'That's right. It's in the blood. Promiscuous bunch. They shouldn't be allowed in respectable places like this.'

Continued Carl.

How could venom flow with such ease from those so young? Mike couldn't understand it. The three of them were so similar in many ways, acting like boys, yet parts of his friends' upbringing horrified him. His mother had spoken of such things but never had he believed them so true, especially the ignorance of such supposedly educated people. Barely noticing it before, especially since they crossed so few cultural boundaries where they hung out, tonight it annoyed Mike.

'I'm still going to say hello.'

'Knowing your luck, you'll strike out with her too.'

Laughter emitted from the two.

Using his usual confidence to hide his uncertainty,

Mike approached the young woman who sat alone with her thoughts. Her eyes veiled in a misty sadness, chin resting on a raised palm, a palm paler in complexion than its reverse side. The tone of her skin reminded Mike of chocolate, not any ordinary chocolate but Cadbury's from home. Not quite shiny but with an incredible appeal. Hairs on the back of his neck prickled, with the thought of the icy stares his friends would have.

'Hi, I'm Mike. Michael Dart.'

'Hi Michael Dart. I'm not interested.'

'That's fine but could I buy you a drink 'not interested'. You see my buddies say that I always strike out with women, and well, they're right. If I could just buy you a drink, then I'll leave. Forever if you like.'

Izzy smiled at his brashness. Over his shoulder she could see his buddies nudging each other, laughing. Adding conviction to his story.

'It's good to see you look so...pitiful, but no. I'm waiting for a friend.'

His charming smile becoming infectious, Mike moved closer leaning on the raised table. At close range this woman was even more beautiful with her pale lips, dark curls and wide emerald green eyes.

'I could wait with you.'

Filling the vacant stool beside her.

'No. I'm waiting for a friend.'

A slow smile spread over his ruggedly handsome face as he swivelled his stool to face her. As Izzy rose to leave, Mike reached out and slid an arm around her waist, as if it came naturally, and casually pulled her between his legs. Then, just as casually, kissed her hello. Her total lack of response made him frown.

Mike turned her to face him. His hands rested lightly at her waist, but his thighs closed until they held her pelvis in a square grip. Mike couldn't quite suppress his smile.

'Please release me Mr Dart or I will make a scene.'

His smile spread to his eyes, as Mike curled his fingers around hers, imprisoning them in a warm possessive grip.

'What type of scene?'

Izzy watched mesmerised, the warm glow in his eyes became a flickering golden flame. Her sense of unease increasing, Izzy's eyes scanned the room for help, but she wasn't sure if she really wanted saving. Returning to his amused face, she could feel herself drowning in his deep blue eyes. Eyes in such contrast to her own.

'Where's your friend?'

The bastard, his eyes were mocking her. Daring her to resist.

'He'll be here any ...'

She didn't get to finish the answer. His mouth closed on hers with a tenderness that took her completely by surprise. His lips were firm yet gentle, asking for a response rather than demanding one. Mike's tongue delicately traced the seam of her mouth, coaxing the lips apart for him, and she forgot – what's his name?

Her hands rejected the instinct to find their way inside his shirt. Mike ended the kiss so abruptly that a soft moan of complaint slipped past Izzy's lips before she could stop it. His eyes narrowed in surprise, but a smile returned to his handsome face.

'And you would be?'

Her lips parted on a silent gasp. Never had she allowed a stranger to kiss her, she hadn't even let anyone kiss her on the first date. Izzy had no way of knowing how tempting she looked at that moment, eyes opened wide in startled comprehension, full, soft lips parted invitingly. She was intensely aware that he hadn't released her wrists.

'I'm glad he's not here.'

Noticing his unabated stare, Izzy's heart sank in dismay. He had suddenly switched to a husky murmur so sensual, so blatantly seductive, that certain areas of her body began to tingle with awareness. As if he knew, he smiled into her eyes.

'Can I escort you home?'

That insinuation was too much. Izzy's emerald eyes burned with anger. Yanking her hands free, stepping back awkwardly, her flailing voice spoke.

'No, you may not! Goodbye Mr Dart.'

As Izzy spun to leave, Mike took her hand, slim, elegant, and normally fully in control of its destiny. Rocking it gently, he kissed it with feathery lips.

'I look forward to seeing you again Miss?'

'Isabelle Lancove. Now let me go.'

'I look forward to seeing you again Miss Isabelle Lancove.'

Releasing his grip, Izzy's composure gathered once more. Glaring at Mike as she left him seated alone. Round the bar, past his laughing friends, Izzy blushed wishing there were another exit. The cool night air offered little respite for the heat that burned within her. Panting heavily, she rested her slim shoulders against the cold brick wall. Her heart palpitated at a million miles per hour. Wringing her hands in disbelief, blood throbbed at her temples.

'Oh, Miss Lancove. You forgot your handbag.'

That mischievous grin was once again beside her. His index finger lazily stroked the outer curve of her breast. She inhaled sharply, as his finger strayed to her nipple. Brushing his hand away Izzy stood square to Mike.

'I would ask that you would cease that, Mr Dart. And whatever game you are playing, please refrain from involving me.'

'It is no game Isabelle. May I call you that? I always get what I want, and what I want is you.'

'And if I don't want you?'

'You don't?'

The growled accusation vibrated through her as he dragged his open mouth up the side of her neck to her ear. His teeth nipped lightly at the lobe. Apologising for the love bite his tongue lingered to make reparation. And all the while his nimble fingers were doing the most incredible things to her breasts, making them throb with a pleasure so acute it was almost pain. As if the torment he was already inflicting wasn't enough, he deliberately tilted his pelvis into the curve of hers.

Reeling with dizziness, Izzy half-heartedly pushed Mike away. When words came she spoke breathily.

'No. I'm not like that.'

'Then let me escort you home.'

'No, it would not be right.'

'I want you, Isabelle. I want to know all about you.'

'No. You just want sex.'

'That's not right. I want you in my life, forever.'

Flashing from Mike's mouth, the statement left both he and Izzy in surprise. Mike had the grace to look embarrassed. Under his tan his face looked ruddier than ever.

'Nice line. No thanks.'

'Let's approach this properly then. A picnic, tomorrow. We can get to know each other first, if you like. We can go through the whole courting process.'

A certain seriousness swept his face, as if he were speaking the words to a long-held lover or friend. Stepping to allow a gap between them, Mike straightened his clothes, and used his thumb to wipe the smudged lipstick on Izzy's lips. Offering his arm, in the way of gentlemen, Mike smiled warmly.

'Please allow me the pleasure of escorting you home, Miss Lancove. I promise to be on my best behaviour.'

Befuddled by the situation, Izzy was prepared to argue until she saw her slimy ex, Jerome, approaching the bar. If nothing else, seeing her leave with a white guy would peeve him off.

$$\sim 3 \sim$$

HOPE

Outer suburbs, Moscow, Russia.

Running through the housing block, Yacob skips down the stairs two at a time. His pace increases, as does his breathing, as he enters the central courtyard. The early morning darkness clings to the sky, obscuring Yacob's shadow as he passes through the gates. Breath curls in front of him desperately trying to rise yet the coldness suppresses it.

Inhaling deeply Yacob accepts the cold that burns his lungs. Training had been long and hard. He was fortunate enough to be accepted at the boxing gym at the age of ten. During the following eight years he had honed his skills. For the first four years they actually did fitness and boxing training.

Some families paid a nominal fee for the privilege of their child attending. For them they saw it as a way for their child to leave the slums though admittedly many didn't. The boys, with their limited training, just became local thugs. Others like Yacob were selected from the street. Boys like him came from disjointed families who did not care or were too poor to maintain any resemblance of a home life. Such boys would normally become petty thieves. To prevent this, a select quantity of boys were paid to attend the gym from the age of fourteen.

The money was not great, yet it was sufficient for boys who had no other options. From the age of fourteen the training changed. Loyalty was already a discipline. Now hand to hand combat training was introduced, as was weapons training and explosives training. By the age of eighteen the selected boys had obtained more specialized training than any elite force in the world.

Yacob understood that to succeed he needed to be the best. Besides, he had nothing to lose. By watching his rivals and training nonstop he had learnt to react as if his muscles were in command, not his mind. This gave him an advantage over his opposition.

As he ran, younger boys would fall in behind him single file. Ahead there were more boys waiting on abandoned street corners. Each stood beyond the streetlights glare yet Yacob saw them. In fact, he felt them before he saw them. That was an instinct the trainers said could not be learnt. They respected him for it. Some he smelt before he saw them. Those boys who wore the cheap colognes would learn, he thought, the hard way.

Feet pounding steadily, Yacob breathes deeper, wishing for the burn to continue. His shoes barely protect his feet from the Russian cold. Ice crystals crack under the soles. Yet they are a symbol of his position, his strength.

The Western sneakers were a gift on his graduation from the boxing gym. He wore them with pride as only ten of the fifty boys at the gym graduated this year. He had graduated with honours. Today they were dispatching him on his first assignment.

Yacob pondered the purpose of the training. As basics go, he understood it. Rich Western investors created the boxing gyms, funded them, and employed the graduates. It was a bit like creating your own personal army, he thought. His friend Gustav had graduated last year. Initially he was posted to Croatia but now he was in Paris. Life was treating Gustav well. He had money, a car and partied in all the flash nightclubs. It was something he and Yacob had dreamed about since they were young.

All of that sounded awesome except Yacob was proud to be Russian, and he dreamed of being respected here, not abroad. To him the others sold their souls to the Westerners. Yacob spat in disgust. The thought of Westerners made the bile rise in his throat, especially ones who thought they could exploit Russia. Those with money who bought their way in to launder dirty cash and run these thug factories.

With a bit of luck, he would be transferred to the woman in Australia. She was the most powerful or at least that is what he heard. Very few went to Australia, the woman was more interested in assigning the graduates around the world. Yacob did not understand why, nor did he care. To gain her trust would put him in a position of strength.

In his mind Yacob was using the Westerners. Taking

their training, gaining their trust but one day he would get his own back. Pulling a knife from his pocket Yacob ran the flat blade down his face. A thrill electrified his spine. Yacob stood taller, he felt impenetrable: to the cold, to the world. He would show them who the real man was. With that Yacob slid the blade down his tongue. A trickle of blood entered his mouth. He tasted the saltiness and smiled. He was the man.

~ 4 ~

TO SEE LIFE

San Francisco, California, U.S.A.

University life hadn't enthused Mike as much as he hoped. Yes, he had argued with his mother about coming to the States, before that it was Rome, which she vehemently opposed. The only compromise was San Francisco, not Chicago as hoped, and changing his name. Ricoldi was a name, which, she felt, could draw trouble. Attention and special treatment were one thing he didn't want. While at it he changed his first name to shirk her. Compromise.

He was always taught to take control of his life, to become a legitimate businessman. How could he tell his mother that the men on Wall Street were more criminally insane than his own family? They were not your traditional crooks and thieves, but their education, strategies and contacts started here, at university. So far, he hadn't met anyone different, except maybe for Patrick, and Izzy.

Yes, throughout the night his mind always drifted back

to Izzy. In those few minutes spent together before she dumped him in some side street, Mike felt spell bound. It had taken him most of the next morning to track her down. Fortunately, he had made quality contacts in his short time in the States. After the first phone call Mike just had to sit back and wait. Last night's kiss was still lingering in his mind when the call finally came.

Jumping into his red '67 Mustang, he followed the directions calmly given by the GPS. Before fleeing the city, Mike stopped at his favourite Italian deli to pick up supplies. Cranking up through the gears the Mustang was soon on Highway 101 heading for the Hellyer Park Velodrome in San Jose. Having the roof down allowed the late summer breezes to caress his excited face. Before long, the exit for Hellyer Avenue appeared. Turning right at the bottom of the off-ramp, and approaching the stop sign with caution he flew straight ahead into Hellyer Park. Following the signage, he finally found the track at the south end.

Sprockets whirred in fury as the blurry figures of cyclists whooshed past the start/finish line. Mike approached the fence with caution, leaning a short distance from an older, stockier gent barking orders to those on the track. His ears pricked up at the coach's comments.

'Come on Izzy. Tuck in tight. What's wrong with you today? That's no way to make the Olympics. You too Sarah. Tuck in.'

Without turning his head, the coach barked at Mike, startling him with the gruffness of his voice.

'Can I help you?'

'I was looking for Isabelle Lancove.'

'So, you are what's distracting Izzy today. Thought her mind was elsewhere.'

The stocky man turned, his frumpy fingers extended to Mike. The lower part of his face was twisted into a partially toothless grin.

'Chuck Kerrigan. Head coach.'

'Michael Dart. Izzy's distraction.'

The two men shared a hearty chuckle. Dragging his lanky frame along the fence line, Mike stood closer to Chuck. Cycling was new to him. Yes, his mother had cycled once, but she rarely spoke of it. Like any new interest, Mike progressively started to drain Chuck of information. Practiced in many lines of questioning, it took Mike extraordinarily little time to extract the information needed.

'What size is the track?'

'Each lap is 333 metres or about 1/5 of a mile. The corners have about 25 degrees of banking to them.'

'Are they special bikes?'

'Yeah. They look similar to road bikes but have no gears and no mounted brakes.'

'Must be hard to stop.'

'Some have trouble.'

He chuckled, more to himself, as if recalling past failures.

As the riders approached again, Mike noticed Izzy leading. Chuck coughed out commands and Mike joined with words of encouragement similar to Chuck's. Shocked by the sound of his voice, Izzy veered away from the others, concentration lost, and careened into the enclosed grassy paddock. Upon hitting the cushioning of the grass at a quick pace, Izzy and bike thumped to the ground. Lying on her side, grass clinging to her face, Izzy maintained the cycling position as her feet remained attached to the bike. Looking up she saw Chuck and Mike darting through the gate, tentatively manoeuvring around cyclists on the track, before approaching her.

'See Mike? Some like to show off when they stop.'

Mike's face showed none of the light heartedness and joviality that Chuck appeared to delight in.

'Are you okay, Isabelle?'

'What the hell are you doing here?'

'See. She's fine Mike. Just trying to impress you. That or get out of the training session for the day.'

Looking up to the now gathering cyclists at the edge of the track, Chuck frowned and stormed over to them.

'Who said you guys can stop training? Come on ten more laps before lunch.'

Helping Izzy dislodge herself from the bike, Mike lifted her to her feet. After dusting her grass-stained legs, he lifted her bike onto his broad shoulder with one hand.

'Light aren't they?'

'Thanks. I can do it myself.'

Tentatively reaching for her bike, Mike clasps her gloved hand in his. Smiling down at her, Izzy gives up without a struggle, drained from a hard training session, she has no strength to argue. Besides, a niggling pain in her right shoulder demanded her attention. Watching her discomfort, Mike freed his hand from hers, allowing him to place his warm fingers on her neck. With a gentle motion he massages the neck down to the shoulder blade and back again. Mike drew close to her, his breath cooling against Izzy's sweaty skin.

'Hungry?'

'Uh-huh. But how did you find me.'

'I have friends.'

He stated with a broad smile.

Seating Izzy and her bike at the base of the grandstand, Mike darted off to fetch lunch from the car. He returned with a large wicker picnic basket, topped with a traditional red and white checked rug. Izzy gave him a faint smile as he returned.

'The picnic I promised.'

'Demanded, I recall.'

Mike's eyes searched Izzy's body to discover the secret behind the spell binding appeal he felt. Her Lycra-clad flesh revealed every bump and nuance, hiding nothing. She was in stark contrast to the fleshy, fabled hourglass figure, the glossy lip sticked mouth and toss of spun sugar hair. Her appeal lay in the attenuated cyclist's body, pale lips, dark curls and those ever-shining emerald eyes. When her anger increased, as was the case last night, the eyes would turn a vivid green, making them sparkle with even more appeal. Disappointedly Izzy covered her body in a warming, yet unflattering, tracksuit. Noticing his attention on the tracksuit's detail, she spoke.

'I'm in training, trying to qualify for the Olympics. I'm part of Team USA.'

'You must be very good.'

Izzy was pleased to see how visibly impressed Mike was. Most people in her life had never taken her sport seriously, except maybe for Jesse. Cycling had always meant a great deal to her, it was the one thing in life she felt she was good at. Previous boyfriends had always enjoyed her Lycra-clad body at first, but in time had become jealous of other leering males. That, and the fact it took time to train at the intensity she needed to make the Olympic team.

'Where would you like to eat?'

'We could go and sit on the grassy knoll overlooking the track if you'd like.'

Forfeiting the fact that Mike had arrived uninvited, assuming she would lunch with him, they trotted slowly to the grassy knoll. Spreading the rug, Mike methodically placed out the food he had carefully chosen for their first meal together. The last objects to be selected from the basket were two crystal champagne glasses and a dark green bottle of wine.

'My, my, what a selection.'

'Yes! A fine Italian selection of linguine with tuna pesto, homemade fusilli with arugula and tomato sauce, calamari and tomato salad, home-style country bread and figs with honey and mascarpone. And the something special I made myself, cuoricini di mais, little golden hearts.' The final plate drawn from the basket held delicate golden heart shaped biscuits drizzled with chocolate.

'I didn't know you were Italian?'

'There is much about me you do not know.'

A cheeky glint in his eye drew Izzy's attention. She noticed, with beating heart, his tall lithe frame, the breadth of his powerful shoulders contrasting with the whipcord slenderness of his hips and thighs in the corded jeans.

'I would have expected you to be the size of King Kong, not that of a grey hound, from eating such food.'

Lean, and tall, Mike patted his bulgless stomach. From his physique she imagined a firm six pack beneath.

'Been away from home too long I'm afraid. I'll apologise in advance that this fare, although of great quality, is not comparable to my mother's cooking.'

'I'm in training you know.'

Nodding at the wine he poured.

'Ah. But this is special. My last bottle of Australian wine, very fruity, you'll love it. Besides, if I call my mother asking for a new case, she'll ask who I drank it all with. It would be far nicer to tell her I shared it with the woman I wish to marry, than just with some of the boys.'

Izzy's green eyes flashed, and she stared at him incredulously. Her heart crashed like cymbals in her chest, reverberating through her whole body, making her deaf.

'Is this another one of your games?'

She asked in husky uncertainty.

'I'm not playing a game.'

Dropping to his knees beside Izzy, Mike's hands remorselessly reached for her. Backing up, shaking her head, trembling but defiant, Izzy's green eyes spat fire at him.

'Don't touch me! You are disillusioned.'

Scampering to run, lustful thoughts flooding her mind. Mike caught her shoulders. Forcing her to the ground and pressing her back against the grass, he enclosed Izzy with his hands on either side of her unmade face. He watched her with bright, inexorable eyes as she twisted and turned.

'Stop fighting it.'

He whispered.

'You know you want me as much as I want you, Isabelle. Your mouth told me that when I kissed you last night. Your whole body told me. Desire came off your skin, a heat I could feel with my fingertips.'

She was hot now, her face flushed, her traitorous body burning, but she wouldn't give in. She couldn't. Not to him or her own incomprehensible emotions. Violently shaking her head, she searched for words.

'No it isn't true. Just because I let you kiss mc docsn't mean I'm easy.'

Mike's normally kind face was a study of dismay.

'No. You have it wrong. I admit, last night, I was just trying to pick you up. But when I sat with you and you stood in defiance, I felt in awe of your inner strength. I know it's weird but there was something there. Even your beauty haunted me in my dreams last night.'

'Please. Leave me alone.'

Her voice quiet and unconvincing.

'I never want to be apart from you again.'

His voice, deep and loving. Izzy felt his arms around her, his hands seeking the gentle lines of her body. Even more shocking was the unexpected weight of his body as he eased himself onto her. She tried to keep stiff and unresponsive, but his mouth was upon hers, demanding her surrender. A wave of weakness flooded through her as she felt the soft curve of her lips parting under the fierce onslaught of his kiss.

Raising himself from her warmth, Mike rolled to the side, then lay on his back staring at the clear azure sky. With a sigh, he turned his head to look at her, his hand stroking her matted hair.

'I'm sorry. It's just that when I'm with you, the attraction is too strong. I know I promised to be on my best behaviour, and rest assured there will be no more attacks on your virtue. Being with you just feels so perfect. I've never felt this way before.'

Hesitantly Izzy admitted there might be something between them, but only time could reveal the truth.

'For now, it would be best for us to get to know each other.'

His hand fell away from her hair and the fearful throbbing of her heart slowed marginally.

'Yes, you are right.'

How well she already knew that twisted smile, the expressive curve of the lips that held, for her, some sexual meaning.

They ate their lunch slowly, relaxing in the warm, heated atmosphere of the velodrome. Relaxing in the fading afternoon and with a little assistance from the heady wine, Izzy spoke freely. Her words tumbled over each other and her face lighting up with eagerness as her sentences rose and fell like waves tossing in sunlight. It was a surprising contrast to her cycling, always characterised by a certain aloof calmness with her long hair and equally long limbs, smooth and mesmerising. In person, Izzy was anything but aloof.

'Tomorrow, if you haven't already cast me into the crazy pile, I would like to take you to Tilden.'

Mike spoke with an eagerness in his voice.

'Tilden?'

Izzy questioned.

'Yes, it's a little park across San Francisco Bay, behind Berkeley. For an Australian, there is no better place to turn one's back on Californian excesses. I would love to wander hand in hand with you amongst the groves of big eucalypts. Together we can inhale the blue gum vapours. Imagine that we were on the wildly rugged coastlines and sculptured ridges, or even on the vast cattle plains of Australia.'

'You sound a little homesick.'

'Very much so. I thought I could learn so much over here, but it's too much like home. Except here I feel, I don't know, further from where I wanted to be. In life I mean.'

'Sounds like you were escaping something.'

'Yes, maybe I was.'

'We all run from something ... or someone.'

Looking up into those eyes, Mike knew his instincts were right. Izzy was the one.

'Not all of my time has been wasted. Maybe up until yesterday afternoon, but from that point on, I've found new purpose.'

Mike looked over her with ill-concealed lust. Izzy felt a deep thrill curve and pulsate somewhere inside her, containing it would take some doing.

~ 5 ~

SANTAPAOLA

Brisbane, Queensland, Australia.

Refreshed from her morning run, Amelia admires her surroundings as she and Rosario leave the apartment and pace through the Southbank Parklands. Whispering with delight, the cool breeze caresses her ruby cheeks while brushing midnight strands across her stained lips. Sunshine dances about them, its rays of light already poaching an assortment of flower buds, encouraging them to burst into colour.

Refreshing days like this reminded Amelia of her youth, cycling through the Alps of France. Her days there were as bright and glorious as this new spring morn. Today everything shining with such vibrant life. Like her body, everything felt alive, including the tidal water slowly eating away at the pontoon as the pair waited for the City Cat Ferry.

A short dash across the river alights them at the edge of the city gardens and QUT (Queensland University of Technology) campus. Walking briskly from under the shade of the freeway, they enter a grove of mature trees. The path they follow circles the whole gardens all while skirting the river's edge. The rising tide had only just commenced to smother the dank putrid smell of mud and rotting vegetation. Just beyond where the path splits towards the café, the pair step down on to a wooden walkway. As it squirmed amongst the mangroves, two men dressed rather formally in black suits and dark shirts waited. With a nod, Amelia proceeded alone to follow the walkway amongst the mangroves. Rosario waited, chatting in Italian with the two men.

The momentary shade made Amelia shiver. Breaking from the mangroves, the walkway expanded into a large viewing platform, bathed in sunlight, the edges surrounded by strategically placed wooden benches. From the very edge one felt as if they were in the river's heart. As the platform was empty, Amelia leaned on the rail. Her eyes wondered along the river to watch an old wooden ferry plod along. Across the water she could see coloured figures clinging precariously to the Kangaroo Point Cliffs. Some pastime she thought.

Startled by a gruff rasping, Amelia spun round to acknowledge the sweat-drenched jogger. Greying chest hair peeking out from his half-unzipped tracksuit, lay matted and wet from his obvious physical exertion. A thick gold chain, supporting a diamond encrusted cross, flapped as the man lowered his head, hands pressing upon his knees. Viewing his platinum watch, he gasped. Amelia was early.

'As always Don Santapaola. Good to see you.'

With an amused grin, Amelia led Don Santapaola to one of the far benches where a towel and a water bottle were set out. Kneeling she kissed his salty hand, admiring the acorn-size diamond pinkie ring as she did so. Looking up she admired his handsome face. Flushed but truly Sicilian. Jet-black eyebrows set above a patrician nose gave his face a roman quality.

'Welcome Don Santapaola.'

Rising to encircle the man in her arms, Amelia embraced him loosely then perched herself at his side.

'And what am I to call you my dear Em? Donna Ricoldi?'

'That is an honour I will never receive, as you know. A woman, no matter how good she is, may never be a man of honour. We can give birth to them, raise them in the code, even marry them and run their affairs while they're away, but never be recognised as one. Thus, I am but a mere messenger for my husband.'

'If all my loyal friends were as good a messenger as you, I would stay home to tend my grapes and olives.'

Squeezing her hand, Don Santapaola sympathised with Amelia, reading her face easily. He had always encouraged her to be open with him. It had taken a while, to earn her trust, but he had succeeded after much persistence. Amelia was someone he wanted as an ally, for she would be a fearsome foe. He knew that if she were a man, she would be in his place, if not higher, in the honour society.

'It is a life you have taken to well. If Nicco could become half the man you have taught him to be, the world will be at his feet.'

'That is what I worry about. He's already rearing to go.'

'Just like his father. Any word on Nicosia's opposition?'

'It's in transition. A past gift from Gordone will complete the transaction.'

'Handling it yourself?'

'For now. But anyway, what brings you to this part of the world. A holiday?' Amelia jested. 'Spring Racing is about to commence.'

'You know why I'm here, Em.'

Looking away across the sparkling river, Amelia sat silent, waiting. Making Don Santapaola work for what he wanted.

'Word is you're about to strike up a new deal with the Columbians. Vito is worried.'

'Vito, huh! He can have his poisonous stock. I have absolutely no desire to trade in that market. As you know, I am against that trade even here, but I allow it out of respect for you.'

'Yes. I understand. Without that trade your income is larger than most who deal in narcotics. That I don't understand or wish to pry in to. Whatever your dealings, they have upset no one else. But if your earnings are on the increase, then...well...'

Finally, Amelia thought, the point of this little meeting. Revelling as Don Santapaola squirmed under his request, Amelia offered a form of release by acknowledging his unspoken words.

'And you want more.'

'Another five.'

'We already give you five out of respect. We always have, even when our earnings were a mere pittance. Why would you possibly need another five? The first five brings in more than many of your other earners.'

'Well.'

The ruddiness of physical exertion had receded but was quickly replaced by discomfort.

'Not another war for control like in the early 80's, Don Santapaola. That too was over the profit brought about by the poisonous stock. Look what happened. Many deaths for nothing and at the end Tommaso Buscetta hangs many a good man. I'm not complaining, it opened a door for me. Fortunately, we were not on the revenge list, that time.'

'No. But it is different this time. Another summit has been called to reiterate things.'

'I should hope so. If the Corleonesi had not won the Palermo war, where would you be? Not invited to the summit I bet. The joining of the Sicilian Mafia and Colombia's Medellin cartel in October '87, led to great things not only for you in Catania, but the other families in Palermo and Gela. Much revenue. And with the idea of moving towards a broader pax Mafioso, we could avoid much conflict and help devise a common strategy. The goal should be to work the planet peaceably together. Greed will destroy us all otherwise.'

A crease flooded Amelia's brow.

'I fear that is coming. We must build strength now in preparation.   I do not disagree with you, but in the eighties our strength flailed, the union made us strong, now we must become invincible.'

Patting her hand.

'As we are old friends, I will voice my concern. But

for what you have done for me, the support and kindness, I will agree to 2.5, no more.' Straightening her back, increasing her perceived height she looked down at Don Santapaola.

'How am I to operate on such a small margin.'

'As you have always done, with dignity.'

Knowing the man as she did, Amelia could see the smugness in Don Santapaola's face. For as long as she had known him, he had always asked for double of what he really wanted. After negotiations, both parties would feel as if they had touched the other. Amelia had no qualms about giving him another five percent, but he would have to work for it.

'Where is my favourite boy? I look forward to seeing him while I'm here. You should bring him to Sicily one day. To his homeland.'

'He's on holiday now. But he'll return soon.'

'Roberto?'

'He's become a fine young man. Unquestioningly completing all tasks given. A very valuable asset. The perfect associate.'

'He's like a son to you, yes?'

'Since his mother's death I have been his surrogate mother, I suppose. So yes, he is a son to me. I love him like one, hold hopes and dreams for him like one and fear for him like one. As I do my own son.'

'Is he ready?'

He asked, reading her eyes carefully.

'Most definitely.'

'Then it is settled. I will personally oversee his transition to a respected man. You must organise everything while I am here.'

'That is an incredible honour for Roberto. I personally thank you.'

With enthusiasm Amelia embraced Don Santapaola. It was an honour, for Roberto to be inducted into the brotherhood by such a man. It would excite him no end. To be welcomed by Don Santapaola was the finest declaration that he was a true, traditional, man of honour. Many, so called, men of honour had lost or disregarded the true purpose of the Mafia.

Once upon a time a Don was the arbiter, a Solomon, patron of the needy and wronged. The Mafia, or La Cosa Nostra, had always enjoyed social consensus since medieval times. The guappo was considered a lawgiver, one who restored order. He interceded when people needed housing, or work, or a duel had to be fought, or a pregnant girl had to get to the alter. The Don made people respect the rules. He moved in a moral universe with which neither the police nor the clergy concerned themselves, the dramas of the everyday life. To Amelia, this side of the Mafia was true and good, but the greed for money and power by individuals was so out of control, it repulsed her. Too numerous unwarranted deaths and malicious crimes had brought the name Mafia into disrepute. Roberto was strong and sound enough in the mind to fight this side of things, but was Nicco?

Her thoughts were disrupted by a loud crack amongst the mangroves. Don Santapaola lunged toward the planks of the platform under the guidance of Amelia's hand. Her body automatically straddling his while swiftly drawing a Beretta from within her jacket, focusing it on a point from where the noise had arisen. A high-pitched whistle escaped her lips as she slowly waddled in a squatted position to the platform's edge.

'Lay still, Vin.'

Mysterious splashing sounds continued from within the mangroves with an occasional branch cracking and falling into the rising water. As Amelia rose, her pistol focused, Rosario's thunderous feet could be heard approaching.

'Ha! Joseph Bodine, what may I ask are you doing here?'

Small splashes swirled on the waters skin as a small dinghy emerged from the thick growth of twisted roots and trunks. Quickly replacing her gun, Amelia turned to see the two men dust Don Santapaola off and raise him to his feet, profusely apologising.

'Spying Mr Bodine?'

'No, Mrs Ricoldi. Just clearing up some rubbish.'

Hearty laughter filled the void behind Amelia and she smiled at the man who had startled them. The man who very nearly could have been another unidentified body found floating in the river. Joseph's uneasiness showed on his face while his hands fidgeted with the oars.

'Joseph, this is Mr Vincenzo Santapaola. A very dear friend to me and unappreciative of your entrance.'

Turning Amelia spoke to Don Santapaola with a slight bow.

'Don Santapaola, this is Joseph Bodine, a friend of mine.'

Coaxing the small boat closer, Joseph unfolded his lanky form to rise to platform level, offering his hand to the man before him. The man, Vincenzo Santapaola, was in his sixties, of medium height, and he walked in a dignified and upright fashion, as if casting disdain on the unfortunate situation in which he just found himself.

'I am sorry to have disturbed you sir.'

'Joseph is the one who makes the gardens look so spectacular.'

Smiled Amelia, without taking her eyes from him.

'It is easy when you enjoy the outdoors. I have a lot of assistance too.'

'Yes, I enjoy my gardens as well. There's nothing like growing something with your own hands.'

Don Santapaola felt more at ease.

'No Mr Santapaola, there isn't. Anyhow, I must go and finish a few tasks before lunch. Enjoy the gardens, gentlemen.'

And with a slight bow, the boat rocking in a passing wave.

'And Mrs Ricoldi.'

'Goodbye Joseph.'

Away Joseph paddled, randomly looking back towards Amelia, then lowering his head to paddle further up-stream.

'That young man puts a lovely sparkle in your eye, my dear.'

'Oh Vin, do behave. I have no time for such foolish fancies.'

A raised eyebrow on that typically Sicilian face thought otherwise. Thought that maybe it was time, she should make time, but he dared not say it.

'It is time I took my leave. Give me time to wash up before my lunch appointment.'

'Yes, but before you go, one question.'

Tapping Don Santapaola lightly on the shoulder, Amelia leads him to one side, away from his waiting escorts.

'Zio (uncle) will make a proposal at lunch. If you feel inclined to disagree with him, I will gladly display my support with another three. Which I am sure will cover any discomfort or damage done.'

Laughing internally, Don Santapaola loved the way Amelia thought. It was cunning, like him.

'You are a soul after my own heart. Of course, I will have to listen to the proposal first, and judge it by its merits.'

'Of course, Don Santapaola. I expect nothing less.'

With a firm handshake, and a last kiss of that acorn-sized diamond for luck, Amelia watched Don Santapaola vanish amongst the overhanging branches.

'Good hunting, Amelia?'

'Yes, Rosario. It was a very good hunting day. Even for Roberto.'

'Don Santapaola is going to make him?'

'Yes, personally. You must feel proud. He offered, I did not have to ask.'

~ 6 ~

ONE STOP SHOPPING

Rambling along the quiet industrial street, the removal truck barely received a second glance. Due to the public holiday, the street contained very few cars on this otherwise ordinary Monday. Echoing off the tin and brick of the warehouses, the engine's rumble sounded louder than expected. Unperturbed, the truck went unnoticed through the chained gate, up to the loading dock of a prominent printing firm. From the cab jumped a young man in drab work clothes. Lighting a cigarette, he casually paced the short distance to the warehouse door.

Back supported by the door, arms folded across his chest, standing as casually as possible, he patiently waited. Within moments a security firm's car arrived. Alighting from the car stood a security officer in his police look-alike uniform. After completing the formalities, a brief negotiation took place. With much ado the young man stubbed out his cigarette before producing a roll of cash. Unwrapping several notes he proceeded to hand them to the guard. Indicating the fatness of the roll, the guard left his hand suspended between them. Another note crossed the palm before a key was handed over, suffice to say the guard promptly vacated the premises.

With key in hand, the young man entered the building to open the large roller door. Alighting from the rear of the truck were two more men with trolleys in hand. As the driver descended from the cab he jokingly spoke to the others.

'I like these one-stop shops.'

With merriment on their faces, the four men entered the building to commence their work.

'Okay guys. Quietly and quickly. Christopher, you keep a look out for any interference.'

Directed Roberto.

'Righto.'

Responded Christopher as he stood on the dock scanning the street, well the part he could see between the trees.

The other three quickly went to work removing every item the printing firm owned. From printing presses, to the computers and forklifts, right down to the telephones and desks. Roberto was very selective in his crew. They had just been promoted, since the ferry incident, to this new endeavour. For a small fee, approximately a third of what it would cost legitimately, a businessman could ask for 'help' in setting up a new business. All he had to do was identify the type of business, and which of his main opposition he would like to emulate. Roberto's crew then entered the premises of the selected business and strip it bare, right down to the last light bulb. Thus, the business-man could set up business with his 'new' equipment and be operational within one week. With part of his oppo-sition removed, and while they waited for the insurance claim, he could attack their business base especially since all the customer's details were on hand.

As a main base for his crew, Roberto had four men, including himself. Slim, a stocky lad from Gympie was the muscle. Built solid from heavy farm labour, Slim's repu-tation was built on his ability to pull loaded farm trucks, with his bare hands, at county fairs. Also of a good build was Joey Mandell, who already, at the age of nineteen, was known as 'Merlin', for his ability to make people disap-pear. Christopher's reason for being on the crew was be-cause of his relationship with Roberto, as the best friend. They had grown up together and broken their teeth on crime together. Estimating that Christopher would take a little work, Roberto felt confident his friend had potential. Besides, he was exceptional at picking locks. It was wise for the others to be on Roberto's crew as he was a mover and a shaker, the one with the contacts, a brain, and the ability, to use them. Hooking up with Roberto meant they were all rising stars.

Having started working together as a crew since about fifteen, except Joey who joined them at seventeen, their ability to read each other was great. Therefore, very few words were required during an operation. Slim nudged Roberto as the purr of a four-cylinder engine approached. Christopher shot round the corner, wide eyed.

'There's a car.'

'Well fix it.'

Nodding, Christopher returned to the dock. 'Hey. Can I help you?'

'What's going on?' Questioned a man's deep voice.

'Just some renovations.'

Christopher descended from the dock and approached the man in a friendly manner. Scanning the area, he noted they weren't viewable from the street. A line of silky oaks hindering the view.

'I'm the artistic manager and I haven't heard anything about this.'

Becoming agitated, the man thrust Christopher aside in time to view his workstation being loaded into the truck.

'What the?'

Extracting his mobile phone from his pocket, the man turned back to Christopher.

'You guys hold it right there.'

One hand held the phone to his ear, the other held Christopher at arms distance. In his arrogance the man failed to acknowledge any danger to himself.

Roberto's voice came as a surprise from behind the man.

'There a problem?'

Turning, the man's face collided with a piece of wood swung by Roberto. Slumping to the ground, Roberto's eyes returned to Christopher.

'Fix it.'

'How?'

Came the stammered reply.

'Shoot the fucker.'

Laughed Roberto. Slim seconded the point.

Drawing a gun, Christopher aimed it at the man's head. With blood spurting from his nose, the man eyed up Christopher before raising his hands in surrender.

'Please no. I have a family.'

Hesitating, Christopher's eyes took in the defenceless man before rising to meet Roberto's set eyes.

'Just shoot him Chris. Every man has to make his bones before he can be a man of honour, this one's just practise. Just do it.'

The words were calm, conversational even. Without warning Roberto swings the lump of wood again, knocking the rising man off balance.

'I don't know, Robbie.'

'Let me.'

Suggested Joey.

'No. It's Chris's.'

Standing by his friend's side, arm wrapped warmly over his shoulder.

'The first is the one you remember, so make it good.'

Turning his head slightly, Christopher's eyes shut as the pressure of his finger increases. With one last ounce of pressure the trigger was pulled to the point of no return. Without looking, Christopher was unsure of where the bullet entered the man's body, but Roberto congratulated him all the same as he sends a bullet, of his own, through the man's left eye, then his right. Only the dull thud of the silencer distinguished the release of the deadly bullets from Roberto's gun to that of Chris's. The other two applaud as Roberto held Christopher's hand in the air like a boxing champion.

'I'll give him to the count of three.'

Yelled Slim, who had barely finished the sentence before Christopher relieved his stomach next to the dead man. Laughing, with the others, Joey searches the body, extracting an expensive looking leather wallet. Withdrawing all the cash, he smiles at his accomplices.

'Hey, hey. Looks like the drinks are on Chris.'

'Back to work now guys.'

Urged Roberto as he tucks the money in his jeans.

'Quickly and quietly Christopher, that's the key. Less painful for the schmuck.'

Quietly the foursome return to work and were nearly finished when the roar of a larger engine approached. Once again, the sky blue police look-alike uniform appeared.

'In the truck.'

Spoke Roberto as Joey circles round to the guard.

'A gunshot was reported.'

Seeing beyond the parked car, the guard gags on his own vomit.

'Oh my God!'

Following the words is, what appears to be, the remainder of his lunch. Reaching for his gun, the guard is no match for Joey who has already drawn his weapon.

The bullet penetrates centrally on the guard's left knee. His body freezes momentarily as if stunned by the pain. Staring incredulously at Joey, mouth open in horror, the guard sinks to the ground as his second knee is shot out.

Crying in agony and begging for his life makes no indentation on Joey's fun, except in heightening it. Laughing like a child with a popgun, Joey yells the word *POW* as each cap goes silently off. Reaching for his dropped weapon, a third bullet enters the guard's right elbow. With a final *POW*, the guards left elbow disintegrates. Like a disconnected marionette squirming on the ground, limbs flaying unresponsively, the guard wiggles in a porpoise motion, in an attempt to hide beneath his vehicle.

'Let's go Joey.'

'Okey-dokey.'

With a final *POW,* the last bullet enters the man's skull squarely on his forehead. The body lays still, eyes staring vacantly skywards as if the man were daydreaming. A light breeze brushes hair over the hole, hiding it from view. Leaning down, Joey sweeps the hair sideways. Smiling joyfully, he joins his companions at the truck.

~ 7 ~

THERE'S MONEY IN IT

Beams of morning sun streamed into Amelia's office as she strode to the large oak desk. Sitting in the high-backed chair, her fingers searched to find the secret latch. Unfastening it, she could feel the secret it held. Her body shivered in anticipation, warmth filling the void inside. Relatching the hidden door, she turned to appreciate the freshness of the morning.

Rosario knocked before entering but Amelia's thoughts were far away. She was recollecting with a kind of twisted sadness, the scene of her own wedding. Even then, Nicco had been too possessive, but it had thrilled her, young as she was. He should have had no fear, for she only had eyes for him. Remembering still, how he had looked at her in those days. Even experiencing the strange trembling that she had felt when his eyes held her in that commanding way. But she had felt safe with Nicco. His protective arms always encircling her.

Unsure of what to do as the phone screamed to be

answered, Rosario's great hand came down to enclose hers and give it a mighty hurting squeeze.

'Your private line, Amelia.'

'Thanks, Rosario.'

There was plenty of time for memories to come flooding back, especially along life's straight monotonous road.

'Amelia.'

She answered briskly, then her voice softened as she recognised the caller.

'Brooke how are you? Yes, the line is secure...Yes yes. India is online and Russia is keen too. Together they can supply the Migs and whatever else Taiwan needs...Tanks? No problem. How many in this daisy chain?...Eight. More than I would like, but that's okay. How about the oil deal?...Four. That's better. Makes a better split. What percentage is the chain getting on the Migs?...1.25. Okay. Each Migs about thirty million. You said they wanted lots? ...Excellent. Should net us about twenty million profit a year. Yes, each...I'll set up a date for the meeting. Yes. India's ecstatic, apparently they're on the same security level as Taiwan with China...Nothing but good business.'

As Amelia discussed her next international arms deal, she could hear Brooke jumping up gears in the background. The wailing momentarily distracts her mind.

'What exotic beast do you have now? A Maclaren! Ha. So you can have a girl either side while you drive I bet.'

Every time she spoke to Brooke he either had a new car or a new woman sitting beside him, or both. She laughed to herself of the time he had stopped at the Sydney Harbour tollbooth to pay the toll. While he was on the phone to

Amelia, the girl in the booth had leant out and asked him if he was somebody she should know. Amelia had laughed and laughed, reminding him of the cheap business cards he had printed when they were in their mid-teens. *Soldier of Fortune* they had read. Followed by a list of unbelievable and incredible occupations.

Specialising in civil wars, Far Eastern Indo China
Special Forces and Jungle fighters Association Limited
Used cars, land, whiskey, manure, nails, bongos,
Dry holes and race guides.
Wind machines bought and sold.
Indoor Sportsman, Hero of the Suppressed,
Women seduced, wars fought, revolutions started,
Assassinations plotted, uprisings quelled, governments run,
Dragon slayer, casual hero, world traveller,
Drinker extraordinaire, bars emptied, virgins converted,
Orgies organised, computers verified and
Privileges abused.

A lot to fit on one card but he had managed it. Brooke's goal in life was to systematically achieve everything on the card. So far, he had achieved about half.

'Oh well. Take care. I gotta go. Another call's coming in. Ditto.'

Amelia winked a thank you at Rosario as he set out the breakfast he had prepared, even against her wishes. It had been a long time since Rosario had seen her eyes glitter with such excitement, all of this since the night before last. He thought the trip to the ferry would crush her, but it hadn't, or she didn't show it. They had known each other intimately for many years, but at times he still couldn't read her.

'Amelia.'

Was her short, sharp response to the new call.

'Gidday, mum.'

Mike imagined the special smile his mother reserved just for him. He knew her face would light up with those simple words, as if he'd walked into the room.

'Nicco. How are you?'

'All's well. Remember its Mike now.'

His voice was not harsh, only forceful in the sense the charade must continue, propped only by his pride.

'And the States?'

She asked. Ignoring his statement.

'Not too bad. Got a few interesting things going on.'

'Excellent. I miss you. Your rowdiness and that sloppy room of yours. There's been no one to argue with.'

No headaches either, or trouble to solve. But still he was only eighteen. There were enough rules in life to restrict him, and with those discovered, Amelia would enlighten him on the realities of life, or more to the point their life.

'Ha. Yeah. Yeah. I've had thoughts about you too. How's business? Robbie said you guys were out the other night. What was that about?'

Making a note to have a word to Roberto, Amelia kept her voice calm and carefree.

'Just some business.'

'Famous last words Mum. Anyway.'

Mike left a pause as if in thought.

'I rang to tell you some good news.'

'I can never have too much of that.'

'Spoke to the Columbians. You would not believe how easy it is for a student to cross borders these days.'

'A warm welcome?'

'You bet. You should see the palaces these guys live in. More secure than Fort Knox.'

'I'm going to Russia soon. How were the Siberians I sent? Trustworthy?'

The ones they had financed through an old cycling contact had so far been excellent. As violence on the Russian streets spiralled out of control, worried parents were rushing to enlist their sons in self-defence classes. Such classes are held in boxing clubs, funded by generous Westerners such as Amelia. The clubs had given many hope, and they had, as a bonus, produced many sporting champions.

Years earlier when Amelia had started using her contact, she had identified boxing and martial arts clubs as the perfect breeding ground for future gang members. Thug factories producing highly trained standover men. Men of this calibre, Amelia found, where in demand around the world. In demand, as standover men, bodyguards and as an elite force available immediately for any situation. Her men, of course, trained to be the best. Giving these youth a future when none other had existed, quelched Amelia's conscience. It amused her that with a single phone call she could have twelve of the most powerful men, and women, in the world murdered by their own bodyguards.

'Beyond compare. I've set them up on campus. A few jobs here and there.'

Continued Mike.

'Not stepping on anyone's toes, are you? I don't want to send Rosario to save you, you know.'

She said, smiling to herself.

'No, nothing serious.'

'So, what about the Columbians? Are we a go?'

'Our reputation preceded us and they're dying for us to handle their transactions.'

'If they only knew. Cleaning money makes more for us than we could possibly make out of drugs. Russia opened up at the right time.'

The right time for many things. By opening the gates to encourage more businesses into Russia, Gorbachev and Yeltsin had unwittingly left the door open for not only legitimate businesses.

'Just a step removed, that's all. Removes the guilt.'

Teased Mike.

'It was your choice to enter the business. You know I would prefer you not to, but the choice is ultimately yours.'

'Don't get me wrong, Mum. I want to be the man my father was.'

If I had the opportunity to know him. One day, thought Mike, I will go to his hometown in Sicily and speak to his family. My family. Mother was always silent on this side of things, so what she won't give, I will take.

'Oh yeah, I'm in love! She's wonderful and perfect. She's going to be in the Olympics, or at least, is trying to be.'

'Marvellous! What's her name?'

Marvellous was not the word Amelia felt. Mike was always her little boy and at eighteen she wasn't sure he was ready, or mature enough, to marry. Yet she and his father were about that age when they met.

Isabelle Lancove. Pretty, hey?'

'Absolutely.'

Mike continued the conversation in the same strain, but he did acknowledge the warble in his mother's voice whenever he asked about Vito and business.

'Would you like me to come home and help?'

'You know I would love to see you, but it's not necessary to fly back. Maybe after the start of Spring Racing I could visit you and meet this special lady.'

'You sure, mum?'

With a heavy sigh, Amelia tried to support the façade she started.

'I'm sure sweetheart. I love you, Nicco.'

'Ditto, mum. Catch you soon.'

Mike's cautionary sense kicked in. His mother was hiding something, as she did. Always in his best interest, she said, but this time it worried him. He had never been so far away from her. For familiar comfort, Mike removed the ragged black and white photograph from his wallet. More precious than any jewel, it was the only picture of the three of them. His father's broad smile revealing perfect ivory teeth. His masculine beauty detracting little from his mother's natural charms. Wrapped securely between the two, a small bundle whose face is twisted, unflatteringly, in a scream. Mike could imagine his father singing Italian lullabies trying to settle his only son.

The photo's smoothness passing gently between his thumb and fingers. Mike imagined the three as they would be today if they were together.

~ 8 ~

DEMONS BEYOND US

'You're being a bit huffy today, aren't you Patrick?'

Sitting casually in the recliner chair in their shared dorm room, Mike watches as Patrick fastidiously packs his bags for the term break. Methodically, he folds each item of clothing precisely to his liking before placing it carefully in the case. Mike detected his sullenness from the moment they rose and had breakfast together.

'You missing me already?'

Jests Mike playfully as he has done many a time before.

'Not likely.'

Cheering up, Patrick's voice rose in its pitch.

'Say why don't you join me? Nothing like the mid-west.'

'To bore the pants off ya. Nah.'

'You aren't seeing her, are you?'

Frowning in amusement, Mike took in his friend. Was that what was bothering him? From that first night in the bar, his friend had acted kind of peculiar. Carl's unbearable teasing restricted Mike from telling him about his future dates with Izzy. Yet Patrick was his buddy, the one who had sat up and listened to him drone on about her.

'For a bit, but then I have some other things to do.'

Mike wanted to be nothing but honest with Patrick.

In an undertone to himself, Patrick murmured a response.

'She's no good for you.'

'Why?'

'For starters she's coloured.'

'I can't believe a man of your intelligence can make a statement such as that. Obviously I have underestimated you.'

Rising in offence, jabbing his finger at Patrick.

'No.'

Sighs Patrick.

'You just don't understand Mike. This is America.'

'The land of the free.'

Interjected Mike theatrically, hand mockingly on his heart.

'Yes. Yes. There's a rumour doing the rounds that her ex, Jerome, is back on track. That, and that she's using you for your money.'

'Buddy. I'm doing the pursuing, so there's no using. Let me tell you. I wish there were!'

Smiling broadly at his friend in a soppy way.

'And Jerome's ancient history.'

Ruffling clothes in Patrick's case.

'Besides, he's coloured.'

Slapping Patrick on the back, the two share a forced laugh.

Unbeknown to the two, Carl was aware of Mike's continued liaisons with Izzy. And he is disgusted by it. Acknowledging he is the only one who can take control, for his friend's sake, he decided to pursue the matter in his own way. To warn her off and save Mike from her destructive influence.

Having felt eyes watching her for most of the day, Izzy was aware of his presence as she entered the park at Tilden. Feeling his cold stare on her neck, even knowing he was there couldn't prevent the goose bumps rising on her skin. The point that he was one of Mike's companions at the bar the other night, didn't ease her mind. There was no reason, she could figure, he would be following her. Unless Mike was disturbed by those insane rumours spread by Jerome. Fortunately, Izzy had the advantage of knowing the park intimately, especially after her forays here with Mike. She was also thankful to her father who had raised her to always have a contingency plan, considering that she was a woman and that cities were never safe. She never had the heart to tell him that a woman wasn't even safe in her own hometown, no matter how small it was.

Walking as far into the park as she dared, Izzy hoped Carl would not follow. In fact, she was hoping to find somebody, anybody that could deter him. Arriving at the most heavily wooded area, she hid her small frame behind the largest gum tree she could find. Pressing her back into its smooth trunk, she felt its coolness seeping into her flushed body. Purposely she did nothing to alert Carl that she knew of his presence only assuming that he was a hundred yards or so behind her. Sure enough, within two minutes footsteps were heard. Carl had obviously lost sight of her but knew she had come this way. When he came parallel to her, she made her presence known.

'Looking for me?!'

Carl was startled. For a moment he said nothing, then he snarled.

'You're the black bitch who should leave my buddy alone.'

Taking a good look at the guy, his heavily built physique, his dapper clothes, Izzy raises her camera and lets it flash.

'You bitch!'

In his momentary hesitation, Izzy begins to run. Her legs are muscular but lack the strength after being drained by a morning training session. Carl's natural athletic ability has him closing in. Spurred by fear, Izzy holds a steady pace. A similar awkward predicament with Danny Lorenzo passes through her mind. If only Jesse was here she grumbles. As they approach the golfing green he collars her arm.

'Listen here you little slut.'

Wheezing from the over-exertion, Carl drags Izzy close.

'Leave my friend alone or else.'

With his thumb hooked into his belt band, Carl displays the three-finger salute of the KKK, Ku Klux Klan.

Snatching her arm from his grip Izzy growls her retaliation.

'Is that the best you can come up with? Some schoolboy's salute. You don't scare me, you low life piece of dirt.'

Her words are strong and pronounced, yet she feels small and weak inside. Turning sharply on her heels, Izzy walks briskly away, knowing that if she stays, Carl will see her shattered nerves. Pursuing her from behind, his breath is hot on her ear as he vehemently spits more words.

'You little trollop. Normally I wouldn't give someone like you the time of day. But heed my words, I've killed your kind before for lesser things.'

He paused to let the thought sink in.

'No matter where you go, I will track you down.'

Riled by his words, Izzy turns abruptly. Her sudden non-movement causing Carl to bump awkwardly into her body. Pushing him away, the hatred displayed in his eyes shocks her. The dark pupils are small and piercing, he was obviously getting some perverse joy from this.

'Listen here white trailer trash.'

The words languished in the air, then his open hand struck the side of her head. Surprised by the sudden physical onslaught, Izzy barely flinches. Carl is yelling something at her with little bullets of saliva springing from his mouth. Words poured out but they made little sense compared to the throbbing in her ear. Without thinking, she kicks him in the shin, as would a frustrated child. Aggravating Carl even more, he grabs her slim arms tightly and begins shaking her, all the time yelling explicites. Releasing her arms, Izzy feels her body collide with something hard. Turning, she catches her reflection in the car window before sliding to the ground. Somehow Carl has forced her to the golf club's car park.

An onslaught of fierce kicks follows until a gravelly voice is heard from the distance. Squinting into the sun, Carl finishes with a final kick to the stomach, then leaves.

Winded and gasping for breath, Izzy attempts to raise herself from the ground. No breath has returned to her, so she settles down on the bitumen. Leaning heavily on the car door, her face rose to the dying sun. Small tears sprinkle her cheek.

Running from the direction of where she assumes she and Carl had come from, was a man. His eyes appeared to be frantically searching for something. Attempting to move once again, Izzy let out an anguished cry. Focusing on the sound, the man approaches Izzy with his hands raised in a non-offensive way.

'Are you right Miss?'

His accent was harsh and strong, a strange combination with such a fresh young face. It was round and open, crowned by bristly blond hair.

Helping Izzy to her feet, the man searches the car park.

'Is he still here?'

Pondering on the point that the man had just appeared from nowhere, Izzy can't fathom the sentence.

'What?'

Her mind was a veritable jumble.

'Is Carl still here?'

'No, he's gone.'

'Good.'

He supported her by the arm.

'Would you like me to help you somewhere?'

'No. No, I'll be fine.'

Pausing for the moment, Izzy looks up at her saviour, an obviously confused look fills her face. She is just about to ask something, but he interrupts her.

'Do you need medical help?'

'No.'

After searching the horizon, his eyes resettle on Izzy. Moving each part of her separately, inspecting every bone and muscle, he smiles.

'You will be okay. Yes?'

His words are static and rough.

'I must go then. Take care Miss.'

With a wave he was gone.

~ 9 ~

OFF AND RACING

Doomben Racecourse, Queensland, Australia.

Crowds milled about the exhibition gardens, the beauty of the day was lost amongst their simmering chatter. The sun, the azure sky and even the half-moon were present. Like a flock of racing pigeons set loose, thoughts of past years flooded Amelia's mind. All vainly trying to find their destination.

As the mind wanders, so do the ever-searching eyes. Yes, there is nothing as blatantly refreshing as reality, she concurred. Spring Racing at its best. Beyond Amelia were groups of women, cackling like hens, wearing summer frocks of garish floral prints. Each participating in a ritual of gathering and dispersing in the endless search for tasty titbits. Easily identified by their hats, an assortment of sizes and colour, feathers and ribbons, wide brims and brimless, bobbing in and out amongst the crowds. Falsely portrayed gents, their silk suits of some cheap imitation make, were hanging around the betting ring bragging about successful bets but managing to misplace the memory of the unsuccessful. Circling her eyes further, two small children, faces smeared in chocolate, could be seen running, screaming up and down a grandstand in an endless game of tag. Each ignoring the half-hearted admonition of their mother and the undisguised irritation of the people they knock off balance.

So much more clamoured to fill Amelia's eyes. Glancing with annoyance she took in each vapid, empty face. All except one. Joseph. Dressed rather informally. Not sloppy, but at ease. Tailored dress pants, accompanied by a refreshing white polo shirt. Such a fine statue of a man with broad shoulders leading to a slim waist, muscular arms resting with staunch hands hidden by trouser pockets. A body adjusted to his hard, laborious work. Not too defined but manly enough.

Having noticed him frequenting the track recently, Amelia always wondered whether he was looking for a rich young wife? Or perhaps, a wealthy terminally ill, aged one? A burst of noise like a small laugh rose from deep within. Amelia manages to suffocate it with a slender hand before it reaches the alert ears of her companions. With a quirky tilt of her head, coal black hair falls to one shoulder, cushioning her amused face. Did she fit into either of these categories?

No time to ponder, announcements for the feature race echoed across the manicured grounds. Amelia, led by the arm, settles in the member's stand where cool long glasses of champagne are offered from silver trays. Shaking her head, Amelia glimpses Joseph entering the betting ring.

Odds on favourite was Bounty Beast. Surely, he wasn't betting on Mafioso. A bleak bay stallion on his maiden voyage.

Time drifts onwards as the red-coated stewards, mounted on grey steeds, encourage the last of the horses into the gates. Men run hectically around, calling numbers, allocating stalls, followed by much wrestling. Revved by what is to come, several muscular giants try to dispose of the annoyance on their backs. One in particular, the last to be jeered in, a horse of immense stature under the guiding hand, or more to the point, under the guiding whisper of a diminutive figure. Body bent over a muscular neck, ears twitching under puffs of voice. Starched white pantaloons, blinding in comparison to the bleak bay colour they're seated on. Blood red silks containing small golden stars, allowing an ethereal feel. A similar redness adorns the helmet, to the centre, a large golden star sits with the ease of a wet cloth.

In moments, the opening gates clang announcing the departure of thundering hooves, cheers from the eager crowd are interspersed with the booming voice of the announcer. Vivid colours all vying for position. Tussling giants round the turn, creating cyclonic movement as each jockey wrestles for the lead out.

Mafioso's name appears several times at the end of a long breathless list. On the straight he slowly jostles for a lead out. Not once does he falter or slip, with head extended, slicing through the competitors. His immense size makes Mafioso majestic, his hooves weightless. With protest, Mafioso takes top honours. Not once does his tiny jockey raise the strap. There is no need, an inner force drives the horse. Besides, Amelia had chosen the jockey herself, for this reason.

Accepting defeat in a gracious manner was not Bounty Beast's owner's way. He flayed his arms and raised his voice, to no avail: the true champion was victor. Trotting back and forth before the agitated crowd, Mafioso is eventually led to the winner's circle. Bowing his mighty head as the ribbon is presented. Amelia waits patiently at the allotted stable unconcerned by the award presentation. Her shadow, Rosario, continues clearing the now gathering crowd. After being rinsed, Mafioso is brought to his victorious owner.

A youthful creature with a gleaming smile bounds past numerous potential champions to the stable alongside Mafioso. Head ablaze with a thick shock of generally unruly red hair, and intense hazel eyes, the jockey greets his employer.

'Did you see the ride Ms Ricoldi? Oh, what ease! Mafioso was as fine as a snowflake floating to earth from the heavens. A messenger from the angels above!'

Thankfully the jockey was selected on riding ability, not melodrama skills. What such life youth carries.

'I did see the ride, Harris. I am pleased.'

Always succinct in answering. Brief and to the point was Amelia's motto. No point leading people astray or entertaining fools.

'My, what a fine ride that was. The best in a long time.'

Her shadow tenses. Caught by surprise Amelia blushes.

She had not expected him to be around, let alone beside her now.

'And congrats to the jockey for sparing the strap. Mafioso?'

He spoke gently. His wafer-thin lips kicked slightly at the ends.

'Strange but truly Italian. A friend of the friend, I'm led to believe it means?'

Rosario was becoming uneasy, hopping from one foot to the other. It was ridiculous to name a horse after the Mafia. Trouble is all it could cause.

'I couldn't be sure, Mr Bodine.'

Suggested Amelia knowing full well what it meant. Nicco had informed her in the early days, when he was a young buck Italian and she, well, a visitor to the Italian nation.

Sensing the uneasiness he had caused, Joseph spoke again.

'A name is just a label we carry.'

An outstretched hand reached towards Amelia who accepted it in a firm business-like manner. Rosario twitched, as he normally did, settled only by Amelia's cold stare. Other than their interlocked hands, a special attraction drew Amelia and Joseph together. Not a physical one, more a curiosity. Each noticing the other from afar, learning the small intricacies of movement and nature. Both recognising the signs of a lost soul. He focused his life and time on the gardens, often catching Amelia unaware as she strolled aimlessly through them.

Sitting in the shade of the members stand, Amelia invites Joseph to sip Muscadean Wine from her favourite vineyard, Golden Grove. It was cool and refreshing with a fruity body that teased the taste buds. White muscatel grapes used in its creation can be tasted in each mouthful, as is the warm Stanthorpe sun, cool winter rains and the granite-laden soils of the region.

'I do hope you enjoy the wine. It is a personal favourite of mine.'

Many a familiar face passes offering congratulations. Faces, which have stolen headlines over the years. Or avoided them depending on ownership and wealth. Amelia graciously accepts the compliments but declines in engaging in conversations for too long. Attempting to stay focused on Joseph.

'A mighty fine drop this is.'

Holding his glass at eye level, spying Rosario's form beyond it.

Rosario, whose presence makes Joseph feel uneasy, is never too far from sight. For as long as he has noticed Amelia, he has wondered why a woman would need a chaperone? Maybe, laughed Joseph, there was an over-zealous, or overjealous, husband causing the interference. Amelia appeared to be at ease with the intrusion, so he attempted to be too.

'Not nearly as nice as the company though.'

A wry smile took in Rosario's disgust.

It wasn't till this moment that Amelia noticed Joseph's chiselled good looks. His face shadowed by a sense of strength tinged with sorrow. A strong jaw set off by a one-sided dimpled smile. Hooded eyes contained in skin tainted by the seasons, framed by mousy short cut hair. None of the body's youthful shape had been lost to the excesses of food or alcohol. To her, if a person had no regard or care for themselves, then they could in no way care for others, in life or business.

In polite conversation Joseph queried.

'Do you frequent the track often?'

'Only to see our horses race. As often as that may be.'

Laconic as ever, decided Joseph. Every phrase that leaves her peachy lips appears elusive. What is she afraid of? A husband? An unseen enemy? Life itself?

Joseph was bewitched by this mysterious woman. A web of intrigue encircled Amelia, one he never could work out. An afternoon was too short to find all the answers and Amelia's surreptitious style only increased his desire to know more. No time had passed before she was whisked away by the shadow.

****

Apart from the murmuring of the wind, Joseph's night passed peaceably, quietly disrupted by tossing and turning that devoured into his gentle slumber. A normally solid sleep, reduced by a strange nightmare about Veronica, his ex-wife.

A few distorted rays of sunlight manage to pry their way into Joseph's pokey second floor apartment. Washing away the last flickering remnants of nightmares, only to awaken him to another. A new day, a new week but the same old bloody life. How could a man go on sanely, to work twelve hours a day, seven days a week, just to avoid life? If only he had known before the marriage. Stupidly assuming that what they had was for life. His thoughts strayed further from the safe confines of today to the darkness cast by the past. Shadows concealing truths and half-truths. A final summation ended with two, possibly three options. Die, move far away, as he did, or was it too late? Had he already lost his sanity?

Plodding to work in his clouded mind, Joseph was unaware fate would offer a suggestion by presenting itself in the form of a black limousine. As the vehicle nudged the curb, a gorgeous creature alighted. Exuberantly perfect legs toned to a delicious irresistibility, was all Joseph could comprehend. A flash of sunlight reveals a small, barely noticeable, gold anklet. Drifting upwards his eyes take in the thighs wrapped precariously in a mini skirt. Ripened breasts invoked a silken camisole to protrude from beneath her jacket accentuating the chest.

In the manner of powerful or frightening people, the woman had a way of commanding those around her. All in her vicinity responded immediately, except Rosario. Amelia's eyes never appeared harsh or unforgiving, but on the same token, they never deceived her.

'Rosario! What were you about? Attempting to end Mr. Bodine's days on this earth.'

The shadow froze in his tracks, a dog scolded by his master, not knowing which way to run.

'Mr. Bodine. You are not too shaken I hope?'

Never had Joseph met someone who was so omnipotent. Not even a man. Still all the femininity was there:

shapely figure, lush lips and flowing lashes. Oh, such beautiful lashes, that reel you into the pools of darkness the depth of which he guessed was limitless. If only his fingers could run down the gentle slope of her jaw line. From the base softness of her ear, down the sensual curve of the jaw, to the roll of the chin. Proceeding down the neck could only heighten the experience.

'No.... I'm fine. Thanks.... Shopping?'

'Just some business.'

Yes, Amelia, just some business. How she hated it all, but that was her life and fortune. Not more than half an hour ago she was standing in her city apartment, depressed by the views. Before her lay a murky brown river overshadowed by indomitable flavourless high rise. Buildings of all eras intertwined in an odd ensemble to create a hive of life. One certain steel blue building taking its image from the fictional Gotham City. Countless corporations were interspersed by a growing number of private residences, entrapping childless couples seeking roller coaster lives, living and breathing where work and freedom collide.

True, Brisbane is the most liveable city with plentiful gardens offering a release from the claustrophobic surrounds, considered Amelia. Streets decorated with native trees and garden beds of unfolding flowers, flashing their refreshing red, yellow and orange stars. Each living element clamouring for the remaining rays of sunlight. Though somehow Joseph's manly figure crouched over seedlings in the City's Botanical Garden always assisted in making Amelia's view of the city more bearable.

Aching to Amelia's eyes was the sun glittering on

mirrored buildings, reflecting the crowded board walk with its multicoloured river of slow-moving humanity. People flooding the riverside cafes and parklands, accepting this as enjoying the great outdoors. Yet she knew this country held so much more.

Wafting past, was the scent of promise from the casino, the echoing sounds raised by the seducing games of chance, mingled with boisterous live music, all adding to the buzz of city life. A scent tainted by the perfume of jacarandas. From the apartment's height, Amelia could faintly hear the mechanical rhythm of the cars travelling the freeway. She really must consider buying a property out Moggill or Redland Bay way. Surely a property of ten acres or more on the river, or by the sea, could keep her settled until she returned home. For nothing compared to her home, Kuntana. The most scenic property in Queensland, or for that matter, Australia. Nowhere else made her feel so comfortable or at ease. It was a different world out there. No disturbances. No threats. No business.

'Just on business.'

Amelia's whisper was barely audible, an undertone to herself. A flash of ingenuity lightens her mood as she continues.

'Care to join me for brunch, Mr Bodine?'

The words flow surprisingly easy, but before Joseph can respond, Rosario enters the circle of conversation looking apprehensive.

'Mrs. Ricoldi, we are already late for our appointment. We are expected!'

'Expected!? For what Rosario? Go. Go tell them I am delayed. Andare!'

She declared abruptly. Rosario stands his ground, as if ready to argue, but thinks better of it.

'Call me Joseph. Mr. Bodine was my father.'

'Of course, Joseph. Feel free to call me Amelia.'

Brunch was to be had in one of the small cafés by the river. In view, a plodding wooden ferry rocks gently on another's wake, each gentle wave distorting the hum of its diesel engines. Seagulls too are left swaying on the water's movement. Newer City Cat ferries make their contribution with twin hulls skimming the water, rising as the speed necessitates. Sails flutter by, offering a silent contrast to their mechanical adversaries. Their coloured flags waving their welcome and intentions. Green and red buoys mingle amongst the entourage to warn of forthcoming dangers.

Décor in this café definitely encompasses the feel of city living, with silver metal tables and matching chairs packing the footpath. Inside, the use of timber, a soaring ceiling and floor-to-ceiling glass windows, creates an airy atmosphere. Tables, chairs, booths, panelling and floor, all in timber, surround the central counter. Two giant blackboard menus span the rear wall where Amelia selects a vacant booth towards one corner.

At this time of morning, not much was happening. Locked safely in the intimidating high rises the workers were commencing their day, while the shoppers had not yet arrived from the suburbs. Amelia enjoyed this time of the day as the city sat in a lull, waiting in expectation of what the day may hold.

Mellow music simmered in the background as the waitress spoke of specials. An array of business folk negotiated intangible deals beyond them. Overall, the waves of conversation raised and lowered with the tide of passing diners. Yet none of this disrupted the conversation going on at the secluded booth. Tucked away from prying eyes and eavesdropping ears.

'Mrs. Ricoldi! How dare you break our appointment. How dare you.'

Taken by surprise, Joseph sat bolt upright while Amelia barely flinched. Here in front of them was a man oozing power. No denying it. Such a bold Italian male, with a ravaged frown, standing above the pair. His black Italian designer suit in no way shoddy like those seen on the punters at the track. This short, brute of a man continued to bark accusations in between puffs of a foreign cigar.

'How dare you, Madame? Stand when I question you. Who do you think you are?'

Amelia rose quietly, a look of boredom on her face. A quick glance preventing Joseph from joining her.

'I know who I am, and so do you. I am your godson's wife. And who are you to ask.' The charade continues.

'Vito Sarmry, my dear. Vito Sarmry.'

Both the persecutor and the persecuted collapse into each other's arms. Kisses on both cheeks, completing the welcome. What a relief.

'Ah. You have a friend.'

Vito offered a Rolex laden hand, accompanied by a gold

studded smile. His eyes barely leaving Amelia. He too, had an appreciation for the finer things in life.

'I had to see who could steal you from me.'

'Vito Sarmry, this is Joseph Bodine. An acquaintance.'

That was it. An acquaintance. Nor in return did she explain further about her husband's godfather. Yes, that is what she said. Your godson's wife. Reservation of such information appeared to be enforced by her business manner.

'How are you, my child? It's been the better part of a year since we last spoke. You and the boy well? Come to dinner soon. Promessa. Promise?'

Vito showed much concern in his questions, more as if a fatherly figure.

'Yes Zio (uncle) Vito. Soon.' Not too soon, I hope.

Relaxing into a cool façade, as others would slip into a martini, Amelia scanned the café to see if they were observed. None of the businessmen had taken much notice, all too engrossed in their own self-importance. A waitress approached with extra menus, discouraged only by Amelia's subtle shake of the head. The coolness was noticeable. Vito continued unperturbed.

'When you're finished. Business can wait. Nice to meet you Mr. Bodine.'

Eventually Vito Sarmry left. Leaving in his place a smoky haze from his Havana cigar. This remnant of his presence hanging around much longer than desired.

'Different business acquaintances you have.'

Joseph jested lightly.

'Your husband's godfather?'

He was fishing but better bait was needed. Amelia sat impassively staring at him, smiling. What was she thinking? His own thoughts were no secret. Wives are not high on his list of objectives, especially other peoples. Was he just a diversion to disrupt Vito's patience? Could it be she was just unhappily married and in need of a friend? Or a distraction? The challenge was tumescent.

After that first brunch meeting, Joseph left feeling invigorated and dubious all at once. Yet it also felt like a breath of fresh air flowing through his life. A call in the afternoon containing mouth-watering descriptions of fresh seafood and homemade pastas worked up an instant appetite, and dangerous thoughts of romance.

~ 10 ~

BREEDING GROUND

Today had been hectic, thought Rosario. Meeting with Don Santapaola, organising Roberto's initiation without him knowing and abating Vito for Amelia. He was always aware that Amelia was overly friendly to the gardener, Joseph. Today though, there was something else. Part of him felt relief and excitement for her, but the other part, well, he was mortified. Was that the right word? Yes. Mortified.

Even now as he stretched out under the covers, a flood of anger welled up in his chest. Was his anger misguided though? Surely Amelia, like everyone else, needed an emotional outlet? He too had desires and needs. Why wouldn't she? No, he was a man, those needs were stronger. Besides, she has been loyal to Nicosia this long, why would she falter now?

In the adjoining room Rosario could hear the soft shuffles of Amelia's feet. In his mind he could see her settling by the window, curled into a tight ball. Knees to her chest, legs embraced by her slim arms. Staying in the city brought forth all of her nightmares. A creature of habit, Amelia would fight sleep until it swept her off her feet. Removing his covers, Rosario wished they were at Kuntana. There her nightmares would not vanish, only subside a little. But a little was all she needed.

Rising, Rosario glimpsed the clock as it rolled over to 2.05AM. Gently unlatching the door, he entered Amelia's room. Without surprise, Amelia sat crunched, hugged only by the moonlight streaming through the open window. Her midnight hair flailed in the cool early morning breeze.

'Sorry. Did I disturb you, Rosario?'

'No Em, you didn't. Would you like me to lie with you?'

'No.'

She whispered as she rose and crawled into the open bed.

Amelia felt Rosario's weight as he settled in beside her. Her protector, on earth and in her own private hell. How many years had it been since they started this charade? Him asking. She refusing: protecting her pride. And Rosario reading her like an open book. Facing the beds edge, her fingers torturing the pillow corner, Amelia bit down on her lip before speaking again.

'Rosario?'

'Yes, Em.'

'Am I heartless?'

'No. Far from it. You care greatly for those around you.' *And weep inwardly for the others every day. I see it, Amelia. Do you know that?*

'Yet some of the things we have done. I have done. The horrible things. I felt nothing.'

'Everything has been justified.'

Yes, from birth you were taught these things were right, expected and justified. But do you know Rosario, the Mafia is the greatest creator of myths. Over the years it has captured the popular imagination with a combination of mythology and terror. I suppose on the good side, myths are cheaper than guns and, in some cases, more effective. Your mother would have raised you in the Mafia propaganda, which has always exalted the values held dear by ordinary people. According to the code of honour, you defend the interests of the poor, stand by your friends, and never harm women or children. Yet you have. Raised as you have, violence, intimidation and imposition of silence is as natural as putting sugar on your Weet-Bix.

'In whose book, Rosario?'

'The code, Em. It allows it.'

Yes, but I was raised by nuns. Maybe that is why my heart feels of stone. Day after day weighing heavily in my chest. Gravity will soon pull it, and me, to the ground. Pinning me there forever.

'Yes, but the code does not allow women or homosexuals. Where does that leave us?'

She had aroused his anger now. His smile would have vanished. Amelia felt a sense of triumph mixed with the thrill of fear. Turning, she saw that his expression was grim. His mouth stretched in a narrow taut line. She whispered.

'I'm sorry.'

Reaching out for his hand. Amelia looked into his eyes that so much resembled those of some untamed animal. Dark, flashing gold and greenish in their depths. Silence flooded the uncomfortable void between them. Beyond the window the stars jostled and danced in a great universe of light. The Milky Way. Million upon millions of stars stretching into the outermost limits of space. Amelia shuddered at the vastness.

'Have I ever told you about my dreams?'

Something was disturbing Amelia tonight and Rosario was unsure of how to proceed. Sure, they told each other their most intimate thoughts, but tonight was different. They were delving deeper into a place they may not return from. Not in all the years he had lain beside her and comfortingly held her, had she given an inkling about her dreams, which were dominated by nightmares. Even in the beginning when he had asked, nearly even begged her to discuss them. She would not. Why would she now be willing to forfeit them?

'There is no need.'

The need is great Rosario. More so than you think. Night after night you have lain with me, holding me when the dreams were at their worst. My life is a nightmare we face together, but the demons within are faced alone, even when you, l'grande protettore, the great protector, is with me.

'One of my first memories was of a time before I went to the orphanage. I must have been incredibly young, probably around three. I remember the smell of freshly baked bread on the morning breeze. While it was still dark, I would creep out to the front chain link fence. Planting my nose into the cool wire, I would peer down the street. Hoping. Waiting.'

Every now and then I feel that now, but I have no way of telling you, Rosario. What I am hoping or waiting for, I do not know. What I do know is if it does not come soon, my sanity may be lost. Even now I feel it trickling away bit by bit, inch by inch. Each day I become weaker because of it.

Noticing the long pause, Rosario prompts Amelia to tell him what she is waiting for.

'My knight in white I suppose. My focus was on watching all the men in white heading home. One, in particular, would walk directly past me and then pause at the corner post. Suddenly turning, he would bow and say *'My Queen forgive me. I have not forgotten my gift for thee.'* From within his apron pocket he would remove the most tasty bread rolls you have ever eaten. Each in the shape of an animal.'

What I don't tell you Rosario, is that I cherished every one of those bread animals. Devouring each slowly and lovingly as if they were truly a gift from a Prince. And that some days, they were all I had to eat.

'That is a good memory to dream of.'

'Yes, Rosario it is.'

It's what sustains me through the rough times. For a man, who did not know me, he gave me several precious gifts. Food and hope. Food for survival and the vain hope for better.

'I tell people this is my first memory as a child.'

'But, it isn't.'

He stated without questioning.

'No.'

A tear trickles down her cheek as Rosario rests his head

on her pillow. Their faces barely an inch apart. There was that odd smile on his lips, and Amelia felt a twist of something uneasy stir in her mind. Eyes, level, she continued.

'Amelia's first ever memory was the darkness of sleep. Then a strange feeling, more a pressure, on her face. She awakened. Opening her eyes, all she saw was darkness. Not of night but an object. A pillow. She tried to scream but the pillow muffled the sound. In her own mind the scream should have woken the entire neighbourhood as it rang loudly in her ears. Grasping with small hands she was unable to move the pillow. Fight as she might, the force behind it was too strong. She was too small, too weak, too useless.'

Rosario wiped another tear from her eyes. He assumed that by speaking in the third person was the only way Amelia could force the story out. Removing herself from the pain.

'Then young Amelia smelled it. Her mother's perfume. It was her mother's pillow and that was who was thrusting it down on her. Trying to take her last breath. Fortunately, she blacked out and never saw that house or the people in it again.'

'But you survived.'

'Yes Rosario, I survived.'

Rolling to gulp air from the window, Amelia hesitates to appreciate the light from the moon. *Yes, Rosario I survived but at what cost? Something was taken from me that I can never have back. Now I pay for it every night.*

Rosario's body presses forth, cupping her from behind.

His strong masculine arms enfold her tightly. Lips to her ear he whispers.

'We all have demons to fight.'

That is the point. I am tired of fighting. Can't you see? I am tired. If it were not for Nicco, I would lie down and sleep forever.

'And now, I dream of Nicosia too.'

So do I Amelia, so do I.

~ 11 ~

DESTINY PREVAILS

Southbank, Brisbane.

Blinking away the morning brightness, Joseph shielded his eyes from the sun's brilliance as it rose from behind the apartment building. Long shadows stretched towards his shoed feet. Tentatively edging backwards, ready to divulge anything and everything trapped in its cool darkness. School boy fear clenches his throat as his eyes ascend the pale building. Balconies lay splashed in colours, with garden settings mixed amongst them.

Compressed living appealed little to Joseph even though each of the hidden cubicles were surely a mansion within themselves, especially here at Southbank. All balconies viewed the city heart across the murky Brisbane River, as well as the parklands that lay at the building's feet. From that height the lagoon would look like a crystal blue oasis surrounded by swaying palms. Glancing at his watch once more, Joseph realised he could not force time forwards. Amelia's words had been direct.

'Do not arrive before ten. Not even a minute.'

Shoulders slumping, Joseph turned and commenced to dawdle around the parklands one more time. Surely that would kill the last ten minutes he thought. A smile rose as he passed the young children in a secluded playground. A small man-made pebble creek wrapped itself amongst palms and play equipment, to the delight of freckled faces. Mothers sat nattering away a short distance to the right in a shaded alcove.

****

'I wish I could attend the initiation, Rosario.'

A subdued smile clouded Amelia's face as she spoke.

'Nicosia would be proud. You should be too, raising such a fine young man.'

'We have raised him Amelia, and yes I am proud.'

Taking her hands in his, Rosario's cheery eyes conveyed happiness to Amelia's dark pools.

'He has come so far in the last few months. I know that look Amelia. He is entering the world where he belongs. You and I both know that.'

'Yes, Rosario, but I still see him as that small larrikin, chocolate smudged from ear to ear.'

Her chest heaved in a sigh riddled thought.

'And now he is a man of the world.'

'And I don't want to see you going out alone while I'm not here.'

Rosario tried to be firm and friendly all at once.

'No, Rosario. I have some paperwork to do.'

With a more serious tone, Rosario leant in close.

'You know it's not safe.'

In a child-like manner Amelia crosses her fingers behind her back as she speaks.

'I'm not going anywhere Rosario. A day at home suits me fine.'

Not quite home but still.

'I can come back early if you want to do something.'

'No no. You go and have a great time.'

She touched his shoulder in reassurance.

'Besides, you deserve some free time. I'll be fine till lunchtime tomorrow.'

Passing a knowing look.

'I'm sure Phil thinks you've abandoned him by now. Catch up with him Rosario. I'll be fine.'

'Sure?'

The prospect of having some free time to catch up with his neglected lover appealed to Rosario. What also appealed was having someone to confide in. Someone who didn't pass judgement.

Separating with one last look, Rosario and Amelia step apart just in time to see the private elevator's doors open behind the glass panelling of the foyer. Straightening his clothes as he steps out, Roberto poised himself, appearing to stare at them momentarily before waving to the pair through the etched glass. His eyes had flowed along the curves and sweeps of the open ranges, focused on the lone horseman and finally came to rest on the wildflowers in the foreground. The landscape encased in the glass was as familiar to him as were the loving smiles reflected through it.

Whistling to himself Roberto approached the pair, uncertain as to why Amelia's eyes sat moist in their sockets. His father's face was solemn, only his eyes deceiving his demeanour. The eyes that settled upon him were beaming. All that Roberto knew was that there was a job to be done and he had been selected to complete it. Rosario had told him not to bring Christopher, which was strange since he was a part of his crew, and they normally completed any job together. By the look of Amelia this job needed a more personal touch.

'Here as requested.'

Sang Roberto as his youthful body swayed to a halt. Slapping his father on the shoulder, his other arm encased Amelia, while his lips brushed her check.

'And on time too.'

Stated Rosario with mock surprise.

'I will not hold you two up for long, as you have a lot to do today.'

Amelia's lips curled in a hidden grin as she thought of what she had to fill her day.

'Come, Sparrow, I have something for you.'

Taking the young man by the hand Amelia led him to her bedroom. For the amount of time spent in the city, Amelia's room was decorated very sparsely. Several paintings hung from the walls, each depicting a scene either of the Sicilian countryside or Kuntana. On the single bedside table sat three silver frames. Each of those frames encased the most important people of her life. The only ones she ever loved, and the only ones she felt ever loved her.

'So, Aunty Em, what's the go?'

'This job must be handled with dignity.'

Straightening his tie as if insulted, Roberto answered confidently.

'Of course.'

'First there is something I must give you.'

Reaching under the bed, Amelia felt for the small cardboard box, drawing it out she laid it carefully on the bed next to Roberto. His childish excitement was getting the better of him as he fidgeted and reached for the package.

'Anh-anh. You have always been too eager for gifts. I remember when you were young and would tear a small hole in the corner of all the Christmas presents. Even if they weren't yours.'

'Come on, Aunty Em. Don't hold me in suspense.'

With intentional care and deliberateness Amelia lifted the cardboard lid to reveal a decrepit, moth eaten velvet jewel box. The box was a swirl of colourings, a rusty red and a once imperial purple. From a distance the colourings were aloof and strange but closer inspection revealed the case had once been a resplendent purple. The additional colour had been added years before, it was the blood of the case's last owner. Lifting the jewel box from its resting place, a sly smile passed Amelia's lips. Her eyes cast to Rosario who now stood a few steps into the room. His hands lay peacefully interlocked in front of his groin.

'I expect you to take care of this Roberto. It was your grandfathers.'

Brushing her hand lovingly over the blood-stained purple, Amelia carefully lifted the hinged lid. Roberto strained to see its contents. Pouncing to his feet he circled behind Amelia's crouched body, just as she rose.

'Aunty Em!!'

His voice pleaded now.

'One would think you were still twelve Sparrow. Here.'

Trying not to snatch the box in his excitement, Roberto studied the gift he was given. His youthful features creased under a hesitant smile.

'Which grandfather?'

'Your father's.'

As she spoke, Amelia reached into the box, lifting the gold chain above head height. The ruby and diamond encrusted crucifix swung before Roberto's eyes, its coolness fading with the warmth of his neck.

'It was his fathers and his before him. And now you are the proud owner of it. Wear it with pride.'

'Why have I never seen it before? Why didn't grandfather give it to Rosario first then?'

A stifled silence filled the room sending Amelia's head into a swirl. Her mouth opened then closed without a noise escaping. It took but a moment before Rosario's baritone voice filled the emptiness.

'It is given to each father's first-born male child on a special day. Your grandfather was killed before it could be passed on. On his death the crucifix went missing. It has taken till now for us to find it and return it to its rightful owner. You.'

'And the job?'

As if he were her own, Amelia brushed a loose strand of

greased dark hair out of Roberto's eyes. Motherly, she ran her fingertips along his cheek, down to his stubbled chin, locked his eyes to hers, and spoke straight faced.

'To make us proud.'

'Proud?'

Enlightenment flashed past Roberto's mischievous eyes, as his strong jaw fell, creating a cavernous opening in place of his mouth.

'You'd best leave now before they change their minds.'

Scooping her into his youthful arms, Roberto crushed Amelia close. His breath was warm and fresh on her ear.

'Thank-you, Aunty Em.'

'Thank Rosario. Today is his success as a father.'

'Yes, I will.'

A small child-like voice responded. Fearful not to say more in case the welling tears broke free.

'Now off with you both.'

Hustling the pair into the elevator, Amelia felt overwhelmed with joy as she watched the metallic doors clink shut on two, of the four, most important men in her life.

She pondered on what a fine young man Roberto had become. He was on his way to that other world. The one in which she was not totally forbidden, yet one that failed to acknowledge her. Even knowing what it would hold for him, the ceremony alone would open his eyes, as it had hers. Fortunately, Nicosia had snuck her to one when they were young.

Oh, how he had made her vow never to tell a soul of what she witnessed. Right before her eyes in the dusky dank cellar of his father's second house. How it was like the religious ceremonies she had seen at the orphanage. A baptismal in a sense. To be initiated a strict ceremony was followed. One which had the new blood reciting the sacred pledge while passing a burning picture of the saint, their saint, from one hand to the other. The lying flat at the true Don's feet.

The mystical Don, who only those in the club knew him to be, the all and powerful. Traditionally the ceremony was the first time the newly initiated met the Don, the head honcho. Previously the new recruits were left in the dark about who was the true leader. Nowadays, with an immense quantity of men claiming to be Dons, each flagrantly flashing their wealth and power about, it was easy. Today, the leaders became obvious (especially to the enemy), ostentatious and dispensable. To many this part of the ceremony had become a farce, but in the tradition of the Ricoldi's, much was still kept secret. The ceremony as a complete had enthralled her so. Yet now? Now, she felt contempt creeping into her fraying soul.

Remembering's of the misty past were vanquished by the buzzing of the lift's intercom.

'Joseph?'

'Yes Amelia. How are you?'

'Good. You're just in time. Come up.'

Stabbing the security box with precise movements, Amelia hit enter and left to find her keys. Fifteen floors below Joseph stood in the private wood grain elevator. Within moments of Amelia saying come up, the doors closed behind him, and the elevator started to move. After what felt like seconds the elevator rocked to a halt and released the doors. As they sprung open Joseph could see the marbled foyer floor surrounded by the most exquisitely sketched glass he'd ever seen. Beyond the glass to the right lay an informal lounge room in soft creamy tones. To the left was a modern kitchen surrounded by windows and, best of all, straight ahead lay an open sight of the balcony, and beyond that a breathtaking view of the city towards Mt Cootha. The green peak to the west cradled an exquisite restaurant, café and the cities most prolific vantage point. Even at this time of day the lights on the television and radio towers could be seen blinking red in their warning to low flying aircraft.

Lost in the view, Joseph failed to notice the approaching footsteps.

'Ready?'

The voice asked as Amelia rounded the corner dressed in figure hugging black jeans, which were externally buttoned. Her black boots clipped loudly on the marble as she neared him. Admiring her half unbuttoned white silk shirt Joseph nodded before being ushered into the lift.

'You scrub up okay.'

Admired Amelia aloud as she scanned Joseph.

'I thought we could go for a drive then lunch somewhere special.'

As she stabbed the button for the basement.

Arriving at the basement car park, Amelia led Joseph to a heart-warming red convertible behind a security gate. With several taps of her long nails on the touch pad the gate released and an overhead light flickered on.

Joseph's eyes absorbed the car, from the long sweeping

lines of the bonnet, around the bold curve of the wheel arches, to the subtle tilt of the rear end with its visor-like taillights and dual exhaust pipes of stainless steel. Its body form was of a pure roadster. Long nose, close to the road and an elegantly purist cockpit. Hints of a classic racing car were present in the simple 'Engine Start' button beside a three-spoke leather covered steering wheel. Hidden was the sequel to the classic styling: an aluminium space frame underneath.

'Wow! It's lovely. A Ferrari!'

Stated Joseph walking up the left-hand side of the car.

'Even better, a prototype Ferrari. Here you drive.'

A clatter of keys took Joseph by surprise as he clambered to catch them before they fell onto the mirror like surface. Returning to the rear of the car Amelia laughed.

'It's left-hand drive.'

'Man. For the money you pay for a nice car you think they could put the steering on the right side.'

'I suppose.'

Laughed Amelia.

'But it's the way that it comes.'

~ 12 ~

INITIATION

Pumped and waiting to explode like raw popcorn in hot oil, Roberto sat agitatedly in the passenger seat as Rosario drove. Both were initially quiet: Roberto from mind tingling excitement and Rosario from thought. Stealing smiles at his father, Roberto had to break the silence.

'This is so exhilarating.'

A forced smile came to Rosario's lips. Preparing his words, he spoke them slowly, cautiously.

'Yes, but there are a few rules you will have to obey closer.'

Ignoring his father's tone, Roberto continues to jiggle in his seat.

'A-ha.'

He responds without truly listening.

'Take that one-stop-shop, for example. Did it have to be handled in the way it was?'

Capturing his attention, Roberto turns to study Rosario's fixed face.

'We had no choice.'

'There is always a choice my son. We have chosen this life, therefore we accept the consequences, whether it be life or death. But they were innocents, they have not chosen this life. Besides wasn't the guard on the cut?'

'He was, yet he decided to play quick-draw with Merlin.'

'Hmm. Not a wise choice at all. The unfortunate thing is that such a situation can spoil the sale. You miss your cut, your crew loses their cut, the captain loses his and the boss loses too. It goes from easy money to no money. In this instance it tainted the sale and we had to take a knockdown. We all receive less for the same amount of work. E` chiaro? Is that understood?'

'Si.'

Letting the silence of before envelope them, they continue to the meeting point. Passing a poorly lit welcome sign, they approach a large boat docked at the far side of the Wynnum-Manly harbour. Having heard about Anthony 'L'Orsa Maggiore' (the great bear) Sasso's fishing boat, Roberto was in awe. It was humungous. Not a small fishing boat as he had always imagined. Aboard were three crewmembers all dressed in identical white uniforms. Sasso greeted them himself, extravagantly shaking their hands and kissing their cheeks. Encouragingly showing them around the deck to the rear of the boat, where they came across a small group of men. Five or six. Roberto only recognised Joey who was beaming from ear to ear as he himself felt sure he looked.

Vanishing to a lower deck, Rosario leaves Roberto to wait for his name to be called. One by one the men are summoned to the lower deck. Roberto is as high as a kite, this being the perceived goal of his young life. His step into manhood. After what seems a lifetime in itself, the call comes.

'Robbie, we want you to come down.'

Nervous as hell, in a happy way, Roberto heads for the steps. Overtaken by a sense of slow motion, he descends into the depths of the boat. Each step lower emphasises the boats rocking motion. Pausing, Roberto clings to the handrail to settle his stomach. Continuing on, nice and easy, he finally reaches the bottom. The room comes into view through the dimness. Clouds of smoke puff about his head.

Before him lies a large, long table with Don Vincenzo Santapaola seated at the head. Sitting to one side is Rosario with Vito Sarmry next to him. People who he knew were captains, capos, are all there as well as others he had only heard about. Those who preceded him also sat at the table. A spare chair sat next to Don Santapaola.

'There's an empty chair by Vincenzo. Just go to that chair.'

'Sit down Robbie. Sit down here.'

Don Santapaola taps the chair beside him. Staring at Robbie he asks his first question.

'Do you know why you are here?'

Answering as instructed by Rosario, the only instruction received, Roberto answers no.

'Do you know everyone here?'

Glancing about the ill-lit room, Roberto takes in every pair of eyes that are, at this moment, focused only on him.

'Yes, most of them.'

'Do you like the people here?'

The questions continued.

'Yes, very much.'

His fingers entwine in nervousness, but Roberto happily answers the questions knowing they will lead to his destiny. The rhythmic lapping of the waves on the ship's hull draws his attention momentarily.

'Do you know that this is a brotherhood, a secret society?'

'Yes.'

Drinking glasses on the raised edged table clink together. Looking beyond Don Santapaola, Roberto spies the horizon in a small porthole. Attempting to focus on the line between sky and sea, a giddiness befalls him.

'In this secret society, there's one way in and there's only one way out. You come in on your feet and you go out in a coffin. There is no return from this.'

Roberto nodded.

'I understand.'

The horizon line vanishes from view, only to rush past in the opposite direction.

'Would you drop all loyalties to everything and keep this brotherhood number one? The first thing in your life, the priority?'

'Yes.'

As had a million other voices echoed out before, so too did Roberto's. Though he glimpsed an odd expression on Rosario's face. It was only fleeting but he saw it. Roberto wondered if it was tied to Amelia in some way, for wasn't it she that called the shots. A woman who was like a mother to him, who had always guided him and known what was best. If asked, could he betray her? Roberto knew his father, Rosario, never would betray her, they had a secret tie, for that he was sure. But would he betray either of them? For any Don? No, he wouldn't. No matter what, they were his number one. Roberto wondered if all new recruits had doubts like him or whether their loyalties to the Don were unbreakable. Whether he wanted to know or not, he was sure he would find out one day.

'Would you kill for us?'

Each word was enunciated slow and precise.

'Yes.' I already have.

The increased rocking of the waves, grips Roberto's intestines. The swirling movement lifting his stomach ever higher to his throat.

'Which finger would you pull the trigger with?'

Holding up his index finger Roberto shakes his mind clear of the horizon's frantic movements in the porthole. Rosario rises from his position. Rising too is Vito and Don Santapaola. Roberto stands while everyone else remains seated. Rosario, as Roberto's sponsor, pricks his finger till it bleeds whereupon he pricks his own finger so their blood can join. Linking each to the other in the brotherhood. If one turns bad, the blood must be tainted, therefore both would die as a consequence. Rubbing the blood onto a picture of a saint, their saint, the picture is placed in Roberto's hands as Don Santapaola speaks again.

'We are going to burn this saint.'

Lighting it with a gold lighter, everyone watches as it caught on fire.

'See the saint burn, so too will you burn in hell if you divulge any of the secrets of our life.'

Repeating the words, Roberto is struck with such amazement that he forgets to pass the picture between his hands. The heat of the flame causes small blisters to form on his skin. After muttering a few words in Italian, Roberto is asked to crush the burnt picture. Its ashes falling to an ashtray below.

Circling the table, Roberto kisses one and all until he is by Don Santapaola's side once more. Sitting down, Roberto is surrounded by the other made men who clasp hands in a 'tie-in'. In Italian Don Santapaola continues the ceremony.

'In honour of our brotherhood, I untie the knot.'

As the practised words pour from his mouth, all the surrounding faces are solemn.

Releasing their hands, Roberto rises, joins the circle where everyone joins hands once more.

'In honour of our brotherhood, I tie the knot.'

Don Santapaola turns to Roberto.

'You are a member with us. You are now a friend of ours.'

Having been informed that a lot of rules and regulations would be explained later, another man is called to come down. Once everyone had completed the oath, Don Santapaola explained that this was a family and therefore introductions needed to be made. Don Santapaola was the representante, the boss of the family. Vito was the acting underboss and Rosario was the consigliere. Vito was classed as the underboss in situations such as this, but everyone knew who Don Santapaola's true underboss in Australia was. No-one dared speak her name, yet she was the one they sourced, via Rosario, for settlement of disputes and grudges. Technically, Amelia could not hold this position, but she could represent someone who could. Many wives and a few sisters had done so when their husbands or brothers were unable to fulfil their duties. Such as when they were jailed or incapacitated.

Next, all of the captains were introduced, and then the new inductees were informed on how to introduce one another. If they were to introduce somebody as 'a friend of mine', that's all he was. But if they were with a made member, they would be introduced as 'a friend of ours'. A third party was needed to do this so there wasn't any way to break into the circle. There was no way they could introduce themselves to a made member as a made member.

Unlike the twenty-six families of America, there was only one main family in Australia. Each state was allocated sub-families with their own captain. These families could operate independently to a point. And a cut from every transaction had to be passed up the line.

Each new inductee was instructed to answer to their captain, their direct father, who would ultimately deal with the superiors. Sasso commenced his practised speech.

'You do everything with him. You check with him, you put everything on record with him. You can't kill unless you get permission from the family. Basically, you can't do anything until you get permission from the family.'

Passing in front of each inductee, glaring menacingly at each.

'You don't run to the boss. You go to your captain.'

That was the protocol.

'Your captain will go to the administration.'

Which is the boss, or in this circumstance with Don Santapaola living overseas, the underboss, the acting underboss and the consigliere.

'There is no God.'

Pacing before the troops ready for war, Don Santapaola leads the next phase in regulations. Each man stands tall and straight, unblinkingly looking ahead.

'We don't have allegiance to any country. Our immediate family, our wives, our children, are secondary. This thing of ours is first. It is above all else. No thought is needed for this matter, it just is. You want to believe in God? Fine. You want to believe in your country? Fine. You want to believe in your own family? Fine. Just remember, that comes a long way after this.'

The Don walked behind the made men, patting each on the shoulder.

Vito, stubbing out his cigar, looks up from his chair.

'Anytime the boss or underboss of the family sends for you, you come. Promptly. No matter if a family member is dying and has ten minutes to live, you come. You refuse, you will be killed. It precedes all else when the boss sends for you. Don't tell your captain, just come.'

Puffing his chest, looking intimidating, Don Santapaola takes his cue.

'I'm the boss. I'm the father of this family. I am your God!'

Honour was spoken of next. Not coveting other's wives and daughters. Never raising one's hand against another made man. Omerta. The law of silence. All punishable by death. The seriousness of the talk died down. Roberto was growing tired of the bosses peacocking their position. It all seemed rather dramatic, and over the top. Like a movie he had seen once. To him the need to belong stemmed from a desire to be taken seriously. To be respected for his views and thoughts. Something he suddenly realised Amelia offered him, but here, in this room, he had just climbed to the level of slime on the floor. No-one would listen to his thoughts, ideas, or views. He had just become a foot soldier who would be ordered to do any dirty work his superiors saw fit. With the final untying of the knot, the party began. Excusing himself, Roberto vanishes to the main deck. Gasping in the fresh air he spied a small open fishing boat a short way off.

~ 13 ~

CRUISING

Exiting the confines of the chilly car park, Amelia and Joseph found themselves on the move in the warm Queensland sun. To Amelia, the view down the long bonnet was pure Ferrari, bulging and swooping far more than you'd think from the outside. Even the sound, the exhaust note now a mellow burble, but soon it would rise to a deep sonorous, Dolby surround-sound bellow under hard acceleration.

'I've never driven a car worth close to $100,000.'

'Neither have I.' Spoke Amelia non-chalantly, as her slender silk-coated arm rested upon the door jam. Snuggling into the leather seat, she unfocused and closed her eyes as the smell of new leather and metal caressed her nostrils. Tasting the fresh air, she could feel her worries dissipate. Sensing the weight of Joseph's eyes, knowing his brow would be piqued in curiosity, Amelia squinted through one eye.

'I said that aloud, didn't I?'

A nod as confirmation.

'This is probably worth four to five times that.'

Before she could resettle, Amelia found herself thrust forward, straining a now tightening seat belt as Joseph hooked the car to the curb. Horns blasted in dismay and red brake lights flashed as if mocking them.

'Come now Joseph, it's just a car.'

'Just a car!'

His voice exasperated.

'Your 'just a car' is worth more than I am.'

'Aren't you under valuing yourself a little there?'

'You know what I mean.'

Trying to restrain his rising disbelief, Joseph's voice rose in an agonised crescendo.

Without annoyance Amelia lowered her sunglasses, snuggled into the seat once more and spoke quietly.

'Yes, and we'll be late for lunch if you don't hurry. Just get going.'

Shrugging in surrender, Joseph forced the six-speed, jammed the accelerator and made a gap in the traffic. On the dry grippy surface, the roadster accelerated effort-lessly, leaving two long, black Pirelli signature stripes and a small puff of smoke.

'Where are we going?'

He asked resignedly. Toowoomba was the response.

After bustling with the mid-week traffic on the Ipswich Motorway, the roller coaster roads of the Warrego High-way came as a breath of fresh air. Wide and welcoming black tarmac invited increased speeds. Sweeping bends begged to be abused.

'Open it up.'

'But the highway is so well patrolled.'

Half-hearted, Joseph felt an incredible desire to do as Amelia asked. Not for her but for the sheer pleasure and wickedness of it. Snubbing one's nose at authority, rebelling against.... What? Thought Joseph. A conformer was he, all the way down to the core and he knew it.

'So? The engines electronically speed regulated to 250 kilometres so you can't hurt the car. Unless, of course, you don't think you can handle it.'

Pressing his foot on the accelerator, the roadster urged ahead with awesome energy, rapidly gaining momentum. The car seemingly attached to the horizon by an invisible elastic band. Green, sunlit countryside blurred past in a repertoire of freedom. Ahead, dark clouds bled from the horizon, offering little promise other than rain.

Taking in the centre mounted instruments Joseph smiled as the needles steadily climbed. The overbearing flickering of red and blue disturbed his study, of the black on yellow faces. 'I told you.' He thought, but dared not say as his foot displaced some of its pressure. A look in the rear-view mirror would confirm his worst fear, so instead, Joseph, with indicator in hand, moved the car into the outer lane.

Acknowledging the jerkiness of deceleration, Amelia peers at Joseph through one eye. The screaming siren punctuating his nervousness.

'Slow down to one hundred and let them pull alongside. Unless you want to try and out-run them.'

Eyes directly ahead, Joseph could not believe his ears.

Surely, she was smirking at him with those last words. Warmth surged through his groin as he felt Amelia's hand run the length of his thigh. Caught by the wind her words were near inaudible.

'Trust me.'

Engine bellowing at full capacity, the white squad car eventually pulled alongside the cruising roadster. A young flushed faced officer in regulation shirt furiously indicated for the driver to pull up. He was further mystified by a passenger being where the driver should be. Sitting in the squad car's passenger seat was a more senior officer, several stripes on his sleeve indicating his seniority. Drawing face-to-face with Amelia, the senior officer, whose greying buzz cut bobbed with the car's motion, frowned.

Amelia's hand fell in a mock salute, a salute returned by the senior officer. With a fluid movement, the squad car, siren still screaming, exited the highway at the approaching turn.

Grasping the wheel even tighter, the roadster commenced to speed up. A quick glance revealed Amelia's approval. Her eyes lay shut, the ruby lips lay in an upward curl and most enjoyable, was her hand resting on his thigh.

Up ahead the Toowoomba range loomed, enshrouded in ominous looking clouds. Minus any perceived effort, the roadster glided up the ten percent grade. Fully laden trucks grunted and chugged as they passed them effortlessly. A certain crispness filled their lungs as the summit drew ever closer. Turning right on the summit, Weis's Restaurant came into view. The building, an old

Queenslander, partially encircled by broad verandas offering shade, from the unrelenting sun, and shelter, from the rains, was transformed into a cosy restaurant decades ago. Set alone on the best vantage point.

Indicating a small line of carports in the otherwise open car park, Amelia gestured for Joseph to park there before the deluge drowned them. Ignoring the 'PRIVATE' sign, Joseph drew into the park just as the skies opened with their farmer's gift of precious water.

'Should we put the roof up?'

'No, it'll be fine here. I'll race you to the door!'

At the disadvantage of not knowing where the front door was situated, Joseph had to trot behind Amelia who darted in and out of false locations. Running down their hair and face, the raindrops faded into their semi-dry clothing, leaving dark polka dots. Finally, at the front ramp, Amelia paused to shake herself off, and jostle with Joseph for the meagre cover. Bursting through the door in a cloud of laughter, many eyes were drawn to them.

'Mrs Ricoldi! What a pleasure to see you.'

'Hello, Peter. How are things?'

'Fantastic.'

Responded Peter in his customary tone.

'Your usual table?'

Walking through subtly lit corridors, Joseph viewed the delectable smorgasbord set up in the main central room. This was the place were all patrons met and converged on the fresh seafoods, fruits, roasts, desserts, anything, and everything that one could desire. Like a spider's web, varying size rooms and corridors led away from the main food area. Larger rooms were filled with boisterous laughter of functions or family get togethers. While smaller, more intimate, rooms were filled with whispers and deep conversations.

Their room was even smaller and more intimate than the others. Once, what probably was a child's bedroom, was now transformed into a cosy restaurant for two. Large windows on one wall viewed an ornate garden while a warming fire crackled in a heritage fireplace. A table for two, complete with silver cutlery and mood enhancing flowers, sat central between the fire and the windows. Each chair having a view of both. Void of electric lighting, candles circled the room. Enhanced by the fireplace and the darkness outside, the room was bathed in an orange glow, giving the impression of early evening.

'It's perfect, Peter. Thank you.'

'Would you like a drink, Amelia?'

Proffered Joseph.

'There is Muscadean in an ice bucket by the table. Both orange juice and chilled water is in a small esky below that.'

Peter spoke solely to Joseph, knowing that this is how Amelia preferred it. Her desire to be alone, even even stretched to the waiting staff.

'Unless there was something else you would like.'

Shaking his head Joseph could think of nothing else.

'And here is your warm bread now.'

A girl of fifteen dressed in the standard black skirt and white shirt, sat a basket of steaming bread on the table.

Leaving without a word she glanced round once to smile at Amelia. Peter followed the girl without a word.

'A nice little place, isn't it? The food is incredible.'

'It has such a warm atmosphere. I think the rain sets it off well.'

'Yes.'

Amelia's eyes absorbed Joseph, his ease of stance, his self-confidence.

'Come stand by the fire near me to dry off before we eat.'

Knowing he could return to the smorgasbord, as often he liked, Joseph still had trouble restricting the food he desired to one plate. After settling on what would become an entrée, Joseph returned to their private room. Amelia had already filled their wine glasses.

'You are welcome to have beer if you'd like.'

'No, the wine is fine. So is the company.'

As they savoured each morsel, the conversation darted from one topic to another. Amelia was very animated in her conversation and mannerisms. More so than he had seen her before. But while she held her hands high, hands that were thin, tanned and thoroughly pleasing, to high-light her point, Joseph noticed her wrists.

From this angle, close to her palms, two vertical scars, jagged and pink, could be seen. Scars about an inch and a half long. Joseph inhaled sharply. His eyes engrossed, locking onto the unnatural marks. Amelia ceased talking. Instantly her demeanour changed. Animated no more, her eyes and actions became cold.

'Forgive me for staring, it was just...'

'Bad manners on your part I'd say.'

'Yes, you are right.'

His unglued eyes were downcast in apology.

'I was just wondering...'

Joseph's eyes were questioning, but words appeared to fail him. Amelia saw his interest, acknowledging that it appeared to be genuine. Thoughts and reasoning tumbled through her head. Should she? Could she?

'No one else can experience life in the way we individually do. Not even our nearest and dearest.'

Lovingly, her index finger ran the jagged pink line.

'In solitude we find our deepest thoughts: our truest selves. If one can push past the fear of being alone, you'd see that, in the end, alone is all we are.'

Soft now, her voice disappeared into the spluttering rain tapping on the windows.

'Amelia, many people tread the safe but shallow path. During our existence we seek distraction from ourselves. Eternally wandering the landscape of our lives without comprehension of what it is to be truly alive. We continuously seek solace in someone else, feeling they are our reflection. Do you know what happens? By hooking our future to their bandwagon, we close our eyes and ears to the silence of our own souls. It is the brave few that stray to the rocky track of self-discovery.'

Laying his palms flat on the table, in a non-offensive manner, Joseph slid them to an invisible half waypoint.

'Solitude is what created these, not fear.'

Feeling the scrutiny of his eyes, she drew her wrists

close. Looking up into his moist eyes, she saw not pity but another emotion rarely shown to her. Holding her trembling self steady, she offered a limp wrist to Joseph who cupped it in his hands. He then stroked the scar with his thumb. His eyes not leaving hers in the process.

****

Each meal with Amelia offered a new release from the tedium of life and, a glimpse of what might be. Over the next two weeks, Joseph and Amelia dined together frequently. Almost daily. Frequenting the track over the weekends for Spring Racing, mingling in the member's stand. Not once did Amelia mention her husband, nor did Joseph ask. If she wanted him to know, surely, she would tell him? During this time Rosario was uneasy. He appeared to resent or disapprove of Joseph. Day or night, he was there. Rosario, the shadow. Only leaving her side when requested, and then only for a moment. Rosario was accepted as a child accepts a birthmark.

If enlightened to Rosario's own personal sacrifice, Joseph may not have resented the man so much. The shadow had forgone his own life in Italy to be the protector of Amelia Ricoldi. A favour asked of him by Nicosia Ricoldi. A man of respect. Never would Rosario abort his post till the death, preferably of old age, of Amelia or by his own untimely departure. He was her shadow for life. Through sunshine and rain. Unless, of course, the Ricoldi family decided otherwise. If any of this were to eventuate, where would he go? Retire. Retire to what? For the last nineteen years, half of her life, he has been the protector, advisor, and companion. He, the only comfort in Nicco's absence. Amelia relies on him heavily. So, what if sometimes she acted brisk and abrupt. Only the city affected her this way. At Kuntana, they were on equal ground.

Saturday was the time of departure for Amelia and her shadow. They were going home. To the disbelief of all, Amelia requested Joseph to accompany them. In the guise that she would like a professional to assist her with the gardens at Kuntana. Not the hardest decision Joseph ever made.

PART TWO

True Self

~ 14 ~

RELATIONSHIPS

Tilden Park, California, U.S.A.

A fool. A complete and utter fool is what I am. Isabelle Lancove, the fool. Life will never be the same again.

Gently lowering my hands, I feel the tiny pricks of the slender grass. My hands search further, pushing through the cushioning until they can travel no more, except for that little unknown give in the soil. Cool dampness seeps through my jeans as I lower my exhausted body into a seated position. Arching my back, it settles into the small smooth groove in the gum's trunk. The smooth bark hugs my body with the familiarity of a well-worn recliner lounge. The eucalyptus scent haunts my nostrils, reminding me of what could have been.

Etching my hands backwards, my fingers hopelessly seek the bulging roots of the oaks back home. Roots, which break the ground, searching. Losing height and mass as they snake away from the trunk. The thought reminds me of Mike's masculine legs and how I liked to stroke them. Seated cross-legged together, face to face, talking, my hands would wander past his fine-drawn toes, encircle his ankles, feel the suppleness of his calves, the hard domes of his knees and eventually arrive at the firmness that was his thigh. A firmness that still sent tingles through my mind, and body. His legs wouldn't have enchanted me so, if they had felt as coarse and as rough as what my fingers felt at the base of my old oak.

Ah, my old oak. Tyre hanging from the broadest limb. Leftover scraps of wood nailed to its trunk for a ladder. And my favourite, a tree house up high in the branches. A secret place for Jesse and me. Oh Jess. More bad memories. Gum trees somehow lacked the warmth and familiarity I remember from childhood.

As the memory lingers and settles into the past, my body tenses. Have I blown it all? With eyes closed I can sense the sun on its morning rise. Warmth cradling my whole body. In the next few hours that warmth will leave me slowly, inch by inch. The coolness of the tree would prevail, as it always did. But soon that warmth would cradle me longer. I can sense it.

The leaves have lost their fresh green smell and at this stage must be turning gold and chestnut brown. As soon as the first winter storms arrive the leaves would fall, carpeting the ground in bronze before the snow transforms the mountains. It sounded so beautiful in words that I did not want to open my eyes and face reality. My reality. California.

Tears trickle down my face now as I recall the week's events. It all started so innocently, until the hand of fate selected my life, slapped it into the puddle of misfortune and wrung it for all its worth. Mike and I had become close during the last few weeks. Considering how bizarre our relationship started, passionately on his part, coldly on mine, it was amazing how compatible we were.

Damn that Jerome and his sweet-talking ways. Mike had only been away for a few days, on an errand for his mother, or something, in Colombia of all places. A small argument took place before he left. It was nothing major or life threatening but it had set my mood for the last week. There was enough on my mind, with training alone. Trying to compensate for the time Mike had taken up. Chuck, my coach, contributed to my mayhem by hassling me about my cycling. Apparently, my results had been far from where the season's goals or qualifying levels were set. If I was to have any chance at the World Championships or Olympic team selection, I had to return to form with hard training. He also said I lacked heart. Heart of all things. Was there no greater desire in my life other than to be the greatest female cyclist? Ever.

As an extra special incentive my parents had rung, stating that if I didn't make it this season, they would pull my funding and support. Yes, they had funded me to move states and set up here, but I failed to see any positive support. But if I chose the career path, they had pre-determined then they would come to my assistance. These are not the words they used, but the message was clear.

Jerome struck just as I had a major blow up with Chuck about not trying hard enough. Had I not given up a major part of my life? My youth? Was I not forfeiting all that now, even my family? Jerome's passionate sentiment filled a void, arriving at a low point. Authentic as it appeared, and as I wished it to be, past knowledge should have won.

Close familiar warmth was what I craved. It was thoughtfully *provided for by Jerome, with his rich coffee-coloured arms. Embracing me close, the warmth of his palm pressing my head to his shoulder. His hands were all encompassing, securing my face, and stroking my long dark hair. A finger raises my chin, our eyes meet. Jerome's nostrils flared as his breathing increased, desire at its greatest, his full lips approached mine.*

From there, I should have brought control to myself. For lacking it I have upheaved more than one life.

In the tradition of weekday soapies, Mike returned early from his trip. Bounding up my apartment's steps two at a time, humming merrily to himself, a large sweet-scented bouquet in his hand, Mike was just about to knock on my door when Jerome made his exit. Swaggering in the style of a gunslinger, a mobile phone the weapon of choice mounted on his hip, Jerome laughed.

'Hey snowflake, women can't resist a homeboy.'

Strutting in the amorous prance of a peacock, tail primmed to impress, Jerome started to do a little jig, blocking Mike's way in the process. In a mixed jump-slide, Jerome sang *chick-a-boom, chick-a-boom,* accompanied with sporadic arm movements as if he dragged a female form to him. Thrusting his hips forwards in wildly perverse movements, his smile split his face in two.

'Nothing but a homey can make a girl squeal all night.'

Pirouetting on the top step of the staircase, Jerome's oversized shorts flared. Brushing down his basketball singlet and reversing his cap, his face uplifting into a final smirk flashing in Mike's face before disappearing.

Turning slowly towards the open door, Mike's eyes take in Izzy, who now stands dripping wet before him. Sticking to her bare shoulders and neck, her normally vibrant hair sits lifeless. Snatched close to the chest, her hands cling tightly to the towel's ends, which barely cover her middle sections. Izzy's face is uncustomary pale.

'So, if I dressed and acted like a heathenistic five-year old, I would have scored better?'

'No. You don't understand.'

'Don't I?'

A ludicrous look on his face.

'Did you not have sex with him?'

Yes, her mind screamed. *I wished I hadn't, but I did. Why did you go away? Why? When I needed you.*

Instead, her emerald eyes flashed regret, drooping under his steely gaze. Feeling the anger surge forth from deep within, Mike knew he had to leave now before it all erupted. Under which his actions would be near fatal. His nails dug deep into his palm's fleshiness.

'Here!'

The piercing scream filled the silent void as a rainbow of flowers scattered on the floorboards.

'Mike. No!'

Pleadingly but of no assistance.

Striking heavily, Mike's feet bit into the stairs with hate. Each step a new dagger in his heart. Her voice floated down on him, wisping about his ears. Pleading, begging as her body slumped to the floor one storey up. Descending quicker now, Mike felt as if he was falling into an abyss.

Seething with unabated frustration, Mike struck out. His fist slamming into the building's front door. The huge oak panel quivering under the force. Intensifying, his rage crashed into the wooden door. Again, and again. Moaning under the barrage the door finally gave way. First in short sharp shards, then in larger splinters. Aching under the pounding, Mike's fist could take no more. Swelled as it was, bleeding at the knuckles, the final strike left the hand limp. Unresponsive. Mike's forehead fell to the bloodied door, as tears trickled down his cheek. The woods coolness appeased his cheek.

An obese lady, lounging in front of the television, dressed casually in a towelling jumpsuit, screamed obscenities at Mike. The heaving of her chest rose and fell rapidly. Lacking anything representing a lap, her breakfast rested on a tray situated between her and the television. The swelling belly's movement disrupted the tray littering the carpet with dry cereal, coffee, and cigarette butts. Her screaming increased, smothering the salesman on the shopping channel. Having not occurred to her to rise from the seated position, the blubberous woman remained seated, yelling through the open door. Mike took one step back to view the woman in the full.

'Shut the fuck up.'

He commanded over her bellowing. Silence finally fell when he reached into his jacket, pulling out a small calibre handgun from his jeans. Fighting to control his anger, Mike's breathing increased as his hand clenched the gun, focussing it carefully at her repulsive face. A whimpering mass replaced the caustic woman in the chair. Mike turned and ran. Ran from the hatred within.

So here I sit under a large eucalyptus tree, feeling sorry for myself. Realising that the sledgehammer of reality has cracked me over the head once again.

Footsteps approach from the distance, shuffling as they go. A whirring accompanies each shuffle. Shuffle. Whirr. Shuffle. Whirr. Closing my eyes tighter, in the vain hope of holding back the warm saltiness that floods them, I listen intently, waiting for each shuffle to come. The way you lie awake at night, waiting for the next tick of a clock. Thinking. Hoping, it will never come. I can envision the young man pushing his heavy bicycle laden down with reference books.

Painfully the shuffle/whirr approaches, stopping a few metres from the tree. A voice, weak and crackling, like a mistuned radio calls. No response. A disgruntled resentment is presented but not received. A blasphemous word is said, and with the presumption that my crumpled figure under the tree is asleep, the shuffling continues. Approaching slowly.

With a heavy sigh I lift a tired hand to my still closed eyes. It matters not whether my eyes are open or shut, either way I am blinded. Blinded by the loss I have suffered and the pain I must now endure.

'Izzy?'

'Yes Patrick. Thank-you for coming.'

Looking uncomfortable, Patrick glances around, a conspirator, he feels guilt with being associated with this Negro woman. Laying his bike on the grass he sits cross-legged a few feet away.

'What do you want Izzy?'

'I need to see Mike.'

Shaking his head, Patrick plucks a small leaf of grass, gently placing it in the corner of his mouth.

'Not possible. He's gone.'

Izzy's eyes spring open, her mind a whirl. A sharp pain strikes the rear of her head. Rubbing it in concentration, Izzy feels a knife lunging through her heart, mincing the remaining fractions.

'Gone? Where Patrick, you must tell me.'

Urgency fills her voice, desperation in its raw form.

'Where?'

Fists close round Patrick's arms. Their force constricting. His arms numbing by the second, the full rich colour of blood abandoning them. In the few fragments of time Izzy gave Patrick to answer, his mind swarmed on the pain the grip of this slightly built woman caused. His body then shook under her urgency.

'Tell me Patrick I need to know.'

Shaking him even harder, Izzy hoped that with enough force the words would tumble from his quivering lips.

'Stop that Izzy.'

With sheer physical strength, of which Patrick was lacking, he managed to pry Izzy's finger from his arms in annoyance. Annoyance that he had to meet here, with her, in such a public place. And annoyance with her public display of desperation. Wiping his hands with a monogrammed handkerchief, Patrick looked up into the sorrowful eyes.

'Back to Australia as far as I know. I don't know what you did. And for heaven's sake I don't care but he said he wasn't coming back in a hurry.'

'Australia!'

That was halfway around the world! A continent that large would make it near impossible to find one man. One in twenty-five million, if she remembered her Geography correctly.

Patrick seeing that Izzy had disappeared behind a mist in her mind rose to leave. Feeling pity for the girl, her devastation obvious, he refrained from speaking.

'His address Patrick. Do you have it?'

'It's very vague Izzy.'

Mike had sworn him not to tell her anything. Anything! Those liquid emerald eyes brought a bitter stinging to his own.

'All I know is Kuntana, Queensland, Australia. That is it.'

'But isn't Queensland a state, say like California?'

'Yes. Apparently Kuntana is the ranch name.'

'How would I ever find that?'

Shrugging and knowing her helplessness, Patrick left, not wanting to watch her wallow in her self-despair. Izzy could hear the pounding of her heart, mocking her with its existence. Regret engulfed her mind, accompanied by a pulse unforgivingly pounding at her temple, while the pain at the rear of her head slithered its way down her back. She barely acknowledged the clouds gathering above, pregnant with their ominous load. From the time when the first drops sprinkled on her toes, till they increased into a sheet of grey, Izzy had resolved to make the trip to Australia. How she was going to achieve this was another problem, but the resolve was there.

~ 15 ~

KUNTANA

Kuntana, Queensland, Australia.

Ah, nothing could beat the smell of fresh country air. The flight, in the Bell 525 Relentless Helicopter, was a bit too turbulent for Amelia, but it was the quickest way to reach Kuntana. Like many other properties in the area, Kuntana was marked as a destination on local maps. As the helicopter slowly reached its final resting point, Amelia's eagerness rapidly unfolded. Showing like that of a small child, eyes darting from window to window, her body perched precariously on the seat. Crossing the range to see the glaring sands, followed by rolling sun burnt hills and patchwork fields, always made the flight worthwhile. A land of such vast contrasts especially compared to the suburban sprawl they had just left.

Kuntana. An oasis, a paradise. The sandstone home-stead, covered in a rainbow of bougainvillea, all climbing endlessly towards the sun. Shading verandas, offering a cool haven from the savage heat. Surrounding the homestead stood lush green spelling paddocks and the full-size grass racetrack they had just landed on. Beyond that stood several fields of golden wild grasses amongst pasture improved cattle country. Land designed for the purpose of fattening cattle and hiding the wild brumbies (horses). Truly a place that breeds champions. Mafioso, just one great example.

On touch down, Rosario went his own way. Choosing not to reside in the homestead but in a small cottage a few hundred metres away. Probably brought about by his association with the cook, Mrs. Greenstone. A widow with plump hands as pale and spongy as the dough she lovingly made. Her face filled with the welcome of many grand-mothers. The centre of her life, the kitchen, was better kept than the rest of her belongings, including herself. Her long hair lay unsuccessfully crammed into a bun above the nape of her neck. Small strands would escape and flut-ter before her eyes as she worked. Gentle puffs from her mouth having no persuasion. Using the back of her hand Mrs. Greenstone would chase the strands behind the ears, but only momentarily. Flour covered everything, giving Mrs. Greenstone and her domain a ghostly complexion.

No finer cook could draw such feisty accolades. Many a fistfight had broken out after a debate about the merits of her steak and kidney pie. Her cooking was the best to be had around. Mrs. Greenstone cooked mainly for the work-ers as Amelia chose to cook for herself. Besides, having lived on cattle stations all her life, she knew only how to prepare bush tucker, meat and potatoes, and bread, which of course all the workers loved. Amelia enjoyed more European cuisine, benefited by the relaxation cooking allowed her.

Joseph's room was plain but elegant, enshrined in the warm colourings of the afternoon sun. The walls were painted in earthy tones, a shade lighter than the golden wheat fields, wrapping the room in its warmth. Standing in one corner was a cheval mirror, offering glimpses of hardwood furniture. To one side, an eight-drawer bureau, provided storage and beauty in one go. Each draw inlaid with exotic timbers, all sealed under French polishing. Standing proudly in the opposite corner, was a traditional porcelain washbasin with matching water jug, each covered with a delicate lace pattern. Central in thc room sat the bed, covered by a hand sewn patchwork quilt made of colours as vast as the surrounding landscape. Curtains of fine mist allowed cool breezes to enter, ruffling Joseph's hair. Louvered doors their only restriction. Its frame enhancing the view of prolific gardens surrounding the homestead. The river clearly visible in the distance. This place was a dreamland. More than he ever imagined.

After busying herself with lunch, Amelia strode along the refreshing veranda to Joseph's open door. A mixture of bird life whisked amongst the shading bougainvillea and other assortment of hanging plants. Feeding and playing as the mood took them. There, upon the white cane setting, she lay out the meal made by her own hand. Looking up, she glanced about his room. His profile was softened by the familiar walls, his hands nimbly removing neat stacks from a rucksack. A laptop was sitting to one side. She silently watched as he refolded each garment again before placing it gently in a drawer.

Feeling the suns warmth on his neck, Joseph smiles with satisfaction. Raising his head, a reflection stole his attention. Amelia, angelically standing in the doorway. Silk dress lapping in the gentle breeze, brushing her golden thighs and rustling about her breasts. Rays of sunlight defining the contours of her body. Tossing her beautiful mane, Joseph finds the reflection momentarily blinding.

'Lunch is ready.'

'I must admit, Amelia, Kuntana is a dream. Surely built over more than one lifetime. It must have cost a pretty penny.' More so, I'd say. 'Forgive me, don't answer that.'

His eyes slid from her to the tantalising view.

Amelia smiled at Joseph's line of questioning.

'I guess I'm lucky.'

She responded. If you mean hard work created such luck, yes, I'm lucky.

Joseph was sincere in his questioning, but the slight undertone was perceptible. He liked her for being strong, and sensed it came from years of necessity. That or loneliness. Thoughts of this nature were initiated by the homestead being over endowed with feminine touches and lacking any masculine feel. As far as he could figure, her husband had left years before.

'The same sort of luck that made me great? Working my butt off!'

His cheeky grin prevailed.

Oh, how much she appreciated his understanding

nature. Needed it too. Most men would have been insulted or disgraced by now. But this man, Joseph Bodine, was different. He was a man. A man Amelia desired. A real man. No! She must not have these thoughts. She was still mourning. What! For eighteen years? Eighteen years without love or tenderness. Without a man's touch or whispers of devotion. Amelia was strong, she had survived. But at what expense?

Joseph knew to continue by Amelia's detour of thought. He had achieved what he wanted, or at least, part of.

'What does tomorrow hold?'

'How about a picnic by the river. We could ride down. If you'd like?'

'Sounds great but I must be honest. I've never.... Well, I've never ridden a horse before. I know what you're thinking.' For once. 'How come a great horse lover like me can't ride? Never had the opportunity.'

Laughing, Amelia showed her sympathy.

'I have just the ronzino for you.'

'Ronzino?'

'Nag.'

Laughter ensued. This fresh country air was relaxing, especially to Amelia. How alive her face came, eyes twinkling with youth, lips uncurling from their malevolence, and muscles losing their hatred. So much more desirable. How could Joseph not fall for such a mysterious woman? This married woman? He no longer cared.

****

Inch by inch the sun crept towards the homestead as

it broke over the horizon. By six the whole property was saturated in its warmth and the promise of what summer would hold. Most workers, strappers, trainers, jackaroos, cattle hands, and labourers alike, had risen early, ready to face the challenges of a new day. A cool morning breeze carried the fragrance of fresh bread. Tantalizing aromas escaping Mrs. Greenstone's kitchen were teasing taste buds all over the property. Hunger, never before felt, screamed with desire.

Amelia rose early, capturing the whole day with its promise. Completing mundane jobs before Joseph rose. Relishing each with delight. Breakfast was ready before movement was heard in the guest room. Benches laden with fresh fruits, cereal and sizzling bacon accompanied by a welcoming smile awaited Joseph when he entered.

'Sleep well?'

'Better than you could imagine. Mmmm, is that a Mrs. Greenstone special I can smell? Smells delicious.'

'Yes. Corn and barley bread today. Fresh from the fields. Sit down, I'm just about ready.'

It had been far too long since Amelia had the opportunity to cook for someone. Yes, it was trivial, but it gave her immense pleasure.

Entertaining himself after breakfast, Joseph strode to the verandah, allowing time for Amelia to complete her chores and prepare a picnic. Temptation to walk the grounds was far too appealing compared to waiting around. For such a vast property, the grounds around the homestead, approximately two acres, were incredibly well kept. From every angle, blossoms in an array of colours were rising from their beds. A beautiful, sweet aroma filling the sun warmed air. Smelling as sweet as the honey the bees were busy preparing. One could not help but relax and drift along, as did the weightless butterflies.

Cities of dull grey monolithic sights could never compare to such a broad landscape. Delicately sculptured by the seasons and kissed by Mother Nature herself. The blooms added selected colour. A mosaic not yet finished. Their fragrance intertwining with the scents of sweat, cooking and horses. Not pungent but alluring in its own way. The smell of the country.

In a light summer frock, Amelia strode down the cobbled path towards Joseph. The gentle breeze tugging at the thigh length hem. Baby blue with a daisy pattern, the frock accentuated her sun-bronzed body. Pausing, she took his hand, pointing out the

main interests on the way to the stables. Their heads drawn together as questions were asked and answered. Looming in sight stood the high loft stables. Breezes flowing freely through its open ends.

Once at the stables, an old man with the features of Father Christmas greeted them. Tumbly round with a big white bushy beard and balding head. A tattered Akubra rested in his hand as he waved a greeting. Perhaps an Australian comparison would be that he looked like that jolly swagman. His scruffy moleskin pants, with their suspenders and R.M. Williams boots, crinkled with age and packed with dust, gave that impression. Under his sun-tanned complexion lies an original olive one, wrinkled not only by age but by far too much exposure to an unforgiving sun.

Selected first was Amelia's carallo. Very grand she was. The mare's thighs oozed immense power. Midnight black, matching Amelia's own hair, broken only by a small white star on its forehead. Shining with such strength, a suitable name had been allocated. Capo, Italian for the boss. An ex-racehorse no doubt. It took no time to realize Capo was Mafioso's mother. With a mother like this, Mafioso's father must be exceptional. And that he was.

Of course, a perfect ronzino had been selected for Joseph. Who felt slightly out of place in his khaki cargo shorts and white Colorado shirt. Nearly all of the stable hands wore the regulation moleskins or Wrangler jeans set off with a pair of riding boots. It was as if he'd stepped into a Henry Lawson poem. The nag was saddled. Cactus Jack his name. There were strands of pure stockhorse in him. Obvious by his boldness and agility. The other part of breeding showed in his mass. Built like a Mack truck, Cactus Jack was part Clydesdale. Hooves like tree stumps and a head that was... Well, enormous.

'Looks aren't everything. His mother worked at the old grain mill turning the stone press. We think his dad was a wild brumby.'

Grinned Santa.

'Tame, as the day is long. Good with children.'

He said trying to relieve Joseph's apprehension.

Good with children. What about adults thought Joseph? Never mind, today he felt like a child. No grey clouds were present in the sky or his heart. Life, at this very moment, offered release from all thoughts of suffering.

After a sketchy start, Joseph managed to hold on tight

enough, to allow the pair to slowly ride towards the river. Cactus Jack and rider mainly in tow. Quietness filled the air, only disrupted by the odd squawking of passing cockatoos. Amelia absorbed the surroundings while Joseph hung on for grim death. Smiling, Amelia spoke to distract him.

'Riding in the bush brings about the realization of many things, especially about trees. How they bend and roar in a gully wind or that soft leafy chatter you get with a light northerly. The way bark shreds and peels or how trunks turn as glossy as a racehorse in the wet. The lime and mulberry tinge of new growth. Trees that give shade. The ones to tuck behind in a squall or those that offer up good wood for campfires. Survival by trees that signpost water. Saplings you can use for climbing, that sort of thing.'

Turning, Amelia noticed Joseph's renewed concentration on the land surrounding them both. So much was taken for granted.

'Take this little nook, for example.'

Indicating the swag of trees ahead.

'What we have here are not neat specimens. Instead, we have a shaggy, scrappy grab bag of a forest. This tall timber isn't just a roof over our heads, it animates the place. There are limbs and crowns. Characters that sway and hum. Oddballs with mottled skin.'

A grin towards Joseph.

'Progeny making their way in the world. Burly types who endure seasons. Old timers stumbling to the ground to rot. Most often, trees are the crux of a place.'

Amelia's voice faded, imagination taking control.

'I've never looked at it that way before. How much character trees offer a place. Riding allows you to see much more than any vehicle could.'

'Yes, this reminds me of my younger days. My husband, Nicco, used to take me riding in the mountains above his hometown. Days so beautiful. And so clear. The views, just breathtaking.'

The opportunity was offered.

'Did you live in Italy long?'

'Several years. Mainly in Sicilia. I was originally in Italy as an amateur cyclist trying to turn pro. But like many before me I just wasn't good enough.... or ambitious enough.'

Quivering, her voice fading on the last sentence, trying to disperse the regret and pain attached to the memory. Not till later did Joseph learn, surprisingly from Rosario, that Amelia was a very talented cyclist. Good enough to turn pro and win. Winning was easy for her, she had even won the Tour de France (feminine). That was until her marriage to Nicco. Then it ceased. It wasn't Nicco's fault but that of the family. Apparently, no good Italian girl cycled competitively. Cycling was a man's profession. Sicilian wives are to be on hand for their husband's every need, and of course, have many children. Despite Nicco's encouragement, Amelia came home one day and cycled no more. Sold her bike and never spoke of cycling again. Only reason given, at the time, was an incident with a drunk driver. Or that was how that part of the story was conveyed to Rosario.

'But that's life, isn't it?'

She accompanied with a half-hearted grin, insufficient to cover the tracks.

'Before Nicco and I were married, we lived in a cottage outside his hometown, Nicosia.'

'Named after the town was he?'

Joseph enquired half-jokingly.

'Actually, he was named after his great grandfather's exploits. As the story goes, great granddaddy Felix Ricoldi was driven out of the seaside town of Cefalu. You see, he stole the heart of a young maiden. Carmalitta Carntino. Her father, Angelo, was very wealthy and powerful. He wanted Carmalitta to marry into the Lombardo family. Together the two families could have dominated the fishing colonies on the north coast of Sicilia. Lovers have different ideas, so the two fled to the mountains. In the process shaming their families. Life must have been good as they bore four sons and a daughter. Unfortunately, the birth of the fifth child was too much for poor Carmalitta.'

'Angered even more. Angelo sought revenge. Thus, the small family moved higher into the mountains to Nicosia. As each child grew, they searched for work in the seaside towns. Being related to Felix made life difficult so they all returned to the mountains, and raised their own families. Only one, the daughter, ever returned to the seaside town of Cefalu. With her husband and son.'

Only to profit from the dying Angelo and an ambition to settle the feud between the Carntino's and the Lombardo's.

'Nicco was their only son. They were disappointed when he didn't marry a nice Italian girl.'

Rosita Lombardo to be exact.

'But he married a nice Australian girl instead.'

Joseph was quick to respond to Amelia's pain ridden face.

She appreciated his company and his attention. It had been a long time since thoughts about Nicosia had entered her head. There were plenty of good times, but boy, there were some incredibly bad times too. Nightmares in fact. For now, she was released from that pain, thanks, mainly to this man, Joseph Bodine. Never before had she mentioned any of this to anyone, except snippets to Rosario.

'Where is Nicco now?'

Time for the million-dollar question thought Joseph. It was an answer he wanted.

'Sicilia.'

Walls continued to surround tender facts. Amelia just a maze needing the right navigation to release the treasure within. Or so Joseph thought. He had learnt. A lot in fact. No more of the past was spoken that day, replaced by frivolous talk, slight humour, and filled peacefully by their quaint picnic by the river. A world away from their first brunch. Clear water, cool to the touch, refreshing to taste, flowed endlessly. Dragonflies skimmed the surface humming their happy melody. An occasional plash was heard as the odd frog, jumping from lily pad to lily pad, missed. Compatibility grew and the first week was filled with similar outings.

Night was the time for relaxation on one of the alluring verandahs, waiting for the cool desert breezes. Laughter and jest was made about Joseph's improved horsemanship.

He was progressing well in his endeavour to become a competent horseman. So daring, that he attempted to ride Capo. As if made of marble the mare stood still. Not responding to any command. Until Santa muttered something in Italian, cibo per cani, and Capo bolted like a horse possessed. Leaving Joseph flat on his back in a cloud of dust. Unhurt luckily, except for his pride, which was grazed ever so slightly.

Moments together were becoming tenderer. Before bed, Joseph took hold of Amelia's hand as they walked in the cool night, turned, swam in the pools of darkness before placing a gentle kiss on her cheek. Unbeknown to him, each touch of his robust hand triggered a nerve ending, sending electric shivers of delight down her spine. Confidence was not only growing in the horse arena. Moving to kiss her other cheek, Joseph's lips brushed gently across Amelia's nose before landing on their target. Resting his forehead on hers, he slowly manoeuvred his lips to her waiting mouth. A hand already caressing his neck, drawing it in.

'Excuse me, Amelia.'

Damn Rosario. 'What is it!'

A tone of uncontrolled harshness leaps from her mouth.

'In private please.'

Reluctantly untangling her body from Joseph's, Amelia strides over to Rosario. Their backs turning in deep conversation. Moments later she returns to Joseph, apologising, saying she must take a call. With a final peck on the cheek, she wishes him good night, ending a promising evening.

By the morning much had changed. Tenseness hung in the air like a foul stench. Amelia's voice took on a sharpness, words cutting the air like a dagger.

'Joseph. You will go into town with Rosario tomorrow.'

More of an order than a request.

'Certainly Amelia. But why?'

A look of impatience washed over her face. Explanation did not come easy. She told, people responded. With restraint, Amelia continued.

'A week is a long time to spend trapped here, with me. Surely you'd like to see some other scenery.'

Or not see what is transpiring.

'I'm sorry Joseph. There is some...business I must attend to. Of course, you understand. Yes? Good.'

With a nod Joseph left the room, as would a scolded child. From instructions, Joseph and Rosario were on the road before six. Joseph having to prepare his own breakfast. The shadow, Rosario, was in such high spirits, probably due to the fact that Rosario didn't have the responsibility of being a shadow today. Much information passed between the two men on this long road trip of 500 kilometres, comforted only by the hummer's grand luxury. Such as Amelia's cycling past and how Kuntana was the largest and most productive property in the district. Plus, Amelia was the reason there was a slaughterhouse, an airstrip and a grain co-op. She had her hand in a lot of other pies, all of them benefited the local community. What a learning curve today became.

Returning late, Amelia's business counterparts where at the homestead when Joseph finished the days exhausting trip. Familiar voices pricked the air. By chance, one of the oak doors leading into the den come office was ajar. Vito Sarmry's large mass was noticeable. Gold jewellery glinting in the lamplight. Now on Amelia's turf, no smoky haze surrounded him. Half obscured by Vito's mass, stood a companion. A lithe young man with chocolaty hair. His face revealing the vigour of youth and suppleness of wealth.

'Amelia, my grandson. Anthony Valentine. He is a lawyer. My new lawyer. My consigliore.' Right hand man, advisor and confidant. 'Un giovane promettente.' A young man of promise.

'Congratulations Anthony. A high honour, usually re-served for an older, wiser man.'

That flat emotionless voice was the last that Joseph heard before retiring to bed. During the night, his dreams were corrupted by sections of raised voices, inaudible to his sleeping mind. Vito Sarmry stood out the loudest.

'But you are not Sicilian. You have no right!'

'No right? I may not be Sicilian, but I am Ricoldi. No matter what, that gives me the right. This alone may not earn your respect. Rispetto. But we have been friends for a long time.' Too long. 'That is why when I say no.' And mean no. 'You shall not and will not question it.'

'Mrs. Ricoldi. Te ne pentirai! You'll be sorry for this. This could be good for all of us. I personally have put a lot of work into this. A lot. I thought.'

A darkness descends Amelia's eyes and Anthony Val-entine is cut short in his futile tracks.

'My boy, firstly you are not qualified to think for me.'

For Vito yes but not me. 'Secondly, never let people know what you are thinking. Otherwise, you will not be a good lawyer. Finally, never, never question my answers. You may ask a reason, but never question the answer itself.' In my own home too. 'Andare! Go now. I am tired of your boresome discussion.'

'But Amelia, you haven't...'

Vito was cut short by an invisible bullet. The stare was cold and struck with practiced accuracy.

Joseph slept late, resigned to the fact that the meetings would continue. Both oak doors lay firmly sealed. Uninviting.

Following the departure of Vito and his companion, many new meetings were held. Each flowing through the night. Rosario resumed his position at Amelia's side, signalling the importance of each meeting. Over the passing nights, helicopters could be heard settling on the grass racetrack. Each landing with a soft thump. By morning they had disappeared, as did the muffled voices they carried as cargo.

~ 16 ~

AUSTRALIAN OUTBACK

Early morning mist began to clear in long, drifting waves across the plain. Pasture improved paddocks could be seen in fleeting patches beyond the stable, much like the earth through a bank of clouds from an aeroplane.

Around Joseph, the men were drinking the last of their tea, strapping on spurs, and climbing into sweat-soiled leather over pants. Each carefully made by their owner. An ideal form of protection against damp underbrush that attacked when they were chasing strays on the gallop. Santa trotted out Cactus Jack.

'Could I ride a different horse today? One not so...Clydesdale.'

A rich baritone chuckle rose from deep within Santa's swollen paunch, bursting uncontrollably from his lips.

'Hey Mr Bodine. Why not try my Ronzino!'

Duke's voice rose above that of the gathered men.

Without fail the remainder of the men joined the bari-tone laugh. Each enjoyed this eventful moment in the morning where Duke's horse invariably revealed a mean streak, by continually trying to toss him off. A spontaneous rodeo display was the treat as Duke's black stallion arched its back and pawed the air with its forelegs. Meanwhile Duke, a big booming, good natured man who stood at almost six and a half feet, sat calmly in the saddle, his stockwhip held loosely at his side, waiting for the animal to complete its morning ritual.

'Like a go? Too bad.'

Duke shrugged, waved to Joseph and moved off down towards the river, his two dogs, Mercy and Bourbon, trotting closely behind.

'That'll do boys. Off ya go.'

With that, the bemused spectators, still chuckling, mounted their horses and trotted off along Duke's path.

'Saddle up Whipple for Mr. Bodine.'

Santa disappeared to the rear of the stable, his chest still heaving with laughter.

'Joseph, I'm Declan. The station supervisor.'

A hand, weathered by the seasons, tarnished by the land, extended to Joseph. Powerfully muscled like the rest of his perfectly proportioned body. His eyes remained hooded by a wide brim, topping a face radiating a cheeky charisma with an old-fashioned sense of prudence.

'Not that ridiculous saddle. Use a real one. My spares just over there.'

Wiping his already perspiring brow, Declan tipped his Akubra jauntily back revealing thickly curled blue-back hair. The startling handsome face with its light grey-blue eyes and ready smile, sized Joseph up.

'You'll like Whipple. She's an Australian stockhorse. Strong, agile, and surefooted. Best you can find anywhere. More suited to the terrain than a Clydesdale unless you just want to stomp round here all day.'

Acknowledging the benefits of such a horse.

'And the difference in saddles?'

'Ha! Your manhood! Them western seats are good for show, but out here. Humph. Say a lassoed bull pulls sharply or the descent is steep, you'll feel it down there. Stock saddles work your legs harder, but man, they sure do plant you in the seat firmer. More control and agility. Much lighter too, so it doesn't tire the horse as much.'

Whipple appeared, short, stocky and eager in her movements. Standing staunch, mounting her was easy. Once secured, Joseph followed Declan out past the stockman's lodgings to an outer paddock.

'Are they solar panels on the roof?'

'Yes. They enable us to provide all the mod cons for the workers while keeping expenses to a minimum. The residence is made up into dorms of up to four bunks. Each room contains a shower, a toilet, a bar fridge and facilities to plug in a kettle, hotplate and a microwave.'

'Wow. Pretty impressive.'

'Yeah. Good tucker, a warm bed for a kip and hot showers is worth more than money after a hard day's work. Mrs Ricoldi knows its hard work out here, so she provides accordingly. Suffice to say our employee turnover is lower than most.'

'Must be a profitable style of business.'

'We do okay. You a tax accountant or something?'

'No, no. Just a gardener. And if there's any time left at the end of the week I do some writing, to exhaust both mind and body. So, you run all of this?'

Sizing Joseph up again, Declan continues in a cautionary tone.

'I run the day to days. Mrs Ricoldi looks after the rest. She has a great business mind but can't be here all the time.'

'She away often?'

'A fair amount of time yes. But other affairs, in the city, tie her up.' Yes, the city. Makes her grumpy as hell too.

Declan visibly shudders at the thought. By now the two men have entered the lush green paddocks, which edge the river. Cleared, except for clusters of trees scattered about, providing shade and relief for man and beast alike.

After achieving so much on Cactus Jack, Joseph enjoyed the new challenge presented before him in Whipple. She was so well trained and experienced, that she anticipated much of what Joseph wanted before even he knew. On several occasions he leant one way while she headed the other, avoiding an unseen danger in the long grass. At times he nearly lost his balance, pretending to be adjusting things when Declan cast his eyes around.

'How long you planning on hanging around for Joseph? Especially since it was such short notice for a holiday.'

Not much passed Declan's ears.

'It's quiet at work at the moment.'

That, and Joseph hadn't taken a holiday in five years or so. Plus, the boss owed him.

'Depending on how things go, I may leave any day

now. Initially I was planning to stay another week. But Amelia's?'

Busy, preoccupied, ignoring me. Take your pick. Joseph had a sulky tone to his voice.

'I understand. How's about you and I improve your horse skills by going bush for a couple of days. Such a pity to be going on your little merry-go-round each day when the real beauty's out there.'

Declan's arm circled the entire property as he raised himself on the stirrups for emphasis. His spontaneous enthusiasm for life and genuine passion for the land, attracted Joseph's attention. Yes, he was up for the challenge.

Returning to prepare for the expedition Joseph viewed the sloping hillside to the river, now all but invisible under a stand of willow trees, many of which have long since reached maturity, collapsing under their own weight. Younger willows, offered the prospect of shade. How easily his life could be defined by these trees.

In the first light of dawn, the many buildings of Kuntana's homestead were toned in rough, uneven gold. After loading the horses, tightening the girths on the saddles, the two men were away, riding down the slope away from the homestead. Climbing the slope on the far side of the gully, Joseph briefly glimpsed the white helicopter settled on the horse track. A light mist had gathered in the snow gums, and the homestead roof glimmered whitely as they turned toward the far-reaching range.

From his room the range could not be seen, but now its presence was constantly before them, even while they made their way through the parched sun-dried Lucerne fields. Patches of strewn rocks were just visible on the higher slopes. Not reaching to great heights, the range gave the impression of immense, impenetrable breadth. So anonymous are the peaks and so continuous are the spurs and ridges, that Joseph doubted the possibility of crossing them. But onwards they persisted.

Travel was slow on this first day. Declan was allowing time for Joseph to condition himself for the much harder pull over the range. In depth, Declan explained how he needed to tone up his muscles in order to adjust to the long hours in the saddle. Knowing the horse intimately was a priority, for surely there would be times when man and beast would be called upon to rely on each other. Sensibility is what horses had, they are sensitive to their rider's relationship to them and will respond accordingly. Apparently the first task was to make Whipple feel at ease in Joseph's presence, but who was going to make Joseph feel at ease?

Following the route along a gully for some distance, Joseph was pleased to see the land rising toward more timbered country. Passing the pasture improved paddocks, they approached a region littered with numerous dead trees, all ring barked. Travelling slowly through this graveyard of gums, their awry trunks and branches etched darkly against the sky, depressed Joseph immensely. Especially after the life Amelia's words had given them. By nightfall, they had climbed into scattered timber and underbrush.

Under a cloudless sky, camp was set up. Unladen and

then hobbled, the horses were left to graze for the night, while Declan started a campfire. Murmuring water was soon heard as the billy came to the boil. No conversation filled the cooling air, except the crescendo of chatter from crickets, the foreboding laughter of kookaburras and the howl of a wild dog in the distance.

Untying the bivvy bags, Joseph rolled each out in a prime position beside the fire. Settling down he gratefully accepted the feed presented to him. Potatoes baked in their skins, a weird broth under the disguise of stew and the best of all, damper fired in foil and lavished in golden syrup. The tea stirred with gum leaves and served in metal cups was the best he ever tasted. Add a little sugar, and it was very revitalising after a long day in the saddle.

'Amelia's a very beautiful woman.' Incredibly. So intelligent too. 'You're a lucky guy, Joseph.'

Spoken in a breathy, nostalgic tone, Declan finally used Amelia's given name.

'Not much more than acquaintances I'd say.'

A cocked eye displayed Declan's disbelief in such a statement.

'You're the first 'acquaintance', she's ever brought to Kuntana.'

'Lucky, I guess. And her husband?'

'Not here.' Heard rumours though. 'I started with Amelia when she purchased the property years ago. Fifteen in fact. We all thought Rosario was her husband at first. The way he hung round and all.' Quite strange really.

'Like a shadow.'

Both nodded in agreement.

'Not an overly friendly chap.'

'No, I suppose not. His job is to protect, and he appears to do that well.' Takes it seriously too.

Spitting and crackling the fire danced into the conversation, its light occasionally waltzing past the faces of the two men. Everything beyond a certain distance lay in darkness, yet everything was full of being around them.

Void of electric distractions, stars twinkled and smiled with neon brightness. The moon, full and silver silhouetted the trees against velvet blackness. Darkened green foliage topped unearthly monsters, eerily reaching into darkness.

After breaking camp next morning, the two riders continued rising towards the scattered rocks jutting out from higher peaks. Towards late morning the peak was crested, accomplishing the first major obstacle for the day. From here, the peak dropped sharply away to a river, too sharply to allow stock, let alone a horse, to negotiate a way down via such a steep descent. No route was visible to Joseph, but Declan knew a way. Not too far away lay a curving, pine-clad spur. Even it appeared to drop suddenly away into the valley below.

At first sight, the horses baulked at the slope, encouraged by the slippery pine needles underfoot. After gentle coaxing they soon gained confidence and chose their own track down skirting the now present pines. Once they dropped below the skyline a perceptible change came over the steep river valley. The green pine clad slopes opposite, stood out in strong relief against the red soil beneath. The sparse undergrowth giving a clear sensation of space between trees. The descent had a fine mysterious quality about it, as though they were entering a secret world never before seen or touched by man.

Finally, through the trees, the river could be glimpsed. A view of a broad, curving expanse of water, pooled and swiftly flowing, with sand and river gravel piled each side near the flood mark. The more sharply angled the track became, the more clearly the flowing river, 200 metres below, could be seen. An uneven rippling current of water fresh from remote springs and winter rains.

Leaning back in the saddles, the horses pitching under the weight, the foursome lurched downwards. Downwards towards something they only half expected: a clear flowing river whose presence seemed to utterly dominate these high slopes. Breaking clear of the tree line, the two men gazed upon the river, at its own level, for the first time.

Stumbling forward over the bank's smooth pebbles, each looked forward to their first taste of natures untouched. Camp was pitched at a junction were a smaller rivulet met the mighty force of the main river. Though there were still a few hours to sunset, neither Joseph nor Declan had the desire to push on.

Observing the river at close quarters took Joseph's breath away. Above the high-water mark was an almost continuous transition of rock, worn smooth and shaped by innumerable floods. Wherever the eyes settled, lay a different cluster of rocks, all curved and cupped with pools of rainwater glistening in shallow crevices, sometimes metres above the riverbed.

Looking further he could see a point where the river flowed around a bend, a place where long stretches of sand had built up over time. Islands of scrub and trees reached down, sipping from the water's edge. Barely noticeable were the tail grazed marks of wallabies and other assorted wildlife. Stands of willows grew on the banks, their lemon green leaves blending with the softer greens of acacias, and the grey greens of the pines further back.

Yes, the day's effort was amply rewarded. Before them stood an almost noiseless world, that was wild yet strangely unmoved by their presence within it. An unspoken whisper, the language of the river, was carried on the still air.

Night descended rapidly, blanketing the valley in orange tones before darkness struck. Upon the small rush filled billabongs, dragonflies could be heard humming as their wings thrummed the surface. Frogs croaked in the reeds while the water mirrored concentric rings as water beetles and tadpoles rose for air. Amongst the pines, the fluted call of a whip bird echoed. A throat filled note, holding in the air for near an eternity, before rising swiftly. Cracking into silence, the gurgling of the river, as it lumbered over unseen rocks and vanished around the bend, was all that remained.

Lying on his back, snugly tucked in his bivvy bag, head resting on folded arms, Joseph took in the vast unknown before him. The Milky Way washed the sky in its brightness, while the Southern Cross pointed to home. Winking and sparkling, the stars flirted with Joseph's imagination.

'This surely is a beautiful land. Why would anyone choose to live in the city?'

'Beats me. Life's too precious to waste anywhere else. The outback is so amazing, yet the fact is life out here isn't easy. People today are soft and don't want to work for the good things in life. Such a view is priceless.'

'What about your family Declan?'

'I was an orphan, my parents died when I was very young. I went from foster home to foster home and ended up a little redneck. By fate, I was sent to a boy's farm and haven't left the land since.'

Declan enjoyed being raised on the land, and the land was the only life he knew or cared to know.

'Never married?'

'Engaged once to a beautiful lass. On her desire to become a schoolteacher she left to study at a university in the city. Got caught up with city fever, never seen or heard from her since.'

'You're lucky to get out of it so lightly. I went through the whole marriage deal with a similar girl. Ended up nasty. No one else on the horizon?'

'There was one special lady.'

A sigh of happy memories escaped from Declan's mouth, drifting up with the last wisps of smoke from the dying campfire.

'Oh, she was so beautiful, intelligent, loved the land as much as I, and..'

Fading into secluded memories.

'And!'

'It just wasn't the right time apparently. Her life is complicated and from her point of view it wasn't to be.'

From mine, there was no better time or person. It could have been so perfect, and yet, still can be. Especially if there were fewer interferences.

'Anyway, thought I might start living like that Dash Starkey writer said in that book. What was it called again?'

'Three Women and a Shed?'

'That's the one. What a beaut!'

Boisterous laughter filled the silent night air. Cattle responded with moos in the distance. Each noise vibrating and echoing through the range, merging into one.

Early morning was shrouded in mist, rising and evaporating as the sun's warmth pierced the valley. The men proceeded along a narrow siding by the river, negotiation was made difficult by a steep and sudden drop to the lower bank. A prospect not relished by the two horses, so they strode deliberately close to the rising hillside.

To mind and soul, the river continued to exercise a powerful influence. In, the now clear, morning air the entire valley appeared incredibly still. Barely audible was the river current as it rippled below. Rounding a bend, four regal white pelicans were slowly cruising across one of the larger pools, their orange beaks looking like blossoms drifting on the dark surface. Startled, the pelicans sounded a futile warning honk. Churning the water with their wings, the birds took flight, leaving the men listening to the rambling river once more. A final flash of their white underbellies was seen as they rounded the bend and vanished.

Slowly, they climbed the track on the far bank after fording at the junction. It was no more than a metre deep where the horses crossed, and below the hooves could be seen mica flecks glittering like gold on the sandy riverbed. Further on, the pass was reached, a narrow track upward over the summit of the range that seemed to lose itself in the sunlight and trees.

Several tracks arose up out of the valley, some passing the summit and on to the plains beyond. As they climbed, the pine-clad slopes were left behind, replaced by a line of gums. A magpie warbled its lone chorus, fluted and melodic, reaching out across the horizon. Lorikeets scuttered in nearby branches, screeched as they tussled for positions, unconcerned by the two horse riders. Lush fertile plains spread before the waiting eyes of the men.

'Shit. Why do I bother working in the city?'

'Beautiful. Isn't it?'

'My word. Makes me want to tell my boss to get stuffed and move out here.'

'Here you go.'

Edging his horse closer to Whipple, Declan handed Joseph a mobile phone.

'As if it's going to work out here.'

'Okay, smart arse. We use satellite phones so that calls can be made and sent anywhere in the world.'

Uncontrollable laughter rose from the two men, dislodging the lorikeets from the trees. Screeching and squawking the birds left to find quieter residences. Startled by an artificial high pitch tone, Joseph dropped the phone. Declan dismounts and reaches for the screaming phone while at the same time scolding Joseph jestfully with a pointed finger.

'Hello? Yes. Yes. But... Of course. I understand, right away.'

With such a short sentence, Declan's tone changed from cheery to annoyance. Hands clenched at his hips and eyes downcast, Declan paused before mounting his horse. Looking despondent he ushered Joseph on.

'The presence of your company has been requested.'

Not even the brilliant view could lighten Declan's now settled mood. Absorbed in his own thoughts, he didn't join Joseph in their usual light banter. In response Joseph now found himself studying the snow gums that appeared to envelope them as they rode. At first glance the trees seemed ill-defined, unstructured, trees without any evident grace. Like all gums, their growth was tangled, anarchic. Their apparent reason for existence, mute obstacles for birds to land on. Yet when the eye and ear are attuned, as Joseph's was becoming, it was easy to recognise that these trees possess an independent life of their own.

Wherever he looked, there were signs of constant warfare between the trees and the elements. Trunks twisted and spiralled upon themselves after prolonged exposure to high winds. Carcasses of trunks that had finally exploded under stress, left remnants across the track. Others were rippled and scarred unevenly, as all the inner violence of long years, the heat and the cold of the seasons, finally surfaced. Each element leaving its signature in the bark's exterior.

Jerking to a halt, Joseph slides precariously on the saddle. Correcting himself, he looked up to see a clearing ahead. Covered in spring blossoms, lush grass carpeting the remainder, the land lay cupped like a basin. Large snow gums encompassed it but dared not to enter. Gentle gurgling from an unseen stream could be heard as it passed through, crashing from the dip of a spur before landing in the valley below.

'We'll wait here.'

For what? Joseph was curious. It soon became apparent as a dull thud echoed in the distance. A rhythmic drumming beating in unison with his heart. Slowly the thuds boomed through the valley and rose to a crescendo on the summit of the range. Trees rustled and folded beneath the artificial breeze. Declan held his hat tightly above his squinting eyes. Cresting the range was a colourful Bell helicopter. Hovering momentarily, like a bee selecting the perfect bloom, the helicopter finally landed.

Two crouched bodies disembarked as the horses became unsettled. One unloaded several parcels a short distance away while the other approached the two men. Dismounting, Declan handed Joseph his reins and approached Amelia. Both turning in heated discussion, their voices muffled by the idling helicopter.

Past intimacies were reflected in subtle movements. Amelia's hand gliding back and forth on Declan's arm. His gaze downcast, reminiscent of a schoolyard tryst. Within moments the conversation died and Declan's hand grasped hers. Kissing her delicate fingers, he momentarily hugged them to his chest before nodding to Joseph. Joseph approached on foot leading both horses, Declan met him halfway taking the reins and mounting his stallion.

Arms folded to deflect the chill breeze of the departing helicopter, Amelia watched the lone horseman until he vanished beyond the summit. Turning, her eyes grasped Joseph's.

'If you'd like to wash up in the stream, I'll set out afternoon tea.'

Chilly as it was, Joseph scrubbed the layered dirt from his body and clothes in the stream. Laying his shirt on the grass, he approached Amelia bare chested. Before him lay a checked woollen rug, supporting an assortment of delectable fruits, cheeses, chocolates and Muscadean wine. Two full glasses awaited next to Amelia's lithe body, which now lay relaxed, supported by one elbow. Flicking her dark locks to look up to him, her hair fell limply as she handed him a glass.

'Sorry for interrupting your expedition, but I finally had a free moment. That, and I felt bad about neglecting you.'

Her eyes studied his response, and managed to fit in his chest, before asking him to lie next to her.

'No trouble at all.'

Lying opposite, appreciating her body relaxed and suspended in youth. Only by looking closely could he see the exhaustion of sleepless nights, the dark shadows beneath her eyes, tiredness in the lines about her mouth. Still, he could not help but admire her physique.

'Strawberry?'

Raising the crimson fruit to her lips, teasing her tongue before letting her bite.

'How was the ride?'

'I'm a natural, I'm sure. Was just about to ring my boss and resign when you called.'

No noise escaped her, but her face revealed the delight within. A breeze drifted between them, tugging at her partially unbuttoned blouse. Touching the unshaven growth about his face, Joseph kissed Amelia's open palm. With a playful flick she toppled his hat.

'Hey!'

Grabbing her wrists in defence, the two playfully struggled. Joseph slowly hovering above her body, her back pressed tightly to the ground. With surprising strength, she rolls him to the grass and gains the dominant position. Amelia's weight pressing his body, her hands pinning his wrists. Shaking her head in a scolding manner, midnight hair falls to fill the void between their faces. The tips tickling Joseph's nose.

'No fair.'

Eyes pitted in combat, Amelia lowers her head. Teasingly at first, she brushes her lips across his. With firmness their lips finally meet in a kiss. Each successive kiss, more forceful, deeper. Tongues intertwined, relishing the touch.

Straddled above Joseph's restless body, Amelia unpins his arms allowing them to wander. Across her thighs they travel, upwards to the line of her back. Untucking her blouse his finger search for the familiar metal clips.

Kisses flow, travelling down Joseph's neck to his bare

chest. Saturated in them, Joseph runs his spare hand through Amelia's long fragrant hair. Raising her face gently to his.

'Amelia.'

Before another word could escape his lips, a shrill shriek rose from the far corner of the rug. That same artificial noise which broke his peace once before, a satellite phone. Ignoring the shrill cries, Amelia continues to focus on Joseph and his partially naked body, her heart beating loudly. Not loud enough to cover the dull thuds in the distance. A tear of disappointment runs along her cheek, falling to Joseph's below.

'Maledizione!' Dammit! 'I hate my life.'

Wiping away the tear gently with a thumb, Amelia disentangles herself from Joseph. Straightening her blouse, she answers the phone.

'Yes.' Despondent recital of what is expected. 'When? Okay. Si. Gia` , facile per te!' It's all right for you! ' It's just cresting the summit now. Va Bene!' All right!

Dejected eyes cast a look of what could have been to Joseph. The helicopter's breeze already fanning her hair in an outlying arc.

In a matter of minutes, they had covered the area that took Joseph three days to ride. Settling on the grass racetrack, Amelia touches Joseph's arm signalling him to stay aboard. Rosario was already loading his rucksack.

'I'm sorry Joseph.'

She said in a partial whisper.

'I'd hoped for more time in your last week. Hope it wasn't too bad for you.'

'Never, Amelia. Thank-you for bringing me here, to your world. Maybe next time, we will have more time together. See you again, hey, Rosario.'

Amelia slid closer to Joseph's ear, the warmth of her breath tickling the hairs on his neck. Her chest was heaving on his arm.

'I enjoyed the company. Your company. See you soon.'

Question or statement, it was not too clear.

With that, Amelia gently cupped Joseph's face in her hands. His body surged with expectation. Their lips brushed then met. Not a memorable kiss, but a lingering one. Their cheeks touched as she spoke again.

'See you soon, Joseph Bodine.

~ 17 ~

FLIGHT OF DISCOVERY

Los Angeles, California, U.S.A.

Noise reverberated through Mike's ears, crashing and clanging with his thoughts. His mind floated in a sea of words, bobbing up and down, dragged this way and that with an unseen current. From nowhere a strong rip would drag him under, the words suffocating. Struggle as he might, his mind would claw its way to the surface gasping, only to be pulled down once again.

People pushed and shoved about Mike, all hustling to departing flights or greeting those from overseas. Safely securing his luggage at the check in counter, Mike proceeded to the Qantas lounge area. A few shots of Mescal later and he was feeling much better. Slumping into an awaiting lounge, he threw his feet up while sculling another tequila. Glancing at his watch, given to him by his mother, Mike smiled at the thought of going home. Home. Just the thought of boarding the Qantas jumbo with Australian accented hostesses, near brought tears to his eyes.

'Hey Nick. Nick. You dreaming, or what?'

'Hey, Tony. Imagine meeting you here.'

Anthony Valentine strode over from the bar, his choc-olaty hair loose and wavy. His supple body displaying a limp as he walked. Shaking Mike's hand, Anthony seated himself in the chair opposite. Composure upheld and back stiff, Anthony crossed his legs. One foot lay suspended in mid-air, bouncing as he spoke.

'Fancy running into you here. Of all places. Come va la vita?'

'Michael Dart if you don't mind Mr Valentine.'

The words flowed in a snobbish English accent.

'Oh, most certainly Mr Dart. I do beg your forgiveness.'

Sly smiles passed between the two men.

Friendly bantering continued until it was time to board. Mike thought it was most fortunate to run into his old friend Anthony, and even more surprising to be seated next to him in the first-class cabin. Anthony on the other hand wasn't as startled with such strange coincidences, especially ones that unfolded under his own hands.

Settling into the oversize chairs and claiming their first champagne of the flight, each man made a toast.

'To homecomings. Ritorno.'

Stated Mike nostalgically.

'To famiglia.'

Enforced Anthony.

Conversation died momentarily as the giddiness of take-off swept over them. Under the captain's instruction the jumbo soon levelled off at flying altitude, hovering precariously above suspended cloud masses.

'So, Mike. I hear Roberto got his button.' Time to plant the seed.

'Really? I hadn't heard.' He what? And no one told me.

'Sorry I thought you would have been one of the first to know. From what I heard, Don Santapaola presided himself.' Time for the knife.

Mike fell silent. Attempting to wear his mask of dispassion, one he had seen many times on his mother, Mike remained outwardly calm.

'Don Santapaola.'

He repeated.

'Yes. Celebrated pretty hard too I heard. Word is he is in training.'

'In training?'

'To replace Rosario. Become the man as they say.'

Smiling internally, Anthony enjoyed the lines of concentration on Mike's face.

'But, of course, you would know of all the plans.'

'Of course.'

Spoke Mike trying to be convincing. No wonder she had agreed for him to travel first, before deciding on his future. I am sick of being kept out of the family business, his mind yelled. I should be the made man, his child's voice whimpered.

Resting his hand on Mike's shoulder in a brotherly manner, Anthony spoke soothingly.

'You are slightly younger than Roberto. When the time is right. It will come.'

'Cosi e` la vita. That's life.'

My turn will not soon enough brooded Mike. Turning

to the ultramarine blueness outside the small window, the colour appeared to blanket anything and everything. Woolly whiteness sat beneath the belly of the plane. Sunlight reflected from the suspended comfort, momentarily blinding him. Shaking his head to regain vision, Mike turns once more to his old friend.

'What did you say?'

'Vito visited Amelia recently with a business proposal that wasn't too shoddy, but she turned him down flat. Vito offered your mother a promising opportunity but failed to show her the respect she deserves. She is incredibly strong, achieving so much for the family. An incredible amount.'

Anthony purposely spoke loosely.

'Many anticipate your arrival, especially having a teacher like her and with the blood that flows through your veins. For no matter how much they respect Amelia, there are still some business areas that are a man's domain. Only a man can achieve true power in this business, only a great man at that.'

Using his eyes as the pointer, Mike acknowledged Anthony's unsaid words.

'Amelia believes that the Ricoldi family, your family Mike, earns enough. But I say, what's money without power. Sure, you can live happily with money, but power means greatness.'

Without acknowledging it, Mike was nodding in agreeance to Anthony's words. His subconscious having summoned this fact previously. Anthony took this as a sign to continue.

'Unfortunately, Vito failed, neglected even, to inform your mother of the full scope of the plan. Amelia never discussed the potential of the proposal, most probably due to his disrespect.'

'It's been that way a long time Tony. Even before she returned to Australia. Were you at the meeting?'

'Oh yes. Didn't I say, I'm an official consigliore.'

'My, my, what a great honour.'

'Yes, but I struggle at times.'

A heavy sigh emphasised a disappointed tone.

'Vito is, how to say it. His respect is askew. His heart does not always think of the family, as it should.'

'Family and respect are one, Tony.'

'Yes, I agree whole-heartedly. I suppose it pains me not to be a made man, as you will be, to follow in the tradition of my family. Vito believes a consigliore should be above reproach. But you.'

Eyes emphasising awe.

'I envy you. I really do. You stand on the threshold of manhood. The world is at your feet. You are bound for greatness, I know it.' And I plan to be a part of it.

'You honour me with your words Tony. What is it you want from me?'

'An opportunity exists Nick. Oops, Mike.'

Laughing lightly.

'It's an opportunity that I think even Vito has under-estimated. Not that I think he could handle it if he did understand the opportunity.'

Leaning in close for emphasis.

'We could Mike. Greatness is within our grasp.'

Snapping his hand shut, as if capturing something thrown to him, Anthony displayed his dazzling pearly whites.

'Greatness Mike. Grandezza by forza.'

'But if mother disagreed.'

'Women don't take as broad a risk as men. Nor do they achieve such power as them. The future of the families comes down to us. The men of the family. Men who will risk all for their family.'

'Tell me more Anthony. How do you see this plan working out?'

'Well.'

In hushed conspiratorial tones.

'As you know Vito controls all narcotics coming in from Columbia. Well, what would you think if we entered into pharmaceutical drugs at the ground floor? The Amazon rainforests are waiting to be exploited and the big companies, no matter how legitimate they appear, have trouble getting a foot in. I have contacts.'

'Be bio pirates? Pillaging jungles for their animals and exotic plants? Never saw myself as a pirate.'

Rubbing the stubble with a sidewards grin.

'Long John Mikey, hey.'

'Something like that, you fool.'

Slugging him in the arm, Anthony continues.

'The Amazon is an incredibly untapped source.'

Anthony's voice deepens as his seriousness bubbles to the surface.

'In 1995, 118 of the top 150 prescription drugs in the United States were derived from plants or animals. Yet the proportion of plant species investigated for their medical properties was estimated at just 1100 out of 365,000. Do you know what that means?'

'Yeah. There were 363,900 duds.'

Ignoring Mike's mockery.

'On average, one important new drug has been produced for every 125 plant species studied, whereas the equivalent rate for chemical compounds is one in 10,000. It could possibly be more lucrative than drilling for oil or the gold rushes of the 19th century. And just think, the ultimate 'strike' could be the discovery of a cure for cancer.'

From past experiences with the Ricoldi's, Anthony was aware they preferred situations where their actions were justified. Assisting society and all that crap, he thought.

'Tell me more.'

Hook, line and sinker, smiled Anthony.

'According to my contacts.'

'I know your contacts, Anthony.'

A single raised eyebrow revealed Mike's lack of trust in Anthony's contacts.

'A professor of forestry at Yale University, and the director of the Institute of Economic Botany, say at least 300 potentially lifesaving drugs may await detection in the Amazon. They value the discovery of these species at $300 billion.'

'In light of this information, wouldn't others also be aware of it?'

A fruitless endeavour considered Mike, especially if it was an already full market.

'Well in a way yes. In legitimate businesses there are around 125 organizations that now have pharmaceutical research interests in the Brazilian Amazon. They are based mainly in Rio or Sao Paulo, and range from drug giants, big brand names, to smaller operations specialising in 'natural' remedies, and institutions, both government and universities. But in smugglers and such, there is no major group of players. Yet.'

'What makes it enticing for us is that there is a backlash from the local Indians and their government. Brazil's laws governing the removal of plants are full of loopholes and new legislation is currently being rushed through Congress to clarify the situation. The locals themselves feel they are being short-changed by the large corporations, abused in a way, as not only do they assist scientists by revealing which plant cures what but they see no income from that. On the other end, scientific laboratories rarely do the smuggling themselves. The information is generally taken from a third party, who doesn't say explicitly where the material comes from. If they don't ask, they're not told. This, of course, makes it very difficult to prove anything if and when it comes to charging people.'

'Another key factor is that plant samples tested in laboratories outside of Brazil make it nearly impossible to keep track of what is leaving the country and where it ends up. What I suggest is that we use the locals as harvesters, pay them minimally for the privilege, then set up hidden laboratories in the rainforest, or on the coast, equipped with the latest test equipment. All manned by native scientists. Have them do the initial research, so that only the good stuff is ready for shipping, and then sell it onwards to the larger laboratories or move it to our own for further research. Just moving the plants is an endless endeavour as the real action occurs with the lab findings. This is where the dollars are.'

'What do you need from us? From me?'

'Two things basically. Both Vito's and my contacts together would be enough to start us in the endeavour. Unfortunately, my contacts cannot be activated whilst Vito is in control.'

Wording it as delicately as he felt the situation could handle.

'Uh huh. I see. The other?'

'Initial funding and the Ricoldi name would not go astray.'

'For doors to open and such.'

Mike was cottoning on now.

'Esatto!' Exactly!

Attempting to look relieved at not explaining further.

'Plus, there's more.'

'More?'

Looking startled yet intrigued, Mike leant in closer. Absorbed in the possibility of gaining his own power base, Mike forgot all about Izzy. Momentarily at least.

For the next fourteen odd hours, Anthony and Mike huddled in conversation, continuously planning and scheming. Breaking only when meals and drinks were required. Upon landing a great plan had been devised. Shaking hands as confirmation the two men went their own way.

Anthony's face was smug as he searched for the silver cigarette case inside his jacket. Removing a sleek white cigarette, he tapped the case three times for luck. Reaching into his pocket he produced a gold lighter and fondled it for a moment, as if it was something more than an expensive trinket. A talisman perhaps, or the memento of an intimate relationship. Cupping his hand around the cigarette and his mouth, his free hand raises the blue flame. White smoke puffs above his head as Anthony's face fills with a mischievous grin. Lips thin and taut across his face.

PART THREE

Business as Usual

~ 18 ~

A HUSBAND'S RETURN

Life after Kuntana was wearisome. Nothing in the city compared to the relentless views or relaxed atmosphere of the country. Unable to find comfort, Joseph initially sat on the balcony, chair tilted back, feet resting on the iron railing before him. But the noise and putrid smell of the city depressed him. Disappearing into the bathroom, the sudden thunder of water helped to drown out the sounds and sorrow he felt

Afterwards, he lulled in the well-worn groove of the easy chair, allowing the warmth of memories, of Kuntana, to fill his body to saturation. Images surrounded his dreamlike state. Cactus Jack with his child like nature. Mrs. Greenstone with a new cooking sensation wafting past his pleading nostrils. And Amelia. Amelia whose reluctant smile had caressed his heart. In the midst of dreaming he was startled by a knock. No, more of a loud banging at the door.

Not till it was open did Joseph see the two men that

stood beyond. The first took a step forward, his mass so mountainous that it blocked Joseph's view of the second man. Unshaven with greying stubble, thinning hair to match, the man smiled ever so slightly. A narrow, near unnoticeable, scar ran from his lip's curve to the upper ear and beyond, into the hairline. Most of his mass was made up of muscles rippling like waves on an ocean under black silk. In youth he would have been quite handsome, as now he still looked distinguished: thanks mainly to the greying temples. Resting his shoulder on the doorframe, he twirled a ruby encrusted gold ring on his pinkie.

'Joseph Bodine? Are you Joseph Bodine?'

A slight nod and a dropped jaw inferred he had found his prey. His lips rolled into an animal like snarl.

'I have a message for you.'

Within an instant the two men were barrelling through the door, pinning him in the room's corner. Their action, was far too domineering for Joseph to go on the defensive. Shutting the door was in no way an option. Too much was happening too fast. A desire to flee filled Joseph's whole body. Brick like fists commenced their pummelling action. Their hands were encrusted with leather skin, built up over years of practice, incredibly experienced in their chosen career. Staccato action led to a sensory overload for Joseph.

Limpness overcame Joseph's body, leaving the second man to hold him up. Managing to let a few kicks and punches fly, Joseph struggled against his attackers. Several attempts were successful as they hit their mark in the ever-soft genital area. Unfortunately, this made the madman even madder. Blood mixed with saliva flew across the room. Joseph's left hook was weakening. Soon no pain was felt as his mind lifted from its shell. Time slowed, presenting sequences as if he were watching a movie of some violent description. Unconsciousness finally rescued him. Fading in and out he thought they said something. Yes, they did.

'Hey lucky boy, you listening. We're only here to make you suffer. Think you suffered enough.' Laughter. 'Saluto. Oh yeah. Nicosia Ricoldi sends his regards.'

Additional laughter fading away.

Nicosia Ricoldi. Amelia's husband was punishing him? This can't be true? Floating in and out of consciousness restricted the assembly of the abstract puzzle. It was a long time before Joseph came around fully.

There was no way he was going to call the doctor. No. He detested them. Besides, they usually only prescribed drugs and he'd seen the consequence they had. All his life, he had tried to erase from his mind, that terrible mental picture of his mother lying so unusually still. Her face whiter than he had ever seen it before and her once sparkling eyes closed forever.

Amelia Ricoldi was the only key holder to the puzzle. With his head the way it was, serious thinking would have to come later, once he had managed to unwind the knot in his stomach and cleared his mind of the tortured confusions that now befuddled his thinking. Was it even worth pursuing?

Yes, she was worth pursuing. But how to catch up with her? Were the meetings finally over? Slowly figuring it out, Joseph came to the conclusion that Amelia would not miss out on Mafioso racing. That name.

Mafioso drew crowds at every meet and was in high demand. The short wait feeling like a lifetime to Joseph. An overcast day greeted the greedy punters. Country lads in their Sunday best, all vying to capture a fair maiden or a winner. Either was okay, especially the latter. Horse stalls recently smothered in fresh hay carried a musky scent allowing the city a taste of country fragrance. This smell was soothing in its initiation of memories for Joseph.

The earliness of the day encouraged a happy and carefree environment. Later, many a sad and disgusted face would be seen as favourites failed to please. One thing punters' had in common was the sole concern for winning that big one. None noticed Joseph's pain, even though he wore a reminder on his right cheek. For fear of what he would discover, his heart ached the most.

True to plan, Amelia was at the track, attending to her melodramatic jockey. The shadow nearby. As programmed, Rosario noticed Joseph first. But unlike previous times, he motioned to Amelia, whispering in her ear. Squadro. She turned sharply and their eyes engaged. Skin crinkled on her forehead as she broke away from her entourage and approached him with the ease of a hunter to an injured animal.

His face? How could it be? The normally handsome face, so tense and full of anger. Oh, the bruising. Take it slowly Amelia. Surely it can't be my fault?

'Before you ask, Nicosia Ricoldi sent his regards. Is that right? His regards!' A good job at that too.

'Nicco wouldn't. He couldn't. It's a lie. Rosario!'

The shadow had never left.

'A lie?'

Fierce flames grew in normally expressionless eyes. Accompanied with a flood of restrained saltiness in sympathy for the body raw with anger. Joseph. For the first time she was speechless. Running her fingers down his battered cheek to ease the tension. Her lips were soon to follow, pressing gently on the bruising.

Aroma of perfume was too much, he just had to touch her. To know, that what she said was true. His arm stretching around her waist, drawing her closer.

'No, Joseph. Not here.'

Rosario stepped in, taking hold of Joseph's free hand.

'It will be taken care of, my friend. Take my word.'

With a nod from Amelia the shadow was gone.

All that was left was Amelia. That and a small card in the pit of his sweating hand. Upon it was written a mobile phone number. An unusual gesture, which was appreciated immensely.

'Come Joseph. I will take you home.'

Amelia linked her arm through Joseph's as if he was escorting her.

'But I have my car. I can take you.'

'No.' A glimmer of a smile displaying, mockery? 'Roberto!'

From seemingly nowhere a handsome young man appeared. His strong, dark looks draped in a quality, handmade black designer suit. A silver silk shirt unbuttoned, revealing curls as dark as his slicked back hair, held flat only by the weight of a solid gold chain supporting an impressive crucifix. Mirror like patent shoes exaggerated his random gait.

'Take Mr Bodine's keys and see that his car makes it safely to his apartment.'

'Yes Mrs Ricoldi.'

A nod from Amelia indicated that Joseph was to trust this man with his keys and his adored car. Hesitantly he passed the clinking mass over, momentarily stalling to remove the apartment keys.

'My address is...'

'It's okay, Joseph. He knows.'

He knows? He knows my address? Amelia's never been to my apartment, nor has she asked about it. But she knows. A sense of uneasiness lowered upon him. Was there more to this than he was aware of?

'And Roberto, treat Mr Bodine's car better than your own. Do you hear me?'

'Yes, Mrs Ricoldi. Better than it's ever seen, I promise.'

A familiar voice echoed from beyond Mafioso's stable.

'Declan. Good timing. I must leave now, so please take care of Mafioso.'

'Certainly Amelia.'

Declan only ever spoke Amelia's first name when his proximity to her was extremely close: never did he use it when other employees were around. But was he an employee? At times he felt like one, but when she asked him to accompany her to the city he knew he wasn't. Declan enjoyed their closeness and was not ready to risk it for anything.

'Joseph, I'll be back in a moment, I must speak to an associate. Please wait with Declan.'

'How's it going Joseph?'

That same familiar sun leathered hand filled Joseph's with sweaty warmth.

'Bad end of the stick hey.'

He motioned to the obvious bruising about Joseph's face.

Believing the matter only involved he and Amelia, Joseph answered with monosyllabic responses to Declan's inevitable remarks, bringing an end to unwanted conversation. It wasn't that he disliked Declan: in fact, he had a lot of respect and envy towards the man. But his mind was so confused about the situation he was in that he had no patience for life's frivolity. Declan accepted this and stood quietly beside him, scanning the passing crowds. Amelia called from a distance, motioning it was time to leave. Declan whispered in Joseph's ear, pretending he was looking at something behind them.

'Be careful. He is watching.'

Puckering his lips in question, Declan shook his head, and rubbed his own eye as an indication. Mind now swirling and giddy like, Joseph stumbled as if he were drunk. He wished he was. As the two men approached the dying conversation Amelia was having with a thin faced elderly man whose light hazel eyes were watery with age, Joseph only heard the closing sentence.

'I want to keep him close to me for now.'

Locking arms with Joseph, Amelia's entourage, of about six, escorted the pair to a waiting limousine. Six was way more than she usually had. What had he gotten himself in to? An open door awaited them. The sun had baked the interior of the limousine, and the warm late morning breeze blowing through the open door ruffled Joseph's hair. It carried little cooling comfort.

Aching with thought, Joseph barely noticed the passing of familiar streets and landmarks. Multitudes of cars blurred by, hurriedly seeking their destination. Amelia occasionally squeezed his hand and offered a limp smile as if to say everything would be all right. But would it?

Silence quenched their ears as neither knew what to say. One burning in anger while the other's anger had subsided replaced with an unknown fear. Each had a new need, but how to fill it? Even in the privacy of his apartment, Amelia couldn't release the anger or emotions she felt.

Hushed as if to be comforting.

'Mi scusi. I'm sorry they did this to you.'

'In the name of Nick....'

'I know. I know. But it just isn't true.'

Her eyes stayed unfocused. Sadness penetrating her face.

'Nicco had nothing to do with it. Maybe the...'

Don't say too much. It would be dangerous. Amelia stopped herself.

'I'd like to explain but... Oh, Joseph. Forgive me?'

As if taking a command Joseph moved closer to comfort her, even though he himself was the injured party. At least his injuries showed. Could Amelia be feeling as much pain as he?

'No, Joseph. It can't be.'

Her hand held his chest at bay, she could feel the increased heartbeat under his toned exterior.

'I'll make us some lunch. Let us think things over a little.'

Her breath touched his face, warm and pleasant.

Watching those tanned legs walking to his pokey kitchen, Joseph remembered his first glimpse of them in that mini skirt. Hmmm. Today she wore a cool summer frock, which hung limply around her shoulders and breasts, its transparency revealing the inviting lace beneath. All her movements were effortless and smooth, seductive in a feline way.

Entering the kitchen, a sink full of dirty plates encrusted with decaying remnants of food awaited. Mottled orange lino on the floor set of the matching orange cupboard doors encased in a Laminex wood grain finish. Much had peeled away revealing the chipboard beneath. Searching the cupboards, she found them half empty, layered with papers from the seventies. Most of the necessities awaited on the far bench top. Cutting board, knife, and a plate. Entertaining would be made hard considering there was only one plate, one cup, and one bowl.

Looking around she was presented with an old, rounded fridge. Across its centre lay a chrome handle, covering from one side to the other. With great difficulty she levered the handle to open the door to a yellowing interior. No light escaped, the bulb burned out years ago and never replaced.

Standing frightfully alone, on the main shelf, was an

unopened bottle of Muscadean, below that, a bowl of muscatel grapes and strawberries accompanied by a box of chocolates. The same as those they had shared at Kuntana.

In the musky kitchen air a sob escaped, echoing its sadness. Without realising it, Joseph stood behind her. His hand resting apprehensively on her shoulder. Moving closer, the fragrance of her hair took Joseph by surprise. Moist, silent tears fell amongst the hairs on his hand as Joseph slid his arm across Amelia's chest. Pulling her closer. Kissing his hand, tasting the saltiness, Amelia occluded her eyes to prevent a flood of tears. Against his shoulder her head pressed.

Vibrating with each of Amelia's heart beats, Joseph's hand found itself drifting below the neckline, prickled by lace, caressing the rigid nipples of desire. Alternatively, Joseph's spare hand had found its way along the thigh, passing the hem unchallenged. Trembling fingers tugged gently at the elastic of her lace thong. With excitement his fingers ventured further, ruffling the softness beneath. Gasping with unexpected excitement Amelia jumped slightly.

'Joseph, I think...'

Spinning her, Joseph examined her eyes, which revealed a peculiar mixture of surprise and seriousness.

'You think too much, Amelia. What do you feel?'

Expressed with concern, his face moved closer to her, and then the feeling of warm, moist lips was on her chest, where her heart might lay deep within. Briefly, lightly, and then they were gone.

'In here.'

Before a word could escape her mouth, even before her mind could discover another excuse, he kissed her on the lips, passionately. Taking her breath away. Reeling with passion's giddiness, no voice came to Amelia. Her mind adrift in a sea of mist.

'Every night, in my dreams, I make love to you. I want you, Amelia. More than I've wanted anything in my life.'

Falling to his knees, embracing her very soul, Joseph kissed Amelia, sinking his face in the folds of her body. Relishing her, the curved fleshiness of her breasts, the rigidity of her darkened nipples and the amorous dish of her belly button. She was all he wanted. And he wanted her now.

Eyes entranced, Amelia sensed Joseph's excitement and promise. Blood pumping through her veins while life itself electrified her body. Touching his chin, she lovingly raised his eyes to her, Joseph's body followed suit.

Standing, looking at each other, silent. Both startled by what had occurred and then without speaking, almost without thinking, as though it were the only natural thing to do, Joseph drew his arms about Amelia and held her close. Amelia's lips first tasted his cheek, and then slid to his mouth. Joseph returned the kiss, his lips parted, tasting the wetness of her mouth. They stood in a tight embrace, their mouths and bodies joined. In the distance they but faintly heard the low rumble of thunder.

****

Brilliant flashes of light illuminated the apartment. Followed shortly by a thunderous crack. A gun sending its deadly message? No, thank goodness. Where was she? The surroundings are not familiar. Then it struck her. Joseph's naked body lay beside her, on his back. His strong, clean profile outlined against the greyish light cast from the window. Joseph slept easily, his full soft lips only slightly parted, his chin firm, his mousy hair tousled. The smooth chest moving slightly with his breathing. There was a small brown mole on his chest, beside the right nipple. Amelia had an impulse to lower her head and kiss it, but feared this would awaken him. Emotions flooded her mind. She had failed herself and the promise she had made. Or maybe it was a life of torture she had set for herself.

A promise of so long ago. Where was the respect for her husband? Nicco was everything a good husband should be, supportive, caring, giving, loving and gentle. He had given up his family for her. Nicco didn't deserve this disrespect. Oh, that fateful night. Could she ever forget it? Salty tears flooded Amelia's reddened eyes as she relived the horror once again in her mind.

****

Nicco's lifeless body slung across her knees. Eyes flickering with life yet to be lived. Amelia cradles the mass to her chest, blood-soaked hands clinging in hope. Hope. Hope for the future. The essence of life escaping. Eyes fixated to hers, in such a loving way, after all that happened. A whisper, closer to a gasp escaped his mouth.

'Dire la madre l'amo. Tell mama I love her. And papa.'

A pause of thought or lack of necessity. Air rasped into his lungs. With conviction.

'Lo perdono. I forgive him.'

'I will Nicco. I will. Si, I'll tell them.'

'Death cannot take me from you. I will always be here.'

A limp hand void of its lifeblood raises and touches her chest.

'I love you.'

Below even a whisper.

'L'amo.'

Breathing as he breathed, trying to bring life into his lost soul. Amelia commenced to weep in despair. This, one of the few times she ever did so.

'I'm sorry darling. Sono il darling dolente. It's all my fault.'

Pained beyond her years.

'Rosario! Where's the help? Hold on. Please.'

'Baciarme. Kiss me.'

The last act of love.

It was all too late. Nicco's eyes flickered once more as the fire of life dimmed. The crumpled body became a limp mass of what was.

'Yours forever Nicco. Enternomente.'

****

Inadvertently Joseph entered Amelia's emotional nightmare. Blurred with sleep his eyes had trouble focusing. Yet such pain was sensed without sight.

'I must leave. This is wrong. I am wrong. I can't stay. I promised. I did. I promessa.'

Rambling words near incomprehensible. Pain of this extent is hard to describe, but it exists.

'Hush. It's okay. I'm here for you. Who did you promise?'

'No, I must go!'

'Because of Nicco?'

Searching her face in vain revealed no new clues.

'Look what they did to you. It could have been worse. It will get worse.'

Her confusion subsided and was replaced with anger.

'Look what they've done to you. I don't give a damn about...'

'You ignorant fool. You don't get it.'

A laugh but not a reassuring one.

'Wake up. I am a part of **them.** There's no escaping it. As my life is, you could never, **never** be a part of it.'

Frustration more than rudeness dominated the situation. Years of understanding colliding to this one point. Her life was crumbling. Nicosia's life was wasted. She could not ruin another. Especially that of someone..? Dare she say it? Someone she loves. There was something almost frightening in the wildness of her eyes. Joseph responded harshly to break her of the invisible hold.

'Your world! Too controlled for my liking. I've seen it and I have seen you in it. What a cruel world it is. Here, I thought you had power and strength of character. Bah! I was wrong. I'm just a pawn in your game. Well, I hope your victory is sweet.'

To sink the final dagger.

'Oh yeah, Nicosia Ricoldi sends his regards.'

The final comment escaped in the heat of things. Joseph now, could not bear to look at her. His eyes darting about the room, as though looking in the familiar surroundings and furnishings for answers. Yes, he loved her. He knew that now. How could she break his heart by not wanting to love him?

'Go Amelia. Go now. If you don't **want** to love me, go. Enjoy your prison.'

Joseph rose and cast one last look at Amelia, turned and left the room. This was good-bye. Unless, perhaps, she would change her mind. Don't leave his heart screamed. Amelia commenced to.

Urges encouraged her to run to him and explain everything. She could not. Pride or guilt held her back. Amelia should have known and trusted the look in his eyes. If only she listened to their calling. He didn't mean what he said. Now Joseph was gone. Gone forever.

Thank goodness she let herself out.

~ 19 ~

LOOSE ENDS

Dockside, Brisbane.

Beep. Beep. Beep. Echoed the reversing delivery truck. Its immense shadow concealing two figures slipping into the hotel's rear entrance. Lost in the afternoon's warmth, two detectives joke and chat with the delivery driver as he hands them two fresh hams.

Darting into a passage storeroom, the two figures remove their overalls to reveal hotel uniforms. Exiting the room separately, the figures meet up at the service elevator. One with a room key and the other with a cleaning trolley. Quietly slipping into the elevator a gloved hand presses three.

With a ding the elevator door springs open on the third floor. Raising his eyes from the magazine, the detective feels uneasy as no one exits the elevator. He rose from his chair, searching the hallway, double-checking the stair well door. Removing his gun he can hear raised voices from the elevator.

'And what do we pay you for?'

'I sorry. I thought no clean.'

Emerging from the elevator stood two staff members, startled by the detectives strained expression. Before the door closes, he checks the vacant elevator, allowing the door to close as his eyes pass once again to the stair well.

'Ah Detective Tomilaris. I'm sorry did we startle you?'

'No. Not at all.'

'Sorry to disrupt you. I'm Phillipe Mack, assistant manager in housekeeping. I believe Maria failed to clean your room today.'

Leaning closer he spoke solely to the detective.

'I feel she may have been a little intimidated by your presence. In her country the police aren't always on the right side. If you know what I mean?'

Laughing detective Tomilaris looked over at the plain woman, cringing behind her cleaning trolley. A uniform sagged over her body like a sack, while her black hair was tied back unevenly revealing black-framed lenses. Her dress gave her no appeal at all or a second look by the detective.

'The room's fine.'

'And have her getting away with not doing her job. I'm afraid I can't allow it. This has been one time too many.'

'See. He no want room clean.'

'Maria. It is our policy to clean all rooms. Do you hear? All rooms daily. If you don't like it, then you can find another job.'

'I need work.'

'Hang on folks. Hang on.'

Stepped in Detective Tomilaris. Unlocking the door he swung it open.

'You must be quick. Okay.'

'Yes. Maria very quick.'

Sidling past the detective with her trolley.

'Thank you for understanding detective Tomilaris. I'll wait to make sure the job is first rate.'

'I always do good job.'

Mumbled the cleaner as her trolley bumped the door closed.

Once in the room, she could hear the shower running. Pretending to dust the side table, the woman looked round to make sure the room was not occupied by anyone else. Kneeling by the bed she grabbed a small plain wrapped package from the trolley's lower shelf. Lying flat on the floor, her arm stretched as far as it could under the bed, her nails digging into the parcel. With an upward force she managed to stick the parcel on the underside of the bed.

Hearing the water stop it's pattering on the enamel bath, she rose quickly, continuing with her dusting and straightening. Emerging from the bathroom was a male wrapped scantily in a white hotel towel.

'What the?'

'Sorry sir. I clean.'

Stricken with fear the man stared at the woman. Her face was wrong. Completely. But the voice was unmistakeable. An uncontrollable shiver took hold of his body.

'How?'

Glancing at the closed door.

Without baulking from her cleaning duties, yet feeling uncomfortable in the custom-made artificial face, the woman spoke.

'Hush Declan. You don't want detective Tomilaris to overhear us, do you? No. Besides, if I was here to kill you, you would be dead now.'

'Then what, Amelia?'

Knowing there was no escape except for the door, Declan stood transfixed. Fucking police. Not even they could keep him safe.

'Don't even think about the door Dec. Rosario is waiting if you want to tackle him. I just came to talk to you. Why run to the police with tales that could hurt us. Especially after all the years we've shared together.'

Shared, you reckon? Kept me around more like it. Baiting me. Teasing me. Flirting even. Uneasiness rested upon Declan.

'Hurt us. I don't feel I could be hurt any more than I am. I'm curious about what we shared? No, you kept me around for amusement, nothing else.'

'No Declan. Is that what they led you to believe? I can't imagine the lies they filled your head with. You are a great station manager, and a special friend. Besides Nicco loves you.'

'And you?'

What could she say to that? From the start she had known he was infatuated with her, but she chose to ignore it. Or was it heartening in her time of despair, that someone loved her. Yes, she had feelings for him, but not as strong as he had for her.

'You are the father he never had.'

'Ignoring the question as usual.'

'I feel strongly for you Dec. Unfortunately, all of my life has been taken up with other people's needs. The timing was wrong for us.'

'It was always wrong. And I realise it will always be. So, what now?'

'Now you are an infame. A man who talks is a traitor, dishonoured, utterly unworthy of respect. Something, which saddens me greatly. I fear something will happen to you or someone in your family?'

'I have no family.'

A cocked eyebrow displayed Declan's piqued brazenness.

'No. I so enjoyed that tale about you being an orphan. Just like me I suppose. Yet you have a mother, father and three baby sisters. That's were all your money has gone over the years. Making up for your renegade youth, you sent all three of your sisters through university. What a caring brother.'

Horrified, Declan's pupils vanished to mere specks. Each fist was clenching and unclenching by his sides. His cheeks were flushed.

Appreciatively, Amelia's eyes travelled Dec's bronzed body. He had always been a man's man. No tattoos. No earrings. As rugged as the Australian countryside he loved so much. He even smells Australian Amelia thought. A mix of honey and eucalyptus.

'You wouldn't dare.'

'I could never harm you Declan. Like you could never

harm me. I just came to enlighten you on this irreversible ideal.'

In her mind's eye Amelia could see a vast chasm divide them. With each passing second it widened and deepened to a point of no return. There was no way of crossing it now, it was too deep, too dangerous even for words. Not even in her mind could she make the leap. Together they had spent many great years at Kuntana. Riding together. Eating together. Laughing even. He had just wanted her to love him and look at the situation he had put them in. The more she thought of it, the more the chasm grew.

Scanning the room methodically, Amelia admired the cleaning job she had done. Reaching into the trolley with a gloved hand, she noticed Declan tense, his mouth twitching. He had a strong desire to call the detective but was unsure of who or what would enter the room.

'Settle down Dec. It's just a bottle of Grange Hermitage 1971. Something to help you think. Your favourite I remember. A gift from me to you.'

Stepping back as she approached, Declan held his breath waiting for the end to come. No end arrived, only a quick kiss on the lips. In moments Amelia was carefully guiding the trolley to the door.

'I do hope you change your mind Dec. I need you at Kuntana.'

When she was in line with the door, Declan noticed Amelia's voice change.

'I done Mr Mack.'

'Right you are Maria.'

Looking in a disguised Rosario grinned at Declan.

'A fine job too.'

Thanking Detective Tomilaris for his patience, the two supposed employees left bickering towards the service elevator.

'Everything okay Mr Dart. You look pale.'

'No. Everything is fine detective.'

As they entered the elevator, they saw Declan's door close, and the detective resettle into his chair and magazine. With the elevator doors sealed firmly, Amelia and Rosario felt free to speak.

'I'm going to miss him, Rosario.'

'Yes Amelia. I will too. But his actions are inexcusable.'

'Will Nicco understand?'

'His actions will hurt Nicco most of all. Besides, the gas is the kindest way to let him go. The timer will go off about one a.m., releasing the gas while he sleeps. He won't feel a thing.'

But I do Rosario.

For the remainder of the afternoon Declan paced his room. From her actions, Amelia had shown that her resources could kill him and his family at any time. Whenever she had the desire. He knew that now. Maybe he always did. Was this his punishment? A slow agonising wait, for his own death. Stuff it! He thought as the cork popped from the bottle of Grange. Drinking the crimson liquid straight from the bottle, Declan stood and stared beyond the window.

If only he had not spoken to that man who presented himself as a punter at the track. Especially on the day Amelia had left with a bruised Joseph. The man, a detective, proficiently manipulating his anger over the situation: she had invited him to be there: and using it against the one person he loved the most. Unforgivable. Then, they had the audacity to threaten his family. Well, not in so many words. Their implications were that his family were in some kind of trouble, of which they couldn't assist unless he furthered their investigations. Declan had patiently waited for Amelia before, but seeing her affection towards Joseph had unsettled him.

It startled him how dark it had become. Pacing back and forth, trying to find a solution, had taken up more time than he realised. Drinking the remainder of the wine, Declan spread his lanky frame across the bed. The towel lay dormant on the floor. Finally drifting off to sleep he dreamt. Dreamt of riding bareback with Amelia through the valleys of Kuntana. Both bathing in the freshness of the river. Making love in the long grasses of the high plains. He had never been happier.

~ 20 ~

VENDETTA

'Mr. Bodine? We were wondering if you could accompany us to the station. We have a few questions to ask. Here is our warrant to search the apartment.'

Narrowing eyes searched Joseph, and beyond, into the darkness of the room. Uniformed officers thrust him to one side as they entered and commenced dismantling the apartment. Unable to fathom the situation, Joseph stood dumb founded, sleep still numbing his mind. The morning's coolness rushed in, chilling his half naked body. How could this be happening to him? Vito Sarmry dead. Murdered? What did he have to do with that!

Forcefully placed into an unmarked car, Joseph sat silently, face sullen. The car moved at a brisk speed through the dark silent streets of the sleeping city. Rain had fallen earlier, under the scattered streetlights the pavement glistened. Joseph watched the empty streets slip by, unaware of light or movement, feeling only his own deep confusion.

Yet only two nights before, Amelia's favourite Italian restaurant, Danny's, on the Gold Coast, was full of song and merriment. At the time Amelia's mind lay elsewhere, her mood surrounding her like a wet blanket. Smothering any joy or laughter within. Vito, once again, was throwing himself an extravagant surprise birthday party. His wife, thirty years his junior, pranced about the room, flirting with anything in trousers. Her hand laden with the latest acquisitions of love from her current husband.

Entering the room, feigning surprise, Vito bellowed a chesty welcome to all present, holding his heart in a pantomime of succumbing to a heart attack. His boister-ous laugh filling the already overflowing room. Catching Amelia's eye, Vito lumbered over, shaking hands with well-wishers as he approached. Forcing herself to be cheery, Amelia raised her arms to the birthday boy.

'Ah, Amelia. What a pleasant surprise! I wasn't sure if you could make it.'

'Wouldn't miss it Zio Vito. Happy Birthday.'

Leaning over to kiss him on the cheek, the sly old fox rotated his head at the last moment, meeting Amelia's lips with his. Repulsed, goose bumps covered her entire body. Acting the game Amelia scolded him like a naughty schoolboy. Blood filled his cheeks with a rosy colour, livening his face with excitement.

'Where is my favourite boy?'

'Not feeling well after his trip.'

It was a lie, but she couldn't blame Nicco for not want-ing to attend. She herself hated it, but it was necessary. Worse still, she knew Nicco was up to something.

'He'll try and get along later.'

'Good. Good. Go and enjoy yourself my dear. I hope to have a dance with you later.'

A leering grin filled his face as he unashamedly settled his eyes on her abundant breasts.

'Yes, a dance would be good. First, go eat, enjoy. You look like you could use it.'

Yes, she had lost weight lately. So much weighed on her mind that she often forgot to eat. *Was it more stressful than normal or was she not coping as well?* She could never decide. Nicco's coming of age didn't help. She worried for him. *This was the life she chose, yeah right, was thrust into and damn the consequences. Should she have pursued it for so long? It was hard to say.* There was pressure from the family for Nicco to carry on from where his father had left off.

Brooke Jeffries approached Amelia while she was in thought.

'Dance Amelia?'

'Sorry.'

'Preoccupied with work again? Come now, come with me and have the time of your life.'

A smile flourished on her lips. Brooke Jeffries always had that effect on her. He was a man who could never be classed or tied down. Having an eye for beauty, a penchant for famous women, a desire for fast exotic cars and in the adage of James Dean, a wish to die young, leaving a good-looking corpse. His definition of young varying each year, even though he had been twenty-nine for far too long. His motto: who dies with the most, wins. Brooke was her oasis in a sea of treachery.

'I was waiting for someone better looking, actually.'

'There is no one more handsome than I.'

His smile alone lightened her mood. They had been friends for a long time. Too long. He could read her moods and responded accordingly. Flicking his blonde locks, Brooke fluttered his lush long lashes. Women would die for such wonderfully seductive lashes.

'I would love to then.'

Looking ravishing in his three-piece dinner suit, blood red rose in the lapel, Brooke whisked Amelia to the dance floor. Clamping her close to his strong sinewy body, they twirled in and out of the other bustling dancers.

'How's Taiwan going? They online yet?'

'Tut, tut. No business tonight. Enjoy yourself, you are with the sexiest man alive, take advantage of it. Grrr.'

Smouldering eyes appraised her body behind half closed lashes. Laughter came easily while she was with Brooke. There was no expectation, no pressure, and no judgement, just a relaxed bond. Enjoying his company didn't detract Amelia's eyes from the signal Rosario sent her. With a glint in her eye and a smile, Amelia whispered to Brooke in a husky sensual voice.

'Save the last dance for me, honey. I'll be back.'

'Sure thing, sugar pie. Unless, of course, something better comes along.'

Displaying playful hurt, Amelia stepped back. Both laughed as Brooke disappeared into the thickening crowd. Quickening her pace, she met up with Rosario behind a palm tree at the rear of the restaurant. Toilet doors were within their sight.

'Is he in?'

'Yes. No one else is in there.'

'You go. I'll watch the door. If all's okay, signal.'

Rosario disappeared into the men's room. In a moment he had returned, his brow furrowed in deep malevolence. His words eagerly escaping in a stern hushed tone.

'He's gone!'

'Where? It's a bathroom.'

'Through the window. I checked it out and it looks like Roberto and his crew got him. They were stuffing him into a waiting car.'

Amelia laughed at the prospect. Simultaneously her mind ticked over deep in thought.

'We must go now and follow. Can we depart without being seen?'

'Same way as them I suppose. A car's already waiting.'

'Let's go.'

A quick glance and the pair were gone. Through the men's toilet and out into a back alley, skipping over the restaurant's waste. Rounding the corner, they met up with their waiting car. The engine already revving to go.

With more skill and caution than the youngsters in front, Amelia's close-knit crew tailed the other car to an old warehouse district. Remaining a safe distance behind, stopping a block away, they watched as the two tall dark figures led the short stocky Vito into an abandoned building.

'Do you have the overalls, Rosario? We might as well get changed. If I know Nicco, he likes his prey to run before he strikes. Tortured many a bug that way when he was a small boy.'

Remembering Nicco as a small innocent child brought warmth to Amelia's heart. He was life, the sun and she the earth. He brought light, happiness and warmth to her otherwise cold existence. Rosario too had fond memories of Nicco, having been present for his whole life. Sadly, Rosario was not always able to spend the time with the lad, as he would have liked. Amelia was his priority.

Rosario assessed Amelia's statement and then considered their surroundings.

'If that is so. I feel Vito will try to escape away from the darkness and head towards the light of the freeway for safety. It may be best if we set ourselves in the darkness in between.'

Amelia's wickedly curved lips accepted the plan. Exiting the car, Rosario and Amelia slipped on the overalls. Blood on their party clothes would not go down well. Dressed as lines men they proceeded to where Rosario guesstimated Vito would run to. It did not take long to hear pounding feet and the puffing of an unfit body.

Rounding the corner, Vito was intently watching for his pursuers, not noticing the two forms in front of him.

'Why hello, Zio Vito.'

Vito's mind unravelled with the events of the night.

****

A streetlight blinked as the non-descript car approached the trash strewn side-street. The night was dark, the moon's face hidden behind a debris of clouds. Without a sound the car pulled to the curb. A neighbourhood generally avoided, especially at night. Thus, it was strange when two young, well-dressed men emerged from the motionless car. Between them was a third. Just as well, if not better dressed. Much shorter and stockier, surrounded by a haze of smoke.

Passing a once proud shop front, now boarded up and decorated with an array of colourful graffiti, they approach a non-descript whitewashed door, that appeared to be a long bolted entrance to an abandoned warehouse. Behind that door was an ill lit staircase that led to a windowless second story loft. Following an unlit hallway, they headed towards the rear of the building where light attempted to escape from a closed room. Without a word the door was opened to reveal light projected by several bulbs hanging loosely from the ceiling.

The room itself was once a main office and like offices of its time, appeared very spacious. Probably helped by the fact the room had been stripped bare a long time ago. Bare of everything except an old teak desk and a high back chair facing the rear wall. Discoloured walls displayed long removed paintings. One man knocked, once they had all entered.

'Come gentlemen. I have been waiting.'

'How dare you summon me! Especially from my party.'

Striding to the desk, the shorter companion slammed his palms against its surface to enforce his presence. A desire to look overpowering, he was waiting for a response from the faceless chair. Creaking as it turned, Vito was taken back. His face quickly draining of blood. Hands shaking slightly. An obvious shiver running his spine.

'I did not summon you, my friend. I asked you to meet me. Like friends should. If you are offended Zio Vito, I am sorry.'

Spoken by a passive face, eyes locked on the visitor.

'But why here? So far away.'

'Far away from what Zio Vito? The city? Ricoldi's hate the city. So impersonal. Here we are equal, don't you think?'

'We are always equal, my friend.' Gulp. 'But so be it. You look tense.'

'I am confused. Maybe you can help?' Like you don't know, you fat slob. 'How is it you dislike Amelia so much. For me you've been a papa. A gold coin you lay upon my palm on my communion day. On graduation an offer of work. You treat me as your own. But Amelia? Eh!'

'We are family. Blood. Your papa and me, like brothers. No son of my own. Your papa, rest in peace, left you in my care. Amelia? Nice girl. Not blood.'

'Not blood Zio Vito? True. Not blood. But Ricoldi! Per riguardo a Ricoldi. Out of respect. As friends rispetto is given.'

'Ahhh, we are more than friends.'

'Then why do you treat me and my family, with such disrespect? Have I offended you in some way? Mistreated you? No. None of that. Yet you steel from me.' Yes you bastard, I know. 'Mistreat Amelia.' I know that too. 'Take matters into your own hands. This is not rispetto.' I will teach you respect. Soon.

'Ah.' Think quick. How does he know? 'The young hearts they flutter. The world is there to conquer. I am wiser. I am older. I know better.' I will win this.

'You know better?' We'll see Zio Vito. 'I understand. You steal from the Ricoldi's in the name of friendship. With your mouth you slander. With your pen you destroy. **No more!'**

Vito commenced to explain himself but was halted by a raised palm.

'Do you think I am blind, Vito? Do you think I am deaf? I can see clearly. I can hear clearly. I too can destroy.'

The voice had lost its edge and dropped to a dull whisper.

For such a tender body, it was making its presence felt, even seated. Perspiration dripping down Vito's forehead. Drawing a silk handkerchief from his jacket pocket, he commenced to dab his face. Pulling at his collar, kick-starting his breathing, he searched the room for a sign of imminent danger.

Slowly the body rose from the chair, his skin tarnished, eyes, oceans of deep blue. Bottomless pits revealing nothing but endless colour. As frail looking as he was, compared to the others, he managed to pick Vito up by the scruff of the neck and drag him to his chest. Embracing his larger counterpart, kissing Vito on both cheeks.

'Andare! Go now. Never utter the Ricoldi name again!'

Turning to end conversation, Vito attempted one last plea.

'But Nicco, we are blood! You can't do this.'

Can't I? Just watch old man. 'You were a blood brother with my papa, not me. Andare! Go now!'

No need to be told again, Vito disappeared at a slow jog down the darkened hallway. Turning occasionally to see if he was being perused. They had not followed. Not for now. They awaited instructions. Nicco satisfied their need.

'Non darla vinta a Vito prima del tempo. Give Vito a run for his money. Go. Go teach him respect. Per rispetto a Ricoldi. In the true name of Nicosia Ricoldi.'

****

Heart beating wildly against his ribs, Vito stopped, frozen to the spot. His mind preoccupied with his pursuers and now muddled with this new situation. Squinting in the darkness, he could barely make out the figures. Going by voice recognition alone, he finally summoned the words to speak.

'Amelia?'

'Yes Vito.'

Her voice steady, as if they were still at the party.

'You must help me.'

Licking his lips in thought.

'There are two crazed hooligans chasing me. They tried to kidnap me for a ransom. Please help.'

'Is that the best you could come up with Vito? A man of your character. No. We both know who sent them. But unfortunately, for them, it is a job I alone must settle.'

Metal coldness rested on Vito's profusely sweating forehead. Darkness covered the face, paling due to a loss of blood. Inhaling in short sporadic breaths, Vito's mouth opened and closed like that of a goldfish.

'No Vito. I must speak now. First I will show you this fine specimen of a Beretta handgun.'

Twisting the gun in the available moonlight, Vito glimpsed the fine craftsmanship in the Italian made gun. Twitching with each slight movement made by Amelia, Vito dared not move. Her eyes were invisible to him, but he could imagine the wildfire that blazed in them.

'It is a one of a kind. Each part lovingly made by a true craftsman, Giovanni Beretta, himself. The gold sets it off well don't you think?'

A question not requiring an answer. Amelia was in conversation with herself.

'It was a parting gift for me when I finally left Italy. A very generous gift, don't you think?'

Not waiting for a response, Amelia glimpsed Vito's left eye twitch. A nervous tick, which only appeared when the robust man was highly stressed or highly excited, or so she had heard. Pressing onwards to increase his agony, Amelia continued to speak light heartedly of the gun.

'The bullet too. A gold tipped wonder. Only one in the gun I'm afraid, so I better shoot straight.'

Physically shaking now, Vito glimpsed once more at the gun, then Amelia, before his anger exploded.

'Why are you doing this to me? I have done nothing to you. You and your foolish son. I spit on you both.'

Wiping her face, Amelia's neck tensed, her veins bulging with fury.

'As I said, this is a special gun. It was given to me in the hope that I would find and destroy the person who killed Nicosia.'

Vito's eyes enlarged, contrasting with the darkness, revealing the shock of discovery. A secret he alone harboured for many years, not revealing it to a soul. His downfall was a job he should have taken care of himself. *Fuck. Sal should have taken them all down.* Vito knew the man's fear had made him run the moment he hit the wrong target, but a professional, as Sal claimed to be, should have finished the job.

'Me? It was not me.'

Two panting figures loomed around the corner. Rosario stepped forward with a slight chuckle. Amelia's gaze not wavering from Vito, her hand steadier than the trembling mess she felt inside.

'Took you long enough.'

Turning he spoke the obvious to Amelia.

'It's okay it's Roberto.'

Signalled to stand back, the two young men waited to one side, unsure of what to do next. In the gloomy darkness they could see the outline of Vito and the outstretched arm holding a gun to his head.

'Just in time for the show, boys.'

Stepping back, Vito looked for assistance that he knew would not come. The two young faces smiled at him with indifference, their bodies relaxed. A metallic click brought his face back to Amelia just in time to see the flash of light, from the barrel, which lit the night for a mere second. The blast echoed in his ears.

Falling to his knees, grasping his bleeding crotch, Vito

raised his agony filled face to Amelia, she viewed him with distaste. A noiseless scream escaped his mouth.

'Oops, sorry. Always knew I was a bad shot. Lucky, I lied before. There are two bullets. See. Wait. Roberto, come here please.'

Handing the warmed weapon to Roberto, Amelia clutched his gun hand in hers. Scaring him, her eyes piercing his.

'Sparrow. Avenge your father and prove your worth as a man.'

A light-headed wave of dizziness washed over Roberto. Looking towards Rosario, his mouth ajar, words froze in his throat.

'Go on son, it is your final task on the voyage to becoming a man of honour.'

Roberto knew that Rosario's distance was too far for him to hear Amelia's spoken words.

Another blast echoed amongst the abandoned warehouses, Vito's head exploded backwards, scattering a mixture of blood and brain matter on to the wall behind. Crouching, Amelia lay the spent Beretta on Vito's still expanded mass.

'Let them trace that gun, and with it declare to all, that Nicosia Ricoldi's death is avenged.'

Using a rag, Amelia wiped splattered blood from her face, acknowledging Roberto as she did so.

'We will speak later, but for now, return to Nicco, and tell him you have completed the task. As a man of honour, it is best not to speak of what transpired here tonight. Just the basic facts.'

'Yes.' His questioning look going unanswered.

'Oh Roberto. Tell your friend Christopher, that if he doesn't remove that look of disgust from his face, it will be the last expression he ever wears.'

Passing a cold unsettling stare to Christopher, the youth bowed his head in humility: or revulsion. Amelia and Rosario vanish into the darkness leaving the young men alone.

'Holy shit man. Are you trying to get us killed?'

'But Robbie, how could a woman do that, to a man. Down there.'

Face showing exaggerated agony, Christopher's hand signalled his crotch.

'Shit she must have hated him bad.'

'Chris, the fucker killed her husband in front of her.'

And my father, he contemplated.

Standing for a moment to absorb the impact of what they saw, Chris looked to his best friend Roberto. They had been buddies for a long time, Chris had an extraordinary amount of respect for his friend, he wanted Roberto to be proud of him too: so far, he had failed. Roberto was more a natural at this, but he would learn, he desired nothing more than to be a man of honour.

'What'll we tell Nicco?'

'We alone completed the task.'

A look of incredibility crossed Chris's youthful features.

'That's right Chris.'

'What did she say to you when she handed you the gun? Didn't she have the stomach for it?'

'Hell yeah. She just wanted me to fulfil my role as a made man, on a name.'

'Cool.'

'You heard Mrs Ricoldi. They weren't here. We completed the task.'

A cheeky grin filled Roberto's face as he tackled his buddy, tousling his hair.

'If you won't tell, I won't.'

'Woohoo! Let's celebrate.'

Excitedly shoving and pushing each other down the alley, the two boys returned to Nicco to tell him the good news. They jostled like two jubilant jocks after winning the Super Bowl. Their detailed blow-by-blow description of their heroics satisfied Nicco.

'You shot the bastard in the balls? Beautiful. I would have loved to see his face.'

As long as Vito was dead, Nicco's plans could come to fruition.

While heading to their local hang out for a few celebrationary drinks, Amelia's car returned her and Rosario to the party where they had not yet been missed.

'Rosario, ring our newspaper friend. I want that gun to make the front page of every newspaper in the world. We need to declare the good news to our friends. '

'Definitely, Amelia.'

Entering the party, Amelia caught Brooke's eye, signalling with a cheery smile that it was time to dance again. Gracefully manoeuvring himself through the crowd, he took her by the hand, pulling her close, and danced through the night. Vito was not noticed gone until a few hours later and it was assumed, by most, that he was playing up with a young filly. The news would not reach Sicily till morning.

~ 21 ~

FAMILY

Repetitious tapping interrupted Amelia's line of thought. Grumpily she looked up, ready to dismiss the intruder until she realised it was Roberto. Hurriedly Amelia rose, and quietly moved across the room towards the young man. Both hands clasping his, Amelia sat them both in the sunlit bay window. She perched herself close to him.

'Aunty Em?' His young face grey with lack of sleep.

'Ssshh. Sparrow. We'll wait for your father.'

Since the night before last, Roberto had been lost. Sure, he celebrated with Chris but his mood had been aloof. For the rest of the time, he had remained alone. Minutes felt like hours, and hours felt like eternity. Now that he was here, he wanted the truth. And quickly.

'I need to know now.'

'You will, my son.'

Rosario stood at a distance, the sun's rays barely touching his polished leather shoes. Roberto remembers being a small child watching for hours as his father polished his shoes to mirror images. The smell of wax filling his nostrils, warming his heart. Looking at his own shoes, Roberto glimpses his own grave face. Why hadn't he noticed the lack of similarities before?

'Was Nicosia Ricoldi my father? Or are you, Rosario?'

'Nicosia gave you the gift of life, but I raised you as my own. Teaching you to appreciate life and all it holds.'

'You were married to my mother. How could he be my father? Honourable men do not covet another honourable man's wife.'

'No, Sparrow, it was not like that.'

Spoke Amelia.

'Before I came along, Nicco had an affair with an incredibly beautiful woman, his childhood sweetheart. Your mother. They broke up as friends. Nicco wasn't aware that she was pregnant till after we met.'

And fell in love she remembered.

'Her father found out and requested Don Ricoldi to find who had put his daughter in this situation so that they could marry her or pay for it.'

Rosario interrupted in a tone meant to be reassuring.

'Your mother knew how in love Nicosia and Amelia were. She actively encouraged their relationship. She also knew how much I cared for her, so named me as the father. Don Ricoldi called me to his home and in a private meeting handed me a roll of bank notes. In his words it was *'either for my wedding or my funeral.'* It was my choice. Handing him the bank notes, I said it would be a great pleasure to marry Natasha. For I loved her very much. We married before you were born. Our life was full of love and anticipation of your arrival.'

'From giving birth your mother became very sickly. Nicosia and I became your godparents so that we could always watch over you and be a part of your life.'

'The two of you got on?'

'Natasha and I got along incredibly well. We became best friends. On her deathbed, Nicosia and I vowed to look after both you and Rosario. Even though it is Rosario who has always looked after me.'

A warm loving smile passed between the two. Unnoticed by Roberto's downcast gaze. His gaze intently following the line of his shoes.

'It went without saying that we would care for you. Roberto you are a son to me.'

'You are my son. All the family that I have.'

Spoke Rosario through a fear-laden face.

Roberto rose unsteady on his feet, a glimmer of a smile fell on Amelia as he dropped her hand. Turning to the only father he had ever known, he stared. Face void of any emotion.

'Am I?'

Caught in Rosario's throat was a lump, to him it felt the size of a cricket ball. Here was his son. His son! Pivoting on his shoulders his head rocked, yet the word could not be forced out. *Yes!* It screamed in him.

'Papa. I love you.'

Hugging each other heartily, the two men held each other with unabated passion. Voices drifted from a far room causing the two to push each other away.

Straightening they laughed and punched each other playfully. Amelia knew her husband would have been proud of his boy.

'Not a word, Sparrow. Not yet. Please?'

'Certainly, Aunty Em.'

Not a word to Nicco or anyone else he thought. Not until the right moment.

****

'Mr. Bodine? I hope I didn't startle you?'

'No. No, you didn't. I was elsewhere.'

Retracing the steps of the last few weeks.

'I am Anthony Valentine, your attorney. I have been sent. By a friend.'

'Aren't you?'

Mr. Valentine held his finger to his lips. Looking round to see who, if anyone, heard. Fortunately, the area was clear, no one was in earshot.

'Yes Mr. Bodine. You are very observant. I do not wish to discuss that here.' It is risky enough to be here myself. 'Please follow my instructions. Have you been charged yet? No. Good. It is believed.' Falsely, I hope. 'Amelia Ricoldi visited your house the evening before the murder. It has been put forward that she contracted you to do the job. As yet, no charges have been laid against you or Mrs. Ricoldi. Answer the detective's questions wisely and you will be out of here by tonight. Once again, do you understand?' I damn well hope he does.

Understand what? Joseph was still confused. He was to be charged with murder. Amelia contracted him. Did she stay overnight to create an alibi? Maybe she never loved him. It could have been a very elaborate plan and he was the fall guy who... My god! Walked straight into it. Damn. Everything was so surreal, especially being forced to trust this familiar stranger.

Transported to a cheerless room for interrogation, white and trembling, Joseph entered, a forced coldness falling upon him. Here lay a room of off white, plain in format, broken by a mirror on one wall and a door on another. Darkness showed outside the room's only window. Artificial light being the only source of warmth.

Joseph sat on a hard-wooden chair beside a small desk. Sitting on its edge, afraid to make himself comfortable, his hands nervously clasped between his knees. Tiny beads of perspiration stood out on his upper lip. Joseph feeling somehow reluctant to lick them away. The only sound was the monotonous ticking of the clock on the wall, its daggers stabbing the time shortly before seven o'clock in the evening.

Two detectives paced the painted grey floor rattling off questions in rapid succession. Trying to penetrate their victim in the style of a machine gun. Joseph looked at the dark-haired officer circling like a vulture, dislike unconcealed in his expression, and tried to speak calmly. Words often failing his quivering lips. Clearing his throat, Joseph forced words to come. Behind the vacant chair opposite, his lawyer stood quietly by, interposing when needed. All entangled in a battle of wits.

Accompanying his interrogation about whether he did or didn't murder Vito Sarmry, was a partial explanation of what occurred at Kuntana while he was there. During that second week, many powerful businessman and so-called crime bosses, from throughout the country, had visited. What for? Their guess was as good as his. Was he the stooge? His heart felt corrupted. For no matter what, he loved her. Even if the feeling wasn't mutual. Lowering his eyes, Joseph stared at the floor, thoughts cramming his mind. The ticking of the clock seemed unusually loud.

Nor did Joseph implicate Anthony Valentine, for which the young lawyer seemed greatly relieved. And thankful. Maybe the life of this stranger lay in the balance of his testimonial. At this point Joseph was more concerned for himself.

A young witless constable interrupted the proceedings to the detective's dismay. Like a pit bull he thought he was on to something. In the absence of officialdom, Anthony winked at Joseph.

'It appears, that your friends are as unhappy as us with Vito Sarmry's destination. So, they've fixed the problem.'

With that snide remark the detective thrust a late city edition of the Courier Mail newspaper to the bare wooden tabletop. Both Joseph's and Anthony's eyes immediately fixated to the headlines.

International Businesswoman slain like sewer rat in City Street.

Could this be true? Situated in the centre of the page was a picture. Three in fact. A minor one of a the now dead Vito Sarmry, as Joseph remembered him. Flashy suit and gold teeth. Eyes transfixed forever. The other one was of...Amelia. Yes, it was her. Not a flattering picture at all. The main photo was of what looked like a body slumped over a fallen trashcan. Even in black and white, the pool of blood was unmistakable. The body was not of a man, it was too delicate and small, but a woman. Oh my God! Nooo! The subtitles read Joseph's worst fear.

Amelia Ricoldi, killed in broad daylight by an anonymous drive by shooter.

Shot? Dead? No, not Amelia. Where, in God's name, was Rosario? This can't be right. Joseph, despair on his white face, pupils dilated, turned to the detective. Words failed his quivering lips. Surely, this must be the cruellest of jokes. No, it was a nightmare of largest proportion

'You're free to go for now, Mr. Bodine. But be careful, we're not the only ones watching you.'

Staring absently at the floor, his mouth dry, his lips parched, Joseph lacked the strength to leave this god-forsaken room. That murderous ticking drilling its way through his skull. Screw it. Screw it all!

~ 22 ~

LOST ARE THE ANSWERS

'It's okay Rosario. I'll be fine. I just need some time to myself.' Please Rosario. I need the time to clear my head. 'What do you thinks going to happen?' He worries too much. 'I promise to be back by two. I promessa. Okay? See you.'

Neither Amelia nor Rosario realized these were their final words together. Instances like this introduce life's fragility and Rosario realised too late that much had gone unsaid between them. To retrace his steps was impossible. Amelia, as with every other soul, is only given one chance at life.

Amelia was on an errand for an old friend when the drive-by shooting occurred. It took place at an incredible speed, yet in her mind, it was like slow motion. Barely had she stepped from the pharmacy, a small parcel tucked neatly under one arm, when the screeching of tyres drew hers, and other passer-by's attention. Instantly realization sunk in, like a repeated nightmare of so many years before.

Who today would hold Amelia in her last moments as she once did for her husband? Had she worked so hard for her life to amount to this? Dead. In a city gutter. Alone.

Time ceased as Amelia lay slumped over the trashcan. Her body frozen. The aching grew with every painful heartbeat. How could she die in a place she detested so much? The city. No! She would hold on. From under heavy eyelids she could see the gathering crowd. All vying for an ideal vantage point. Vultures! Shot down like a dog, creating perverse entertainment for them. Surely it was obvious that she needed help.

Housewives dressed gaily in their summer frocks pointed and whispered to one another. One or two shot off to be the first to convey the exciting news. A girl of twelve stared engrossed, her mother half-heartedly attempting to shield her devouring eyes. More consumed herself by the grisly scene. Several small toddlers screamed for their mothers, one little boy at the chemist's door had urinated in his overalls, leaving a dark stain down the inner part of one leg. Several men were prominent at the front of the crowd, arguing over what should be done. Disputing the pros and cons of such a situation, each having no real intention of assisting in any way.

You bastards! What are you looking at? Scio! If only I could... Her mouth moved but the words tumbled out together, creating a long sonorous groaning noise.

Life was so vibrant for those who were still youthful. Life had no tragedy or perceived ending. Living for the moment with never ending love. Love of life, love of self and love of all things beautiful. Where had Amelia lost it all? Maybe it was when she lost the love of her life, or when she lost the will of her own. Only one person knew the answer. Amelia. Like most, she chose her own destiny in life. Yet it was so long ago.

****

'Rosario, can I ask you a question? Just between you and me.'

'Si Signorina Amelia.' Not too personal I hope. 'My English not so good yet.'

'You speak it fine, Rosario. Why do the Ricoldi's hate me so much? Have I offended them?' I've tried everything to follow their rules, but nothing works.

'They not hate you, Signorina Amelia.' Just dislike.

'Why don't they want me to marry their son? I love him.' With all my heart. 'Don Ricoldi asked me not to, personally.' And forcefully, I must admit.

'Nicco is their only son.' He carries the family name. 'There are big plans for him.' To settle many a rift. 'His future is here. One day he will be Don.'

'But I don't want to take him away. We can live here in Nicosia or even in Cefalu, if they want.' I don't want to change his future, but become a part of it.

'If Don Ricoldi says no, then that is the way. I cannot question that.' I dare not. But look how sad she looks. She is so sweet. 'It different here, Signorina Amelia. Tradition, family and blood. All very important.' The only thing. 'It may not be safe for you to stay.' It would not be safe for Nicco, you are his greatest weakness. A Don cannot be vulnerable.

'I don't understand, but I will leave today.' As if I had a choice. 'Please give Nicco this note.' It will explain as much as I understand. 'Rosario?'

'Si Signorina Amelia?'

'Tell Nicco I love him.'

****

Morning broke the same way the previous day had settled. Rainy and gloomy. Befitting for a funeral, Amelia's funeral. It was by fate that Joseph discovered the tattered card given to him weeks before. Days of deliberation passed before the tentative call was made. He had to say good-bye, as the last one was not favourable.

For Amelia's departure, the family had selected a quaint chapel set amongst an orchard in Stanthorpe, several hours from Brisbane. Not too far from her favourite vineyard in Ballandean, Golden Grove. Distance could not stop the endless procession of cars, which now surrounded the small chapel gardens. Crowds of people overflowed from the rustic pews. Amelia was going to be missed, not only by Joseph it seemed. Yes, there were a few familiar well-worn faces from Kuntana, and those select few from the races had given up their precious time at the track.

Mafioso stood patiently outside, waiting to escort Amelia to her final resting place. A magnificent white topless carriage intricately decorated with gold leaf imported from Japan, set on luxurious black wheels, awaited its passenger. An array of the most beautiful flowers and buds adorned three sides. A whispering breeze rustled through the colourful presentation, collecting the redolent aroma and dispersing it amongst the guests.

Rosario stood still at his designated position. A shadow with no body. Eyes searching the gold encrusted coffin for some answer. Any answer. His skin was near translucent, paler than was characteristic of his complexion. Pressure and guilt weighing heavily on his now slumped shoulders. A mere glimpse of a smile in acknowledgement of Joseph's presence.

'Did you know her well?'

Joseph turned with surprise. The crackling, tear ridden voice was directed at him. There stood a hunched old lady in a black sixties style funeral gown. Layers of satin brushing the floor. A misty black veil hid her tears. Droplets of water on her chest the only indication. Unsure how to answer he paused.

'Not well enough, I'm afraid.'

'I knew her well. Maybe too well. Amelia had a very troubled soul, you know?'

'Yes. I hate to say it, but I too saw that side of her. If only I was there, maybe...'

Memory flashbacks haunted his mind. Some favourable, some less so.

'She was very strong willed you know. You cannot blame yourself. We pick our own destiny. Good or bad.' Right or wrong.

'Yes. Yes, you are right.'

His voice deceived him.

'I'm a lonely old lady, maybe we could share our happier memories over, say, some supper?'

Trembling with sadness, the old lady grasped Joseph's arm. Steadying herself with a frail almost translucent hand. A hand marked with a lifetime of use and abuse. Yellowing nails, small patches of white and the murky red spots of lifeless blood. She opened her bag searching for a pen. Upon completing her scrawling, she passed the torn slip of yellowing paper to Joseph. It contained an address. Presumably where she lived. Without another word she disappeared to settle herself into a now vacant pew.

Looking up, Joseph saw Rosario approaching. Sensing Rosario's dilemma, Joseph took hold of him, a remnant of a man once known, and cleared a spot for him in the closest pew. To comfort another when his own pain surged unforgivingly, was a struggle.

****

Destiny had taken hold of Amelia's life so many years ago. The clearest moment being her time in Italy.

'Come in Signorina Amelia. Sit down. Sit down my dear. We must talk'.

'Talk about what Don Ricoldi?' I wish Nicco was here.

'It is time you returned home. To Australia. Nicco needs to concentrate on his life and commitments to the family.' Ones my wife and I have painstakingly organized.

'But Nicco has asked me to marry him. I have said yes.' With great delight.

'My dear Signorina Amelia. Please understand, we are a family of tradition. As with all tradition there is a lack of self-need.' Or will. 'This is known from a very young age. Tradition binds the family together.'

'I am not welcome?'

A very hard question to admit.

'Not welcome in your tradition or family?'

No. 'Please understand, it is for the best. Nicco cannot deny his heritage.' And my chance to finally merge both the Ricoldi's and Lombardo's. What a dynasty that will be. 'His marriage has been planned since birth. To someone else.'

'Is money and power the only assets you wish for your son? What about love, happiness and all those other terrible aspects of life?'

'Of youth. Not life. A sacrifice like this could achieve so much more for Nicco than you ever could.'

'But aren't you afraid...'

'Nicco is blood. He will respect my will and so must you. Our countries have differing values, but here my judgments are respected.'

'I do not doubt your respectability. Just the legitimacy of your claim to your son.' And your love for him. 'I know him well, he will not succumb to this.'

'He will and you will. E senza speranza. He is beyond help. You are leaving today and that is final. You will be compensated of course.' You are young it will suffice.

'Money!' You monster. 'I am insulted, that you consider me so cheap. Obviously, you have mistaken my motives.' Why does love have to hurt so much? 'For this I feel sorry for you and your son. But as you request, I will leave Nicosia, but not Italy. This is not to satisfy you, it will allow Nicco to decide for himself, with no influence from me and hopefully not from you. Good-bye Mr. Ricoldi.'

'It will be futile for you to wait, but I thank you just the same.' Her will is stronger than even I expected. My son had picked wisely. 'Please do not think too badly of us Signorina Amelia. Show her out Pauly.'

From the outcome of the meeting, it was obvious that Nicco's business trip was planned to coincide with Amelia's forced departure. She felt no betrayal in leaving Nicosia and Sicily. Without Nicco the town had lost its sparkle. He had once said he would travel to the ends of the earth to be with her. Here was the opportunity.

Rosario was selected to be the bearer of the bad news. Amelia trusted only him. A note, with carefully selected words, was, to some degree assist Rosario in explaining her disappearance into obscurity. The rest of the family wasn't to be trusted.

Leaving her heart in Nicosia, Amelia fled the mountains to a haven by the sea at Palmi on the Gulf of Gioia. It was decided that she would wait three weeks, and three weeks only. Nicco was required to declare his love in that time, otherwise she would return home. Broken. An easy option this was not. Weeks passed and Amelia's despair found new depths. Maybe family and tradition always won. The weight of sadness was too much. She was in desperation to leave this horrid country.

Against the wave of people at the station, she ran, tears streaming down her hallowed face. Just a short trip by train, and then she'd be gone. Flying home. No fight was left. Her cycling days were snatched away and her heart was broken, all by one man. Don Ricoldi.

But wait! Reminiscent voices lapped at her ears. Could

it be? No, it was just her mind's feeble attempt to salvage the heart. Was that it again? She turned, eyes firmly sealed in prayer. Not wanting to face any more disappointment, her mind held them occluded. Bumped by the rushing crowd, Amelia swayed. Hands reached her shoulders and panting warmth caressed her face.

'Amelia, don't go. I love you.'

****

A cold sweat awoke Joseph. There was a sense of urgency as he arose and dressed. The funeral, fresh in his mind as he strode into the darkness. Some unknown force drew him to the old lady's house. Was it too late in the night? The cottage was inviting. White clouds of smoke puffed from the chimney. Holding their random shapes as they rose in the cool night air. Flowerbeds lay dormant, waiting for spring's early warmth. A traditional white picket fence held the image as a frame does a painting.

Unlatching the gate, Joseph treads carefully on the cobblestone path. Pausing for a second, he ponders why he is here. How could he deny it? He was looking for answers. The answers. Creaking open slowly, light burst from the house saturating the path in front of him. The shadow of a plump Negro woman stood in the doorway. As she raised a lantern from a side table, he could see her inviting smile accentuated by her salt and peppery hair. She wore a plain loose-fitting dress, complemented by a crisp white cooking apron, quoting a verse from the New Testament.

'Mr Bodine, is d'at you?'

'Yes, it is. How did you know my name?'

'Miss Hearton, sir. She said you'd be a visiting tonight. She always right, Miss Hearton. She's waiting for ya in the lounge.'

'Thank-you?'

'Betsy, sir. They call me Betsy, like me great grand-mamma.'

'Thank-you Betsy.'

Betsy led Joseph to a door and pointed. For her courtesy, Joseph was thankful, for as far as he could see her heart radiated such warmth, more noticeable than any sun. The room was more of a library than a lounge. At least three of the walls were shelved, each shelf holding books to its fullest capacity. Large French doors filled the fourth wall, probably opening to a back garden designed with spring in mind.

Amongst one group of shelves lay an open log fire. Screened to prevent sparks bounding in all directions. Logs crackled as Joseph surveyed the room. His eyes finally settling on a wheelchair tucked snugly near the fire. Its occupant lay still, only her hands showing beyond the tartan rug on her lap. Entering the room further, her face came into view. Her cheeks had become rosy from sitting too near the fire's warmth. More warming still was her smile.

'Amelia!'

'So glad you could make it Mr. Bodine. I've been cooped up in here for too long. Thank goodness for Betsy. My only ray of sunshine.'

'Here is da tea. If you be needing me ma'am, just a holler.'

'Thank-you Betsy. You've wasted enough time already. Go home to your family. Have a lovely night.'

'You too, Miss Hearton and Mr Bodine.'

'Thank-you Betsy I will.'

Turning to the occupant of the chair.

'Miss Hearton?'

'Yes, Joseph. The nun who raised me in the orphanage, you met her today, it was her maiden name. Mrs. Ricoldi no longer exists, as you are aware.' A mixed blessing I'm sure.

'Should I be sad or happy?'

'Happy, I hope.' I dearly pray you are. 'I had to ask you here. So that you know the shooting was not a set up. Trust me, I'm still wearing the scars!'

And they weren't the only ones. Joseph could feel the pain in her eyes. Iced over no longer, he could see the torment of the bullets followed by their consequence. Dare he ask?

'And Rosario?' No don't cry, I just needed to know.

'It saddens me to think of wonderful Rosario. My saviour over the years. I feel I have betrayed him, and at the same time, set him free. When I knew I could survive, I thought it best if I didn't. The greatest proof of my true death was Rosario's sorrow. He was my shadow that I adored.'

Raking through the mound of wood on the floor, Joseph thrust another log into the fire. Turning to her now, he saw the pain and misery her life had caused. Oh, how the flickering fire relieved her of years of loneliness. No one else understands him so well or makes his body tingle in such a way. Could they make a life of this? Why not. He had nothing to lose, she now had nothing to lose. Could the past remain where it was? He was just thankful she was alive. Opening his lips to speak, he thought better of the situation.

Sensing his pause, she spoke softly. No longer able to project her voice. With a long blink she focused on the fire, not him.

'There is so much I would like to tell you. Much of it, I can't.'

Sensing he was about to contribute: she raised her eyes to his. She had so much to tell but she couldn't. It burst inside her, forcing, tugging, dying to be released from its cell. She couldn't. Deep down she was still a Ricoldi. Maybe in time this wonderful man before her would understand. Maybe not. If she told, how would she face that look of disgust, which would cloud his eyes? It's bound to. No, she couldn't. This had been her destiny not his. Never again would she burden that responsibility on anyone. That life was sealed when the coffin was.

Without warning the French doors opened intrusively. Momentarily the icy breeze of darkness froze the pair. Upon the entrance stood a man. A man of slim athletic build and the familiar olive features. His eyes flashed round the room as his lips broke into a smile.

Joseph knew instantly who he was, Amelia's eyes could barely hold back the love.

'Joseph, this is Nicosia Michael Ricoldi. My son.'

PART FOUR

Streets of Shame

~ 23 ~

RETURN TO SENDER

Stanthorpe, Queensland, Australia.

Life's journey is long and arduous. But I contemplate. I contemplate whether we are the cause of our own misery. Is it not in our own actions, or lack of thought, that these miseries come about? Yes, mistakes are part of life, for from where else would we learn, but shouldn't we have sense enough not to anger the gods, the God? My life is a journey for here I am in Oz. Australia that is. Chasing a dream.

When I was a small child Jesse and I would chase the butterflies around Ma's garden. Round and round we'd go until we were so dizzy, we'd fall over in a bundle of laughter. Ethereally hovering on the wind, the butterflies, rainbows of nature, would flutter here and there oblivious to our endeavours. If Jesse and I ever got our act together, we'd find a net and bound round the garden till we caught one of god's greatest creations. Quickly we'd pop it in a jar and stare in awe. Awe of the magnificence.

To our disappointment the butterfly would be dead the next morning. Should we not have had the sense to provide food or oxygen for the small creature? Or would it have died anyway? Trapped and alone. I sit here now and wonder. Wonder if Mike is that butterfly. In my bones I feel this trip may become a nightmare, but I may regret never trying.

Having patronised my family for a short period before my adventure. Done all the hoo-ha, visited relatives, and everything else expected of me, I have now made my way to Ballandean. For it is here, that the first bottle of wine Mike and I enjoyed came from. It is also a place he recalled visiting a lot. Ballandean is a wide-open area inhabited by a scattered population. A patchwork of small ranches and homesteads. Each encompassed by brilliantly coloured orchards and vineyards. Even the smallest property, grows plentiful crops of grapes, olives, stone fruits and apples.

Thankfully, the people are friendly, making my improbable journey easier. With so many Italian descendants here, I feel that I may be in Europe. So far, my aim is to gain employment on the outskirts of the local town, Stanthorpe. An ordinary Australian country town, which is made up of one main street. A street designed, quite simply, as a thoroughfare for tourists, catered for by a small line of shops, restaurants and motels. I am happy to cook, clean or labour away in the fields as a fruit picker. Whatever the Gods may offer. I have been fortunate enough, probably due to my colouring, to have been sent in the direction of Mrs Newton who has kindly put me up in her house for nothing until I can find a paying job.

Mrs Betsy Newton, a widower, has the soul of a saint. Her vast girth jiggles as a continuous stream of laughter pours from her mouth. Above her curled lips sits a crinkled nose made worse by her merriment. Sparkling brown eyes, a blessing to her African heritage, touch warmth to everything they settle upon. Immediately I am taken by her, and she, with me. Reminding her of the children never to be had, she adopts every stray. Cats, dogs, wallabies and lost travellers alike.

Her small cottage is a monument to anything that was ever lost. On the mantle sits ill matched figurines, while the sideboards are crammed with china of which no set is complete. Each setting at the dining table differs from its neighbour, yet the house exhibits a homeliness, as if everything there belonged. Everything was needed, used and loved for what it was. Together they formed a whole, but each singular piece was appreciated for what it alone represented. As eccentric as she may be, Betsy was what I needed. Someone who accepted me for who I was, no more, no less. As a thank-you, and under her constant goading, I called her Aunty.

Here I sit now waiting for my new aunt. The kitchen of her employer is cosy, warm and country like. A beautiful iridescent blue sets off the walls against the whitewashed wood grain furniture and door panels. Running my hands along the granite benches, I can feel the coolness. My pores hunger for its freshness, its purity. Do I belong here? Who knows? I'm here now so I might as well take advantage of it. My original plan was to have a break from everything: training, men and other people's expectations.

In the last few years, I haven't gone anywhere without my bike, the weight of my parent's disappointments and expectations, and the sorrow of losing my best friend. Having no one to confide in has had the effect of making my problems tenfold. Each festering within me, growing and compounding till I am ready to burst. I'm starting to feel this break is for me. For me *to find my soul, wants and needs. Till now they had all been planned out, or had they? When Jesse left, oh Jesse. My life fell to pieces. I realize now that I'm stumbling on the path of least resistance. Australia is where I thought I'd find myself, but the truth is, you never lose yourself. No matter how far I run.*

'Ready for da tea now, Izzy?'

Betsy's rotund figure cascades into the small kitchen, filling all available space with the love that radiates from her. Retying her apron, she sets the kettle on the gas stove. The flame pops into life, hissing its heat forth.

'That'd be lovely Aunty.'

'So, where was we before d'at fellow came to da door.'

'My riding, I think.'

'Yous' do well to train up near Girrawccn National Park. Just up the road tis.'

Sounds echoed in through the open kitchen door. Crickets chanted their mantra while frogs croaked towards the sky, singing for rain. Sitting with her back to the door, Izzy could hear and smell the cottage garden. During the day it was a delight to behold, but at night it transformed into something special. Just as Izzy was about to respond she heard faint footsteps crunching on the granite stone path. Looking up she saw her Aunt's face brighten. Rushing as fast as she could in the small kitchen Betsy moved to the door.

'Here comes one o' my chilen now. Nicky!'

Betsy's arms rose with the word 'chilen'. Izzy had little interest in the person entering the door and who was now locked in Betsy's embrace. In fact, she failed to see the young man who strode to the door, his face full of concentration. Head bent, he in turn failed to see Izzy and only raised his head as Betsy's figure loomed before him. His lips rose in a half smile.

'Betsy. You know I'm too big for that now.'

'Never!'

'I've come to see how she's going.'

But before he could go anywhere, Betsy had his face cupped in her hands as Uncle Timba did with toast. A motherly look passed over Betsy's face as she looked down the boy in front of her.

'You's needs some fattening up by the looks. Sit by my new niece and I'll git you something.'

Smiling, knowingly.

'I'm fine.'

'No no.'

The man turned to the table, ready to draw a chair out for himself. Looking up, Izzy's eyes sunk into a familiar blueness. Liquid at first, the eyes that stared back went hard, brittle even. The pupils withdrew in hate, a hate that penetrated deep within her.

'Izzy. D'is is Nicky. D'at scallywag I did sit for when he was d'is high.'

Her hand fell way below her waist, stating the time she first started looking after the boy.

'Nicky, d'is Izzy, from America. Isabelle Lancove. She was straying around the countryside. Fortunately, some good soul sent her my way. She such a good girl.'

'Nice to meet you, Miss Lancove.'

'You too, Nicky?'

A self-satisfied grin befell Mike's face. This game was going to be played to the full.

'I'd shake your hand, but I had an unfortunate accident.'

He stated patting his plastered right hand that lay limp in a starched white sling.

After taking the full brunt of the landlady's dismay about her young companion terrorising the apartment building, Izzy's eyes fell in guilt. She felt as if she had broken his hand.

'How long you in Australia for Miss Lancove?'

His voice pleasant but informal. *The bastard!* He'd caught her by surprise and now what was she going to do.

'For a short while. The American winter is too harsh for me to train successfully so I have come to Australia to train.' *Not completely true but two can play at this game.*

'Train? Train for what?'

You smug bastard. You know for what. 'I'm a cyclist.'

'Any good?'

Damn good until you arrived on the scene. 'Yes. Unfortunately, this season I had some distractions, but luckily, they have all gone now, so I can get back to what I love most in the world.' *Oh, sorry, did that take the smugness out of your smile. I do apologise. Like hell Mike.*

So, as you can see my dream, or nightmare, didn't follow the path I expected but nothing ever does. One must work with what they have. After declaring my intention that I was here to train, and with a strong desire not to be left in 'Nicky's' company, due to Aunt Betsy's persistent matchmaking, I commenced cycling daily, in between assisting Betsy with the chores about Miss

Hearton's house. Miss Hearton appeared to enjoy my company immensely. Frequently becoming nostalgic whenever we spoke about cycling, which was often. I enjoyed her company, for even though she was caught in a wheelchair and had a sickly pallor, a vibrant life jumped from her. To look at her was to know she had once been exquisitely beautiful, but what remained of that beauty was an interesting ruin. Over her slenderous bones, the pale skin was so tightly drawn, one felt they could tear it with the slightest touch. Beneath her eyes were deep purplish hollows, a sign of hard living, late nights, illness, suffering, or some combination of all these. Still, an aura surrounded her of hope and life, I found this energising whenever we spoke.

My impression of her was a prisoner trapped in this small cottage and its garden. Her outlook was cheery enough, but her words lacked certain spontaneity. It was as if she was forbidden to leave: yet she came across as a once strong personality. This strength peeked through at infrequent intervals. Whenever Mike visited, she would just purse her lips tightly and nod. This action was accompanied by a slight tapping of her fingers that would eventually lead to their embedment in the chair's wood.

Just yesterday, laughter emitted from Miss Hearton's garden. I had just completed 200 kilometres on the bike and was coming down the side path when I heard it. It was light and contagious with happiness. Miss Hearton's voice carried on the subtle breeze, whirling about my ears, enticing me to laugh along. A man's deep rumble erupted as I entered the garden.

'Oh Isabelle, meet Joseph Bodine.'

'Mr Bodine. Miss Hearton.'

'Joseph please Isabelle.'

His smile was warm and inviting and the affect he had on Amelia was shattering.

'Yes, use our first names Isabelle. We are all friends.'

Amelia's face contained a lively pink hue, her lips bold and red, and arms animated in a way Izzy had never seen. A switch had been turned on and Amelia had come to life. Pinocchio, a puppet, come to the land of the living. Words and laughter intermingled in the air's coolness. As the afternoon dragged, the conversation mellowed and I could see the pair needed some peace, so I rose to excuse myself.

'Isabelle. Bring your track bike tomorrow, Joseph is returning to Brisbane for the day, so I thought we could go out to the velodrome at Chandler. You don't mind us tagging along, do you Joseph?'

For the first time that afternoon, Joseph's face darkened into a frown. It darkened not with anger but an obvious concern.

'Are you sure that is wise.'

A sideways glance to Isabelle.

'Your health and everything.'

He hastily added, for which Isabelle knew was for her benefit. For why, she did not know.

'Yes of course. You up for it, Isabelle?'

Izzy could not bear to disappoint the excitement held on Amelia's face. A trip would do them both good. Prisoners united in freedom.

'Why not!'

Accepting the invitation while avoiding Joseph's concerned glare, Izzy hurriedly disappeared up the garden path in the search of food.

'A lovely girl isn't she Joseph.'

'Yes, but don't change the subject. Mike dislikes you returning to Brisbane in case you are seen.'

'He dislikes me being alive.'

It was hard to believe but her eyes still had the ability to quieten him with one look. He smiled as he realised the harshness they had once contained was gone, yet a certain reserve of strength lay hidden beneath the eye's blueness.

****

The velodrome was an old cement type, but it was more than suitable for my training. Nigel Williamson, a slim athletic looking man in his late thirties, from the Queensland Cycling Association, unlocked the gates for us and stayed to chat with Amelia or Emma as he called her. Commiserating with her about being waylaid in a wheelchair. From their conversation and the facts I had gathered in the back garden, Amelia was quite a cyclist when she was younger. The pair traded stories while I warmed up. My first lap brought to my ears Amelia's joke about entering the Paralympics if she could not walk properly again. In a more serious tone, Nigel agreed whole-heartedly, stating this would be a very sensible idea and well worth pursuing.

'Maybe if everything goes to plan, you could ride in the Masters Games.'

'Now Nigel, how many years has it been since I last rode. Twenty?'

'But you were so good. You used to beat the pants off me and I'm sure you still could.'

'That says something about you, not me.'

Amelia smirked in a friendly way.

Their voices raised and lowered, echoing throughout the velodrome. The whirring of Izzy's wheels broke through the conversation as she passed frequently.

'Why don't you give the poor girl some competition?'

'I'm getting too old for that.'

'No older than me Nigel. Younger in fact.'

Voice low, Amelia's gentle persuasion won out. Leaving for his office at the rear of the track, Nigel returned with a custom, locally made, Frezoni track bike. After warming up for a few laps, and hoping that Izzy had tired a little, the pair lined up for a sprint race. The idea for a sprint race is for two riders to jostle and psyche out the opposition over two laps and sprint for the line on the third and final lap. A winner was decided over three races. Starting with a track stand, each cyclist rolled out slowly, alternating who would lead out each race.

Izzy had age and speed on her side, yet Nigel had experience and foresight. Cycling was a great equalising sport as the fittest was not always the winner. From the lead out, Izzy easily won the first sprint. She had dominated the whole race and her confidence showed. During the second race her confidence diminished as Nigel used his head and counteracted any move she took, by the final lap he was in the lead and won easily. Amelia signalled her to the fence during the cool down laps.

'Izzy, use your head. At the moment it is working against you. You don't believe you can win from behind even though you are the stronger rider. By far too.'

She stressed as Nigel's red panting face passed them. Izzy's body had only raised a slight sweat and in under three minutes her breathing had settled back to normal. Izzy's short recovery time was one of her greatest assets.

'It is better to be behind the enemy. If you are in front, you cannot see them coming or who they are until it's too late. Then you are gone. To come from behind, you hold the upper hand. You can surprise them, take them off guard. You are the power. This is very important Izzy.'

Amelia's hands went forward, grabbing Izzy in a frantic manner.

'You do understand, don't you? You must control every situation. Strength will only get you so far: out thinking their every move will mean victory. You are not safe otherwise.'

Panic rose in Izzy's throat, Amelia spoke as if this race was life or death itself. Not fully understanding, Izzy nodded in agreeance.

~ 24 ~

TO CARRY OUT A MASSACRE

Doomben Racecourse, Brisbane.

Near the member's entrance, a smartly dressed busi-nesswoman, in an immaculate white and gold pants suit, sat with a cocktail. Her heavily ringed fingers casually turned the pages of the form guide. Yet her eyes deceive her, as they glance for any potential prey, maybe husband number four.

Standing on the threshold of the member's private room, Mike glanced further as the woman tried to capture his attention. Nearby, an elderly man on a bench sat with an abandoned Australian Financial Review spread over his ample paunch. Rimless glasses balanced precariously on his forehead while his sleeping head hungs over the chair back. Mouth suspended open, revealing yellowing dentures and producing a slight snoring sound. Similar to the droning of an angry wasp.

A rippling laugh draws Mike's attention. A pretty blond, her bright print dress doing nothing to conceal her ample charms. Charms, which have captured the enthusiastic attention of two visiting U.S. sailors. The darker, leaning on raised knee, eyes eagerly exploring the cleavage revealed by height. The fairer sailor, hand resting on the young girl's shoulder, whispering sweet nothings in her ear, was receiving little of the girl's attention. Straightening his tie, Mike strode past the expectant businesswoman to the pretty blond. Her eyes gleamed as he approached. Brushing off the excess baggage of her two companions, the blond rose to meet Mike.

'Michael Ricoldi.' With an easy fluid movement, he bowed taking her slender hand into his, kissing it as he rose. Eyes locking solely on hers.

'Elizabeth Smeraldi.'

'Well Miss Smeraldi, would you care to join me for lunch in the member's lounge, say, about eleven thirty.'

Her peachy lips opened in a seductive manner, tongue tracing its circumference. Long lashes fluttered, as if in answer to his thoughts. Disgusted at losing their potential entertainment, the sailors rose, using their mass to block Ms Smeraldi. Jabbing Mike with a pointer finger, the darker sailor sneered.

'She's with us buddy.'

'Until lunch then.' Ignoring the sailor, Mike kissed the blonde's hand in a slow manner, his tongue lingering long enough to entice her rippling laugh. Purposely, his shoulder nudged the sailor as he commenced to leave.

Resenting the blatant snub, the sailor broadened his chest, rose to full height, glimpsing forlornly at the blond as he grabbed the offending shoulder.

'Did you not hear me?'

'If you do not remove that now, my associates will do it for you.'

Speaking without facing the sailor, Mike's voice was firm, in a low forceful tone. Unshaken the sailor momentarily gripped the shoulder even tighter until a stockily built man grabbed him from behind. Twisting his arm in a painful manner.

'Having trouble Mr. Ricoldi?'

A deep husky Russian murmur enquired.

'No trouble Kristov. Is there?'

Glaring at the sailor mockingly. His head shaking, Miss Smeraldi's nervous giggle completing the American's embarrassment.

Through the air drifts the theme to the Godfather. Mike retrieves his cell phone as he heads toward the member's stand.

'What do you mean you've lost her? How could you lose a woman in a friggin' wheelchair?'

'She was not here when we arrived, sir. Here comes Betsy. Yacob's questioning her now. One moment please.'

Muffled voices could be heard, rising with each word. After clearing his throat, the caller returned to Mike.

'Apparently she left with Miss Lancove and Mr Bodine. Um. They left for Brisbane at first light.'

Wincing in anticipation of an explosion.

'For where? Brisbane! God dammit man, go and retrieve them from wherever they may be. Bring Bodine to me and take care of any witnesses who may have seen them. Do you understand?'

'Yes, Mr Ricoldi. Straightaway.'

Turning to Yacob, Klaus looked stern. His face seemed designed to inspire terror. It was square, jowly, and the colour and texture of unfinished concrete. The cheeks were slashed with knife scars. Yet they were random in shape, as if caused by broken bottles.

'Send for the helicopter. We must go now.'

'Ya Klaus, but where?'

'To the gardens where this man Bodine works.'

Placed with full urgency the call was sent and as requested the helicopter arrived pronto. On board were three other solidly built Russians. All having the build and consternation of an army's elite force. Quietly they awaited orders from Klaus. Each man hiding the bulge of a reserve handgun under his trouser cuff. Similar bulges would exist in the small of their lower back, cleverly hidden by their loose-fitting jackets. Nearly all carried a concealed knife, either a sharpened flick knife or a curved karambit. Trained to kill a man, in as few as ten different ways with their bare hands, these machinations were mere accessories.

With military precision they landed at the heli-wharf and proceeded to wrestle the information they needed from Joseph, loaded him into an awaiting car and departed on the second errand. The most important.

Amelia was not pleased to see them arrive however it was half expected. Izzy and Nigel were heading into the final lap when the four men surrounded Amelia.

'It's time to leave Mrs Hearton.'

One man had already commenced to wheel her towards

the gate. Grabbing the wheels to slow his process Amelia struggled against the inevitable.

'At least wait till the race is over!'

'It's over!'

Yelled Klaus as he stepped on to the track.

'Yacob escort Miss Lancove to the cars.'

Grabbing Nigel's handlebars as well as Izzy's, Klaus stood firm, his strength supporting both riders.

'What the...'

Bellowed Nigel as he nearly lost his crown jewels on the top tube of the bike.

On command Izzy was escorted to the awaiting car alongside Amelia. Klaus approached flanked only by one other man. Not Nigel. Izzy could see the distress on Amelia's face as the two men joked and laughed while lighting a cigarette.

'Where's the fourth man?'

'He will follow us shortly in the other car. Yacob, you will assist.'

'Lei non puo fare questo a me.' You cannot do this to me. 'Lei puo't.' You can't. Amelia spoke in hurried Italian tones, trying not to upset Izzy. 'E un vecchio amico.' He is an old friend.

Panic and fear filled her eyes.

'Non facciamo niente a lei signora.' We are doing nothing to you. 'Eccetto l'escorting lei la casa.' Except escorting you home.

He looked matter-of-factly at his watch, a thin disc of gold, secured by a band of tiny overlapping gold scales, like those of a snake.

'We should be home in time for a late lunch.'

'Il bastardo! Lei puo't fa questo.' You can't do this. 'Disdire i suoi cani adesso!' Call off your dogs now. 'Farlo non chi sa sono?' Do you not know who I am?

'Si.'

His smug smile mocked her.

'Sono uno delle sue prime storie di successo da Russia.' I am one of your first success stories from Russia. 'Signora Ricoldi. Ma gli ordini sono degli ordini.' But the orders are orders. 'There is **nothing** you can do.'

'There isn't?'

Mustering what strength she had, Amelia steadied her weight on her arms. Rising out of the chair she took one tentative step after the other.

'Lei il forfeited la suo control.' You forfeited your control.

Her eyes bit into him with a sharpness that chilled. The twinkle that shone in Amelia's eyes was a mere glimpse of her past strength. Staring at her now, Klaus could feel the hairs prickle on his neck. She was taunting him, her will forceful. Klaus had only seen such unemotional, and impenetrable, eyes once before, on a cold-blooded murderer. At the time he was unable to read those eyes, like now. A near fatal mistake, he thought, as his hand absently fondled the scar on his left cheek. One he would not wish to repeat. Never had he experienced Amelia's strength firsthand. Beyond that, it was just terrifying stories.

Izzy rushed to Amelia's side as her left leg gave out. Her body folded like a concertina. No one else came to her. The young girl was flustered and Amelia could see her confusion. She also saw the man approach with the syringe.

'Is that necessary?'

Questioned Izzy.

'No. Everything is fine.'

Amelia held up her hand to ward off the needle. The man looked toward Klaus.

Glaring at Amelia.

'Nessuno piu guasto?' No more trouble?

His voice was strong, like before, but it cupped a little self-doubt.

'No.'

A soft whisper responded. A voice not her own.

'Help Mrs Hearton and Miss Lancove into the car.'

~ 25 ~

TO FILL THE SHOES

Months had passed, the world had turned on its axis and like always the bright morning sun still beamed in on the large oak desk. Roberto swung in the high back chair imagining his Godmother sitting here, in this exact spot. Conforming to his shape, the seat held no memory of her. Its inhabitant did. Gazing wistfully at the line of photographs, one sepia picture took his eye. An extremely young Amelia, accompanied by her husband, his father, were holding a screaming baby. Trembling, Roberto's hand rested on the frame's edge. Lovingly he let it fall along the man's face, coming to rest on the baby.

Scraping the tears away with his cuff, Roberto straightened as the footsteps in the hall approached. Today represented his first major meeting and it was to be with Sam 'The Monk' Mandell. Sam had many favourable traits such as his genteel nature and jovial manner in all situations. He was almost a caricature of an old-line hoodlum, with his cap and baggy trousers, teeth invariably clenching the stub of a cigar and an undershirt peeking above his unbuttoned collar. Plus, he was the best hardball player Roberto ever had the honour to meet. Take his last assignment for instance. His mission was to gain sensitive information from a supposed federal informant, Phillip Tocco. By snatching Tocco on a Friday, Sam had the whole weekend to play his games. It only took a matter of hours though.

Patiently, Sam had waited at the airport for Tocco, who was heading out to Melbourne for a sojourn with one of his many girlfriends. Abducting him with apparent ease they transported the ex-league player to a meat processing plant across the river. There, Sam and his assistants hoisted Tocco's one hundred and sixty kilo frame wrapped in duct tapped a few feet above the ground. While Tocco wrestled with the tape, they went further. Sam personally beat him in the kneecaps with a hammer. After this preparation, they questioned him. Was he a snitch? A rat?

Unfortunately for Tocco, he couldn't comply with their demands because he wasn't an informant. He was unable to admit to snitching because he wasn't. The torturers weren't satisfied. Their endeavours increased. Applying a cattle prod to his body, the electric current was turned up. As Tocco screamed and screamed in the greatest of pain, Sam went further by pouring water on the body, thus causing an unbearable electric shock. This did it: Tocco passed out and never again regained consciousness. Hanging from the ceiling, he was left to expire, not to be found until work started on Monday morning.

With great expectation Roberto waited for Sam to enter. Staying seated until the older man did so, Roberto

264 ~ DASH STARKEY

held hope of respect. Deep down it was obvious the respect shown was for his father not he, yet one day this would change. The affairs of Amelia were obscure for such an organization. Considering the set-up of the business, both Roberto and Mike inherited their positions. Under normal circumstances, Mafia circumstances, the next strongest player would have moved up into the top position. Possibly Rosario. Possibly a son who had already earned his respect and place in the organization.

The battleground was set. Yes, the legitimate businesses would remain under their control, just. The others would take some fighting to hold on to. So, Sam 'The Monk' was central to the plan. To gain his respect would go a long way in the organization. To have him working for them exclusively, even further.

With a jaunty step, the middle-aged man entered the room, his eyes fixed momentarily on Roberto. Rising from his seat, Roberto shook the older man's hand with both of his.

'Mr Mandell, long time no see.'

'You too young Roberto.'

Sam's appraising eyes took in the surrounds. Nothing had changed since her rule.

'Joey well?'

'Travelling the world he is.'

Nodding with fatherly pride, Sam slid his spectacles up the bridge of his nose before he continued.

'And what is it I can do for you today?'

Under his happy-go-lucky manner, Sam was all work. Since the death of his wife over ten years ago, he had gone celibate. Rumour had it that his torturous fun replaced that section of his life. During situations like those with Tocco, it was said, Sam would foam at the mouth and the bulge in his pants would grow. Another abnormality was that Sam always demanded to be left alone with the victim after the job was completed.

'We need a new 'Mr Outside'. As you may be aware, we need someone better suited to the position.'

Outside the casinos and gambling clubs. The Ricoldi's had dozens of men inside their Royale Casinos, other clubs, and the like, who directed the skim of money. The sole reason for backing smaller clubs: the expected returns. Mr. Outside made sure all the Mr. Insides towed the line. If one of the inside gambling recruits had any kind of problem, it was Mr. Outside he consulted to make sure the recalcitrant shaped up. Or else. Mr. Outside was the muscle, the enforcer of the rules. The default boss. Nobody screwed around when in his presence.

'What are your stakes? I hear they're rocky.'

Sam's ear to the ground had produced many interesting rumours.

'Considering we own the Royale Casino's, God help anyone who tries to step on our toes there. For the others, we have been building up on our original holdings. A burst of juice into the Mt Gravatt Stadium will see it kicking again. We are traveling as well as ever.'

Roberto spoke, sounding confident and non-plussed by the rumours.

'The new Mr Outside will also need to oversee the merger of Vito Sarmry's investments with our own.'

'A takeover is in the wind.'

Sam, still smiling his jovial smile, spoke casual, trying not to be offensive.

'One not in your favour.'

'We have a lot of respect for you and your work Mr Mandell.'

Roberto used the term Mr, out of respect for Sam's loyalty to Amelia. Instead of reverting to Sam's first name, as he would with anyone else to enforce his position.

'We are not willing to concede any, not a single one, of our holdings. Those who continue with us will benefit greatly, those who don't...well?'

Shrugging his shoulders, revealing his bare hands, Roberto looked unfazed, before throwing out the temptation to Sam.

'That would be up to you.'

Nodding at the imposed threat not directed firmly at Sam, but directed at his insatiable desire to torture. Using long strokes, Sam rubbed his sweating palms along his thighs. An excitable desire filled his body.

'When would one start?'

Displaying an excited edge to his voice.

'Now.'

Roberto couldn't bring himself to caution Sam to keep a low profile. Debating over the situation and disrespectfulness in his own mind, Roberto was saved by the unexpected figure in the doorway.

'Remember Sam. You make no noise out there. As one famous chimp once said, *speak soft and carry a big stick.*'

That's what we want you to do. A problem comes up you handle it.'

Licking his lips in response to the thought Sam squirmed in the chair, Rosario continued.

'But nobody gets hit in one of our places. You decide somebody's got to get whacked, you talk to us. We don't want to scare the punters. If it wasn't for the suckers who come to make a play at our tables, and the old ladies who pull the levers on our slots, we couldn't get the skim. Without the skim, we have no reason for you.'

Pressing his hand into the seated man's shoulder. Speaking slowly and clear.

'So don't be scaring the friggin' players. Keep your head down.'

Looking as if he'd say something, Rosario continued, keeping his voice thick with authority.

'All the people inside the casinos and clubs will know who you are and what you are. There's no need to tell them. You don't have to scare them because they already are. Every Mr Inside was put there by us, so they know what will happen if they step out. And they'll know you're the guy to do it.'

Pupils dilated with excitement, Sam's head nodded rapidly, seemingly unattached from his shoulders.

'Fine.'

Is his only word before shaking Roberto's hand and kissing Rosario's. After pausing momentarily, he embraces Rosario, kissing him rapidly on both cheeks.

'I'm sorry for your loss.'

Within seconds he has fled the office, returning to the sanctuary of his waiting car. Sweat still dripping from his forehead, he loosens his trousers and digs inside to release the built-up expectation.

~ 26 ~

A FUTURE YET TO BE HAD

Stanthorpe, Queensland, Australia.

Standing at the French doors, Mike's eyes fell upon Izzy who was in deep discussion with his mother. Hunched together, they spoke in whispered tones. Amelia's resonated in a soothing manner while Izzy's was sharp and confused. Patting the younger girl's hand with her own, Izzy laughs, throwing her head backwards in enjoyment. Her hair flowed in a solid arc.

From the first moment that Mike had seen her, all he wanted to do was drown in that mess of hair, smelling the salty sweetness of her skin. It surprised him how quickly the old feeling rekindled. There had been many a fantasy in those first months. His hand rearranged his pants, as he thought of her. Imagining the feel of her skin on his tongue. But his fantasies had remained just that.

Watching her, he felt flushed. The want to look at her was strong. Yet he hoped she didn't see him in case she fled. The images pounded on, one after the other, until that final moment on the stairs. Stroking the moistness from his eyes, Mike leaned on the door's handle for support. Looking up again, Izzy was staring right at him. His newly unplastered hand slipped, ramming his shoulder into the glass of the door.

Amelia struggled between motherly concern and anger of what had happened at the velodrome. In context, what he had done was the right decision, but forgiveness would not come easily.

'If you'll excuse me. I've had a long day.'

Her frail almost translucent hands gripped the wheels of the chair. Forcing them round, desperate to leave his company. The small patches of white and the blue lines of veins became more obvious with each effort.

Izzy moved towards Mike, as close as she dared. He could feel the heat emanating from her body, catch the scent of her breath here and there as her lips moved in and out of range.

'Yes. It's fine.'

Deeply her fingers massaged his shoulder, slow circular movements intermingled amongst it. He could see some of the skin underneath her shirt. There was a strong desire to touch her. Catching his eyes on her chest she gave Mike a look he would never forget. Mischievous, daring, and haughty. Mike could have died.

'Would you like a lift home?'

'If it's not out of your way? Aunt Betsy still has a load of chores to do.'

To face his mother, or give Izzy a lift home, the choice was obvious. Waiting in the kitchen, Mike helped himself to a few servings of chilled water. Which was much too cold and hardly enough to quench his thirst. Mike laughed at his nervousness then his mother spoke.

'Why, Nicco?'

Near startled, Mike spluttered on the water, as its trickling coolness rushed into the wrong passage.

'You created the situation.'

Nonchalantly he remained with his back to her.

'Is your heart stone only towards your mother? Or Izzy too?'

'Funny. I got that trait from my mother.'

Turning, he faced the figure in the darkness. Standing, his mother had lost none of her height, yet her body seemed shrunken to him. Her presence was no longer as he remembered.

'It's only a shell you know. It can break.'

'Yes, mother.'

Stepping into the room, the light caught her face momentarily, returning the youthfulness she had once savoured.

'I know about your plans. He will bring nothing but trouble to you. Promise, you will have nothing to do with him.'

'Promises are like diamonds mother. Men freely give them away while women, women cling to them fiercely, holding them close, never letting go.'

Supporting herself on the bench, Amelia used controlled precise steps to approach Mike. Once she was near, her bony arms reached out to encircle him. The warmth of Amelia's lips settled on his cheek.

'I love you Nicco. I will always love you.'

'Yeah Mum. Ditto.'

Standing in the embrace, neither dared to move. Becoming uncomfortable, Mike cleared his throat.

'Oh yeah. I spoke to Joseph today.'

The words activated a trembling motion in Amelia. Mike could feel it against his body. Close to his ear, her breath caught in her throat.

'We just talked, Mum.'

Taking Amelia by the shoulders, he moved her to arm's length.

'Maybe it's time for him to disappear too. The two of you could go somewhere. Travel even. Be somewhere other than here.'

His eyes were compassionate and loving.

'Go and recover, Mum.'

Amelia smiled at him limply, then plod off into the darkness from where she came. Standing in a lull, Mike's expression changed rapidly as he felt something behind him. Mike turned to see Izzy's arm pressing on his shoulder.

'Bike's all secured. Let's go.'

They were off to the car and with a few rough directions they arrived at her new Aunt's small house near the centre of town. Dusk was descending yet all the lights were off.

'Betsy lives alone.'

Answered Izzy to his questioning look.

'If you don't allow for the animals.'

Izzy took a moment to see to Betsy's menagerie of

cats and dogs. Patting them exuberantly, and then setting them out the back with food and water. Coming back inside, she asked Mike if he'd like anything to drink. Nodding, he took a seat in the dark living room as Izzy found the kitchen and poured them both a glass of cold spumante from the fridge.

Bringing the drinks out on a tray, Izzy lit a single lamp and proceeded to sit opposite Mike on the couch. Izzy wanted to be perfect, romantic and ravishing. She prayed Mike couldn't see her nervousness. To her, he seemed perfectly at ease, his usual friendly self, telling her about his day at the track. Omitting only a few minor details. Mike's voice echoed off the walls as her mind raced around in circles. Trying to figure out how he really felt about her.

In her heart, she hoped that maybe deep down he forgave her, and that he just hadn't really considered that possibility yet. Maybe it had never crossed his mind. And never would. Izzy just had no idea, which left her full of nerves and jitters.

They filled in the noticeable silence with old jokes, sipping their wine and giggling nervously. The words finally came that they both dreaded. Leaning forward, settling the glass on the table, Izzy spoke first.

'I'm sorry.'

There were no other words. Words to describe that terrible feeling in the pit of her stomach. Nor were there words for the pain of agonising over the situation, day in, day out.

Positioning himself on the coffee table's edge, Mike reached out to stroke Izzy's hair.

'I know.'

Looking down, she blushed.

'Really?'

She asked, looking into Mike's eyes for a moment.

'Yes.'

He whispered, stroking her head and neck.

'Even though you are my curse.'

She chuckled, then sighed, shifting her weight towards Mike. Relieving her of the wine glass, he cupped Izzy's face. She looked so innocent and pure, just shining, and wholesome, and unpretentious. Pure, yet smart and real. Mike knew that his careful study of her personality meant although he wanted her deeply, he wanted more than just casual sex. If they were to fool around, he wanted her to remember him forever.

He leaned in for a kiss. And what a lovely kiss. Her mouth was soft, giving and at the same time full of fire. Changing position, Mike moved in to hold Izzy. Her weight shifted and the pair fell slowly backwards into the soft cushions. Ravenous now, his mouth was all over hers, his hands squeezing Izzy's breasts, her hips grinding into his. Disengaging from the kiss, Izzy snuggled into Mike's neck, biting a little. He cried out in pleasure.

Removing her thin shirt revealed her luscious breasts encased in a silky new bra. Mike's hand rested momentarily on her stomach, her skin felt warm and soft. And sensual. He wanted to kiss and fondle the belly ring that had been hidden all this time. But he lay there for a while gently stroking it, lazily running his hand back and forth along her side. From her hip, up a little, and then down and around to her belly button. And back again. With each motion, Mike started to apply a little more pressure, digging his fingers into her skin. This action stirred both of their desires. From under hooded lashes Izzy held his stare intently.

'Stand up.'

She whispered.

Mike slowly complied. Izzy lifted his shirt slowly, peeling it up and off his skin. Then she moved down and unbuttoned his jeans. Once again peeling the clothing from his now sweating skin. His skin was so pale, almost glowing, compared to hers. She paused, looking at him for a long moment. Standing there was strange, the feeling of moving through her Aunt's house near naked. Izzy began to remove her pants, walking towards the bedroom. Mike followed, kicking off the remainder of his clothes and shoes.

'Better bring them. Don't want to go around shocking Aunt Betsy.'

Lighting some candles on her dresser, Izzy turned to see Mike turning down the sheets. Naked, he was glorious. Immediately upon entering the bed, their passion was re-ignited. Flesh greedily touching. Chests rubbing together. Kissing with wet forceful tongues.

****

'Sneaking out, are you?'

Leaning seductively on one elbow, Izzy's nakedness

was incredibly appealing under the loose cotton sheet. Light streaming in from the window behind her only highlighted the fact.

'I've got to go. I'm flying out at two.'

'Flying out?'

'Yes.'

Mike dragged his eyes from her lushness.

'Out of the country.'

'Oh.'

Izzy's disappointment was obvious.

'It's not like that.'

'Like what?'

With a heavy sigh, Mike perched himself on the bed. Reaching across the rumpled sheets, his fingers barely touched Izzy's slender form before she recoiled away. Away beyond his reach.

'Last night.'

'Ah huh.'

'It meant something to me. But.'

'But?'

'This business trip is very important. I must go.'

'For how long?'

'Hopefully only three to four months.'

He shrugged.

'But who knows?'

Pulling the sheet higher, Izzy slouched to her back. Her voice was small. Disappointed.

'Go then.'

'Izzy.'

Moving closer, his arm caught her shoulder before she

turned away. Away forever. Nuzzling her neck, he kissed the hollow at the base of her throat.

'I have forgiven you.'

Pausing to separate the two statements.

'But this is important. Maybe if I can find a free moment, I could send for you. If not, I promise to come back and work all of this out. With you. I want to be with you. I promise.'

Drifting on the stagnant air the words hung suspended. He promised. Eyes of concern caressed her, yet there was something.

'Is that a diamond you are offering?'

Flushing anger, then understanding, Mike pulled her closer, his breath warm and moist on her lips.

'No. When I offer you a diamond, I will be down on one knee.'

Above her now, the kiss was passionate, loving and promising. A future yet to be had.

~ 27 ~

OIL AND WATER

International Airport, Brisbane.

Seated in the departure lounge of the Brisbane International Airport, Roberto stared at, what amounted to, his stepbrother. Mike was dressed in one of his expensively made suits, looking old style Italian. Basically, a decent suit accompanied by a tie with a matching handkerchief in the breast pocket. His hair cut in the style of a marine completed the picture. Standing above him now, in a mildly threatening manner, Roberto's only response was the intent study of his own nails.

'You may have inherited control over the transport and shipping from mother. But as the new family head, I am in charge. You will follow my decisions.'

'Those words aren't yours Nicco. They must be someone else's.'

Speaking flippantly, Roberto's gestures indicated his feeling of equality with Mike.

'You've always been a follower, not a leader.'

'You may be right.'

Saliva formed silently at the corner of Mike's mouth, foaming to white as he spoke.

'But at least I'm not a fall guy like your old man.'

Feeling the searing pain of teeth nipping the tongue's end, Roberto tasted the bitterness of hatred in his sealed mouth. The remark not only pained him in its reference to Rosario, but also of what lay unsaid about his true parentage. He as the elder child should, and is, entitled to take over the helm of the Ricoldi family empire.

Growing up together, like brothers, had not changed the fact that Mike resented being the younger of the two. The constant comparisons had gnawed their way endlcssly through his young, blooming, self-esteem, to the point of his fleeing to America, under the guise of studying. For which he felt as if he had returned as a stronger man. Amelia, in her own way, had endeavoured to guide each boy into his own destiny. Yet to her dismay a strong rivalry had grown. It had grown silently in each, only showing itself at random intervals. That was until matters were brought to a head by her sudden demise and their subsequent inheritance.

'Nicco, we are family, are we not?'

As the elder, Roberto knew it was his job to placate Mike's fiery temper. As a child he learnt how and when to aggravate Mike, and with such an intimacy came the knowledge of how to dampen the anger before it festered.

'Now is not the time to bicker over such ills. Amelia always placed us on an equal footing. Her will was a testament to that. You may not agree, but it was her desire for each of us to acknowledge our strengths, and to promote them. To promote them well for the sake of the family.'

'Yes, you are right. But see it as I do. We must achieve several deals of this magnitude if we are to consolidate our power. To let them know they are not dealing with just a couple of schoolboys.'

Resting his palm on Roberto's shoulder, Mike's fingers gripped hard as if pressing the spoken point.

Roberto's easy smile and cold eyes made people uncomfortable. Twitching under his glare, Mike knew Roberto to be a man of honour who would not risk family for personal gains. If he had to leave for a few months, as he desired to, there was no-one else to trust.

'Go then, but know I will do all I can to eliminate the wolves at the door.'

'I know you will do well by the family.'

The lifetime bond they shared had exceeded any known words. An embrace was all that was left for them.

'Farewell Nicco. I will look after things at this end. Promise to call if you need anything. Anything at all.'

'Yes Robbie, I will. Take care.'

Without a second glance Mike departed for his flight. Kristov met him at the top of the escalators, tickets in hand. Just before they descended completely into the customs area Mike turned to see Roberto leave with Klaus. Their heads bowed in deep conversation. He quietly prayed they were both successful in their respective missions. As young as they both were, their knowledge of the workings of 'the business' was outstanding. In the coming weeks their youthfulness would be a detriment in many business deals, yet their cunning would pull them through. Hopefully. Clashing with Roberto had become more frequent since Amelia's 'death', Mike found it hard to retain himself in some instances, though he had to as he knew Roberto was important to the family's plans. And his.

Passing through the customs checks, the pair turned towards the café that looked identical to the floor above. Except only departing passengers were allowed in this waiting area. Those not drinking alcohol at the café's bar were either seated in the formally laid out chairs, glancing nervously at the large televisions filled with flight schedules, or puffing away on their last cigarettes.

'Welcome gentlemen.'

Spoke Anthony Valentine as he leant casually against the bar.

'This is my associate, Joey Mandell.'

Licking his lips slowly, Anthony's eyes darted about as he spoke. His hand brushing the hair along one side of his head punctuated every third word spoken.

After the brief introductions, the four men settled into a table near the ceiling high window, which overlooked the departing aircraft. Positioning himself about a foot from the table, Joey sat quietly in a brooding manner. At frequent intervals, his left hand would rise and tug at his starched collar. After much struggling and apparent indecision, he undid the top button, loosening the tie in the process. His shoulder length hair sat neatly brushed in a ponytail giving the impression of short-back-and-sides from the front.

Kristov, bored by the conversation, rose and made his way to the bar. Not rushing back, he made small talk with a skinny lass behind the counter. At first, she barely responded to his joking manner and lopsided smile. Just as he turned to leave a gurgling noise rose from her mouth, but her hand smothered it before the full extent of laughter escaped. Smiling anyway, Kristov returned to his position at the table.

'May I?'

Anthony indicated to the fresh pack of cigarettes that Kristov was tearing the foil from.

'Certainly.'

Kristov leaned forward, throwing the pack's wrapping into the ashtray.

Anthony's hand hovered over the open pack, his tongue darting quickly about his mouth. His fingers dove towards a cigarette, froze and moved to the one on the left of the original. Slowly drawing it out, Anthony studied it momentarily before tapping his lighter three times with the cigarette's butt.

Recoiling his arm, Kristov was about to select a cigarette for himself when Anthony's hand grabbed his.

'May I have another?'

'Sure.'

Kristov shrugged in confusion.

Placing the first cigarette behind his left ear, Anthony started the selection process again. His hand hovering, falling suddenly then freezing before selecting the cigarette to the left. After tapping this cigarette's butt three times, he leant towards Joey who had a lighter waiting.

Waving away the smoke in annoyance, Mike glanced away from Anthony's leering face.

'Is the first meeting set up?'

Squaring himself to Anthony, Mike waited for an answer.

~ 28 ~

LET THE JOURNEY BEGIN

Ryde, Sydney, New South Wales, Australia.

A loud commotion containing the sounds of metal on metal and the whining of an engine woke Brooke from his light sleep. Looking at the curvaceous body beside him, his lips rounded. The morning's endeavours fresh in his mind. Glancing at his watch, his forehead furrowed. It was too late in the afternoon for the garbage collection.

Casually untangling himself from the bedcovers, he sauntered to the window. Sinking into the luxurious carpet, he could feel each soft fibre as it wiggled between his toes with each step forward. Without urgency he drew the drapes to one side. Squinting, the afternoon glare daggers to his eyes, Brooke looked towards where the noises arose.

'What the...'

Without taking into consideration his attire, or lack of, Brooke scrambled with the sliding door's lock. Yanking the door aside, he burst onto the balcony screaming.

Standing barefoot, and bare everywhere else, on the cool tiles did nothing for his authority.

'Clear off! Get away from my friggin car, you, you... heathens!'

Already the Maclaren was halfway up the tilt tray. One man, dressed in blue overalls, shaded his eyes as he peered up to the balcony. His mouth grew wide in amusement when his eyes levelled with Brooke. Without speed the still air brought laughter to Brooke's ears, muffled with the whirr of the winch. A second man leant from the truck window, pointing and laughing in line with the first. Shamed into action Brooke moved through the apartment, grabbing a robe as he passed the bed.

'What's the matter sweet cakes?'

Came a woman's voice from the bed.

'They're stealing the Maclaren. Some bums are stealing my Maclaren.'

'Well, you aren't going to make it downstairs in time, not with that lift. Besides, shouldn't you be wearing something more...um...masculine, than my robe?'

Resigned to the inevitable defeat, by the poor picture of manhood he looked in a mauve floral silk robe, Brooke dropped his body into a waiting couch. Automatically his body starts a rocking momentum, his hands cradling his head. A mixture of words and mumble trickle from his mouth. His manicured nails, massaging his skull, a soothing pink amongst the blond locks. Looking up his face is pale, aged looking.

'Let me think.'

Inspiration enhances his face, clarity overtakes the features.

'Pass me my phone.'

Shrugging, unconcerned either way, the girl leans across the bed, her breasts squeezing into his pillow, as her eyes appraise him invitingly. Noisily now, beyond that of his anger, Brooke's breathing hastens as he watches her enticing movements. In a fluid motion she retrieves the phone from his side table and flings it through the air towards him. With eyes fixed on her now jiggling breasts, the phone catches him unawares, landing harshly on his private regions. Smiling, the girl rises from the bed, her long legs leading the way. Pirouetting before Brooke, she smiles seductively, wrapping herself in his robe which, till a moment ago, hung loosely from the second chair, before sauntering off to the bathroom. Listening carefully, he can hear her movements, the picture still frames in his head. The almost silent drop of his robe, its ties landing tangled upon her feet. A click followed closely by a burst of water rushing out to meet the tiles. Water pattering like rain, its sound softening as her body moves beneath it. He can almost taste the water beading on her skin. Instead, he dialed a number.

'Yep.'

'Roberto. It's me Brooke Jeffries.'

'How can I help?'

'Some bum has just stolen the Maclaren. On a tilt tray! In broad daylight!'

His voice rises in amazement, interspersed with anger.

'Ahh. Luckily, we installed that navigation chip. Thought it might come in handy.'

Roberto smiled to himself. Since taking over Gate's Transport, his first priority was to install tracking systems in all of the trucks. It was a great system not only in the prevention or recovery from theft, but in keeping overheads down. The system could reveal whether a driver was leaving the air conditioner run while on breaks, whether the truck was idling in neutral for too long and whether the drivers made detours from designated courses. All of this information had not only saved him time, fuel, and excess wages but had made it easier to 'sell' shipping to certain companies who knew the stock would be continually monitored. The control room could even adjust the temperature in the freezer trucks as they travelled around Australia. The drivers none the wiser, especially if a shipment arrived spoiled. Thank goodness for insurance smiled Roberto.

'Don't worry Mr Jeffries, we'll get onto that right away.'

'Lord Jeffries to you Roberto.'

Joked Brooke.

'You're kidding. Right?'

'That's the problem when the Poms owe you a favour, you get a bloody knighthood instead.'

Brooke could hear the boy suffocate a chuckle.

'Amelia would have gone crazy over that!'

'Yes.'

An involuntary sigh escaped him.

'She would have laughed forever over it, at my expense.'

The sudden void slowly filled with silence as they each contemplate, from their respective angles, the story of Amelia's life.

'I miss her too. Sparrow.'

Drawing his lips in tight, Roberto can feel the bitter sting in his eyes. Drawn as his lips are, the small tuft of hair left uncut under his bottom lip juts out horizontally. Stroking it with his pinkie while still holding the phone, Roberto forces himself to speak.

'Yes. Your car will be returned to you shortly Lord Jeffries. I promise you that.'

Without another word the line falls dead. As if weighted, Brooke is unable to rise from the chair. He can hear the sweet tones of her voice coming from the bathroom but has no desire to move. No desire at all. Leaning on his elbow, chin resting on his knuckles, he stares forlornly at nothing. He is this way when the girl re-enters the room twenty minutes later.

****

Being sure that his voice will not deceive him, Roberto makes a call.

'Control room.'

Came the crisp reply.

'Pursue ATX690.'

'Engine is off, but it is moving. Passing through Ryde, Sydney.'

'This is a priority. Don't lose track of it. I'll ring back.'

Roberto was happy that Klaus is driving. Giving him

an opportunity of staring out the window to conceal his discomfort as he speaks.

'Do we have any chop shops in Sydney?'

'No. None. Is that where the car's been jacked?'

'Yes. Who do we owe a favour? In Sydney.'

Without taking his eyes from the road, Klaus chews his bottom lip in thought. His mind going through a Rolodex of names and faces. Finally, it rests on one.

'Detective Sargent Davis is having a hard time of it lately. He has some 'interesting' contacts.'

'Right. And the number.'

From his mind, Klaus lifts the number, rattling it off as if it were his mothers.

'Detective Sargent Davis.'

The phone is answered in a tired disinterested way.

'Ah. Davis. I hear you are having a tough time of it lately. Thought you might need a hand.'

'What do you want in return?'

'Nothing.'

'Nothing.'

Davis's monotone repeats the word. His tongue tumbling it about in abandon.

'It is a favour, to repair that tarnished image of yours.'

A grunt is the only reply.

'Lord Jeffries' car has just this moment been stolen. And I have the capabilities at hand to track it.'

'Lord, huh.'

The monotone once again reducing a word to its joyless state.

'Didn't heist it yourself did ya?'

'I am a legitimate businessman, why would I need to jack cars.'

In a laugh the monotone sounds nearly humorous.

'Okay, okay, what's the score?'

After clearing this detour in their predetermined plan, Roberto and Klaus continue to pursue their number one priority. As the minutes tick by, each man's mind runs over the evening's undertakings. Playing every scenario, making sure nothing escapes them. To make a mistake, to leave evidence, any minor fraction could be their downfall. In normal circumstances it would not be them that would complete such a plan, but tonight was not normal circumstances. Head against the car window, misting it with his breath, Roberto's finger tapped inconsistent dots of doodlings from his mind's flurry. An hour of the car's gentle hum is all it took to rock his eyelids towards the closed position.

Dozing in and out of wakefulness, Roberto reclines relaxed, arms folded loosely about his chest. Swaying with the cars motion his head looks as if it is about to topple from his shoulders. Yet his unconsciousness appears to pull it back before it does. Klaus on the other hand is the embodiment of concentration. His broad shoulders hunched over the steering wheel, eyes fastened to the road taking in every street name and corner.

They have long left the main coastal road that crossed them over the border to New South Wales an hour ago. Here, the roads are narrower making the big sedans manoeuvrability less. Picking off the corners one by one, the bitumen suddenly disappears, replaced by corrugated gravel. The sudden jerkiness awakens Roberto from his slumber.

'Nearly there.'

States Klaus without a sideways glance.

'Good. I want to get this over with.'

'He was a good friend of yours, yes?'

'Was. Don't worry. Nothing is stopping me from completing this job.'

Klaus' preselected route takes them within a hundred metres of their destination. A hundred metres of climbing. Looking into the dense scrub, Roberto imagines the point of their destination, and ever so faintly he can see a flickcr of light.

'Something to guide us, I suppose.'

A little dejected with the task at hand.

'The main entrance to the house is off the other road. If any trouble strikes that is where it will come from. There are neighbours too. This abandoned track has none. We can slide in unnoticed, complete the task and vanish into the darkness. No one will be the wiser.'

Trying to justify his selected point of entry, Klaus leads the way. He paces back and forth before deciding on an entry point into the denseness of the overhanging trees and long wild grasses. The climb is slow until they come across a small track leading from a lower dam to the house. The track is narrow with no perception of height, probably created by a wallaby thought Roberto.

Gaining entry to the house is made easy by an open door just beyond the decking. Slipping quietly through the lounge room, Roberto, followed by Klaus, proceeds down the hallway in search of his prey. Having no idea of the layout, or location of light switches, the pair play it by ear. Studying for signs of life Roberto waits for sounds to come to him. Nothing. To his left is located the bathroom, the moon reflecting sorrowfully from its tiles, illuminating the room in a soft glow. Next to that the toilet. Ahead to his left another door leading to a bedroom. Empty. A small flicker of light catches Klaus' attention. Pointing, Roberto can see the flicker of light under a partly opened door further down the hallway. Advancing with a sense of dreadful anticipation, the pair press themselves against the wall. Spreading the fingers on his right hand, Klaus gently pushes the door open.

Revealed to them is the source of light. The dancing flame of the candle momentarily holds a face, a face Roberto once considered a brother, before relinquishing it to the darkness. Christopher's brow is smooth with sleep, his lips are bowed in a smile. His face innocent with youth, angelic even. Beside him lies his girlfriend. An unexpected surprise for Roberto. May had nothing to do with this. Yet it could quite possibly be the end of her too.

As if his sad thoughts penetrate her sleeping mind, May stirs. Her movements slow under the heavy quilt. Rolling towards the light, Roberto can see her eyes flicker before resettling to their closed position. As he and Klaus enter the room, he can see her body stiffen. Within moments the room is filled with a blood-curdling scream as May throws back the quilt and presses her body hard against the backboard. Wakening more slowly, Christopher rolls towards May, his arm limply reaching out for her.

'What's the matter babe?'

With a trembling arm she points to the figure now standing at his side of the bed. Upon seeing Roberto, Christopher wakens immediately.

'Holy shit! Man, I can explain.'

Christopher's palms, open wide, face the shadow.

Roberto stands deathly quiet. His only movement is to indicate to Klaus the removal of May.

'Don't hurt her man. Please. I beg of you.'

Shivering, her hair falling limply about her face, May tucks herself into a tight ball. Yet when she hears Christopher yell *Run!* She uncoils rapidly like a spring and flies from the bed. Taking Klaus by surprise, she shoots under his gloved hand and through to the hall. Angered by this sudden action Klaus follows.

Under casual observation May appears to have a limp. But closer scrutiny reveals her left leg acts as if it was continually climbing a step. For someone with such a handicap, she could run extremely quickly. Nearly to the point of being agile.

Klaus pursues, sifting through furniture that has been thrust at him and jumping objects meant to slow him. Turning right at the hall's end he comes to two doors. One closed, one open. The open door reveals the bathroom, its dull glow vanishing beneath a cloud, and from the closed door he can hear a panting voice hurriedly giving directions. With the sole of his foot he kicks the door inwards with seemingly little effort. Before him sits the frightened May, huddled on the toilet seat, clasping a mobile phone. Down her legs trickles a yellow stream of urine, the closed toilet lid preventing its escape.

All that could be heard was the first part of *no* as the bullet seared through her left eye. The impact delivered by the Heckler and Koch momentarily suspends May above the toilet seat, while at the same time pitching her back against the wall. A fearsome crack echoes in the closed room, amidst a spray of blood and grey matter, as her head hits the hard surface of the cistern on its way down. Legs folding beneath her, May's body slides from the seat to the tiled floor. Suspended from the walls are the last remaining remnants of May's life.

Wiping any over spray from his face, Klaus returns to the main bedroom. Down on his knees, Christopher is begging. One look at Klaus has him sobbing and falling to the floor. Roberto holds steadfastly to his friend's hair, refusing him the privilege of relaxing his body.

'He asked me to do it!'

'Don't speak such rot to me! How could you after all we've been through? You of all people. '

'I just wanted you to respect me.'

Came the sob saturated reply.

'I wanted to be a man of honour like you. And he asked me to. How could I refuse?'

'You have shamed us all. At least you could end it like a man.'

Pressing the gun firmly into Christopher's temple, Roberto comes eye to eye with his one-time best friend.

'Oh, I nearly forgot.'

Echoes a chilling reminder.

Within seconds of the words spoken, Roberto let the tip of the gun sink. Before the bullet even penetrated the skin, Christopher's throat dried while his mind bordered on hysteria. Clinging to his lower, genital region, in pain and through gritted teeth he persists with his plea. Raising the guns nozzle once again to Christopher's temple, Roberto pauses. In that moment of thought, Christopher raises a bloodstained hand and places it on the cold, gloved hand holding the gun. Sliding his thumb along the cool under-belly of the Beretta, he forces Roberto's trigger finger.

~ 29 ~

SHINTO WISDOM

Stanthorpe, Queensland.

Leaves rattle aloft in the breeze and underfoot. Staring up into the filtered sunlight, Amelia could feel nothing but pleased. Days had passed before the final fragments of a plan had drawn themselves together in her mind. After three months, the fright of a near death experience had somewhat faded. But Amelia figured that to be little comfort since her new life, thus far, appeared only to be a fore view of herself as an old woman. Especially awash in the solitude she found surrounding her, and the feeling of diminishing capabilities. And today, the first day of autumn, had signalled the end of the dimensionless life she was leading.

The sun's growing warmth cradled her face, adding conviction to the strength, which grew inside. As her eyes fluttered shut, Amelia's lashes trembled as her pupils darted under their scant lids. Moving slowly her lips mouthed promises only she could hear. From a distance it would have appeared that Amelia was in prayer, for her hands sat clenched tightly at chest level.

Not wishing to disrupt her obvious bliss, Izzy approached slowly, dragging her feet reluctantly. Mike's departure had left Amelia in a moody state. As the days had grown into weeks, the mood had mellowed slightly. Izzy's mood was indeterminate as her last moments with Mike were exciting and held much promise.

'Come Izzy.'

Using her senses other than sight, Amelia felt Izzy's presence.

'I have decided.'

'Decided on what?'

Patting the seat beside her, the younger took her place. Amelia reached across taking Izzy's warm hand in hers. Stroking her smooth brown skin, she looked towards the sky.

'I think we should travel. Make you a woman of the world.'

Frowning, Izzy couldn't see the point. Or the reasoning. First California, then Australia had been her biggest moves to date. She was unsure if the rest of the world could hold anything significant for her.

'Let's fly to Japan. I'll show you, and Joseph around and then we'll catch up with Nicco. He's due there in a week or so.'

There was something for her.

'How do you know he'll be there? He was unsure of his time frames.'

'He'll be there. Trust me.'

****

Without question Izzy did as she was instructed and within days she, Joseph, Amelia and, strangely, Yacob were in Kyoto, Japan. From the airport they had gone straight to a ryokan, a traditional Japanese inn. To Izzy it was incredible, beyond anything she had seen before. From the outside the building looked much like any other, but on the inside it was unique. The first thing to catch Izzy's eyes were the sliding paper doors, and that wasn't all. Upon entering the apartments, as such, there were no walls but more paper sliding screens, which, if desired, could be removed completely.

'You should always remove your shoes when walking on the tatami mats.'

Amelia stated while Izzy was lost in her bewilderment.

'What mats?'

'The straw mats on the floor. You must always remove your shoes. Slippers too. Socks and bare feet only.'

Amelia guided Izzy about the apartment. To the right was a small alcove, which barely contained a hanging scroll and a flower arrangement, ikebana she thought Amelia said. The words were foreign and strange yet they rolled off Amelia's tongue with such grace: Izzy found herself repeating each one. Veering around what passed as a kitchen: a gas cooker, a rice cooker, a microwave oven and a refrigerator, they entered another tatami room. Although she had not been raised in the lap of luxury, Izzy found it strange that this was where she was to sleep, but for the life of her she could see no bed.

Turning away from Amelia's chuckle for help, Joseph just offered a shrug. Izzy, not one known for making a bed frequently was disgusted to find that the bed, or futon, was kept in a closet during the day and was laid on the floor only during the night. She was further disgusted by the fact that the room functioned not only as a bedroom but a living room and a dining room. To make matters worse Yacob was in the next screen over.

Still chuckling, Amelia led Joseph through another sliding door into an adjoining apartment. Yacob protested and commenced to follow the pair. Amelia turned in the doorway, smiled at Izzy who had commenced to unpack, and said a few private words to Yacob. His face fell, and his few protests were met with harsh whispers. Looking sullen, he dragged the paper screen closed behind him, before returning to his room.

Out on the Kyoto streets that afternoon, Yacob was delegated to walk at least ten paces behind Amelia and Izzy while they shopped. Yacob was one of those things Izzy dared not ask Amelia about. She had tried asking once but Amelia's brow had creased and a certain expression crossed her face, an expression that sent waves of shivers along Izzy's skin. It was enough to scare Izzy off the subject and several others. Like why when Amelia trimmed her nails or hair, she burnt the clippings? Many a time she had seen Amelia light a fire for the express purpose of burning the clippings. Amelia had stood there, staring into the fire until there was nothing left, and then, and only then would she turn and walk away. Much of Amelia and Mike's life confused her, yet she knew that if she persisted it would all make sense.

Frustration filled Yacob's face as Amelia visited and spoke to people in a tongue he failed to understand. Several times he attempted to pull her aside and have a stern word, each time she laughed him off. And when she entered a teahouse, her eyes glinted with mischievous fun as she sat the pair down and excused herself. Yacob rose but was informed he was not welcome in the little girl's room. Izzy and Yacob were brought steaming cups of green tea accompanied by some sticky rice sweets. Izzy devoured them hungrily unlike Yacob who sat agitatedly, continually looking at his watch. His eyes darted the busy room where a mix of languages wove themselves into one blanket of noise.

'Why do you worry so?'

Izzy's question was innocent.

'What harm could come to her?'

His glare was intimidating.

'It is what I am employed to do. You should not ask about things you do not understand.'

His accent adding to the severity of the statement.

'I understand she's had a hard life and you don't make it any easier.'

Looking as if he'd say more, Yacob pursed his lips tightly, his eyes darting once more to the hallway leading to the bathrooms and beyond.

'Would you mind checking on her for me?'

His expression changed slightly.

'Maybe she is ill.'

Looking as if she'd object, Izzy paused before rising to her feet. Sarcastically smiling at Yacob she dawdled towards the hallway purposely taking an interest in any object that would slow her progress. Once she was out of Yacob's line of vision she hurried towards the lady's toilets. Amelia was nowhere to be seen. Panic rose in her throat. The saliva that circulated in her mouth tasted metallic. Had she risked Amelia's life with her own arrogance? Exiting the toilets, Izzy searched the hallway, the main tearoom was to the right and a swinging kitchen door to the left. As she hesitated in her choice to retrieve Yacob, the kitchen door swung wide. Out strode a small waiter with a silver tray held above his shoulder. An assortment of Japanese chatter followed until it was locked away behind the door again. In the moment before the door settled Izzy thought she caught a glimpse of something.

Nearly knocking several waiters over, Izzy threw the swinging door open and scanned the room. Steam rose from sizzling woks blurring her vision. The clash of utensils distracted her but in the far corner there was something. Yes, it was Amelia and a Japanese businessman. She was bowing to him, her head remained low as she stepped aside for him to pass.

'Amelia.'

She gasped.

'Why Izzy, you look flushed.'

Her smile was warm as she took Izzy by the arm and led her to the hallway.

'What.'

Gulped Izzy.

'What were you doing?'

'Securing my children's future, my dear. That's all.'

With no further words, the pair moved towards Yacob who was now standing. His fists drumming into his sides. Failing to return Amelia's hearty smile, he just glared at Izzy.

'Klaus would kill me if he knew.'

'Knew what Yacob? That I went to the bathroom.'

'You and I know better than that Ms Hearton.'

'Yes, we know that it is Klaus you respect not Mike.'

'Respect must be earnt.'

'Then surely I have done enough. Saving you from gang life on the cold streets of Moscow, Leningrad or God knows where else. Maybe even saving you from a coffin. Yet you cause me nothing but trouble.'

'I am under orders.'

'One day soon you will step too far over the line.'

Amelia lowered her voice beyond Izzy's hearshot.

'And that will be your last day on earth. I promise.'

'Your threats mean nothing to me. You are just a powerless, weak, old lady. What you had is gone. You do not scare me.'

The return trip to the ryokan was quiet, with Yacob refusing to walk behind them. On their return Joseph greeted them with the words *Irashaimase* and presented them with a light meal of miso soup, sushi and noodles. Removing their shoes, they settled on the tatami mat at the lowered table. Amelia said *Itadakimasu* before they commenced eating. While Yacob shovelled noodles into his cavernous mouth, and Izzy investigated what the green stuff was between her prawn and rice sashimi, Amelia and Joseph clasped hands before gazing wistfully into each other's eyes.

'There's something we need to ask you both.'

Started Joseph.

'It would mean a lot to us.'

Continued Amelia in a quiet voice.

Screwing up her face, Izzy searched hastily for something to wash the green wasabi from her mouth. Looking up, she noticed the conversation had stopped and all eyes were settled on her, she blushed and asked Joseph to continue.

'We would be honoured if the two of you could witness our marriage tomorrow.'

It was now Yacob's time to choke. Joseph leant over the table, pounding Yacob's back. Holding up a hand, Yacob composed himself.

'Tomorrow?'

'Yes.'

Smiled Amelia.

'At a Shinto shrine, in the traditional Japanese manner.'

'And Mike?'

Amelia's light heartedness faded.

'He is not my keeper. Nor yours, apparently. You would do well to remember that Yacob.'

****

Early the next morning a fitter arrived with Amelia's wedding kimono. Izzy was instantly taken by its delicate beauty. The perfectly white silk was made even more incredible by the intricate design captured upon it. Her pulse jumped while her fingers hesitated above the fabric. The fitter, looking younger than her considerable years, nodded encouragingly. Her own dark clothing rising the kimono above mere white. A toothless grin showed her approval. Delicately tracing the pattern, Izzy's fingers hovered hesitantly before tracing another pattern.

'I've never seen anything so beautiful.'

'Yes. It's called a shiro-muku. A special kimono just for the wedding ceremony. Later I will change into this iro-uchikake. It too is handmade.'

Nodding profusely, a rocking horse grin plastered to her face, the fitter produces another string tied bundle. From the second wrap of brown paper Amelia lifts a kimono. It was more colourful than the first, yet just as magnificent. Flinging it across the futon, the fitter slides a bamboo pole through the arms so the full design could be seen as it is raised. Izzy takes a step back, the breath inside her vanishing. From the base hem up diagonally for about a fifth of the kimono the colour was a strikingly deep blue. In the foreground a grand white heron observes the setting of a bold golden white sun. Dispersing into incredible tones the afternoon sky disappears into the brilliant oranges and reds of a true Australian sunset. Ghostly silhouettes of mountains come to mind, obscured partly by the dying rays of light. Watching his companions rise and float, speckled across the horizon, seemingly within reach. The observer is left wondering whether the heron too will rise and join his kind into the unknown.

'It is time to ready oneself.' Spoke the small, hunched fitter.

'Yes. You too Izzy. There is something special for you behind that screen.'

Sliding the paper screen to one side, Izzy discovered a third kimono. It's silk just as wonderful to touch, the fabric sliding noiselessly through her dark hands. The intensity of the pearl green fabric shifted in its curved movement. Embroidered upon it were the branches and flowers of a tree not known to her, yet its simplicity created a certain elegance.

'I thought the colour would match your eyes.'

'How can I thank you?'

'Your happiness is enough for me, my daughter.'

Raising her eyes, Amelia reached out for Izzy and wrapped her tightly in her arms.

'Do you think?'

'Yes Izzy. Just be patient with him. His life is not his own at the moment. But soon. Soon, it will be yours.'

It took a while to dress as the fitter demonstrated how the traditional shoes, socks and underwear were to be worn. As she helped each into the kimonos she spoke of the traditions of each piece and its importance. Finally, she tied the obi belt, sighing with great satisfaction as she did so. Her next task was to complete the ensemble with a proper hairstyle for each. And finally make up. As the women readied themselves so did the men.

Yacob dressed in a traditional western suit while Joseph squeezed into a formal kimono. First, he slipped into the traditional pants for bridegrooms. The hakama were not like any pants he had worn before, but to his surprise they were quite comfortable. Next came the short jacket kimono, the haori. Both were dark in colour, the jacket dyed with a family crest in five places. Situated on the back, two on the breast and one on each sleeve, the family crest was in a distinctive shape.

'Joseph. I thought the motifs were usually of plants.'

Yacob asked pointing at the monochrome crest on Joseph's sleeve.

'I'm not sure to be honest. Amelia insisted on this one.'

Joseph tugged the sleeve around to a better viewing point.

'Said it was a special family crest. Cho or something.'

'Meaning?'

Yacob asked straightening his tie not adverting his eyes from the mirror.

'Butterfly. I think. She said that old Japanese people believe the butterfly protected the soul.'

An involuntary chuckle escaped Yacob as he murmured to himself.

'She needs it.'

'Pardon?'

'You'll need it too I'd say.'

He slapped Joseph's back, his husky laughter rose even more.

****

Walking was a more conscious effort in the kimonos, especially for women with a western gait. Izzy found it difficult to change to the smaller, delicate shuffle of Japanese women. The foursome was escorted a short way from the city to a small Shinto shrine tucked neatly behind some trees. Sacred trees. From her vantage point, Izzy found the shrines to be very plain and simple. Each part, though, was distinct from the other. Some had reed-thatched rooves while others had a gabled or hipped-gable roof. The one Amelia led them to, the one she appeared to be familiar with, had natural trees that retained their bark, used as supports. Between the supports, Izzy dragged her hand gently against the earthen wall.

'I'm speechless Amelia. This place is beautiful.'

'Yes. Shinto is the indigenous faith of the Japanese people. They have objects of worship, or kami, which are sacred spirits. These can take various forms such as natural elements like the sun, mountains, trees, rocks, and the wind. Even abstract things like fertility, plus ancestors, protectors. I adore a religion that cherishes nature.'

'Is there a god?'

'Well yes. Shinto only contrasts with western religions in that there are no absolutes, yet there is a most important goddess. The sun goddess Amaterasu Onikami. It is an extremely optimistic faith, as it is thought that all humans are fundamentally good, and that all evil is caused by evil spirits.'

'A nice sentiment.'

'Anything to clear one's conscience.'

His tone an aroma of amused sarcasm: Yacob's jib is firmly aimed at Amelia.

'Yes, well. The Japanese' use of the gardens.'

Her finger pointing to a traditional garden beyond more trees.

'As with much else is to bring harmony.'

Glaring at Yacob.

'Such as the gentle trickling of water. Strategically positioned not only for its beauty, or purpose, but also for the gentle lull emitted.' Amelia continued speaking her voice becoming terse.

They were walking casually now, around the shrine selected by Amelia. Before they entered, she pointed out different features and the history behind each. As they approached the outer resting place of the shrine, a priest dressed in his own kimono, insigne with a religious family crest, awaited them. Pointing towards a small pavilion outside the building, they see two bowls of water, Joseph hesitates.

'Go Joseph. We must purify ourselves.'

Amelia shows them how by cleaning her hands then her mouth with the clean water. All follow suit except Yacob who stands back. Amelia faces him and searches his features.

'Please.'

She whispers.

Standing firm, Yacob does not move. His hands rest peacefully behind his back. The muscles in his jaw move to open his mouth, though tighten instead to seal it shut. Taking a step back, his head rocks in the universal sign of no. Izzy twists a small bag in her hand, nervous about the questioning look from the Shinto priest. Her father had always said, no matter whose house of the lord you go into, you must respect their traditions, as they must yours. Joseph approached, stopped only by Amelia's hand. Rising to full height Amelia stood square to Yacob and spoke in a very harsh language. Neither Joseph nor Izzy could follow the sentence as it was foreign and not any they had heard before. Yet a similar accent lingered in Izzy's mind, from a day that seemed distant now.

Yacob though, pales at the thought of an assassin standing outside the apartment his mother and grand-mother share. It may be a façade, on Amelia's half, but her family still had the contacts to do such things. Would he risk the lives of the two he most loved to prove her wrong? Besides, how had she known that other detail about his girlfriend? Face pasty white he slowly draws his hands forward as he approaches the bowls to purify himself.

Entering the shrine, Joseph and Amelia stand next to a small wooden altar while Izzy and Yacob stand to the side. As the priest is purifying the couple, to protect them from future harm, Izzy spots a movement at the door. A man, looking somewhat familiar, enters wearing a casual kimono. Detracting from the traditional look of his clothes was a diamond-studded watch. As the priest asks the gods to grant them long life and happiness, the man moves through the shadows behind Izzy. At this point the couple exchange a small cup, sipping from it several times.

Joseph clears his throat, and in English, reads some words of commitment. Accompanied by an ancient Japanese harp the pair exchange wedding rings. A handful of people have filtered into the shadows, much to Izzy's surprise and Yacob's anger. To further alarm him, the bride and groom momentarily proceed to the sanctuary to offer twigs of 'sakaki' sacred tree in worship, as a small offering, to the gods.

The service though short and simple has a very solemn atmosphere. All in the room are deathly quiet until the couple return. As they re-enter, young women clothed in red and white dresses serve sake to the guests who are now congratulating Amelia. Yacob gives her a cold stare as the man Izzy can't place gives her a kiss and a small envelope. He speaks to Amelia briefly in his own tongue, before congratulating Joseph in English. The other people are introduced as family.

Stepping forwards to congratulate the couple, the tiny shrine's warmth wraps tightly around Izzy's body. Before her blinking eyes swarm hundreds of black dots. Each absorbing the sense of gravity from her. Sinking into the feeling of weightlessness she stumbles into darkness.

~ 30 ~

REVELATIONS

Flying into Brazil was an uneventful trip. Rio was a bustling city, not that Mike was able to see much for they were soon hustled onto a light aircraft for Manaus, capital of the Amazon. Nearing their destination, he found it enthralling for his eyes to trace the coal black river as it snaked its way to the Atlantic. The numerous cuts it made in the forest turned the terrain into a green mosaic. Recognising that they were being leered at in their suits, Mike insisted that he and Kristov change. Anthony refused claiming he brought some civility to such a primitive place. Mike could only shrug.

With a silk handkerchief pressed upon his nose Anthony led the way. The path led them down to the ebony riverside, far away from the city's docks and commercial districts. Arriving at the small market they took in their surrounds. There were no more than two dozen stalls, some with blue plastic awnings to protect their owners from the inevitable rain. But despite its size, the market appeared to sell everything: from batteries to bananas, copper piping to Chinese firecrackers. And among the cornucopia there were animals. Lots of animals.

Sniffling, Anthony lit a cigarette.

'Oppressive, isn't it? Every week, traffickers from across the region travel here to buy and sell beasts of every kind.'

Mike felt uncomfortable for he noticed that not only were there regular stallholders, who were all banter and boisterousness, that there were other men interspersed in the market. This second type remained quiet, searching the crowd with their eyes. As he stood and stared, one of the men surreptitiously caught his eye. It was like a trigger bringing the man alive.

'Olha! Look at this.'

Said the old man, who swiftly opens a carrier bag for inspection. Inside were two brilliant blue parrots.

'See how fine they are. How healthy.'

Stroking them with a grubby finger, he pointed to their eyes.

'Look at these. How shiny! How clear!'

Despite the old man's pitch, to Mike the birds look anything but healthy. Most of their tail feathers were missing and they moved listlessly.

'Where are they from?'

'You want to buy? Good price!'

'No. Where did you get them?'

His manner changes abruptly as the bag is squashed shut.

'Never mind where it comes from. You want to buy?'

Stuffing the bag up his jumper, he shuffles off into the crowd when no answer is forthcoming.

Strolling around the market, the old man soon returns with a much younger man who is trying to look fashionable in a shell-suit.

'If you're interested in animals, you should talk to me.'

He says.

'I have many dealings with foreigners.'

As if this were some kind of signal, the old man makes himself scarce. Meanwhile, his shell-suited companion produces a scrapbook. He begins flicking through the pages, which show pictures of birds and snakes and monkeys. Every imaginable type of Amazonian animal, including jaguars.

'Anything you want from the rainforest.'

He states looking into Mike's astonished eyes.

'Anything at all. I can get it for you.'

'Be gone with you Drauzio!'

Cut a strong English accent.

'These men are gentlemen, not your style of deviate.'

Recognising the voice of his detractor, the shell-suited man hurriedly closed his scrapbook and disappeared amongst the crowd. Turning to see from whom the voice had come, Mike saw a wiry man approach.

'Our scientist.'

Stated Anthony.

Looking more like an English tourist than a scientist, Dr Barossa approached his obvious contacts.

'Pome git.'

Whispered Kristov to Mike as he took in the scientist's attire. Dr Barossa's pale shorts swept just above his knees, while his socks were stretched to just under the bony knobs. Wet and dark under the armpits, his shirt swung loosely on his body. To top off the ensemble was a traditional safari helmet. He looked as if he'd just stepped out of a Tarzan movie, not spent the last twenty years of his life in the Amazon jungle mixing it with the natives. When Dr Barossa wiped his forehead with a handkerchief, Kristov could not stifle his laughter any longer.

'This man could possibly be connected to our future, Kristov. Therefore, we must greet him with an open mind, no matter what our personal prejudices are.'

Taking a pace back, Kristov left Mike to greet the scientist.

'Pleased to meet you gentlemen.'

The scientist offered his hand.

'And you too Dr Barossa.'

Spoke Anthony refusing to lower his hand from the handkerchief on his mouth.

Mike leant forward with a friendly smile.

'Dr Barossa. I have heard great things about you. Your work with the Wapishana Indians decoding the ingredients in their traditional remedies is a prodigious read.'

'Yes yes. A lot of intellectual effort, a lot of money, thousands of my own, and no one takes any interest. Typical I suppose.'

'Yet your fortune may be changing my dear Dr Barossa.'

Finally, Anthony took an interest in the conversation.

Waving his hand flippantly, Dr Barossa indicated they

must leave to catch their boat upstream. An Indian native waited for them aboard a long dugout canoe. Balancing themselves, the men settled precariously into the canoe. Mike found a spot behind the doctor at the front of the boat. Appreciating an audience, a captive one at that, the doctor's mouth moved continually. His voice, a dull drone, buzzed about their ears. Anthony yawned, lit another cigarette before wiping his forehead for the hundredth time. Joey scooped at the water, inspecting its contents carefully. Annoyed by the persistent insects, Klaus brushed his arms before selecting a bug to torture. The only one to take interest in Dr Barossa's words was Mike.

'Manaus is so exciting, located at the confluence of the Negro and Amazon rivers. It is the point of the clearest dramatic union of a black-water stream and a white one, where the Rio Negro flows into the muddy Amazon.'

He turned to Mike specifically.

'For many miles the black and white waters flow side by side in separate, clearly defined streams before they finally intermingle. Incredible.'

'Sounds unique.'

Offered Mike.

'Yet today.'

Continued the doctor.

'We are travelling upstream, until we are hidden in the canopy, for that is where the real work begins.'

Tapping the side of his nose with an extended pointer finger, the doctor winks at Mike.

An electric motor on the canoe drove them along at a steady pace. Soon any sign of civilisation was left behind as they cornered bend after bend along the mighty river. Tropical vegetation grew thick and strong along the banks. Frequently the songs of birds, monkeys chattering and the squeal of death flooded their ears. Under the muddy banks the croaking of frogs rose. Mike absorbed his surroundings, appreciating the clarity only nature could provide. Anthony on the other hand muttered continually about *this mosquito-infested swamp.*

When it appeared they were as lost as could be, the native directed the canoe to a bank, aiming it towards a fallen trunk. Without slowing the canoe's pace, he yelled *Duck!* when they were a foot from the moss-covered remnant of a tree. Immediately obeying, the men were surprised to find themselves travelling up a smaller stream. It narrowed rapidly with the overgrowth striking severe and stinging blows at them. As the growth closed in, blocking any possible light the native yelled *Duck!* again. Responding in unison like a well-trained bobsled team, their heads barely missed another fallen trunk. Yet this time they lifted them to see a small lagoon bathed in sunlight. On the far side were other canoes dragged uncaringly ashore. Beyond that a narrow path cut roughly through the growth.

Quietly following the chatty doctor, the men were led to a collection of buildings. The smaller cabins were obviously for housing while the larger contained a well set up, yet outdated, laboratory. An incredibly large, incredibly dark African dressed in a traditional baggy gown and pants with a small circular matching hat on his shiny hairless head greeted them at the door.

'You made it safely then?' He spoke in a heavy Liverpool accent.

'Thank-you Axo. We did. Please meet, Michael Ricoldi, Anthony Valentine and?'

Here he paused, looking at the two men.

'Joey Mandell.'

Offered Joey with a smile and jaunty wave.

'Kristov.'

Huffed Kristov screwing his nose up with his surrounds.

'Welcome to our humble abode. Please join us for some tea.'

Bowing deeply, Axo swept an arm to direct them to a small table along the laboratory's verandah. It was enclosed in the white cloth of mosquito netting.

'Gomes.'

He indicated towards the native who was carrying their overnight bags.

'Will place your things.'

'Man Axo, I have never met anyone so tall.'

Blurted Mike's youthful mind as he offered his hand.

'You are way taller than the basketballers in the US.'

A row of straight pearly whites greeted Mike's remark.

'I have only met two men who came close to my height, both blacks. The whites only pale in comparison.'

A rumble rose from his belly, exploding from his mouth. Comparable to a small dozer, the noise startled not only a couple of macaws in a nearby tree but Anthony who sweated profusely in his suit.

Arm around Mike's shoulders Axo led him to the table,

drawing the netting aside for him to pass. The other men were left to follow. Kristov kept eyeing off the native.

'Are they trustworthy?'

He asked the doctor.

'They have all they need here. Your few measly possessions would mean little to them.'

Around the table the men sat sipping English tea and ate freshly made scones. Anthony was eager to discuss business because he had no desire to stay in this place too long. Cigarette after cigarette trailed to his mouth. Twitching in his seat he squatted his neck repeatedly.

'So, what is it you need doctor?'

'Relax, look around. Take the time to see what I have and can offer before we rush into anything.'

'With the time restraints we have doctor, the sooner we are out of this miserable place the better.'

Shooting smoke through his nostrils, Anthony leant towards the doctor.

'Besides everything has a price.'

Enduring the smell of an endless chain of cigarettes, Mike happily accepts Axo's invitation to peruse the lab, and more specifically, the work they did. Axo was friendly and quick with a joke. His patience for Anthony was lacking but Mike surmised most peoples was. Anthony always believed in the quick fix solution. Throw money in people's face. Mike on the other hand was taught to learn about the person you were dealing with. Find their strong, and weak points, and play upon those.

'Only a tiny percentage of Amazonia's millions of species of plants and animals are known to science. But those few that have been studied have already yielded valuable foods, medicines and commercial products.'

Stated Axo as he gestured Mike to look through the lens of a microscope. Adjusting the viewer Mike studied the miniature landscape.

'How do the native Indians feel about that?'

'We have worked with the local Indians for over twenty years and during that time have catalogued many of their traditional remedies. No one is trying to stop people using the specific remedies discovered, but this knowledge has always been with the Indians such as the Wapishana. It's part of their heritage and they are afraid it will be taken from them without payment.'

'Payment in what form? Money? Education? What is it they really need?'

'No one has ever bothered to ask that before my young friend.'

Axo's large fingers slap Mike's shoulder. Mike was sure that if Axo so desired, he could crush his skull with one hand. Its immenseness was incredible.

'Maybe we should get you out to meet the natives.'

'I would like that but I'm not sure how my companions would cope.'

'Not to worry the doctor will keep them entertained.'

The glint in his eye gave it away to Mike who looked Axo squarely in the eyes.

'What is it you are looking for Axo?'

'Did you not come all this way to ask the doctor that?'

'No, I was more inclined to ask the man who had given his life and soul to a people who could not defend themselves. A man who graduated with the highest honours at Cambridge. A man who likes to be underestimated.'

'Ah. So, my little secret is out. You are a wise young man, Michael. Now your reward. I have spent my life creating a register of natural remedies. Cataloguing which plants the tribes used, where they grew, what time of year they should be harvested, their Indian names, the part of the plants used, and how to prepare and administer it.'

'And I take it that should not be passed onto just anybody. Considering the recent rash of wide-scale smuggling of genetic material by unauthorised companies and how the government has taken to that, not to mention the local natives who inadvertently assisted the companies.'

'A man who has done his research. Yes, each year, 24 million cubic metres of timber is illegally removed from the Amazon. Genetic material is far easier to take because it is smaller, so I have no doubt about the extent of biopiracy.'

Rubbing his chin Mike thought for a moment. Axo studied him with massive arms crossing his chest.

'But the plant isn't as important as the intellectual effort. The decoding process?'

'I will have to watch myself with you young Michael! You are a keen observer. We will get on well.'

Mike involuntarily stepped forward from the force of Axo's hand slapping his back, again. Accompanying each slap was the thunderous laugh.

~ 31 ~

IT IS YOU OR I

Kyoto, Japan.

My head feels so heavy, but not an ounce of alcohol has passed my lips. The last thing I remember is the striking figure Amelia and Joseph looked in their wedding kimonos. That's right, I was just about to congratulate them when I felt funny. Those blurry black dots, like flies swarmed around me and then... Then, I felt as if I was floating, drifting down in a spiral of darkness. My eyelids are heavy, even now, it takes all my might to pry them open.

'Oh, Izzy I am glad you are okay.'

States Amelia, wringing out a cold cloth and resettling it on Izzy's head.

Afternoon light teams through an open window, savagely biting at Izzy's eyes. Slowly she raises her arm, the movement forced, before resting it across her eyes.

'What happened?'

'You fainted, my dear.'

Responds a voice filled with motherly concern.

Repositioning herself on the futon, Izzy involuntarily

throws both arms to her sides, her hands clasping to gain hold of anything stable. Sending a request through a paper screen, Amelia holds a second wet cloth firmly to Izzy's forehead until a girl returns with a bucket. Taking that as her cue, Izzy violently turns to the futon's side and expels the contents of her stomach. Straightening herself out on the futon again she squints at Amelia who is smiling.

'What?'

'Nothing dear. Nothing at all.'

Her smile compounded. *She would find out soon enough.*

'Where are we?'

Till this moment Izzy had taken little notice of their surrounds, but now as she glanced about the room it was obvious, they were not at the ryokan. The room was richly decorated with antique vases, early Japanese armour and the most exquisite paintings Izzy had ever seen. Nor had she seen so much gold leaf.

'Mr Kanazawa invited us to his home for a wedding meal.'

'The one at the shrine with the watch.'

Nodding with a bemused smile, Amelia looked at Izzy adoringly.

'I'd seen him before, but I couldn't place it.'

Yes, nodded Amelia.

'The kitchen! The kitchen at that teahouse.'

A tap at the screen interrupts the pair. It was the young girl again, this time she brought a message for Amelia. With her hand she directs Amelia's gaze to the window. Beyond it was Yacob, his mobile phone drawn, raised in the air. He was searching for a signal strong enough to use the phone. Excusing herself Amelia slips quietly from the room. Joined by one of Mr Kanazawa's men, Yasue, they head towards the foyer. Passing the party on the way, Amelia is stopped by Joseph. Tenderly taking her arm, an inquisitive look clouds his features.

'Care to dance with your husband?'

Eyes watery from the generous servings of sake.

'I'd love to my sweetheart, but Yacob awaits me.'

Scooping her in his arms, Joseph swirls Amelia about the floor, intermittently stumbling on the tatami mats. After the fourth stumble, Amelia squirms loose from his grip. Leaning close, she kisses his moist lips.

'I know that look Amelia. I thought you had given up that life.'

'What? We are just going to have a chat.'

Rolling his eyes, he rocks her hand in his.

'Will he come back alive?'

What could she say? Did she have the answer to that?

'Will he?'

His voice resigned now.

'Yes Joseph. Yes.'

Searching her face, her eyes were set in the distance, seeing an unknown spot above his shoulder. A look he had seen before. Sighing in surrender Joseph drops her hand a finger at a time.

'I know that look. Your mind is made. Please don't humour me, not on our wedding night.'

'You think so poorly of me, do you?'

Joseph turns from her.

'I am going to have a chat, nothing else. Mike will be here in a day, I will have him replaced.'

'He is not Rosario! He never will be. Nor will the next poor fellow. Give it a rest. From what I can see, you are your own worst enemy. Nobody can protect you from yourself.'

'Maybe you are right Joseph, but I fear what might happen to Mike. Yacob is the key to that.'

Cupping his face in her hands.

'I promise you, I will not do anything stupid.'

Moving her face towards his, she tilts it slightly.

'I love you with all my heart.'

Their lips meet fleetingly, a tear traces a lonely path along her cheek. The kiss lengthens, neither wishes to release the other.

As they separate.

'Let's leave all this and find ourselves. Go as far away as it takes. Just you and me.'

'I'd love to Joseph, but my children need me.'

Walking away from Joseph, Amelia feels a stabbing pain in her heart. If only she could do as he asked. Walking away from it all, was that an option? Was that not what her death was about? Her life had been a self-destruct missile and, she promised herself, Mike's would not be the same, even if it took her dying breath to help him.

****

Yasue accompanied Amelia to the underground station, for it was here that she knew Yacob would be. Dropping her off at the entrance, Yasue insisted she wait, but she was unable to, the matter was too pressing. Descending into the artificial light of the subway station she spies Yacob. He, a solitary figure, standing a full foot or two above the other travellers. Phone pressed to his ear, he urgently walks in a small invisible circle as words congest in his mouth. Hurriedly he tries to expel the information he has.

She, herself, was not hard to notice. Her hurried steps down the long escalator, the traditional kimono restricting her movement as she forces her way through the growing crowd. Eyes turn to take in the magnificence of her gown, hands reach to touch. Each individual movement slowing her down.

Mutual anger displays itself on each of their faces. Yacob stares at her before flipping his phone shut. Panting from the extra effort caused by the kimono, she waits to regain her breath. His face bears down on hers.

'Mrs Ricoldi what can I do for you? You don't mind me using your real name, do you? You seem to have no need to conceal it, the way you have been flaunting yourself around Japan!'

His questions require no answers for they are sarcastic little statements that heighten his reddening face.

'No fear, I have just come off the phone from Klaus.'

'What did you tell him?'

'Oh, nothing too thrilling. Just that you were hanging around a Mr Kanazawa, a Don of sorts himself, really.'

'You had no right. I have been lenient with you so far but now!'

Breath finally came to Amelia, yet the destination of this conversation had not.

'Lenient. Ha!'

His nose pressed right into hers. A film of sweat and city grime the only barrier between their skin.

'I am the one in control. You are not!'

Eyes level. Staring with pure hatred.

'You haven't seemed to grasp that you don't exist. Let me show you.'

Fingers encircled her throat. Each digging in tight to the pale skin of her neck. Raising her slightly, her toes barely touch the tiled floor. Yacob commences to hustle her towards the platform's edge.

'If I kill you now, no-one will be the wiser. And you know what? They couldn't sentence a man for killing a person who was already dead.'

'Yacob, no.'

Each breathe fading rapidly. Supported only by shortened inhalements, made more difficult by his pressing fingers. Gasping, other passengers stand by agog. Their bodies frozen by the terror in her eyes.

'Sorry, it must be an evil spirit or something.'

In his red sea of anger Yacob clasps Amelia's throat even tighter. He begins shaking her with exaggerated movements. Unlike the other women in his life, she does not go limp to soften the coming blows. She stands firm, as firm as her tippee toes allow. Her eyes defying him. Clipping her face, his fist is set to mesh with her skull again when a breeze fills the subway tunnel. It is a coming train. Grimacing like a madman, Yacob shakes her over the platforms edge.

Teetering on the edge, the traditional shoes she wears fall to the steel track below. Barely making a sound as the whistling of the oncoming train overtook all rational thought. Frantically trying to remain footed to the platform, Amelia squirms in Yacob's grasp. Bulging from their sockets, her eyes can barely focus yet in the distance she sees something. Forming the word with her lips, Yacob loosens his stranglehold a fraction to see what she sees. In that millisecond Amelia's senses come together. A searing pain explodes in Yacob's groin as her knee connects with it. Doubling over slightly, Yacob releases his grip enough for Amelia to touch firm ground. As her feet touch the cool tiles, her hands claw Yacob's face. Searching frantically, her thumbs find their mark. Penetrating the eye cavity, she feels his eyeballs pop. Falling to his knees Yacob drags Amelia with him.

Rich, oxygen infused blood flows down his cheeks like tears, but his grasp on Amelia is consistent. Rising to his unsteady feet, Yacob can feel the train upon them. Swinging her in the direction, of what he hopes is the track, he feels her sink. With all the might she has left, Amelia clasps Yacob's forearms, and using the momentum from his strength, swings in the direction he's pushing. The pair pirouette a full 180 degrees and as Yacob swings round his shoulder and head collide with something metal.

Still possessing a certain amount of speed, the slowing train collides with Yacob carrying him several metres before dropping his body limply to the track. Dragged at first, Amelia is eventually thrown from the impact when Yacob's grip could hold no more. Echoing screams filled the underground station. Terrified commuters ran hysterically from the platform.

****

'Amelia!'

Bouncing through her head the voice was somehow familiar.

'Amelia.'

There it was again. Somehow Amelia knew that she should know the owner of the voice yet the spinning sensation wouldn't allow the pieces to come together. When the nauseum of the spinning had settled slightly, she ventured to open one eye.

'Joseph?'

Weak and unsure, her words scratched past the dryness in her throat.

'Yes, my love. It's me. Stay still, Yasue is getting a private ambulance.'

'I didn't mean.'

Attempting to rock her head in the universal no, Amelia could feel a dampness in her hair. Coolness coated her skin, feeling like the evening fog of the Brisbane River. How the white nothingness wrapped around her body, she felt its touch now.

'I know. I know. Save your energy my love.'

Stress filled every syllable.

'I didn't mean to hurt him.'

'Ssshh. It's okay.'

Muttering the words as soothingly as he could muster.

'I promised, to you, I wouldn't.'

Her words punctuated by short gasps of breath. She felt the warmth about her eyes but was unsure whether it was tears or blood.

~ 32 ~

MONKEY MADNESS

Dining alone in the privacy of Axo's cabin, Mike refilled their glasses. Swirling the crimson liquid, the large man drew in the scent of the wooded grapes. Eyes skimmed the rim of the glass, Axo finally sips the fluid.

'Mmm. So, tell me Michael, what is it you are really after?'

Acting coy, Mike felt Axo's studying eyes upon him.

'With the plant extracts? What we all want, to find a cure to the shocking diseases in the world.'

'Your mother said you were a smart one.'

Wagging his finger.

'But you can't fool Axo. No sir.'

'You knew my mother?'

Inexperience coupled with eagerness shoved the words out.

Reclining, Axo acknowledged his captive audience as the story of he and Amelia unravelled. Encumbered with child Amelia had returned to her homeland, Australia.

Using certain contacts and funds appearing from apparently nowhere, she managed to purchase a segment of what is now known as Kuntana. Working hard, she laboured on the overgrown earth, trying to reclaim the rich soil beneath. This is where Axo first met her. Recalling the moment with fondness, he pauses, reminiscing, until Mike prompts him to continue.

'Ah. She was like the women of my youth. For I was not born in England you know?'

Straying from the path it takes several minutes to lead Axo away from Africa and back to his mother.

'Yes, she had you wrapped tightly in a sarong, which she tied about her body. Nearby under a tree was Roberto. When she could, she would suspend you both in the sarong from the branches, swaying the two of you asleep. As she moved through the backbreaking work of clearing the land, she would sing songs to you.'

Tales of Axo's Mama doing this for him shone above the main story Mike was interested in, but he listened politely. For it appeared a long time since Axo recalled his youth. Skirmishes in the dirt with his half-brothers brought a shine to his eyes, while myths his grandmother told reduced his features to humbleness.

During this backbreaking work was when Axo found Amelia and her 'husband', Rosario. Both toiled night and day, trying to improve the land enough to be self-sufficient. Axo, himself, was backpacking through Australia before his final year at university. Asking for work, he was told all they could pay was food and board. Seeing the fatigue in Amelia's face, he gratefully accepted, being the

English gentleman, he was. Not once though, did he hear her complain, nor see her shirk any share of work.

As the last rays of light died in the horizon, the five of them would return to the slab hut ready to devour anything possible. Axo recalled that each meal shared with this small family was very special. Every meal was a unique experience. Each night the table would be set with a clean linen tablecloth, and linen napkins were folded neatly at each setting. Her finest china, delicate crystal, polished wedding silverware were all featured. Fatigued as she was, Amelia would prepare a hearty meal, presenting it in a way that made them feel as if they were dining in the best restaurants. To assist her the men would entertain the boys.

'I was so fortunate to become a part of their world, your world.'

To Axo, no other time was more joyful than the time he spent with Amelia and Rosario. The work was hard, the days were long, yet there was plenty of laughter. Laughter was the key he said. Laughter alone could brighten any day.

'Some would say it was complete isolation. But truly it was a world in itself. Mind you we had some fun too. Your mother sure can dance. Often, we would make the long journey into town, hitching a ride if we could. You boys loved it too. Fussed over by the woman and all. Ah yes.'

'A world in itself.'

He repeated. His next words revealed his fear for Amelia, thus displaying his genuine affection for her.

'Never again did I see Amelia as happy as those times.

God rest her soul. I hope she found that happiness again before she died.'

Rolling on, the tale included details Mike had never even considered before. His childhood memory could not recall any antics involving monkeys and himself in Amazonia. Persistently Axo declared Mike had visited him before when he was much, much younger.

'She took such a keen interest in the tribal people. With her help this lab was set up and steps were taken to halt any biopiracy and the like in this area. An incredible feat really.'

'Securing the market, making it profitable. That's all she was doing.'

Disgusted that his mother was one step ahead.

'Don't be so critical Michael, weren't you considering doing the same!'

Holding the glass forth for more refilling, Axo's smile vanished.

'Look around you Michael. This is all yours already.'

Bursting from his mouth was a small sound similar to laughter, its tone was more mocking than humorous.

'The natives around here love you. Your patronage has saved them. It's saved their forest. It's saved their heritage.'

This fact was true, for in the area where they now sat, no organics or animals were ever stolen or sold. All the local natives were well educated, as were their children. In a whole, they had acquired a lot from this controlled research. Yes, the Ricoldi's had made money from this investment, gained political power and presence, defeated adversaries, but at the ground level the Amazonian people, in this area, were controlling their own lives, making their own decisions.

Quietness filled the room. Small, unknown feet scuttled in the far corner, neither man cared to look. Swirling the fluid once more, Axo's mouth opened wide allowing the liquid to vanish in one bob of his Adam's apple.

'Under her wishes I returned to England to complete my Masters, and with her help, we set up this laboratory. The rest, as they say, is history.'

Studying the boy's face, Axo was dismayed. Changing tone, he continued.

'You are so much like her.'

His hand waving Mike's words down.

'No, no, you are. I can see you chomping at the bit to prove your independence, your strength, your individuality. Flaunting convention, if you like. But, my boy, remember this. Rebel as hard as you like, the more you do, the more you replicate her.'

Mike rose without a word. Looking Axo in the eye, he spoke.

'Thank you for a most enjoyable evening. I will retire to my room now. Good night.'

Turning to leave, he could hear Axo suck air through his teeth. The tone that pursued him to the door was heavily serious.

'Use it to your advantage Nicosia. Quit fighting it.'

****

Moonlight gleamed through the high leaves, crisscrossing the path before him. He was tired from the day's events, but bed held no appeal at this moment. His ears had burned under Axo's tutorage for the last few hours. His desire now was for peace and quiet where he could stew alone.

Was he really the reincarnate of his mother? Could others only ever see that in him? Mike's mind tossed the question about. Over and over it rolled. What annoyed him the most was that this should offend him, but it didn't. In fact, he felt a little parcel of pride well up deep inside. Taking lungful's of the rainforest air, Mike felt like screaming. The pungent smell of decomposition continually drew him to home. Kuntana.

That was the problem. His mind had touched it before flicking it aside. Now that smell brought it all back into focus. Kuntana. Why if his mother had never been happier, than those earlier days, did she take the path she had? Mike wanted to return to that time of his youth, see it again with adult eyes. Draw the happiness close to him and hold it tight. Was she like that with his father? Or was she even happier then? Reaching into his breast pocket, Mike withdrew the worn photo of the three of them. All smiles except for him. Shifting it slowly, his thumb traced her smile before coming to rest on his father's. What if?

****

Morning descended with a clatter of squawks and screeches. The native, Gomes, stands in the clearing between the huts, clicking his tongue. From a satchel at his waist, he draws an assortment of vegetable scraps, fruits, leaves and berries. Flinging the bag's contents across the ground he continues to click rhythmically. Viewing the activities from the screened doorway, Joey watches as the weirdest assortment of animals he has ever seen, congregate in the clearing.

Gaily coloured birds flock in the nearby trees, cautiously swooping down to pick up little delicacies. Large animals arrive from amongst the deep foliage. Several rodent-like creatures scamper past Joey's door, tussling over a large piece of fruit. Laughing, Joey invites Kristov to see the antics. Kristov just huffs and rolls over in his bunk.

Grabbing his camera, Joey makes a move to get close to a small monkey attempting to crack open a nut. Crouching down as low as possible, adjusting the focus as he does, Joey moves within range. Gomes commences laughing just as Joey realises he has been hit by a small pickpocket. The monkey's playmate snuck behind Joey and relieved him of his satellite phone. Racing around like a lunatic, man following beast, the other monkeys join in with what sounds like chanted laughter. Being of no assistance, Gomes is crippled with amusement. Joining the foray came a collection of laughter from the other cabins.

Eventually, to Joey's delight, the game came to an end when the phone releases a shrill squeal. Startled, the monkey drops the phone and joins his friends in the tree-tops, staying close enough in case the game starts again. Retrieving the phone, Joey pants his name into the handpiece. Inhaling deeply, Joey fails to take a breath for the remainder of the call.

****

Having missed the morning antics, Mike is startled by the knock at the screen door. Rubbing sleep from his eyes, he sees Joey's outline enter the room. Frowning, he smiles lopsidedly at Anthony's assistant as he raises his body onto one elbow. Settling into the chair beside the bed, Joey rubs his palms, his eyes studying the floorboards.

'I hope you're not here to kill me Joey, because it's too early in the morning for that.'

'No Mr Ricoldi.'

A glimmer of a smile flashes past.

'I've had some news. About your mother. Mr Bodine rang.'

'My Mother? Why would he call you?'

His interest was piqued.

~ 33 ~

A ROAD LESS TRAVELLED

Kissing her gently, he notices she does not withdraw from him. Instead, her body presses harder into his chest cavity. Tasting her, his tongue explores their linked mouths. Caressingly one hand tumbles across his chest. The other ruffles his hair, drawing him closer. Desire grows with each prolonged touch.

'I love you, Joseph Bodine.'

The words escape in the momentary lapse of touch.

'And I love you, Amelia Bodine.'

A brief laugh escapes before their lips meld. Oblivious to the world outside their embrace, neither notice a tall lean shadow enter the room. An obvious cough startles their moment.

'Mother, good to see you are okay.'

Viewing Joseph's back, Mike stands in a far corner of the hospital room, his head slung low, disgusted by the flagrant devotion.

Straightening his back, Joseph rises, kissing Amelia's

cheek, he turns to Mike. Mike's eyes have not moved from where Joseph had been. His view now encompasses his mother. Her eyes are as dark as the marks that circumnavigate her throat. Two thick purple black lines cross under her chin, where Yacob's thumbs had overlapped. Intermittently between the darkness is the pale skin he remembers. Bloated lips offer a weak smile.

Staring at the changes Mike is speechless. The once glorious hair had been shortened dramatically. In a section from just above Amelia's left ear, circling towards the back of her skull, it is shaved bare. The sparse hair above the only covering for the stitches. Feeling his piercing eyes, Amelia touches the spot. Drifting across the prickliness her fingers trace the stitches, one by one. Counting them as she has before.

'We were just changing the dressing.'

She justifies.

'Here sit beside me.'

Patting the blanket.

Eyes transfixed, Mike moves to his mother's side. Cupping his hand in hers, Amelia rubs them gently, all the time smiling at her son. Silence revolves around them.

'How was Axo?'

Dramatically his features change. Tightening, his lips purse into a disappointed pout she remembers from his childhood. Furrowing, his brow creases down between his eyes.

'Why didn't you tell me?'

Fleetingly he attempts to withdraw his hand from her grasp.

'It was your secret, remember. You were going off to conquer the world.'

No bitterness punctuated the words.

'How did you know?'

His frown had turned inquisitive.

'Anthony can be very persuasive at times. He was disappointed when I rejected his plans. I knew he would pursue it elsewhere. And he did.'

Her face was not harsh, it captured understanding sprinkled with motherly love.

'And this?'

Hesitantly he touched the bruising on her cheek and throat.

'Lack of foresight.'

As her shrugged shoulders droop, so do her dark eyes.

Both sat staring at their hands for a long period. No words needed to pass between them. Unknowingly Joseph had slipped from the room. He was met in the hallway by several of Mr Kanazawa's men and Joey. Joey was very anxious to see Amelia but was advised by Joseph to give her a few minutes.

****

Preoccupied with his mother's situation, Mike failed to notice when Kristov allowed Izzy to enter his hotel room. He sat on the bed, head slung low, trying to lock all the pieces together. Yet the more he discovered about his life, and his mother, the larger and more unfathomable the puzzle became. Seeing him there in such a depressed state, Izzy moves quietly towards him. Her footsteps whisper across the carpet. Untying the loose belt, she lets the kimono fall about her feet. Silently the fabric crumples.

Bare delicate toes catch Mike's attention. It was in the middle of the process of studying her glittery toenail polish that the falling gown glimmered before him. Without looking at her body, the warmth surged through his veins. Raising his head, he found his face within inches of her chocolaty skin. His eyes rise to meet hers.

'I've missed you.'

She whispered in her slight accent.

Pulling her closer, his ear rests upon her belly. Minute hairs tickle his lobe. Her scent is strong, consuming, overpowering. Tracing the bumps of her spine, his fingers come to rest on her fleshy bottom. Mike can feel his arousal. With a gentle tug, he pulls her down on top of him. Sprawled on the bed, Izzy's naked body flutters upon his, like a winter's leaf.

Straining her hair with shaking fingers, their lips meet. Allowing the hair to drop, conceals their smiles in semi-darkness. Tracing his lips, her tongue darts within his mouth. Vanished from her face, Mike's hands are beneath her trying to loosen his trousers. Rubbing herself against him, his preoccupied hands struggle. Thrusting upwards his desire for her is strong. Holding her tightly, Mike's face contorts with desire.

'I love you.' *I truly do.*

Panted into Izzy's ear, the words are what she's been dying to hear. Guiding him, she initiates their lovemaking. It is all encompassing, nothing penetrates their sphere of desire.

With as much energy as he used in the bed, Mike leaps from its sheets. Enlightenment dawns upon his face. Izzy resettles beneath the covers her body drenched in sweat. Kneeling beside her in all his splendour, Mike takes up her hand. Biting his bottom lip, his face has changed. A serious hue has taken control.

'I Nicosia Michael Ricoldi, would like you, Isabelle Lancove to be my dutiful wife.'

Erased is the seriousness with that prevailing cheeky grin.

'Dutiful? Huh. And what about this Ricoldi? I thought your name was Dart.'

'Well yes, at times it has been.'

Clasping both hands about hers.

'For business purposes, but my true name is Ricoldi. And I am proud of that.'

'What would I be known as?'

'Mrs Isabella Ricoldi!'

'Isabella?!' *Are you kidding?*

'More Italian hey.'

Slapping him playfully, she realises he is joking. Taking his original tone, he continues with his plea.

'So will you marry this poor Italian male?'

'Poor! I've struck out all the way round, haven't I? Lucky, I love you.'

Kissing him seductively.

'Yes, I'll marry you.'

Throwing back the sheets.

'So, get in here and fulfil your duty, again.'

****

A rusty morning haze clings to the window. Rising in the sky, the sun sends its arc about, yet only its light energy can penetrate the glass. Gliding through in droplets, it manages to coil itself around the two entwined young bodies. Feeling the morning's coolness, Izzy tugs on the blankets. Her eyes remain closed as Mike rolls to enclose her in his arms. Lying there, feeling his breathing on her back. Inhale, pause, exhale. The exhaled breath puffs about her neck. Still warm, it has lost the sweetness of the night before.

'Come with me when I leave.'

'What about your mother? She will need assistance.' *More so than before.*

Drawing her in tighter.

'She has Joseph.'

'Yes, but.'

Selecting her words carefully.

'What about your business? I don't want to sit around in a hotel waiting for you. Amelia needs my help.'

Turning slightly to view his reaction. A small pout exists.

'Suppose. But I'll miss you.'

Kissing her, he can see the worry in those emerald eyes. The care she shows Amelia scares him slightly.

'That was a lovely kimono you wore last night for all of...ah...three seconds.'

Nuzzling into her now, Izzy's face filled with enchanted dreams. Her smile grew broad in the memory of the event.

'Your mother gave it to me to wear to the wedding.'

'What wedding?'

'Hers.'

Her eagerness to divulge the special ceremony was lost on him. Rattling on Izzy failed to notice the consternation on Mike's face. His hands fell cold and unwelcoming. Describing in detail the facts, as she knew them, Izzy failed to comprehend why Mike rose and hurriedly dressed.

'I'll be back soon.'

Slipping out the door before a protest, Izzy was confused. *Surely, he knew about the arrangement, he was her son for goodness sakes. Family stuck together.*

Without waking his constant companion, Mike ushered himself into the hospital unnoticed except for a couple of Mr Kanazawa's men. Recognising the young man, they allowed him to pass freely into Amelia's room.

'What's this?'

He shouted.

Amelia was barely awake. A nurse was assisting her in wiping her face with a fresh washer, trying to avoid the sorer parts. Her shaking hands unable to keep the cloth steady or in place. Mike's entrance startled her, and with a quick pat to her hair, she settled the hands into her lap where they continued to dance. Forcing them lower into the blankets, Amelia carried on as if nothing was amiss.

'What's what, Nicco?'

'This marriage thing!'

Nodding gently, Amelia's dark eyes looked out from their pale sockets. The random bruising gave her a mottled look, for the skin that was not bruised was as pale as porcelain. Not her natural, effervescent shade.

'You told me to do something with my life. So, I'm no longer a Ricoldi.' *What more could I do?*

Arms flailing at his sides, Mike could not find suitable words. Sound escaped him momentarily, his brain somersaulting on the facts.

'Fuck mum, you didn't even invite me. Did you think I would oppose it?'

'No.'

'You treat me as if I don't exist.' *And it hurts.*

'Well, you aren't inviting me to yours. Are you?'

'You're dead! Or supposedly so. How could I invite you?'

'Not seeing my only child marry the woman of his dreams, you think that doesn't hurt.'

Watery eyes looked up at him. They held none of the strength or majesty that he remembered. Fear grew in them. A fear he would never understand. Raising a hand to her temple, Amelia was barely able to control it. Falling, it failed to hide her tears.

'Mum.'

Rushing to her side, Mike thought he glimpsed her vulnerability. After all these years, she was human. Breakable.

A small voice he didn't recognize tumbled from her mouth. Soft, in a selfish manner it fluttered past his ears. Leaning closer he asked her to repeat the words.

'I want to go home.'

Her eyes were pleading now.

'Kuntana? That wouldn't be possible.'

'No. Home.'

His shrug was an indication for her to explain.

'That small slab hut, some kilometres to the east of Kuntana's homestead.'

'The one the jackaroos use during round up.'

Hidden away in a small valley, the hut had existed for as long as Mike could remember. It sat regally halfway up the valley wall, overlooking the creek and land below. For an area of about three acres, the land was clear of any scrub or trees. The grasses were long on the occasions no cattle were grazed there. Looking as if long ago it had been purposefully cleared. Was it the secret place he and Roberto hid when they had done wrong? Could this be the place Axo spoke of? Somewhere close and familiar all along?

'Yes there.'

Her eyes had unfocused beyond him. They were in the time she remembered, they were in the place she called home.

'When you're asleep, the mist sneaks in to blanket the land, trapping the land smells. Eucalypt oil from the big gums, dingoes, manure from the animals. All of that. By morning the mist has lifted, taking with it every odour and scent, leaving the day renewed, fresh.' *My place. Mistyvale.*

PART FIVE

The Final Journey

~ 34 ~

LET THE JOURNEY END

New Farm, Brisbane.

It had amused him to think that he had been responsible for many murders, and many illegal acts. Yet inside he was interested only in the simplest things. Basic things, such as his small vegetable garden at Kuntana, being loved for who he was, loving indiscriminately, raising his boy and enjoying good meals with great friends. Amelia's death had taken much from him. Most of all his best friend and confidant. From all points of view, he was her rock, her confidant. The great protector, Rosario.

On the flipside, her death removed a burden, opening a life he had only ever dreamed of. For here now, he sat in bed with his long-time lover, sharing a newspaper. A simple everyday thing for most but an extraordinary event for him. Lowering his feet to the floor, Rosario looked up to see his reflection in the mirrored dresser.

Once proud and strong his face was now stained by an indulgent and sometimes stressful life. Somewhere along the line, the laugh lines surrounding his mouth had changed themselves into deep creases. Extra skin hung about his jowls, apparently slipping from beneath his eyes. With his fingertips, Rosario pushes the skin up beneath his colourless eyes, as if the action would reconnect the skin in its original place. Lines, more like deep gouges stream from his eyes towards his ears and beyond to the hairline. Running his fingers higher, Rosario attempts to smooth out the gouges in vain.

Rising to his feet, his view encompassed his complete body. To him it looks tired and in need of a rest. Like always the wispy hairs on his chest conceal the nipples. Yet the colour had changed, from the strong black of his childhood to a more muted grey-brown. Pulling the waistband of his boxer shorts, Rosario shook his head.

'This body is in serious need of attention.'

'Then what was last night?'

Responded a pouting Phil.

'No. I need to get back into shape. Go running like I used to. That type of thing.'

'Shaping up for someone new, are we? Sick of me already? '

In a joking manner the words were said but Rosario knew Phil partially believed what he was saying. His insecurities were always surfacing when he felt Rosario was about to walk out the door and not return for a month, or two or even three. Partially standing with one knee resting on the bed's covers, Rosario slid Phil's hand into his. Raising it to his mouth he gently kissed it.

'Nothing could match that of which I already have. Why go out for takeaway when you have steak at home.'

Blushing under the complement, Phil's face lit up with a dazzling smile. The same smile that had caught his attention ten years ago. Rosario paused at the thought of their first meeting. It wasn't romantic, exciting, or appropriate.

Amelia and he had flown to Japan to contact a man with similar business interests. Rosario was unsure of how the man felt about dealing with a woman, but in such circumstances, Amelia easily transformed into the submissive role, catering to the male ego. She alone performed the tea ceremony to the man's obvious surprise. Her knowledge of the customs commendable. In a matter of hours, they had achieved an alliance that was solid, and would be reinforced at every opportunity.

Despite their tiredness from a hurried schedule the pair managed to fly out early the next day, to be home in time for one of Vito's birthday bashes. Rosario could not see why Amelia made such incredible efforts to attend these parties. Especially with her strong dislike for the man. But every effort was made, and they arrived in time.

'I know that look Rosario. You give it to me every year. Remember, you keep your friends close to you, and your enemies even closer. That is all we're doing.'

'Yes, but these things are such a farce.'

'I know. I know. Look, there's a cute waiter over there eyeing you up. Why don't you find another way to keep yourself amused tonight?'

Her smile was warm and without contempt.

Glancing over he could see the young waiter who would have been all of twenty. He could see the boy blushing under his scrutiny. The boy's head was tilted with his chin close to the chest, yet his eyes followed Rosario through a scraggly fringe. To Rosario this was not the appropriate time to cater to any personal needs, especially not in front of his contemporaries. As way of compensation, Rosario stood in the rooms outer shadows watching the partygoers go by, and the young waiter making his rounds.

Slowly the evening died down. Amelia was carefully picking her way through the remaining crowd, hoping to avoid much more contact with the drunk or the boring. As she made her way to Rosario she stopped. He frowned at her and was about to approach when his arm accidentally knocked a tray from a waiter who had unknowingly walked up beside him.

'So sorry.'

The words came automatically to Rosario's mouth as he knelt to help clear up the items spilt.

'That's okay. I don't think you saw me.'

Raising his head, Rosario's eyes met with the face he had been watching all night. The heart shaped face with the sensuously hooded eyes was staring at him. The boy, making no attempt to clean up the fallen glasses.

'I did see you.'

The words were a husky whisper.

On their haunches, Rosario and the boy sat, looking at each other and smiling. The boy's cheeks reddened slightly, adding a romantic glow to his face. Rosario could feel a warmth fill his face too.

'Well, we better clear this up, hey.'

'Yes.'

Responded the boy. Without separating their eyes, the pair slowly collected the glasses, whole and broken, from the floor. Then the warmth of the boy's hand was on Rosario's. Inhaling deeply, reluctant to move his hand, Rosario froze and waited.

'My name's Phil. I'll be finished in half an hour. If...'

The boy paused, Rosario was unsure whether it was from embarrassment or uncertainty. Biting his upper lip, Phil continued.

'If you'd like to get a coffee or something?'

Nodding Rosario shook his hand free and rose to his feet. The way the boy was looking up at him was so innocent, trusting even. And so god-damn seductive. As he did now.

'Anyway, you look divine to me, darling.'

Moving closer to his lover, Phil's lips brushed Rosario's as his hands encircled him, dragging him in to bed.

Settling his body next to Phil's, Rosario's hand drifted, at first fondling Phil's smooth flat chest, then lower towards his belly button. Slowly wiggling his fingers, all the time knowing this could induce Phil to laughter. Swirling his fingers in ever descending circular motions, Rosario leant closer to taste Phil's porcelain skin.

With his passion ignited, Rosario barely heard the knock at the door. Phil pretended not to hear it. Fortune was smiling on him and he had no desire to stop it now. The knock came louder the second time. By the fourth it was a bone rattling thump. Rising in annoyance, Rosario covered himself and skipped the steps two at a time. Swinging open the door he was confronted with a down and out scruff. An elderly man, his oversized pants tied in a bunch at the waist with coloured cord, stood meekly before Rosario. Not only were his trousers ill-fitting but his skin looked three sizes too big. Atop his pale head the grey hair grew in wispy patches. Obviously homeless, Rosario could not believe such a man could make such a noise.

'What is it old man? What's so important for you to come knocking my door down?'

'She give me this.'

Patting his jacket pocket, a glass clink could be heard, shaking his head he patted his other pocket. Nodding at Rosario with a conspiratorial wink he continued, his speech slurred by the effect of alcohol.

'A secret.'

Looking as important as he could, the old homeless man swayed before steadying himself on a rail.

'Are you?'

Raising his bony finger towards Rosario, leaning in close. Rosario's stomach nearly turned from the waft that drifted from the man's mouth. Rosario had smelt better corpses. Whispering for effect now.

'A Mr Rosario?'

'Yes. And who wants to know.'

'I have a letter for you.'

Reaching into his pocket, Rosario had to grab the man before he tumbled.

'Much obliged.'

Slowly and majestically, he withdrew the envelope

from his pocket. Rosario recognised the paper immediately, even before he could see or feel the embossed letters on its top left-hand corner.

'Ah.'

Snatching the letter away from Rosario's impending grasp.

'Couldn't spare a penny for an old man's cup of tea, could ya?'

Even knowing that if the letter were real, the old man would have already been taken care of. Rosario darted inside to return with a fifty-dollar note. There was an incredible urgency to take ownership of the small cream envelope.

'Take it.'

Rosario practically screamed as he snatched the letter, slamming the door in the old man's face.

'What's the matter, hun?'

Questioned Phil from the top of the stairs. His body seductively wrapped in the bed linen.

'Leave me be.'

Panting heavily now, Rosario could feel the rush of blood through his temples. His legs, at first, failed to take their commands, but he managed to stagger to the lower floor bathroom. Locking the door behind him, Rosario came to rest on the toilet seat. The delicate patter of Phil's feet down the stairs and across the room soon approached the door.

'What is it, hun?'

His voice high and panicky.

'Nothing. Let me be.'

A hint of anger had crept in unannounced.

The patter of footsteps slowly receded allowing Rosario the peace he sought. Gently his fingers traced the outline of the embossed letters. Seeping into his fingers was the familiar texture of the paper, disturbed only by the flowing smoothness of the letters. Shaking back and forth, Rosario's cheeks were streaming with tears. It took him the better part of an hour to slide his finger under the back seal to open the envelope. Paper, identical to the envelope lay nestled within. Pinching the letter out gently, Rosario flicked it open as if it were rabid. A tear accompanied each word read.

Emerging from the bathroom sometime later, and slightly more composed, Rosario made his return to the bedroom. Without acknowledging Phil, he proceeded to pack a bag.

'No.'

Pleaded Phil.

'You said it was all over. No more travel. No more leaving me.'

With his back towards his lover, he continued to pack the essentials. When that job was done, Rosario lowered a shoebox from the manhole in the ceiling of the ensuite. From it he took a Smith and Wesson.

Tears streamed down Phil's face now.

'Are you coming back?'

'I hope so.'

Rosario looked up at his distressed lover. Taking in the puffiness of Phil's eyes, the redness, and the plea they held.

'I must go.'

He had been summoned. Whether it was a hoax or not, didn't matter. He had to go. To find out. How could he tell Phil it may be a trap? He couldn't. Taking Phil into his arms he held him tight. The embrace was returned three-fold.

'I love you.'

The whisper of the words he had always desired to hear, offered no comfort to Phil. For deep in his heart, he knew his lover, his partner, his best friend, may never return.

~ 35 ~

HELP, DEAR FRIEND

Dimly lit, the corridor suffered from the claustrophobic stench of antiseptic. Gasping at the scent, Amelia could feel the stench clinging to her nostril hairs. Actively forcing its way into her body. The eucalyptus fragrance was unable to sooth her rising nervousness.

Casting an eerie glow, the lighting dances in the corners of the doorways. Barely touching the blanketed feet, which hide in the shadows. A scene disturbed only by a low bilious moan rising from the corridor's end. Quickening her step, she approaches the far doorway. Beyond in the darkness lies Izzy, her body tormented by the agony of destiny. She hovers reluctantly on the edge of waking. Somewhere in the back of her mind nightmares swirl dimly. Izzy tries to catch them as she once had attempted to catch the butterflies in her mother's garden. But they drift further from her grasp with each attempt.

Amelia notes how Izzy has lost weight, despite her condition, since her return to Australia. While Izzy had never been fat, as such, the loss of just a few kilograms is enough to alter the angles of her face dramatically. It was as if it had acquired a depth, or merely the faint imprint of tragic experience. The collection of Izzy's features was no longer merely beautiful, it was that of a woman. A woman capable of great passion. A woman with secrets to conceal. A woman who knows something about life. Others would be puzzled with the transformation, possibly attributing the change to the birth experience and its now fatal consequences. Amelia, who had been unfailingly sympathetic throughout Izzy' s illness, knew better. Experience her guide.

Taking the limp hand in hers, Amelia strokes it lovingly. Running her fingers along Izzy's cheek she brushes a stray curl from the girl's eyes. A voice weak and distant responds to the warmth of touch.

'Is d'at you Mama?'

'Ssshh. All is right.'

Bending closer, Amelia's breath washes at the curls near Izzy's ear.

'Is there anything I can get you?'

'No.'

Crystal tears grow in the corner of her left eye.

'My son?'

'Yes. The nurse is bringing him now.'

As if to signal the truth in Amelia's words, small wheels can be heard approaching. The patter of the nurse's soft-soled shoes is interspersed with a faint squeaking noise that grows progressively louder. Louder and louder until it stops in the doorway.

'Remember, he can't stay long.'

Speaks the scowling nurse as she makes her retreat.

With the assistance of Amelia, Izzy manages to raise her body slightly from the bed, allowing Amelia time to position a few pillows. Reaching unsteadily towards the side table she manages to clutch a hairbrush. Involuntarily her hand releases the brush before she could raise it to her hair. Ignoring the sob of frustration, Amelia catches the brush. In long progressive sweeps, she gently prepares Izzy for the performance of her life.

'Ready?'

A faint nod has to suffice for an answer.

With all the care in the world, Amelia lifts the small bundle from the humidicrib. Returning to the bedside, Izzy's flailing strength is noticeable. The face once vibrant and healthy has a taupe paleness to it. Shaking hands, over which the pale skin is so tightly drawn, reach out. The suggestion of the bones beneath the flesh is uncomfortably apparent.

'My beautiful grandson. Here's your mummy.'

Gleaming with the happiness, only a first-time mother can feel, Izzy holds the bundle to her chest, concentrating firmly on not letting her arms fail. She is reassured by the pillow Amelia places beneath the child, allowing for less exertion by her trembling arms. Managing only to produce a few breathy cooing sounds, Izzy looks to Amelia.

'It's time.'

Without a word Amelia backs away to the room's corner, but not before switching on the table lamp. The sudden brightness unsettles the baby, causing him to whimper

like a small pup. Speaking softly into his ear, Izzy manages
to settle him as Amelia switches on the video camera.

'I'll wait outside.'

Receding to the gloominess of the corridor, Amelia
wraps her arms tightly about her body. An involuntary
shiver runs along her spine, shaking her shoulders and
head. Turning to the darkness of the opposite room, she
speaks.

'Rosario?'

From the darkness steps a less bulky form from what
she remembers. This has been harsh on them all. How long
had it been since she had seen him last? Or even spoken?
A feeling flooded her body which made it slump. A sinking
feeling that made her nauseas. She had not spoken to him
since before the shooting, her shooting.

His tongue circles his teeth beneath the skin. Drawing
his lips into his closed mouth, he sucks them momentarily.
Thinking in his own manner.

'Amelia.'

An emotionless monotone the only response. Rosario's
face held steady except for the small crease in his forehead.

'I am ashamed to ask a favour of you, especially after
causing you so much pain.'

'And you should be.'

'Yes. As you can see, I am alive.'

Arms sweeping down her body to emphasis what alive
meant to her.

'A shell of my former self.'

Appraising eyes follow her movement. Yet Rosario

does not approach. Stepping towards him her voice falls to a whisper. A plea.

'I missed you, Rosario.'

No response.

'I'm so sorry. You know how much I love you.'

'I no longer serve you. Why did you call me here?'

A cold wind had blown into Amelia's soul. She knew this was not easy. For either of them. Contact should have been made months ago, under the right circumstances.

'The favour I ask is incredibly important.'

For the first time Amelia could see the disgust on his face. The once caring eyes were possessed with hatred. Hatred for her.

'Can you trust me?'

He mocked.

'Always.'

But not with her death she could hear his thoughts say.

'Trust is a tightrope. Both ends need to be held taut, otherwise it is just a flailing piece of rope.'

'I've always been there to catch you, Rosario. Even after my death.'

Turning not to see her, his hands settle into his pockets.

'What do you need?'

'Izzy has given birth to my grandson. He is premature, but I am assured he will survive. Unfortunately, she may not.'

As heavy as her head felt she raises it high enough to lock eyes. Surely, he felt her pain. Reaching for her forehead she massages the pain, which steadily grows worse.

'Does Nicco know?'

'No. And he must not.'

A frown of confusion shadows Rosario's face.

'Why?'

'He is in danger. There is nothing I can do.'

The tears fall now.

'If nothing else, I must protect the child. We must Rosario.'

A stream of tears descends Amelia's face, yet Rosario does not approach.

~ 36 ~

MOTHER

Indianapolis, Indiana, U.S.A.

Hot and humid weather that was typically a feature of the NHRA (National Hot Rod Association) US Nationals was prevalent, as Jesse slipped into her leathers. Temperatures in the 90's meant that there were no spectacular numbers in qualifying and in many cases riders, and drivers alike, got their best shot in the relative cool of Friday evening. The sweat was already trickling down her body, soaking into her fireproof undergarments. Thoughts of how far she had come, from just cruising on a half painted Indian, to this hotted up, imitation of a street legal machine, interspersed her thoughts. She was pleased to see that the weekend marked the first time since '97 that three women had qualified for Top Fuel at Indy. Not only that, but in her class of Pro Stock Bike, two women had qualified. Herself and Angelle Seeling.

As the Vance and Hines crew prepared Jesse's Suzuki, she set about psyching herself into the next run. Running and rerunning the quarter mile scenario behind her closed eyes, her mind focused solely on the win.

'Excuse me are you Miss Jesse Dakota?'

'Do you mind?'

Stated another voice from behind the first. Jesse recognised the second voice immediately. The accent was European, a throaty guttural voice appropriate to some other, harsher, language. Its tongue unwilling to curve around the sharpness of the American accent. She smiled at the thought of Felicity ready to pounce on the intruder who also had an accent. A softer, more gentle tone.

'She is preparing to race.'

'I must speak to you Miss Dakota.'

Stated the voice without any effort to make it sound like an apology.

Before her opening eyes, Jesse saw a well-built middle-aged man. Silvering at the sides his hair looked striking but not as striking or peculiar as the handmade suit he wore. Most Drag Racing fans seen strolling the grounds were in a t-shirt and jeans. A suit was way out of place in this environment, especially in the pit area.

'Nice suit.'

Mocked Jesse.

'My name is Rosario, I have been sent with important news. Can we speak in private?'

'News from who?'

'I dare not say in front of these people.'

With a wide sweep of his hand Rosario showed his displeasure of being the ogled object of all around.

'Teach you to wear a suit to the drags.'

Jesse smiled as she rose and indicated the team trailer as a place to speak. Leading Rosario up the narrow steps Jesse seated herself in the booth of a small kitchenette. Rosario sat opposite as Felicity ascended the steps.

'Alone.'

Stated Rosario without taking his eyes off Jesse.

'But Felicity is...'

'I know, your lover. But this is private.'

Felicity was dismissed with a reassuring smile from Jesse. Looking rather displeased with the request Felicity turned to leave but not before saying

'I'll be just outside if you need me. We'll have to go around to the lanes in five to ten minutes.'

Nodding, Jesse turned her attention to this unusual visitor. For the first time in her life, she felt intimidated by a man's presence. It wasn't a fear she felt, but this man looked as if he could and did command respect from those around him. Power oozed from his mere presence.

'Rosario, is it? What can I do for you?'

'I have been sent with a special request.'

With the word request, his head fell while his hands set about the task of cracking his knuckles.

'This is a very delicate matter. I am sure you recall a Miss Isabelle Lancove.'

'Izzy? How is she? Where is she? Is she here?'

Excitement rose in Jesse's voice.

'I regret to inform you that Miss Lancove is no longer with us.'

Falling sickly pale, Jesse sat stunned. Words failing to form between her lips. Rosario paused to allow the first shock to sink in. Focusing on her face, he realised this was something he seldom saw. Yes, in his time he had rubbed out a few people, but never had he been the one to inform the next of kin. The pain in Jesse's eyes saddened him.

'Her parents. Do they know?'

'Yes, I believe so. I only flew in yesterday.'

'Flew in?'

Falling to the table Jesse's forehead banged to a halt.

'From Australia.'

'Australia?'

Shoulders heaving, Jesse's whole body sobbed in misery.

Rosario smiled sympathetically as Jesse's brain waves failed to function by themselves. Her mind was only capable of taking one key word in at a time. He too recalled the blanket that descended on the mind when the death of a loved one occurred. A similar thing occurred to him when Amelia died. Reaching out across the table he cupped her shaking hands.

'I'm sorry for your pain. But there is a more pressing matter.'

Red-rimmed eyes rose to meet his steely gaze. Snatching her hand from beneath his, Jesse looked at Rosario curiously. His face, as from the start, was void of any emotion.

'More pressing than death?'

'Yes. Life. Here is a letter to help explain.'

From an internal pocket, Rosario removed a custom envelope initialled with a flowing A and an R. In a rounded handwritten script was her name. Placing it flat on the table he slid it over to her. Hands falling from the table, Jesse avoided any contact with what was presented. What could be more pressing than the death of her best friend and her only true love?

'I will return after the final round for your answer.'

Without searching for acknowledgement Rosario rose and descended the narrow steps, closing the door as he did. Hearing Felicity's light footsteps approach, Jesse hurriedly tucked the envelope into her leather team jacket. One lot of bad news was enough for now. It was time to refocus on the task at hand. Racing.

Nerves withheld her from opening the envelope through the semi-final rounds. With such adversity in her heart, Jesse was surprised that her professionalism had carried her into the grand final round. Once at the starting line, her mind always clicked into automatic mode. The Christmas tree lights (starting lights) always triggered an intense desire to win. Over any competitor.

To gain peace and quiet for the final round, Jesse sat in the small kitchenette by herself. Working hard outside was her crew, making sure the Suzuki was ready for the final and most important round. Felicity was out and about preparing for the party, which was sure to follow, whether they won or lost. Between her fingers sat a slightly crumpled envelope being twisted round and round. Its corners now dog-eared and damp from her perspiration. With a sigh, she slid a nail under one flap and let it be guided by the firmness of the paper. Inside the delicate, almost transparent, paper contained gold embossed initials identical to those on the envelope. Words flowed in purple ink, written by the same person who had written her name on the outside.

****

Dearest Jesse,

I am sorry this letter bears with it such sad news. One thing for sure is that both our lives were greatly improved by knowing Isabelle, with her kind ways and loving manner. Isabelle spoke so highly and lovingly of you, that I feel right in the choices she has made.

As you may already see this is a very delicate matter, for with you I am sharing a great secret. Gone is Isabelle Lancove from our lives, yet a special part of her remains. She gave birth to a child, my beautiful grandson. You may think it mean of me not to inform the other grandparents of his birth, but his life depends on their ignorance. For the sake of the child, they must never see or know of him. I am praying this will change at some later date. Tears flow now as I write this. With great regret I too must give up any right to him.

Thus, this letter to you. After discussions with Isabelle before her departure, it was decided that what was best for the child was you. Her greatest and most loyal friend. Isabelle's heart felt wish was that you would raise her son as your own. I am aware of the great burden this request represents but for the safety and integrity of the child it is necessary.

A decision not to be taken lightly, yet one that needs to be completed most urgently. Sorry for the tight time frame given. But, for the sake of the child, it is imperative that these decisions happen quickly and quietly.

In accepting Isabelle's request, both you and the child will be financially taken care off. I feel that in the circumstances this will be of no concern or influence upon your decision-making. However, substantial trust funds have been set-aside for the child, one for now and one for later in life. His complete family history is also securely locked away for a special day, hopefully a day in the near future. Any other paperwork will be taken care of.

Once again, I offer you my condolences and apologise for forcing such a request upon you. It is a hard time for us all. I trust, no, I pray that you can assist Isabelle in her time of need.

Yours Sincerely,

Amelia R.

P.S. My beautiful little grandson's name is Michael Jesse.

****

The final round of racing was called. Jesse ran the quarter mile in a daze. The words of the letter haunted her. Sitting at the bottom of the shutdown area, astride her Suzuki motorcycle, its headers crackling and popping from the heat generated by the short run, Jesse's thoughts about losing the US Nationals Pro Stock Bike Finals, after snapping a throttle cable, were soon replaced by a more pressing matter.

If the cable had not broken, she would have driven up the return road. An unusual move for her style of bike but not impossible. Why was the tow crew taking so long? Under normal circumstances, her crew stalled for a period so that Jesse could cool her normally self-depreciating temper at losing, even more so now that it was the Nationals. After enough time had elapsed, they arrived to collect her and the Suzuki. All was silent as they returned to the trailer.

Surrounding the trailer was a barrage of fans, each seeking autographs and photos. Passing thanks to well-wishers but not seeing them, Jesse's eyes scanned the crowd over and over. Becoming frantic for fear of missing him Jesse rose onto the mechanics toolbox. In the distance she saw the man emerge from the shadow of two other team trailers, acknowledging her with a nod of the head.

Unable to untangle herself from promotional commitments, Jesse had to wait till the man loped across the tarmac in a crisp and vigorous stride. Grabbing Rosario by the wrist she pulled him behind the protective ribbon of her pit area and up the trailers open ramp.

'Yes. The answer is yes.'

'I'm glad.'

Rosario's head turned momentarily as he raised his arm, pointer finger extended and indicated the ground near his feet.

Scrunching her eyes Jesse could see nothing. No one in the distance, just shadows from which Rosario appeared like a phantom.

'He has a carer whose employ is paid for. Feel free to keep or dispose of her as you see fit. This cylinder contains the boy's birth certificate, your name is listed as his birth mother with the father unknown. This can be changed if you require.'

His face business like, Rosario handed Jesse the cylinder followed by a thick legal looking envelope.

'This has all the information you need on the trust funds and contacts for legal, or any other purpose, relating to the boy.'

'Is all this necessary?'

Searching his eyes, Jesse could see no emotion, the eyes that returned her gaze were blank, vapid, and empty.

'Yes.'

He fell silent as there was nothing more to be said. The letter had revealed the situation, and the envelope would complete the exchange.

'All I need before we hand him over is for your signature. Just here.'

'What is it?'

'Formalities. For the child's protection. Yes, here's your copy.'

A timid looking woman now appeared from behind the trailer door. Held closely to her chest was a small bundle wrapped tightly in a blue bunny blanket. Downcast, the woman's eyes took in Jesse's presence. Her skin carried the darkness of southern Europe. Hesitant to come forward, she moved no closer till a man equipped with a baby seat and a backpack, spoke to her sternly in a strange language. It was completely opposite to Felicity's, soft and rolling. On his command the lady approached Jesse placing her delicate bundle in this stranger's hands.

'Tenerto questa maniera.'

'What's going on?'

Startling Jesse, the voice from behind made her jump as she tentatively held the warm bundle in her arms. Never had she held anything so small and fragile.

'Felicity, what did the lady say?'

'Hold him this way. Why? You don't like babies.'

'This one is special. Very special.'

Looking up at the meek lady, Jesse smiled. At first the lady cast her eyes away unable to lock to Jesse's. Persistence won out and the lady curled her lips slightly while her cheeks blushed with shyness.

'What is your name?'

Looking at Rosario before answering the woman spoke again in her mouse like voice. 'Il mio Rosa del nome.'

'Rosa? Well Rosa, you'll have to help me with this little bundle.'

Unable to speak the english language did not hold Rosa back from understanding. Smiling warmly at Jesse, Rosa was glad to be wanted. She had only been Michael's carer for a few days, but in that time she had come to realise how special he was. Indicated not only by how he was treated but how he had arrived in her life so soon after the death of her own child.

Felicity leant over the bundle in Jesse's arms. Babies disgusted her, especially at this young an age. They all looked like boiled monkeys as far as she was concerned.

I suppose that was another benefit of being a lesbian she smiled, no mishaps such as pregnancies. Looking into Jesse's eyes though, she became worried. There was a look she had never seen. It radiated a warmth, a tenderness she never knew Jesse possessed. Not even as a lover.

Folding back the blanket, Jesse could see the outline of the small fragile body over which a pale blue jumpsuit was loosely drawn. Michael had his mother's sensuous mouth, high cheekbones and as far as she could tell, her delicate structure. Obviously he was not pure negro, his colouring neither black nor white. His skin was a smooth rich colour, slightly darker than olive. Surprising though was his light spray of hair. Blond locks contrasting strangely with his fragile dark looks. What came as the greatest shock was his eyes. How vivid they were. Felicity released an audible gasp despite Rosa's evident disapproval. One eye was the rich emerald colour of his mother's, yet the other was blue. Not just blue but a striking bottomless blue. Each eye, a precious jewel, highlighted the other.

Daring to hold him in the crook of one arm, Jesse raised her free hand to Michael. His skin was soft and warm to touch, and as she drew an invisible line down his body he grasped her finger. A shudder of pure pleasure ran through her, with one smile from his cheruby face Jesse was committed. She had made the right choice, the only choice.

In her absorption of the baby she had failed to see Rosario and the other man disappear into the darkness. *What would she have said to him anyway. Thank you? Thank you for bringing me such sorrowful news, yet at the same time bringing light and meaning to my life? What could she have possibly said that would have conveyed what she felt at this very moment? She had lost the US Nationals to Angelle yet she felt the victor.* Felicity's rough voice prompted her back to consciousness.

'Better hand him back now.'

'He's mine.'

Jesse whispered with Rosa nodding in agreeance.

'He's what! Have you gone crackers?'

~ 37 ~

THE MARRIAGE

That day.

Here I sit. A modern reflection looks upon me from an antique mirror. Is this not meant to be a woman's happiest day, yet I feel? What? Empty? My chest feels hollow, a black hole of existence, of which my throat seems to be descending into. There is nothing. My mood is neither happy nor sad. Just numb. My body passes through the motions of a woman readying herself for such a wondrous day, my mind though, sees only the beautiful face of a child lost. Fate's cruelty has competed well with the joy in my life. A never-ending struggle of dark and light.

Strength, beyond any that I have known has led me to today. A marvellous man waits for me outside, at the far end of the garden. Of my pain, he knows nothing. Over two hundred guests wait to see his choice for a wife. And from what I hear, their top pockets contain envelopes stuffed with cash. Envelopes, which will shortly, be crammed into a medium sized silk bag given to me by Mrs Greenstone.

For reasons unbeknown to me, I must not mention either

Amelia or that she exists. Mike's life appears to be complex, a maze with riddles at each turn. But my love for him is what leads me to today. Everything else is secondary. To overcome that phase in my life, I will hold back one, and only one, secret from my future husband. The child he will never see. No matter how many children we are graced with, in my heart I know I will never forget that beautiful boy who was blessed to me for such a short time. He is in God's hands now. My faith does not allow me to question why he was here for such a limited stay. One day I believe the answers will come.

'Izzy, my dear child, are you ready?'

Wiping away the last remnants of tears Izzy rose to be embraced by her father.

'Yes Papa. I am ready.'

Holding his fragile little girl at arm's length, Izzy's father tilted his head, his eyes overflowing with affection.

'My little girl is a woman. It only feels like yesterday that you and Jesse were chasing butterflies in your Mama's garden. Such free spirits the two of you.'

With the heavy movement of his broad shoulders, a sigh escapes him. His eyes flicker like a late-night television when the channel is lost. Swirling in them are the memories he will always carry of 'his little girl'.

Behind the pair, the wedding march is being tapped out on a grand piano. The piano, as with much else, the guests included, were flown in for the special day. All flown to the most remote ranch she had ever seen. Kuntana. The mystical Kuntana of Mike's lively youth. Looking around, Izzy feels as if the place is already a part of her. Home.

With the commencement of the lone piano, the guests

fall quiet. Slowly one by one their heads turn toward the homestead waiting for the first glimpse of the future Mrs Nicosia Ricoldi. Today is a momentous occasion. The Ricoldi name is to survive another generation. Their strength intact. People have come from everywhere to pay their respect. Foreign Princes stand amongst the dusty Jackaroos and Jillaroos, Sicilian businessmen are seated next to Amazonian natives, while turbaned Arabs jest with the gospel singers.

Mike feels nothing but pride as Izzy makes her way down the aisle to his side. Promising himself that he will do everything in his power to make their lives rich and full. The first glimpse of her flowing white gown takes his breath away. The strapless creation shows the smooth domes of her shoulders to their fullest potential. Hugging her closely, the corset, beaded with diamonds reflects a rainbow of colour in the morning light. *Yes,* thinks Mike. *All my dreams are coming true.*

The traditional Roman Catholic wedding is long and arduous for Izzy who is accustomed to her father's energetic sermons. Kissing the wedding bands before giving them is a gesture she savours. A display of their commitment and love. On completion of the ceremony a shower of white sugared almonds befalls them. Small children frantically scavenge the treats from around their feet, tripping Izzy. Holding her firm, Mike leads her through the crowd stopping frequently. Kissing and hugging, especially the Italian males, the couple are congratulated by one and all. Steadily the small limp bag at Izzy's wrist plumps out like a stuffed bird.

Patrick offers her a quick peck with his lips barely touching Izzy's skin. His lack of confidence with women showing in his own flushed cheeks. A characteristic made worse by the day's rising warmth. Carl, on the other hand, stands in the distance. Izzy notices him momentarily before averting her eyes. The cold dark sneer already penetrating her skin like a poison. Capturing Mike in his gaze Carl's expression changes dramatically. Fortunately, Mike rescues Izzy from the awkward position she and Patrick have found themselves in. A lack of similar interests other than Mike.

'Izzy, I'd like you to meet Sir Brooke Jeffries, an old friend of my mothers.'

'Not too much of that old either young Mike.'

His words may have been directed at Mike but his eyes remain firmly on Isabelle.

'Ah Isabella, you are simply wonderful.'

Bowing his head in a gentlemanly manner, Brooke brushes his lips over her hand. Holding tight, he stares into her emerald eyes.

'Dance with me?'

Bowing her head in shyness, Brooke laughs. Tugging her gently, Brooke leads Izzy to the temporary dance floor. Holding her in his arms, they waltz slowly together.

'I have something for you.'

His hand slips into a pocket and returns clenched.

'A special friend, Mike's mother, asked me to hold on to it till this special day.'

Izzy's confused look causes Brooke to laugh softly.

'No, I am unable to speak to ghosts. She put this in my

care before she passed away. I was her lawyer amongst other things.'

Raising his hand between them, the contents tumble out, all except for the part looped over his finger. A delicate gold chain swings before Izzy's face. Glinting in the sunlight, her eyes descend to the apparent charm hanging from the opposite end to Brooke's finger. Lifting it gently in her palm, Izzy takes in the small gold key. Within its fancy loop sat a reasonably sized emerald. Identical to her eyes.

'It's beautiful.'

'Yes, and it's yours. Apparently, the key works, you just need to find what on. Don't look at me, I have no idea. Amelia said you would know when you found it.'

With a flurry of kisses, Brooke allowed himself to be swept away in the crowd. Leaving Izzy standing alone with the necklace.

****

Curiosity has always been one of my downfalls. After our marriage, I took a few days to explore Kuntana before our honeymoon to Sicily. Mike's origins. The wide expanses attracted my attention to begin with, but eventually I found myself indoors. To the rear of the house, I discovered a locked room, which, I'm happy to say, I managed to pry open. Slumped in the corners, like vagabonds, were canvas-covered boxes. The room had not been entered into for many months, if not years, for my feet left distinct imprints in the dust.

I felt a child again. Searching into things that did not belong to me. To my disappointment, some of the canvas only covered books, which I could not read. They were in Italian, I think. One was a beautiful bible though. A brief family history appeared to be scrawled in the back. I would have to ask Mike about it.

A familiar form catches my eye. Lifting the canvas sheet reveals something exquisite, an early racing bicycle lovingly restored to its former glory. Painted by hand, the pearl white base coat is highlighted with the world champion's rainbow of colours. Compared to my own bike, the equipment is crude, not as aesthetically pleasing, and yet very functional. Showing an elegance of its era. Along the top bar in a beautiful scroll is the name 'Emma Hearton'. A slight breeze from the open-door ruffles something, taking my attention. On the handlebar is a small card tied by a rainbow ribbon. Feeling nervous, I tentatively reach out for it. My hand shakes as I feel its roughness between my fingers. I feel as if I am invading somebody's privacy. A bold script greets me.

****

Il mio Amelia caro,

Strolling in a market in Florence I came across this special gift for you. Unfortunately, it was not found in the condition that you kept it. Abused by time, it was a special remnant of your former glory that I felt needed to be preserved. From what I could remember, from the photos I could find and Brookes help, we restored it, hopefully, to how it was. The same bike you rode to Olympic gold and to your first junior World Championship. It is a part of you that should be held close. None of us should ever be forced to let go of our dreams. I cannot replace those lost years but I hope this will bring back the good memories you have of those times. The ones I myself hold. Happy 30th Birthday.

Il mio amore sempre, Rosario.

****

Rosario. The man I had just met yesterday. It is hard to imagine him passionate about anything. Such a sullen face belongs on a grieving widow. And the way he looked at me. Through me. Mike commented that he had come out of retirement to watch over 'things' while we were honeymooning. But I am unsure, there is something about him.

Dropping the cover again on the bike, I stand and listen to the silence of this strange country. Voices on the wind haunt me so. Amelia had told me several times never to give up my dreams. I see now that she was speaking from painful experience. Sometimes we are so enclosed in our own lives that we find it hard to imagine that other people have their own, if not worse, experiences. Let alone anything important to say. What we say to each other seems limited, due to the lack of words and concepts of common experiences and understanding. I suppose that is how we unwittingly destroy each other's lives.

Searching further, lifting the covers one by one, it feels like Christmas. Behind a couple of the back boxes, I find a tin chest. An old military style. Since it was locked, I tried the small key Brooke had given me. I must admit, since that day, I have been on the lookout for a suitable lock for it to fit. As with all the others, the chest needed a larger key. Lacking one, I had to make do with a piece of metal wire I had found. And hey presto! What was inside this box took me back a little. Unsettling it was. There were photos, hundreds of them, of me. Riding my bike, picnicking with Mike at the Hellyer Park Velodrome, walking at Tilden and astoundingly, me being pursued and attacked by Carl. I have trouble taking my eyes from them. None are happy snapshots, they are of my daily activities. An unaware me, traipsing through life.

Beneath the photos I discover a strange box. An exquisite box at that. It is metal, intricately carved with an assortment of characters with a small gold lock built in. It is about the size of a sheet of paper, with the thickness of a lunchbox. My fingers can feel the sharpness of its pattern as I attempt to lift it from the chest. Considering its size, the weight is deceptive. Leaning closer to inspect the pattern, the small key on the chain about my neck taps ominously on the box, prompting me to consider using it. Fondling the key in indecision, a loud scream rocks the house. Frightened, I am unaware our lives will change forever.

~ 38 ~

BATTLE FOR THE CHILDREN'S SOUL

The sky over the plains were sprinkled with high, fluffy white clouds. By the time they reached Kuntana, the clouds had formed a dense, low hanging mass. Its dirty grey belly ominously close and heavy looking. Amelia's thoughts were being disrupted every few minutes by rumbling thunder overhead. She was so miserable that she could summon neither the desire nor the energy to make idle conversation with Rosario.

Amelia laughed nervously in her disbelief, thinking that perhaps it was a joke, that her very own son had summoned her here. But here she was, in her own home, treated like any other guest. Rosario was distant, yet only a few feet from her. Life this past year had taken every turn possible, vexing Amelia more than she thought possible.

Behind the large oak doors, stood her office. As Brooke Jeffries would say, a cauldron continuously on the boil. With her forced absence, not much had changed. Amelia moistened her lips with her tongue, her sense of unease increasing as the doors creaked open. Framed by the sill stood her son. No longer was he a boy, his carefree smile replaced with a solemn face. His once lanky form filled into a chiselled physique.

'Nicco.'

Her voice was a little shaky, and more than a little breathless.

'Mother, glad you could come.'

In contrast, Mike's voice was deep and alarmingly steady.

'Do come into my office.'

Absorbed in her thoughts, Amelia failed to notice Mike's fingers locking around her wrists as he greeted her. After a motherly peck, his grip remained. It was firm enough to hold her when she made a half-hearted attempt to pull her hands free, but not so tight that it hurt. Amelia was certain that Mike could feel her accelerated pulse. She made a second more determined effort to tug out of his grasp. The pressure of his fingers increased slightly, letting her know that he wasn't ready to release her.

'Rosario, could you organise some lunch for mother and I.'

Cringing at the use of the word mother, Amelia yanked harder at her hands. At the same moment Mike released them, allowing Amelia to lose balance in an exaggerated movement. He turned and entered the room, indicating for his mother to follow.

Following him, Amelia's eyes scanned the room, taking in the luxurious furnishings, the cool, peaceful atmosphere, unlike the tension within her. Plants hung in little terracotta baskets from the walls, shrinking from neglect. She stood shivering, surrounded by antique wooden furniture. The only concession to comfort was the one solitary leather armchair.

'Drink? Muscadean?'

Amelia nodded, her hands trailing over the luxurious feel of the thick leather armchair in the centre of the room. Memories flooded her, as her eyes stung with held back tears. Her heart glowed remembering Mike, as a small infant, playing peek-a-boo amongst the cushions. How he sat on her knee and demanded one more story before bed, or when she would nurse him all night in the hope his fever would break.

'Do you know why I asked you here?'

His eyes watched her with a shade of anxiety. Obviously uncertain of what her reaction would be.

Amelia bit her lip, her hands clinging to the smooth surface of the glass.

'Well, it's not to thank me for giving birth to you, or making you a wonderful life. Obviously, you think removing me will fulfil your plans.'

A tide of red stung Mike's cheeks, and he looked away, shuffling his feet uncertainly.

'In a way yes. My plans are under way and nobody, not even you, could stop them. Vito's death and your supposed death gave me time and now all is going to plan.'

'Very fortunate my shooting then?'

'The timing perfect.'

'Was the shooter aiming to kill?'

The question came at him from out of nowhere, catching him off guard. And though she'd spoken softly, he sensed that the answer was important to her. She confirmed the impression when she added, just as softly.

'The truth Nicco.'

He only hesitated for a moment. She wanted the truth, Mike didn't have to search for it, the truth was within easy reach, waiting to be recognised and accepted.

'No. Just to waylay you for enough time for me to take control. I was unaware Christopher hated you enough to go for the kill.'

Amelia looked perfectly composed, damn her. Calm and in complete control as she had always appeared to him.

'Doesn't say much on how I raised you does it.'

Mike stared at Amelia dazedly for a moment before collecting his wits and hastily turning his back. Not trusting his voice, he didn't say anything.

'You picked a lousy hit man then. Any Don would have hired a professional for such a contract, or done it himself.'

Amelia watched closely, alert to every nuance of expression on his youthful face as it turned towards her. She sensed that his pride was ruffled, but that he was stubbornly resisting the urge to defend or explain his ways. There was arrogant disdain in the strong line of his jaw, and a hint of resentment. Yet she thought she saw a glimmer of surprise beneath his lowered lashes. So she continued.

'Do you hate me that much?'

His eyes narrowed, but a grin tugged at the corners of his mouth.

'No. I've always loved you.'

'And I've always loved you, Nicco. More than any man on this earth.'

Amelia spoke quietly, as if resigned to an answer that would go unheard or understood.

'You were never the patient child. Always wanting things now. This business needs to be learned. There is an etiquette, one you don't seem to care for. Roberto knew. He was learning the trade. He was earning respect.'

'I have respect and I have the power to make them respect me.'

Mike defended himself with strong words though the small pout on his lips said otherwise. He stood tall and firm trying to look intimidating. He did not.

'Oh, Nicco, this is where you are wrong. The Ricoldi name does have respect but those out there, the ones you are relying on, like Sam Mandell, they respect those they trust and know. Like me and Rosario. Beyond that they can be bought. The handover needs to be slower, not taken with force.'

Mike's voice crackled like he was about to go into a rage.

'Those who oppose me will be dealt with.'

'Sounds like you are under the influence of Anthony Valentine. He has his own agenda you know?'

'I am not under the influence of anyone. To be honest, I am sick of being in a room with you, and every order I give, they look at you for confirmation. I want to be the man my father expected me to be. I want to not only carry his name, but to carry on his legacy.'

Rubbing the burning pain in her forehead, Amelia continued.

'But how did we end up here, like this.'

'I want more.'

'More than we have? I have spent my life building an empire, for you. At every step, I have attempted to turn the business into a legitimate endeavour. All of this so you wouldn't have the persecuted life I had to undertake.'

Amelia spoke looking out the window, wishing she had just built Kuntana and nothing else. No kingdom that would tear her family apart. Nor one that demanded the need for retribution. All she ever really wanted was a simple life.

'I know mother, but I simply want more. Money alone does not demand power or respect. You, of all people, should know that.'

'I never wanted to see blood on your hands. Let alone my own blood.'

Mike, feeling the upper hand, grew more confident in his words.

'Those in glass houses should not throw stones mother.'

'I admit I was wrong, but it was for survival. Yours is for power.'

'It went past survival a long time ago. You could have stayed in Nicosia and allowed me to have my heritage!'

The growled accusation vibrated through her. An audible intake of air, followed by a single tear, was obvious as Amelia steadied herself on the desk corner. A slow smile spread over his ruggedly handsome face. At this age he looked so much like his father. His father being only a few months older when he was maliciously gunned down.

'You can have your damn struggle for power in a new Mafioso war. End up like your father if you like.'

Her heart sank in dismay, as he suddenly switched to a husky murmur.

'Like Declan?'

'He was not your father!'

She snapped back.

'He was the only father I knew, thanks to you.'

Amelia's jaw hurt from the tight rein of control she was exercising over herself, while her heart ached with emptiness. A familiar pattern, unrequested sacrifices made for children who don't know, don't want to know, or don't understand.

'That had to be done. You know why.'

'No. I don't. Maybe it was because I loved him as much as I loved you. Maybe that was the threat.'

Mike's voice changed momentarily to that of a spoilt child.

'And Roberto? Hey, Nicco. I loved him like a son.'

'That was an accident.'

'He was your brother!'

'What?'

'Your blood brother. Your father had two sons.'

'You lie mother.'

'No. Did you ever verify the date of your father's death? You were not even born.'

'But the photo.'

'How could I tell a child of three, who was over the moon to find a picture of his mother and dead father and a child he thought was himself, that it wasn't him but his father's illegitimate son. A son claimed by a loyal foot soldier.'

Mike had been almost incoherent in his shock, staring at her with horrified eyes, his body rushing with fear, panic, and anger. He inhaled sharply, attempting to jolt his torpid brain out of its stupor. Crackling, his voice was harsher than a whisper.

'Rosario. Il protettore. The protector. You really screwed up his life too, didn't you mother.'

Reaching under the large oak desk, Amelia felt for the switch to the secret compartment, which she alone knew. Both her desks, the one in the city and the one here, had special compartments to conceal Amelia's secrets. Her hand searched frantically, fingers finally resting on the cold blue metal.

'Do you recognise this?'

Amelia held the ornate gun forward for Mike to see its details.

'Isn't that the gun that killed Vito?'

Looking on in disbelief, Mike was genuinely curious.

'Yes, my son, it is.'

'Why do you have it? And here?'

'The polite detectives sent it to Beretta in Gordone for identification. Giovanni returned it to its rightful owner. Me. Yes Nicco.'

A wicked grin filled the edges of her mouth.

'Your brother and I shot Vito. More blood on my already stained hands.'

'What would make...'

His throat constricted, choking off the rest of the question, his ears not wanting to know the answer.

'He killed your father!'

'But I sent Roberto and Christopher...'

'Yes. For the wrong reasons.'

'I should have been the one. For my manhood and honour was at stake. Yet you did not say a word.'

'You too would have cringed, as they did, when I left your father's mark. Could you have finished Vito off? As you said, yourself, you sent your men to extinguish someone you were close to. You did not have the balls for the job.'

Amelia vehemently spat out the last remark.

'You made my access to the honour society more difficult.'

'Yes. And I did it for the right reason.'

Stunned silence surrounded the pair. Mike admired his mother's powerful presence, noticing her youthful silhouette as she seated herself at the large bay window. Life on the land, Mistyvale, and its toil agreed with her. As did her marriage to Joseph. Farm work, the sun and love. Amelia seated herself in the sunlit bay window, her head bent in thought, speaking as if to herself.

'It's amazing really. I had the gun engraved VIVA LA MALAVITA! (Long live the Mafia!) Throughout the years I have supported something that has persistently taken so much from me. And now it will take more.'

Mike felt that he had heard enough. Years of pain gurgled to the surface. Like a child he stomped his feet, clenched his hands, and snorted in disgust. Her undermining had aggravated his temper more than ever this time.

'No mother, you are what has taken so much from our lives. First my father. Then Declan. You even hid that I had a brother! You alone have stopped me at every path to becoming who I am meant to be. You alone have created this persecution.'

Mike's piercing eyes held her on the bay window seat. His eyes burned with such hatred and scorn. He continued to speak.

'You are what's evil in this world. Nothing could quench your desire for power. It was above all else, even me, your only son. You had no desire to share it. You never did. That is why those around you meet a violent end. Using the Ricoldi name to hide your own personal bloodlust.'

Amelia rose facing her child. A sharp slap ensued. The brisk sting on his cheek belied the frailness of her hand. Her voice was not frail, it had the strength it once had.

'And what of your family Nicco. What of your wife, your son?'

Here Amelia paused then corrected herself. Her voice was hesitant, searching for replacement words.

'Your future children. Will your thirst for power destroy them?'

Mike was not fooled. He heard her stumble on the words.

'You said my son, as in present tense. What did you mean?'

Amelia turned from him.

'Nothing.'

Mike knew that his mother's nothing was definitely something. She had that odd look on her face. One he knew from childhood when she was trying to hide something from him without fully lying. Grabbing her roughly, Mike spun Amelia to face him. His voice, though desperate, had softened slightly.

'My son?'

'I'm sorry, I had to make him safe.'

Amelia spoke in an apologetic tone though she did not regret her actions, only the pain it would cause to her beloved son.

'I knew what your plans were, I know what Anthony's plans are, and I couldn't have him in danger.'

Mike thought he heard a small explosive pop in the distance as the window behind his mother instantaneously shattered. A stain seeped across Amelia's chest as her body fell to the floor. An eerie echoing pained his ears. Crimson blood slowly soaked into the speckled plush pile. The stain crept further and further from its source. Lifeless, the body lay unflinching.

'Don't leave me mummy.'

Tears streaked Mike's face, as his wish for power and control became lost to him. The moment's clarity revealed the loss of all he genuinely cared for. Holding his mother's limp body, Mike realised, he had a son to find.

****

The satellite phone vibrated silently next to his trigger

hand. Removing his eye from the scope, the sniper viewed the caller ID then answered it. Sitting quietly, he waited for the caller to speak.

'Is it done?'

'There was a problem.'

'What do you mean a problem?'

The caller was concerned. A lot of plans were pinned to this moment.

'The woman. She was there.'

'What woman?'

'Amelia.'

The line falls silent, her name taking the caller by surprise. It takes a moment before they can recompose themselves.

'Is Nicosia dead?'

'No.'

'Why not?'

'The woman took the hit.'

The sniper was unsure what would transpire next. Initially he had sought Mike through his scope, yet the boy had vanished under his view when his mother dropped. He must have been holding her limp body below the bay window's ledge.

'Shall I try again?'

The line remained silent.

'I repeat. Shall I try again. I have another minute before the helicopter launches in search of me.'

There was commotion on the other end of the line. Suddenly the voice returned.

'Do you have a clear shot?'

'No.'

'God help us all.'

The line dropped dead. Picking up the shell casing, the sniper cleared his position, removing any trace of his presence.

Dash Starkey

Born and raised in Brisbane, Australia, Dash Starkey melds imagination with personal experiences to create lively stories. Paying homage to the state of Queensland in every book, with most having a home base of Brisbane, the stories have a personal feel, even when the characters travel the world.

Dash mulls over a novel started over 25 years ago, along with other works in the pipeline. Free time is spent between writing and van life. Dash's two greatest passions outside of family. Travelling with Elle in an old Toyota Hiace called Howie, Dash has many more adventures, and disasters, to divulge.

Backed by years of experience as a technical writer Dash Starkey has written articles for several magazines across the world, including Mountain Biking Australia, Australian Cyclist, Guitar (US), Bass Guitar (US) and Game Informer. Articles have also appeared in trade magazines and international inhouse magazines.

www.ingramcontent.com/pod-product-compliance
Lightning Source LLC
Chambersburg PA
CBHW070159120726
47909CB00001B/179